HERETICS IN OCCUPIED EDEN

The **HERETICS IN OCCUPIED EDEN** Trilogy

Book One: **THE FLOATING BOY**

Book Two: **THE STRANGE ANGELS**

Book Three: **THE DANCING CHURCH**

The **HERETICS COMPANION** Works:

Book Four: The Mansion of Our Undressing

Book Five: Chaucer Dickinson and the Timberscape of Memory

Book Six: The Book of Zara

Book Seven: Emma Round and the Holy Rowlings

Book Eight: The Heretics Appendix

HERETICS IN OCCUPIED EDEN

BOOK TWO

THE STRANGE ANGELS

A NOVEL BY

KENNETH ALAN MOE

STRANGE ANGEL PRESS
Phoenix, Arizona

Cover, interior design and author photo by Ethan Moe
"Angel" figures on cover Copyright © 123RF Stock Photos
Cover photo is Window Rock, Navajo Nation, Arizona

Printed in the United States of America
Second Printing

ISBN: 978-0615710440

For Shelly

No, no, it is the three strange angels.
Admit them, admit them.
D. H. Lawrence

CONTENTS

I

CLOUD AND TERP

The soul, it seems, is enabled by our Body.
John Donne

To teach thee, I am naked first.
John Donne

Let her breasts satisfy thee at all times, and be thou ravished always with her love.
Proverbs 5:19

If a little dreaming is dangerous, the cure for it is not to dream less but to dream more.
Marcel Proust

CHAPTER ONE

Numinous energy surged through Terp's body as her mind registered the words Cloud had spoken. "Why did you say that particular phrase? 'All shall be well.' Have you encountered it somewhere before?"

"I think it's from a T. S. Eliot poem," he replied, "but I don't remember which one. I have no idea why I said it. It just popped into my head."

"Of course!" Terp said. She smacked her forehead with her right hand. The movement of her arm caused Cloud to wince from the laughter-induced pain in his side. "Oh, sorry," she added. "I'm sore too. It's from ***Little Gidding***, the last of Eliot's ***Four Quartets***. When we studied that poem sophomore year, I thought Eliot must have had a mystical experience, like I did, because I'd ***heard*** those words before -in an extrasensory way. The Christmas Eve after my father died, I felt abandoned and was wondering if God really cared about people. I was standing alone outside the church at midnight, and all at once the sky seemed to brighten, and a sense of warmth enfolded me, and that message echoed through my mind. All shall be well."

"I'm tempted to say that's a spooky coincidence, but after all the overlapping prescient dreams and experiences we've had, I suppose this is merely one more example of something beyond our understanding that brings us together," Cloud offered.

They climbed into the Volkswagen Beetle and started back to his apartment.

Terp said, "I feel like I've known you my whole life."

"In an extra-sensory way, you have," Cloud answered. "Most of your life anyway. But there's one more thing you need to know about me. Next week I'll be twenty-nine, and for half my life I've chosen not to believe in God."

"You told me that last night," Terp said.

"For a long time," he continued, "I've wanted to believe but something in my mind held me back. That purple cloth is the catalyst I needed to believe in God again."

Terp reached across and caressed the side of his face with her left hand. "Oh, Cloud, that makes me happy."

"That doesn't mean I suddenly believe in a whole package of Christian doctrine. Or the doctrine of any other religion, for that matter. My sense of God is more energy than matter, more power than substance. Believing this much only opens the door for thousands of questions about the nature of God.

"I've seen it happen when a person has a transforming spiritual experience, people with narrow theological agendas swoop in and claim the event proves their particular dogmas. It does no such thing, but momentary elation can make one vulnerable to being sucked into a parochial view of God. I won't fall into that trap. To force boundary-dissolving, transcendent encounters inside rigid doctrinal walls is...arrogant...and stupid!"

"Your insight makes me happy too," Terp said. "It means we two have an exciting theological quest ahead of us."

"Do you realize how calmly you've spoken of ***us*** rather than you or me?" Cloud asked.

"Yes," she said. "It may be presumptuous, but it seems so effortlessly natural to think of us as a couple. How does it feel to you? Does it frighten you?"

"It should, I suppose. But it seems perfectly normal that we've become established in a relationship in less than twenty-four hours," Cloud confessed. "On the other hand, much of my life has been lived beyond the range of the ordinary, and your life too, so I guess we should just thank God and get on with whatever awaits us."

"That we shall," Terp declared. "Now the story truly begins."

They were famished from their trek into the desert in search of relics, so they stopped at Woody's for Mexican food before returning to Cloud's apartment. As they entered his living room, Cloud said, "Well, here we are." He was tempted to add home at last but thought it premature. "Now where do we go from here?"

"I know I ***don't*** want to go back to my dorm," Terp said, "but I think I'd better do that anyway, to get my...bearings." Her unspoken thought was to get her things.

"Of course," said Cloud. "Would you like me to drive you over or would you prefer an old-fashioned stroll over to campus?"

"A stroll, without a doubt," she said, lacing her right hand into his left.

Rather than linger over saying goodnight in the lobby, Terp escorted Cloud up to her room, where her roommate, studying at her desk, was astonished to see a man with Terp. "Dagmar, I'd like you to meet my guardian angel, Cloud Morgan," she said.

Dagmar extended her hand. "Far out! I've never met an angel before. How do you come by that title?"

Cloud took her hand and said, "It's good to meet you. I'm about as far from being an angel as one can get. But that's a story for another time. I'd like to say that Terp has told me all about you, but she hasn't. We've had other things on our minds."

Dagmar surveyed the older man, whom she judged to be about twenty-five. "My guess is that you're a graduate student," she said.

"Right you are," said Cloud. "PhD candidate in Asian history." He turned to Terp. "Well, I suppose I should be going."

"Please wait a few minutes. I'd like you here while I tell Dagmar how we met. I'll tell the short version," Terp said. By this Cloud knew she would not reveal any of the intimate extrasensory information he and Terp had confessed. She described her return to the empty dorm room the previous afternoon, her decision to take an overdose of over the counter medicine, and the manner in which she bumped into Cloud in the drugstore. She took some time telling Dagmar about the New York City blackout seven years earlier and how she recognized Cloud from that chance meeting.

As if they had rehearsed the tale, Cloud then related how he had seen Terp at an anti-war rally two years before, the poem he wrote, and how her image had remained in his mind ever since. He omitted the part about seeing a golden aura around her head.

"It turns out, we have a lot in common," Terp said with a gleeful lilt.

Dagmar's knowing eyes scanned Terp's face and saw what she had never seen during the time Terp had been involved with Kirk Trilby. Terp was already deeply in love with a man she had known for a single day. She turned her attention to Cloud's face and saw the same thing. But there was something odd about both of them. Their countenances were not those of infatuated new lovers but of a couple who had loved each other for decades. Dagmar sensed she was staring at a mystery with more layers of meaning than she could ever grasp. I may as well throw all my advice out the window, she thought.

Terp led Cloud downstairs past the dorm lobby and pirouetted into his arms. They kissed with passion and grace, as if they had done this a thousand times before and couldn't wait to do it again. When their lips parted, Cloud gazed into Terp's eyes and recognized a depth of intellect and personality he had never seen in anyone else.

"I'll see you tomorrow," he said. "We've both got studying to do."

"Tomorrow," she said. "In the meantime, I want to say something you already know. I love you, Cloud."

"The only reason you know that I know you love me," he said, "is because you also know I love you, Terp. Now that we have that out of the way, we can take as much time as we need to make sense of it all."

Released somehow from an inner vault of memory, the pop song "My Special Angel" played in Cloud's mind as he walked home. He felt lifted into an otherworldly sacredness he had known before only in his imagination.

The next evening, Cloud produced a vegetable stew, which he and Terp ate with French bread in the corner of his apartment that passed for a dining room. Over dinner they swapped war stories -not their own but their fathers' tales.

Cloud said, "So, your dad and mine both served in the Eighth Air Force in England. Was your dad's name by any chance Tommy?"

"It was Tom," Terp said. "I never heard him called Tommy."

"Well, my dad told me he lost a bombardier in a tragic accident on one of his bombing missions. The guy who was killed was Tommy Olson, and his replacement was Tommy Person," Cloud explained.

"Oh wow!" Terp exclaimed. "My dad told me about that. He flew one mission with a crew right after the bombardier had fallen through the bomb bay doors. And then the pilot didn't show up for the next mission."

"That pilot was my father, and he didn't show up because he had a mental breakdown brought on by guilt. He thought he was responsible for Tommy Olson's death, and he didn't want to kill another Tommy," Cloud said.

"You'll have to tell him that Tom Person...Tommy...made it through the war without a scratch," Terp said.

"I think you should be the one to tell him," Cloud said. "I wonder how he'll react when he learns that I'm in love with Tommy Person's daughter?"

Together they washed the dishes, and when the kitchen was clean, Terp said, "If you wouldn't mind indulging a young girl's fantasy, there's something I'd like to do."

"You have my full attention," Cloud said.

"I told you yesterday about the dream I had where I danced for a sad poet. I want that dream to come true," she said.

"You only told me part of the dream, but I can't think of a better way for the evening to unfold," he said. "Although I'm not at the moment sad."

"But you were sad two days ago, and you're definitely a poet," she said. Terp pulled an album from the crate where Cloud stored his long-playing records. Removing the disc from its sleeve, she placed it on the turntable. "Now, clear a space for me to dance."

When the furniture and area rug had been moved to the side of the room, Terp said, "Take off your shoes and socks and sit in the middle of the floor." He did as he was told. She set the stereo arm on a band of the ***Dr. Zhivago*** soundtrack well known to her, kicked off her sandals and removed her glasses.

As strains of "Lara's Theme" filled the air, Terp began to dance. In graceful turns and elegant swoops she moved around the room, arms outstretched, head high, led on by the rhythm of the music, circling the man resting attentively in the lotus posture.

Cloud's eyes were full of her form. As she danced, she unbuttoned and pulled off her blouse then unzipped her skirt, letting it slip to the floor. Now I test the truth of the dream, she thought, as she unhooked her bra and tossed it across the room. She peered into Cloud's eyes to see if her breasts, which she felt were too small, would nevertheless please him. In an instant she knew that the dream was true. The poet loved the dancer's breasts. She stepped out of her panties and continued to orbit the room in stately sweeps until the song came to its end. Standing still before him, she asked, "Any words from my metaphysical poet?"

"May I have this dance?" he asked as he rose, quickly undressed, and moved the tone arm back to replay the piece. Cloud held Terp in a waltz embrace as they swayed to the melody, bodies slightly apart, gliding lightly across the floor.

As the song ended the second time, she said, "The next dance, dearest poet, will be ***a capella*** and horizontal." She pressed her body against his and whispered, "Ravish me, Cloud Morgan."

He lifted her into his arms and carried her into the bedroom. With teasing caresses and kisses all over her body, he brought her to the heights of arousal, and then Cloud entered Terp with strength gained from years of unrequited passion, and she received him eagerly as a bride experiencing the fullness of love for the first time. The lovers burst into concurrent orgasms, and then lay still in peaceful connectedness. No word was spoken for many minutes, but joyous grins covered each of their faces.

"Did your dream come true?" Cloud asked, breaking the silence.

"Oh much more than that," Terp replied.

Cloud rolled on his side, moving Terp with him so that he remained inside her. She threw a leg around him, clasping them together. "More than one dream was fulfilled when you danced for me," he said. "Eight years ago I dreamed of a long-haired dancer from the East. But I was confused about where the East was, because I could see palm trees in the background. I assumed the setting was somewhere in the Orient. It didn't occur to me that the East would be New Jersey. Yet never has a mental image been imprinted in my mind more powerfully than the woman I saw in my sleep eight years ago. Now I see palm trees in the moonlight through my window and that lovely dancer in my bed."

"I knew I was answering your dream too, but I wanted you to say it to me," she whispered. "And in the spirit of Proverbs 5, may my breasts satisfy you always and my love ever ravish you."

"Amen," Cloud said. "Now there's something else I want to tell you, dearest dancer. Legal and ecclesiastical technicalities aside, we have just conducted our own wedding ceremony."

"I guess that means it's too late for you to propose to me," she said.

"Way too late," he said. "We've managed to get married without anyone proposing to anyone."

"But what sweet vows we've made!" she said. "It all seems so...sacramental, graced with prescient dreams, dance, and physical love." She paused to reflect on this image and then added, "Of course, my mother will want a formal wedding in Metuchen." She paused again. "And so do I. I'm going to be greedy about this, Cloud. Promise me someday you'll marry me in a ceremony at Second Calvinist Church."

"I promise," he said.

Three important tasks fell to Terp with the dawn. Considering the timing of her menstrual cycle, she was not worried about being pregnant from their lovemaking, but she wanted to be sure for the future. Therefore, she visited the campus health clinic and obtained a prescription for birth control pills.

The second task was gathering her things at the dorm and loading them into Cloud's car for transportation to his apartment. "Don't worry," she said to Dagmar. "The room and board has already been paid for the rest of the year. I haven't told my mother about moving in with Cloud, and I'm not sure when I'll get around to that little detail."

"The room and board stuff doesn't worry me," Dagmar said. "Common sense says you're in way over your head and setting yourself up for a big fall, but my intuition tells me everything will be OK. I just hope my intuition is right. Keep in touch."

"Oh I'll still be around. Once I get settled in, we'll invite you over for dinner," Terp replied. "And two more things, Dagmar. One, I owe you a lot for taking care of me when Kirk messed me up. Thank you. And two, reviving a conversation we had eighteen months ago, Cloud finds brainy women -how should I phrase this?- sexually attractive. So I've found that there is one such male in the world, at any rate."

"Only one? Then I might have to go after him myself," Dagmar quipped.

The third task was calling her mother for a chat in which she casually mentioned she was dating a graduate student. Terp had never spoken about the relationship with Kirk, but she gave Penny a carefully edited description of Cloud, setting the stage for another call in which she would tell her mom that she and Cloud were getting serious and provide a little more information about him. This would be followed by yet another carefully spaced call to announce they were engaged.

After marrying Nissa, Lloyd Morgan sold his townhouse in Scottsdale. The newlyweds moved into a Spanish ranch house in the Town of Paradise Valley, a desert landscaped atoll of wealthy individualism shimmering between the vast tracts of Phoenix and Scottsdale.

Cloud and Terp stood before the home's enormous carved oak front door, awaiting a response to the chimes that served as a bell. Terp thought she detected an angel emerging from the dark stained wood, similar to the one she had mentally manipulated in Salisbury Cathedral several years earlier. A good omen, she thought.

That morning Cloud had called and said he wanted his dad and step-mom to meet the woman in his life, and Lloyd had immediately invited them for dinner. Since Lloyd and Nissa were naturists, it suddenly occurred to Cloud as they waited before the door that they might be greeted in the nude. He was glad he had told Terp about their lifestyle.

Terp secretly hoped they would be undressed, but Nissa was demurely clad in a long-sleeved blouse and jumper when she escorted them past the courtyard and into the sunken living room. Lloyd wore white slacks and a blue polo shirt.

"Dad, Nissa, this is Terp Person," Cloud said.

Nissa took Terp's hand and shook it warmly. As Lloyd grasped her hand in turn, Cloud continued, "Dad, Terp is Tommy Person's daughter."

For a moment Lloyd did not know what to make of this information. Tommy Person? The bombardier? And then the realization engulfed him. Lloyd had quit flying because he did not want to kill Tommy Person, and now his son was in love with Tommy's daughter. And that daughter would never have been born if Tommy had been killed during the war. Suddenly his confinement in a mental hospital in England all those years ago seemed like a meaningful sacrifice. Tears appeared in his eyes.

"Oh my Lord!" said Lloyd. He looked carefully into Terp's face and then embraced her in a wide hug. "Thank God. Thank God. Thank God," he repeated over and over. "Forgive the blubbering of an old man," he continued, "but this is so unexpected. I could never have imagined something as wonderful as this."

Terp found herself hugging Lloyd back and crying along with him. "I could never have imagined being greeted like this, either," she said. "But it makes me happy."

Releasing her, Lloyd asked, "And how is your father?"

Terp replied, "He made it through the war without a scratch, but he died from heart disease in 1966."

"I'm so sorry," Lloyd said, feeling genuine grief for a man he had barely known, but whose existence had loomed large in his conscious mind for nearly three decades.

Nissa served lean sliced beef, rice, and artichoke hearts for dinner. The four toasted the meal with glasses of Spanish ***Rioja***, the first wine Cloud had tasted in years. Tears of gratitude flowed in abundance that night, along with burly laughter.

Toward the end of the evening, Terp, feeling more at ease and mellow than she sometimes felt around her own mother, said, "Cloud tells me that you two are nudists. What's that like?"

Nissa said, "That's a dangerous question to be asking someone like me. I'm an evangelist for naturism, and I can talk your ears off about it."

"Go ahead. I'd like to know," said Terp.

"I have literature about the Natural Christian Church," Nissa said. "Let me give it to you to read. It'll give you the doctrinal details that I'm not very good at explaining."

Lloyd said, "Being naked in a social setting frees the mind and alleviates anxiety. And I'm glad you brought it up, Terp, because this provides an excuse to have you over again soon to talk about naturism. In the meantime, Nissa and I turn into pumpkins by ten o'clock, so you two need to scoot."

They exchanged hugs at the door, and Nissa pressed a fat manila envelope into Terp's hands. "Here's a whole bunch of information about the NCC," she said, "including pictures of naked people. In the old days the church literature didn't include photographs, but nowadays they're more open."

As a result of perusing the material Nissa had given her, Terp decided to go naked around the apartment. This did not mean a radical change, since she usually slept in the nude. Now, she simply did not bother getting dressed until she was ready to go outside. While living alone, Cloud had generally not bothered to don clothing unless he felt chilly or was expecting visitors, so Terp's experiment with family nudism seemed natural to him.

Soon after moving into Cloud's apartment, however, Terp insisted on a major change in his lifestyle. "You've got to get a telephone," she said. "You can get an unlisted number if you like, but I need to be able to call my mother and Dagmar from time to time."

"I use the pay phone outside the manager's office when I need to make a call," Cloud said.

"If my mom calls me at the dorm, Dagmar needs to be able to alert me so I can call her back, and a pay phone won't do for that," Terp explained. "Look, dear, I know graduate school is expensive and we need to be careful with money. I'm very happy to live modestly as long as we're together. So if money is the problem, I have enough for both of us to live comfortably. I'll pay for the phone."

Cloud chuckled gently. "Your offer of enough money for both of us has made my day. I love your generosity, Terp. You're welcome to contribute as much or as little as you wish to our commonweal. I'd be happy to live off your income or mine. It's all the same to me. Call the phone company and order what you want. But first sit down. I have something to tell you. This is not a secret, but it's a subject I seldom think about.

"Terp, I live off the GI Bill checks because I think that's a prudent thing to do. I need very little and am content with simplicity. But the fact is, because of my father's generosity, I'm fairly well off financially. Dad manages my money, and he's a pretty astute and careful investor."

"Well, how much do you have?" Terp asked.

"I'm not sure what my portfolio is worth right now. I don't watch it very carefully. I leave that to Dad. But it's more than $350,000."

"And to think I was worrying about how to pay for your airfare to New Jersey at Christmas to meet my mom and sister," Terp said.

"Not to worry," he said. "Between the two of us plutocrats, we'll find a way. And that reminds me. Someday soon you're going to have to meet ***my*** mother. I've been putting it off, but we've got to face it. If you still want me after meeting my mother, you are truly a saint."

When the telephone conversation began, Cloud had just finished his morning calisthenics and yoga routine. To avoid being decisive about a visit to Narcissa, Cloud said, "Time for my shower now."

"Mind if I join you?" Terp asked.

As the hot water cascaded over Cloud's face and chest, Terp stood behind him and took this opportunity to caress the large scar on his left butt cheek. "You haven't told me about this," she said. "I presume this is a war wound."

"It's one of them," he said. "The other is on my forehead, but that one has faded. It's really hard to see it unless you're looking for it. And nobody knows to look for it anyway, so in a sense it's not really there."

"Turn around and let me see," she said. He turned, and she traced her fingers reverently across his brow. "Yes, I can feel it. How did you get these injuries?"

Through all the self-revelations Cloud had made to Terp -about out-of-body experiences, religious doubts, and his love affair with Xuan- he had not told her about being wounded in Viet Nam. Having seen the long scar on his bottom, though, she suspected he had been shot. Now it was time for him to confess the truth.

Cloud hesitated. This was a subject he was clearly uncomfortable with. But he had no desire to withhold anything from Terp. And this seemed important to her. He sighed. "I told you about being with Xuan when she was killed. What I failed to add was at that same time a bullet grazed my head, which caused me to bang into the wall and suffer a concussion. It was a minor wound. Not much to talk about. The damage to my butt came from running across a hot landing zone with a chopper pilot slung over my shoulder."

He described his rescue of the pilot from a burning helicopter and the sniper's bullet that had pierced his left cheek while he was running. "It was rather comical," he said, making light of a frightening situation. "There we were lying in the mud, and me with a big pain in the ass, literally."

"So, you have two Purple Hearts," Terp said solemnly.

"I used to," Cloud acknowledged. "I gave one of them away. When Dad married Nissa, I presented him with a Purple Heart. I think soldiers who suffer mental wounds should be honored with a medal every bit as much as those with bodily wounds."

"That was a wonderfully loving thing to do, Cloud. It gives me goose bumps to hear about it," she said.

"Quick, get under the hot water," he said, rotating her into the shower's stream. "I don't want you getting the chills." He hoped this would end the conversation.

It didn't. "Well, what other medals do you have?" Terp demanded from under the torrent of water.

"The usual," he said. "National Defense ribbon, a couple of campaign ribbons. They give those to everybody who serves in a war zone."

"Is that all? Didn't you get anything for saving the life of that pilot?"

"OK," he admitted. "They gave me two Bronze Stars. One was for meritorious service as a translator and analyst, and the other for...valor. I suppose you would have found out anyway. My mother has a framed newspaper article about me in the entryway of her house, and you won't be able to miss seeing it when we go there."

"Why didn't you tell me these things?" Terp asked, bewildered.

"Because this hero stuff is way overblown. I was only acting out of instinct. Lots of people were far more courageous or suffered much worse wounds than I. I'm simply not that deserving. More than anything, I was just...lucky."

Terp peered into his eyes and gently asked, "Lucky for the years of grief that followed your tour in Viet Nam?"

"No," Cloud whispered and lowered his head. "Not lucky for that. But grief doesn't make you a hero."

Terp wrapped her arms around Cloud. "Oh my love, my love. I

am in awe of your humility." She turned the water off. "Come to bed and let me ravish you before I head off to class." He allowed her to ravish him.

CHAPTER TWO

Narcissa was glowing, wearing a belle of the ball gown, when Cloud and Terp arrived at her home in the Palmcroft district. The framed and matted newspaper article still hung in the same place.

"Mother, when are you going to take that thing down?" Cloud asked, with a hint of irritation in his voice. "That's old news."

"It's not old news to me," Narcissa protested. "I am still very proud of my hero."

"Me too," Terp whispered in his ear.

After a round of white wine and vegetable munchies, Narcissa decided Terp was a refined young lady and therefore approved her son's choice. Terp represented a huge improvement over that Oriental woman Cloud had gotten mixed up with in Viet Nam, she thought. Narcissa made mental plans to invite Terp, and perhaps some of her college girlfriends, to a Ladies Patriotic beauty supplies sales party.

"Has Cloud told you we are friends with the Goldwaters?" Narcissa asked Terp.

"No, he hasn't said anything about that," Terp replied.

"I suppose he wouldn't," Narcissa continued. "As a matter of fact, I played an important role in Barry's presidential campaign. I served on his staff. Oh, you can imagine how crushing his loss to that boorish Texan was to ***all*** of us."

"Mother, you were only a volunteer who passed out leaflets," Cloud interjected.

"I did far more than that, young man," Narcissa corrected. "Barry and I were quite close. He turned to me quite often as a personal confidante."

With impish intent, Terp said, "I didn't share your sense of loss in that election. I'm a lifelong Democrat. And I cast my first ever presidential vote for McGovern, by absentee ballot of course, so I resonate with you in how it feels to lose in a landslide."

Narcissa found herself reconsidering her premature approval of this young woman. "Well, Cloud, of course, is a lifelong Republican. I suppose he's told you that."

"Well actually, Mother, I'm not a Republican anymore," Cloud said.

Narcissa gasped. "This is news to me. When did this...this...betrayal happen?"

"Not long after I returned from the war," he said. "But if it will help ease your heartburn, I'm not a Democrat either, although I too voted for McGovern last week. He was a B-24 pilot, you know, just like Dad. For what it's worth, I've registered as an Independent, and I'm intrigued by the Libertarians on issues of personal behavior, but I won't join their party, because I've come to see that a mixed economy is simply more healthy, effective and equitable than either a pure socialist or pure capitalist system."

Narcissa was addled by her son's reference to Lloyd as a B-24 pilot, and she failed to grasp mentally all the rest he said, so she dropped the subject. The dinner went fairly well. By prior agreement, Cloud and Terp determined that they would speak as little as possible, letting Narcissa do the talking, and this strategy worked splendidly.

In the car on the way home, Cloud sought Terp's impressions of his mother.

"Well, I really like your dad and Nissa," she said by way of preamble. "Your mother is aptly named, but let me assure you she's not anywhere close to strong enough to pry me away from you."

Cloud laughed heartily. "That's certainly good news."

"Of course, we'll have to invite her to the wedding. Do you think she would fly to New Jersey?" Terp asked. "She could potentially be a major disrupter of peace there."

"I doubt that she'd come," Cloud said. "Despite her pretense of worldliness, in her entire life she's never set foot outside Arizona. But I think Dad and Nissa would. Dad would want to meet your mom and find out more about your dad."

"I've been thinking about a date," she continued, "and it seems like a Saturday next June would work out well. We can make specific arrangements over Christmas."

"Sounds good to me," Cloud said.

"And once we're legally married, I will at last have a middle name," Terp added. "Terry Person Morgan. I love the way it resounds in trochaic trimeter."

As she and Cloud were getting ready for bed that night, Terp asked, "Will you demonstrate floating for me?"

"I've never done it in front of anyone before," he said. "I don't know if I can do it with someone watching, but the thought of you guarding my body while I'm out of it makes me feel very... blessed."

Cloud lay supine on their bed, while Terp assumed a lotus position beside him. "You probably won't be able to see or hear anything," he said before starting his deep breathing preliminaries. She watched in silence and a few minutes later she noticed that the animating spirit was missing from Cloud's face.

"Where are you?" she asked, but no answer came. She listened attentively to the sounds of the air and experienced a profound sense that Cloud's spirit was quite near. Then she felt his love penetrating her entire being.

When Cloud floated from his body, he followed a habitual path toward the ceiling. From there he looked down on his beloved Terp and called her name. But no sound came from him, for his larynx remained with his body on the bed. Apparently she could not sense his location, for she spoke, asking him where he was. He descended to her place on the bed, looked into her eyes and nestled his soul into her body.

Each cell of her physical being was drugged with the knowledge of his love. It was almost more than she could bear. Almost. Terp's mind and body were aroused to a level of mystical passion far beyond the merely sexual. The ache in her muscles was exquisite. The feeling of joy went beyond the limits of words to describe. And then his spirit faded from hers and she saw the animation return to Cloud's face.

"Did you sense my presence?" he asked.

"Yes," she said. Her eyes were deep pools of liquid crystal. A gold aura shone around her entire body. "More deeply than I can begin to express." A warm silence bathed the lovers for a time, each enjoying the sight of the other without need for speech.

After an unhurried interval of quiet, Cloud whispered, "Like John Donne's mistress going to bed, you are a mystic book, drawing me irresistibly deeper into your pages. And by the way, beloved muse, I see a golden aura surrounding your frame."

Terp shivered with pleasure at Cloud's reference to the metaphysical poet. Lovingly she traced the contours of his face with her fingers. "I see the same around you," she echoed. Another silent era passed before she said, "Can you teach me to float? I want to show you what I felt when you were inside me. Not now. I don't want to mar the exquisite enchantment of this night with a tutorial. But soon."

"With you I'm willing to try anything. I'm not sure I can explain what I do, but when you're ready to experiment, I'll do my best," he said. "There's a lot about floating I don't understand, though, so don't expect me to be a very good teacher."

"Like what?" she asked.

"Well, when I'm out of my body, I can see and hear, but I can't speak, smell, or taste. I ***can*** feel, but it's not the ordinary sense of touch. It's completely different -all diffused, with no pain. And I don't need to breathe, either. The thing is, I can't figure out how I can see and hear, when my eyes and ears are back in my body along with all the other organs."

"Curious," she said.

"And another thing," he added. "Walls are no hindrance. I can move right though bricks and steel with no effort, but I can't seem to travel very fast. Most of the time I move outside my body about as rapidly as I do in my body. I've tried accelerating but haven't been able to go more than what I estimate to be two hundred twenty miles an hour. The sound barrier eludes me."

"Time for sleep, my love," Terp said. She kissed his eyes and ears and snuggled contentedly into his arms.

The invitation to a June wedding in New Jersey pleased Lloyd and

Nissa. Lloyd was now retired from the bank and had a flexible schedule as well as a desire to travel. Once the date was set, they would book airline reservations.

The four sipped red wine in the sunken living room of Lloyd and Nissa's home. Cloud and Terp had come in response to another dinner invitation.

Nissa was excited that Terp had read all the material about the Natural Christian Church.

"I've been going naked around the apartment to see how it feels," Terp said.

"So how ***does*** it feel?" Nissa asked.

"Great," said Terp. "And truthfully, the idea is not new to me. Two years ago my roommate Dagmar and I scouted for safe places on the ASU campus to sunbathe nude. We didn't find any there but did locate a secluded spot in the Salt River bed. Anyway, your church is intriguing, and I'd like to meet Adam and Evelyn. Could you take us to a service in New River someday?"

Nissa looked at Lloyd and said with a wink, "What do you think? Is there any chance we could we arrange a meeting with our pastors?"

"I don't see why not," he responded. "What do you think, Cloud?"

"The last time I saw Adam and Evelyn, I still didn't believe in God. Now that I believe again, I'd like to get back to those fascinating theological discussions that Mother truncated a long time ago. I have a broader and deeper perspective on religion now."

Having anticipated this possibility, Nissa was prepared. "How about this Sunday? You can stay here Saturday night, and we'll drive up together early Sunday morning."

"It sounds like you've got it all planned," Cloud said.

"Yep," Nissa confessed. "Our pastors are looking forward to meeting Terp and seeing you again, Cloud. They didn't get to talk with you much at our wedding. All I have to do is give them a jingle and say when you're coming."

"That's short notice. It's up to you, Terp," Cloud said.

"Most certainly," she said enthusiastically.

"Wonderful! Now that that's settled," Nissa said, "I'm going to get natural." She stood, unbuttoned her dress, and removed it, revealing her complete tan. "And by the way, Terp, you and your friend Dagmar can sunbathe nude on our back patio any time you want. It's totally private here. Anyone need a refill?"

Two minutes later, without a word spoken, the others were also naked.

Nissa had put an end to Lloyd's burger and fries habit. Dinner was broiled salmon, asparagus spears, and baked potatoes, which they all enjoyed in the buff around an oval oak table.

Terp relished not having to fret about food stains on her silk blouse or wool skirt. "I wish it were this simple in a restaurant," she said. "Just remove your clothes before dinner is served. Why should anyone object?"

Nissa laughed heartily. "It's amazing how even a little exposure of flesh in public can generate huge objections."

"But I can dream, can't I?" sighed Terp. "So tell me, Nissa, how did you become a naturist?"

"I was born into it," Nissa replied. "My parents were pioneer naturists in this country in the 1920s, although they called themselves gymnosophists in those days."

"What was that like?" Terp wanted to know.

"Oh, I guess it was mostly pretty fun," Nissa replied in vague fashion.

"She was something of a practical joker," said Lloyd. "A real imp."

"Like what?" asked Terp. "We want details."

Nissa grinned in remembrance of her days of elf-like behavior. "Well, for a couple of years my dad managed a nudist dude ranch out Wickenburg way. I was ten when he started working there. One time I filled the hot tub with a whole bunch of blue Easter egg dye tablets."

"And?" said Terp.

Nissa's grin deepened. "I guess you could say a certain Hollywood starlet gave new meaning to the song "Blue Moon" and the studio executive who was with her provided a vivid illustration of the term blue balls. They never found out who did it. Based on my previous behavior, my dad figured it was me, but he didn't let on. There were other kids around the place, some of them spoiled rotten, so I wasn't the prime suspect."

"What else?" asked Terp.

"One time I found a box of whoopee cushions in the store room of a beach resort where my dad was assistant manager. That was when we lived in California. When certain snooty people got up from their towels to go into the water, I would slip the cushions under their towels. That was great fun to watch them blush and gesture innocently when they artificially farted."

"Tell them about the sunscreen," Lloyd prompted.

"Well, actually it wasn't sunscreen," Nissa explained. "In those days we used sun tan lotion or oil. We didn't know about protecting our skin with sunscreen. When I was in high school, there was this one girl at the nudist club in Phoenix who thought she was better than everyone else. She was in the habit of snatching my tanning lotion when she got out of the pool. If she'd have asked, I would have given it to her, but she never asked. She just felt entitled to whatever she wanted. So, one day I mixed glue in with my lotion. And sure enough, little miss brat came by and helped herself to it. That was such a hoot! When the stuff dried, her face and chest were a mess. She looked like an old lady with a skin disease. She accused me of being malicious, but nobody would take her side, because she treated everyone else like servants too."

"That reminds me of something I've been meaning to ask you, Nissa," said Cloud. "Some people who have sunbathed for years, naturist or not, develop wrinkled and leathery skin. Yours is nicely tanned but soft and smooth. What's your secret?"

Nissa glowed at the compliment. "I'm tempted to say good genes, but it's more likely three decades of good habits. I never stay very long in direct sunlight at any one time. Usually no more than about thirty minutes before returning to the shade or going inside. Plus I always use sunscreen before going out and moisturizing lotion after showering. I log enough sun time to benefit from absorbing vitamin D, but I avoid getting sunburned like the plague."

"Wise words I must make a point to remember and heed," said Terp. "But back to your life story, it sounds like you moved around quite a bit."

"Mostly it was in the Phoenix area," said Nissa. "Except for a couple of years in Southern California. My dad was always looking for a better opportunity. He owned a nudist golf course near Cave Creek in the early fifties. The ground was naked too. That was the gimmick.

No grass, just desert landscaping. Unfortunately, that went belly up. Most of the time he managed resorts and private clubs for other people."

"There's something else I've been curious about for a long time," said Cloud. "Did you ever know that the nudist magazine with you and Onan in it circulated rather widely around our neighborhood in the late fifties?"

"Oh sure," said Nissa. "Working at the Post Office, I also knew who had subscriptions to that magazine, including some people in our neighborhood, like your friend Quincy's father, for example. He was a cop, if I remember correctly."

"That's probably where Quinn got it," said Cloud. "He never would tell us how he managed to acquire so many girlie magazines."

"That was no girlie magazine," said Nissa a tad defensively. "Girlie mags display the models in sexually provocative poses. Nudist publications don't. They show people of both sexes in natural recreation and everyday life. It's a very important distinction."

"Yes, you're right, of course," said Cloud. "Please pardon my glibness."

"This is a serious matter," Nissa continued. "In 1960, a man in Florida lost his job at the Post Office because his photograph appeared in a naturist magazine. They claimed that it was conduct unbecoming a Government employee. Bosh! The Government's discrimination and persecution of naturism was the unbecoming conduct if you ask me!"

"Well, I want to know if you've kept up with your practical jokes at New River," said Terp, seeking to return to the earlier playful subject.

"Oh, I've thought about it," confessed Nissa. "But somehow it doesn't seem right to engage in pranks in a church. Besides, I'm an adult now. As the Bible says, there comes a time to give up childish ways."

"I don't know why. It's not inappropriate to joke around in church," Cloud opined. "I can think of certain pastors who are existentially themselves practical jokes, though no doubt as unintended as Freudian puns. Childlike is not the same as childish."

"I don't have the slightest idea what you just said," Nissa responded.

"It's a compliment and affirmation," said Terp. "Cloud thinks the world of you."

"She's right," Cloud said. "Nissa, you are a real gem, and I'm so glad you fell in love with my dad and vice versa."

"Speaking of the Bible and humor in church," said Terp, "since my early teens, every Easter when they read the passage about finding Jesus' linens in the empty tomb, it makes me think that the risen Jesus must have run around naked till he could find a robe somewhere. Maybe he borrowed one from the gardener. Is that a blasphemous idea?"

"Well I don't think it would be to Natural Christians," said Nissa. "Unlike some of his later disciples, Jesus was not ashamed of his body. And if he did borrow a robe, I guess that means someone else had to walk home naked."

"I don't think Jesus would take someone else's only garment," said Lloyd. "He'd sooner go without than deprive another person."

"It would only be blasphemous if Jesus' body were in some way corrupt or vile," said Cloud. "And if any idea qualifies as blasphemous, it's that God would create Jesus with a shameful body."

After dinner, Cloud volunteered to help Nissa clean up. While loading the dishwasher, he said, "I've been thinking about your comments about the Healthy Nudist magazine. You said Quinn's dad had a subscription. Did anyone else in the neighborhood subscribe?"

"Well, Onan and I did, of course. We liked to see pictures of our friends and find out what was going on at other camps and read the interesting articles. But about other people, you're asking something that's confidential," she said. "Actually, I shouldn't have told you that much, but it really bothers me when people equate naturist photography with pornography. But I don't work for the Post Office anymore, so I guess it won't hurt to say that a lot of people who subscribed were naturists that I knew."

"Sorry," Cloud said. "I don't mean to pry into anyone's confidential business. But all the naturist magazines I've seen are clearly ***not*** in any way pornographic, so it shouldn't be any big deal."

"Yet it was a big deal to the Postal Service for many years," Nissa said. "Have you ever heard of the Comstock Law?"

"Sure," said Cloud. "It was an anti-obscenity statute passed by Congress in the 1870s, if I remember correctly."

"Right," said Nissa. "In 1873 to be exact. It was named after Anthony Comstock, who founded the New York Society for the Suppression of Vice. How's that for a self-righteous name? Anyway, lots of states passed copycat laws. The problem was the various Comstock laws were applied in all sorts of idiotic ways, prohibiting real works of art from entering or circulating in this country. They were all incredibly prudish. What boils my butt is that my own employer, the Post Office Department, or United States Postal Service as it's known now, got into the act in 1941 by deciding to enforce Comstock in an especially restrictive way."

"That was during the war," said Cloud. "I thought social mores loosened up in wartime."

"You thought wrong," Nissa said. "The POD decided that nudist publications with nude photographs were by definition obscene, no matter how artfully the shots were taken or even whether they were airbrushed. They could not be legally sent to subscribers through the mail. Naturist magazines were confiscated and publishers were threatened with huge fines. Postmaster General Frank C. Walker declared war on nudists."

"So how did people get the magazines?" Cloud asked. "I know they were published in the forties."

"Newsstands," Nissa answered. "That really limited circulation. Nudist organizations sued and repeatedly won in court, but it took two decades to settle the matter. Arthur E. Summerfield, Postmaster General during the Eisenhower years, invented administrative obstacles and sporadically and arbitrarily refused mail service to particular issues of nudist magazines. And that bears directly on your question about subscribers in our old neighborhood.

"January 13, 1958 is a kind of Independence Day for naturists, or at least for naturist publishers. That's when the Supreme Court finally ruled that nudist photos are not obscene and nudist magazines can be legally sent through the mail. The magazine with Onan and me in it that Officer Queensbury subscribed to was the first issue to go out after the Supreme Court lifted the ban."

"That was providential timing for my developing psyche," said Cloud. "That magazine was my introduction to a wonderful lifestyle."

Nissa beamed at him. "You're such a nice bright boy," she said, "even if you do say good things in strange ways."

—o—

In the car on the way home, Terp began to sing a gleeful rendition of "A Natural Woman."

"You put a lot of vitality into an already energetic song," Cloud commented.

"It's a favorite from my ***Tapestry*** album. Of course, I don't think Carole King had naturists in mind when she wrote it, but you and your family do make me ***feel*** like a ***natural woman***. Oh, Cloud, I feel so free and loved. I feel like I'm becoming the woman I was meant to be."

"Well, get used to it," he said with a grin. "There's plenty of natural life ahead."

Terp's first call to her mother about going out with a graduate student had gone smoothly, with Penny delighted that her elder daughter was at long last dating. Terp's sister Mary, three years younger, had already gone through half a dozen boyfriends, so Penny felt relieved by Terp's news. The second call, however, hit a snag. When Terp said she and Cloud were getting serious, Penny was ready with sobering advice. "Slow down, Terp! As far as I know this is the first man you've ever dated. You're at the high school crush stage only starting a bit late. This relationship will most likely run its course and you'll find a better one sometime down the road."

"Actually, Mom, Cloud is not my first relationship," she said. "I dated another man for a while but...he wasn't my type."

"So you met Cloud on the rebound. That's even more dangerous," Penny replied.

Intuitively, Terp knew arguing would not help the situation, so she sighed silently and said, "OK, Mom, I'll keep my eyes open and take things slowly."

She decided to postpone the third call until mid-December.

CHAPTER THREE

Cloud called his mother from the new telephone in his apartment, although he failed to tell her such an instrument had been installed. "Terp and I are planning to get married next June," he said, "and we want to give you advance notice so you can clear your calendar."

"What happy news," she said without enthusiasm. "What day are you planning?"

"We don't know yet. The service will be in Terp's church in Metuchen. That's in New Jersey," he explained.

"Oh...well...I don't know if I can promise my attendance. I'll have to check my schedule. I think the Ladies Patriotic Beauty Society has a convention in June. Let me know when you have a specific date. And...uh...congratulations. I'm sure you'll be very happy." Narcissa hung up. At that moment, she remembered that her parents had declined to attend her wedding before a Justice of the Peace in 1942, and this provided her with all the warrant she needed for avoiding her son's nuptials.

"What did she say?" Terp asked.

"She won't come. She'll find an excuse not to be there," Cloud said. "And the funny thing is, I am simultaneously relieved and disappointed."

—o—

Adam and Evelyn were delighted with Terp. Were it not for the looming eleven o'clock service, the clergy couple could have spent all day engaging in vigorous conversation with Terp and Cloud. As it was, they filled their allotted hour with talk of literature, theology, psychology, anthropology, and matrimony.

"Oh, Cloud, she's lovely and literate," Evelyn said to him in a moment aside. "She's a perfect match for you. I'm so happy for you both."

"Do you get this excited about all the engaged couples you meet?" Cloud asked.

"You don't know this," Evelyn said, "but Adam and I have a great deal of affection for you, Cloud. You're almost a son to us, wayward though you may be. We still talk about our theology sessions with you and your dad in the late fifties. You asked profound questions that we still remember." She put a hand on his shoulder. "You are an especially gifted human being, Cloud, and I want only the best for you. And it looks like you've found your soul-mate. What pastor wouldn't be excited about that?"

The service included Communion, with parishioners coming forward to tear a chunk from the loaf of bread in Adam's hands and dip it in the cup of wine that Evelyn held. They placed the wine-soaked bread in their mouths as they returned in silence to their pews.

Debriefing the service from the back seat of Lloyd's car on the way to Paradise Valley, Terp said, "Never in my life have the words 'This is my body given for you' affected me so powerfully as today when I saw all those naked bodies -all those different shapes and sizes and ages, taut skin and wrinkled, scarred and clear- all those trusting and eager people lining up to take part in the Lord's Supper."

"Wait till you see a baptism," Nissa said. "I cry sweet tears during baptisms. Back in 1961 when our pastors baptized their own twins, Abram and Sarai, I cried a bucketful. So, I take it this means you'll be coming back to church?"

"I'm sure of it," said Terp.

"We have a lot to talk about with Adam and Evelyn -theological stuff," said Cloud. "They have a meeting in Scottsdale next week, and we've invited them to our apartment afterward for dinner."

Nissa was very pleased with this development.

In Cloud's car en route to their apartment, Terp said, "I thought I was being greedy insisting that Argyle Watts marry us in Metuchen. But now I'm going to be really, really greedy. I want three weddings."

"Let's see. The first was our self-conducted service at the apartment last October. The second will be at Second Calvinist next June," Cloud said with a note of intuitive expectation in his voice. "What could the third one possibly be?"

"I want Adam and Evelyn to officiate at a wedding at their church. There is no doctrinal or ecclesiastical reason to prevent us from saying our vows as many times in as many services as we want."

"A doctrinal argument against it wouldn't hold much water with me anyway," Cloud responded. "But if you want a naturist wedding along with the traditional one, then you shall have it. We'll talk to Adam and Evelyn when they come over for dinner next Wednesday."

"Thank you, dearest," she said.

"No need to thank me. It's a great idea." Cloud grinned. "In fact, to quote my favorite dancer, 'it makes me happy.' Earlier today Evelyn told me she thought you and I are soul-mates. I think that's an understatement. Our love goes deeper than that."

"That reminds me," Terp said. "I think you should tell Adam and Evelyn about your out-of-body experiences and precognition."

"I was thinking the same thing," he said. "And you should tell them about meeting the Old One."

"I'll tell them my thing if you'll tell them yours," Terp quipped.

Terp planned a simple meal of green salad, hearty soup, and cheesecake for their dinner guests. Over salad, Evelyn and Adam quickly agreed to do a wedding for Terp and Cloud. No decision was made about a date for the service, but they all agreed some time in the spring would be good. Terp suggested May thirtieth. "If I'm going to be married in my birthday suit, it may as well be on my twenty-first birthday," she said.

"So, how exactly did you two meet?" Evelyn asked over soup. This was the cue Cloud and Terp had agreed upon for telling their secrets. A long time passed before they got to the dessert, as the two ministers sat spellbound by the overlapping tales that Cloud and Terp poured out.

"I am stunned," said Adam.

Evelyn said, "Last Sunday, Cloud, I told you that you were gifted. I had no idea how incredibly gifted. And you, Terp -a face-to-face conversation with...with what I can only conceive of as an angel. I feel like I'm sitting in the presence of a holy mystery, and I have so many questions I don't know where to start."

"It feels so good to talk about these things with people who don't think we're crazy," Cloud said. "Please, ask away."

"You're not crazy," said Adam.

"I feel as light as a feather, having revealed the Old One to the two of you," said Terp. She had adopted Cloud's name for the mysterious creature she met in the desert, deeming it superior to Big Head, which she had used as a child. "And I sense the more I tell the lighter I'll feel. If you ask enough questions, maybe I'll float out of my body too."

"Before you go floating off," Evelyn said, "Give us a more detailed description of the Old One. As much as you remember. You said that you couldn't see whether the Old One was male or female."

"That's right," said Terp. "The Old One was covered from neck to feet with a purple robe. It had long white hair and a large, triangle shaped face. Wide forehead, big eyes and ears, small nose and mouth, and pointed chin."

"Could you see hands and feet?" Evelyn asked.

"Yes, I touched one hand. It was dry and warm -and soft."

"What did the Old One's voice sound like?" Evelyn continued.

"I can still hear it in my head. It sounded just like mine only...older and deeper."

"And you asked the Old One's name and the Old One said...?"

"Never mind my name. You couldn't pronounce it," Terp spoke from memory.

"From which we can infer," said Adam, "that the Old One does indeed have a name. As opposed to being a functional but nameless manifestation of the Divine, the Old One is an actual, presumably flesh and blood, creature."

"May we see the purple cloth and boards you found in the shack?" asked Evelyn.

Cloud led them to a corner of the living room and removed a

decorative runner that disguised his Army footlocker. Inside were the relics. The pastors' eyes were full of wonder at the sight of the bleached white lumber and colored fabric. After years in the desert, the purple hue in the cloth remained bold and unfaded. Adam picked up a wood slat while Evelyn ran her fingers over a piece of the cloth. Both felt jolts of energy.

In a rush of euphoria, Evelyn gushed, "This makes me feel like dancing."

An equally euphoric Adam added, "And I feel like singing."

"This sounds like a scene from a musical," said Cloud. "So, Adam, why don't you sing something your wife can dance to."

"We'll be your audience," said Terp, "and absorb the joy of your art."

In his flowing baritone Adam sang "I Danced in the Morning," the new Sydney Carter hymn based on the old Shaker hymn "'Tis a Gift to Be Simple." Evelyn spun around the room, joyfully unencumbered by clothing, spreading her arms, bending and rising, enacting the story of Jesus' life through her motions.

When the dance was finished, Terp's mind and heart were racing. Excitedly she asked Evelyn, "Do you ever dance in church?"

"No. This was entirely spontaneous and improvised," came the reply.

"Someday, I want to dance in church," said Terp. "I have choreographies worked out in my head. But I've never actually seen it done."

"Oh, there are places that use dance in worship," said Evelyn. "You should look into Pacific Crossroads Theological Seminary. They have a liturgical dance curriculum."

"I think I've found my graduate school," said Terp. "My assumption has been I'd go to Princeton Seminary, to please my mom. But if Pacific Crossroads offers the right kind of dance curriculum, Princeton would be a definite second choice."

"How do you feel about Terp going to seminary, Cloud?" Adam asked.

"Thinking about being married to a minister feels odd," Cloud said. "But there's a sense of inevitability about it. Almost -dare I say the word in front of a Calvinist- predestination. It seems the most natural thing in the world for Terp to do. I hung out at San Francisco Seminary when I was stationed at Monterey, and I loved the atmosphere of the place, where academics wrestled with spirituality. I'm looking forward to following Terp wherever she wants to go."

Cloud closed the lid on the footlocker and they returned to the table, where Terp served the delayed course of cheesecake.

Adam asked, "Cloud, do you think the being Terp saw in the desert is the same one who communicated with you the first time you left your body?"

"Yes, I believe so," Cloud said.

"I wonder if you were dead that time and the Old One sent you back to life," Adam continued. "What do you think?"

Cloud said, "I don't think I actually died, but I was probably close to it. There's no way of knowing for sure. Of course, I've been quite healthy every other time I've floated out of my body."

"When was the last time you left your body?" Evelyn asked.

Cloud blushed. "Last week," he said, volunteering no further information.

Evelyn recognized she had intruded upon a sacred intimacy and changed the subject. "Or a prescient dream? Have you had any more dreams about national events?"

"Lately we've been experiencing the pleasant fulfillment of old, very private dreams," Cloud said. "It's been a long time since I've dreamed about any tragedy involving public figures. I hope those nightmares are over."

"I hope so too," said Evelyn, "but I wouldn't count on it."

"Time to pepper Terp with questions," Adam said. "When you made that little wooden angel move around Salisbury Cathedral, did anything else unusual happen?"

"Hmmm," said Terp. "Apart from nipping that obnoxious tourist's rump? Let me think. Oh yes, in Hyde Park, I thought I saw someone who reminded me of the Old One, only wearing a white alb. I was a good ways away, so I'm not sure. I wanted to get closer, but my mom wanted to go shopping, so we left the park. There was a sense of peace emanating from the direction of whoever it was in the white robe."

"What else?" Adam asked.

"Well, this wasn't in England, but on the plane back to New Jersey, a guy across the aisle was smoking like a chimney. I'm pretty sensitive to the issue of smoking, because my dad died from smoking related heart disease. Anyway, I got up to go to the lavatory, and the plane hit an air pocket and I bumped into the guy just as he was about to stick another cigarette in his mouth. Then the strangest thing happened. I put my hand on his shoulder to catch my balance and he put the cigarette back in the pack and didn't smoke another one the rest of the flight."

"What were you thinking at the moment you put your hand on his shoulder?" Evelyn asked.

"I was thinking about my dad dying too young and how he'd been a heavy smoker."

Adam and Evelyn exchanged knowing looks.

"Have you ever had any similar experiences?" Adam asked.

"Now that you mention it, my freshman year at ASU, on the flight from Newark to Phoenix, I sat next to a woman who was opening and closing her seatbelt compulsively and counting the number of times she did it. She was getting on my nerves. I think she was up to thirty-some. It was really strange. I touched her arm and offered to help. Actually, I did more than offer. I clicked her seatbelt together and told her it was OK now. And she stopped fidgeting and was a peaceful companion the whole trip."

Adam and Evelyn exchanged knowing looks again.

"Any other times?" Evelyn asked.

"Well, this isn't about me. It's about my pastor in Metuchen, Argyle Watts. When I was a kid, one Sunday I was waiting in line to greet him after church, and a really agitated man, I'd guess a derelict by appearance, came bounding up to him. The stranger had a crazed look in his eye and wasn't about to wait his turn. But just as Rev. Watts turned to look at him, the man calmed down and was very polite. I was amazed that one look from my pastor relieved the man of his nervousness."

Adam said, "Did this agitated stranger have any contact with you, Terp?"

"No, he didn't say a word to me." She paused, dredging the image of the paranoid schizophrenic to consciousness. "He bumped into me, though, because I was next in line to shake my pastor's hand."

"Your pastor didn't calm the man, Terp," Adam pronounced. "That was undoubtedly you!"

"No, it couldn't be," Terp responded.

"Terp, you have the gift of healing," said Evelyn. She turned to her husband. "Adam dear, we are in the presence of two extraordinary, dare I say holy people."

"Whoa," said Cloud. "Gifted...maybe. Not holy, at least not me. I know better than to use the word holy in connection with me."

"We need to be heading back to New River," Evelyn said. "But this conversation must be continued. Can we talk more about your experiences? Both of you?"

"Sure," said Cloud. "And I want to restart our conversation about the Trinity."

"We'll be at church this Sunday," said Terp. "Maybe we can talk after the service."

"Come to our apartment for lunch," said Adam.

Early Thursday morning, after a restful night of sleep, Terp asked Cloud to teach her to float.

"Lie still," he said. "Right here on the bed, face up. Relax and breathe deeply, hold the air in your lungs for a moment and then let it out slowly and completely. All the way out. Take your time. Don't try to hurry anything."

She had observed Cloud performing this preparatory breathing and was able to mimic his technique perfectly.

"Now," he said quietly, "focus your mind on the ceiling. Imagine yourself hovering next to it. Concentrate all your thoughts on rising out of your body and floating toward the ceiling."

Cloud watched her for a long time. He could see her knit her brow in an effort to force the needed mental energy. Her breathing was right but she seemed to be calling upon intellectual strength to accomplish the task. After twenty minutes without success, she said, "I give up. We'll have to try again another day."

"It's all right, my love," Cloud said. "There have been plenty of times when I couldn't do it no matter how hard I tried."

"Well, maybe it's simply not my gift," she said with a sigh.

—o—

"OK," said Cloud over lunch at Adam and Evelyn Rarom's apartment, "before we get to solving the manifest problems of the Trinity, I have a question about sex, specifically pre-marital sex."

"Whatever your question, I'm against it," Adam shot back.

"Well, you said that rather strongly in a sermon in 1958. I remember it well," said Cloud. "But now Terp and I are living together, and you haven't said a word against us."

"Let's say I've had to accommodate to modern reality," Adam confessed. "Today ninety percent of the couples who come to us to get married are already living together. I believe it's better to bless the existing union and perform the marriage ceremony than to send them away with moralistic condemnations. I still believe that sex belongs only in the matrimonial bed, but I'm not hardnosed about it."

"Tell them what you said on the way home from their apartment last Wednesday night," Evelyn said to her husband.

"I said," Adam responded with a hint of smugness in his voice, "I thought the two of you were already spiritually married."

"That confirms it," Terp said. "On the day after we found the remnants of the Old One's robe, we decided that we had become husband and wife in the eyes of God; that is, we'd said our wedding vows without words. And that was without either one of us proposing." She then blushed remembering sensate details of the event.

Adam did not notice her change in complexion, for he had turned to peer at Evelyn. "I rest my case," he said. Changing focus then to Cloud, he said, "Speaking of the relics connected with the Old One, I think it would be good to store them in a safe, archival facility. Some place dry and cool with temperature controls."

"I'll bet someone at the Hayden Library on campus can help me find a facility to protect these things," Cloud said. "I'll look into it."

"The Trinity has waited for years," Evelyn said. "I'd like to talk more about Terp's gift of healing. Every situation you described, Terp, related to mental or addictive illness. I've done some research since last Wednesday. You have the gift of psychiasis, that is healing of psyche - or soul. But it seems that experiences of healing resulting from brief touch are temporary. Without prolonged attention, people usually revert to more primitive states of mental health."

"In other words," Cloud said, "these are not cures but respites from affliction."

"Right," Evelyn said. "But with longer physical attention and prayer, especially from someone like Terp, outright cures can occur."

"Hence the need for intentional healing services," said Adam. "Not like those phony tent shows where cripples throw away their crutches and prance around the stage shouting 'Praise the Lord!' I'm talking about intimate services where hurting people, especially mentally and spiritually wounded people, can be anointed with oil and experience the laying on of hands and profound prayer."

"Terp, we'd like you to officiate with us at such a service," Evelyn said.

"I'd be honored," said Terp, "but it will have to wait until next year. We're going to New Jersey over Christmas break, and I have finals and a dozen other things to do first."

"No hurry," said Evelyn. "We just want you to think about it."

"It looks like the Trinity and the divinity of Christ will have to wait till next year also," Cloud added.

Dreading the reaction from her mother, Terp nervously placed the third call to tell Penny that she and Cloud planned to marry. "Well, Mom, I have news," she said soberly. "I watched carefully for signs that the relationship with Cloud might be -How did you put it?- a high school crush or on the rebound."

"That's a normal situation," Penny said sympathetically. "Don't worry, though. Somebody better will come along, and you'll be better prepared for the relationship."

"It turns out, Mom, that this is neither crush nor rebound. Cloud is the love of my life. I'd like to bring him home at Christmas so you can meet him. We're engaged."

Penny was silent for an uncomfortable interval but finally said in a controlled voice, "I think that's a good idea, Terp. I definitely want to meet this man."

Dagmar took Terp to lunch at Monti's. "This is the place where that rat Kirk Trilby made his first pass at you," Dagmar explained. "So I'm redeeming a great restaurant by providing you a different memory of the place."

"Thanks, Dagmar." Terp said. "And I want you to know that Kirk is thoroughly expunged from my system. I hardly remember what he looks like. I'm so happy now there's no room in my brain for thoughts of him."

"So, tell me what's been going on," Dagmar said.

Terp told Dagmar about their looming Christmas trip to Edison and the plans for a June wedding in New Jersey. Then she talked about Lloyd and Nissa, Narcissa, Adam and Evelyn, the Natural Christian Church, and their plans for a naturist wedding in May. Much was required to render Dagmar speechless. Terp's tale accomplished the task.

"Hey, I've been doing all the talking," Terp said. "What's happening with you?"

Dagmar said nothing. She found organizing her thoughts difficult. After a time of pregnant silence she said, "Forget my prosaic life. Terp, your story is incredible and I'm jealous as hell. For all my negative feelings about religion, I confess I'm morbidly curious about this nudist church. It sounds delightfully debauched. Can I go with you sometime?"

"It's far from debauched," Terp laughed. "I'll check with the pastors. They'd need to interview you. They're very careful about prospective visitors."

"In the meantime, you promised to invite me over for dinner when you got settled," Dagmar reminded her former roommate.

"We're flying back east in two days, so why don't you come over for dinner tomorrow."

"Are you sure? I was teasing. It'll wait till January," Dagmar responded.

"I'm sure. Cloud's very efficient about these things. Most of our packing is already done. It'll be fun. Tomorrow around five."

"What's the proper dress?" Dagmar asked with lewd inflection. "Can I run around your apartment stark naked?"

"Certainly," laughed Terp. "Plan on it."

Terp was nude when she answered Dagmar's knock on the door, and so was Cloud as he enfolded their grinning guest's right hand around a glass of wine.

"You weren't kidding," said Dagmar. Since morning she had been nurturing a fantasy about how this evening would unfold. Now the prospect of her first sexual threesome aroused her libido as she unzipped and slipped out of her denim dress.

Mentally, Cloud noted what Terp had told him. Dagmar did not wear undergarments. "Terp was right," he said, reflecting on something else she had said. "You have a classically proportioned body, ideal for an artist's model."

"Can I hold it against you?" Dagmar purred as she shuffled seductively toward him, pursuing an amorous embrace.

CHAPTER FOUR

Cloud raised a hand to his chin and assumed a professorial demeanor, artfully obstructing the oncoming embrace. "My mother had a gorgeous body when she was young, but Sigmund Freud to the contrary, I never wanted to relate with her in a sexual way," he said.

"Is that a put-down?" Dagmar asked with a startled and hurt tone in her voice.

"Not at all," said Cloud. "It's really a compliment. Look, Dagmar, I hardly know you, but my intuitive first impression is you use sexuality as a way to attract and relate to people, maybe even manage them. You don't need to do that here. Terp cares about you a great deal -even loves you as a sister. And I would like to be your friend, and perhaps someday love you as the sister I never had."

Dagmar now realized her fantastic misjudgment of the invitation to socialize nude and was mollified but not subdued. "I guess incest is out," she retorted. "Well, I can see that you're gaga over Terp, so I may as well settle for being the chaste little sister."

Terp said, "It's not a matter of settling for anything. We want you to feel welcome here, where it's safe to run around naked without any pressure to perform sexually."

Cloud added, "Just be yourself. We want to know the real Dagmar."

"Well, part of the real Dagmar is a highly sexualized being," Dagmar noted.

"Any time you feel an overwhelming need for sexual gratification," Cloud said, "you're welcome to use our bedroom to satisfy it -as long as we're not there. Go in and close the door and no one will disturb you. And we'll never say a word about it."

"But you'd know what I was doing in there," Dagmar replied provocatively.

"I suspect you'd enjoy us speculating," Terp said wryly, "but we certainly have no objection to self-pleasuring. As for group pleasure, dinner is ready. Let's gather at the table."

"Give me a minute, please," said Dagmar. She went into the bedroom and shut the door. Sixty seconds later she emerged. "Curious about what I was doing? Actually, I didn't do anything. I just wanted to experience the freedom -see what it felt like."

"I would think you already know a lot about sexual freedom," Terp said.

"Not with people I honestly care about," Dagmar confessed with subdued voice.

After dinner the three bumped into one another cleaning up in the tiny kitchen. When they had finished, Dagmar said, "Now I want to give you two a gift. It involves physical touch but don't get your pubes in a knot; it's not sexual. I learned it in drama class as a relaxation technique. Have you ever heard of reflexology?"

"No," said Terp and Cloud simultaneously.

Dagmar explained, "It's a kind of foot massage, where pressure is applied to certain points on your feet. This relaxes corresponding places all over your body." She picked up her purse and pulled a bottle of massage oil from it. "Do you have an old towel I could use?" Terp provided it, and Dagmar moved her chair in front of the couch, sat down and spread the towel across her legs. "You first, Terp. Plop down on the couch and put your left foot in my lap."

Dagmar slowly applied pressure to various points on Terp's foot and individual toes, and then conducted a general massage, moving her thumbs up and down the length and across the width of the foot.

"This feels wonderful," Terp sighed. "And nothing hirsute to get knotted."

"I get it," said Cloud. "It's like treating trench foot."

"Like what?" Dagmar asked.

"In high school ROTC," Cloud explained, "they showed us World War II training films. The most famous one was called ***Trench Foot.*** It showed actual soldiers peeling frostbitten toes off their feet. Really gross! It was supposed to scare us into taking good care of our feet. The preventive for trench foot is for soldiers in the field to take off their boots and rub each other's feet for at least five minutes by the clock. General Eisenhower made foot rubbing mandatory in the European Theater."

"Similar principle," said Dagmar, "but different context."

After fifteen minutes of attention to her left foot, Dagmar began the reflexology technique on Terp's right foot. She then turned her efforts to Cloud's feet. Cloud felt so relaxed he thought he might pop out of his body but decided he wanted to stay in it to savor the experience.

When Dagmar finished Cloud's foot massage, Cloud said, "Thanks, Dagmar. That was a tremendous gift. Now let us reciprocate. Get over here on the couch."

"No need. This was my present to you," she said.

"We accept your gift," Terp said. "Let us give you one."

"You've already given me the gift of affection without sexual expectations, so apparently you care about me more than my body," Dagmar said. Despite her protests, however, she wanted the tactile attention and slid obediently onto the couch while Cloud placed a chair beside the one Terp now occupied.

"Give me your right foot," Terp instructed Dagmar, "and put your left one in Cloud's lap. We need to practice this reflexology and hear from you if we got it right. Don't be shy about critiquing and guiding our efforts."

Twenty minutes into the dual foot rub, Dagmar had drifted into a deep meditative state. Two hours later she awoke to find herself stretched out on the couch with a blanket over her. Cloud and Terp sat across from one another at the dining room table. Terp was reading an assigned novel, while Cloud was making notes on index cards for his dissertation.

"How long was I out?" Dagmar asked.

"A couple of hours," Terp said. "You're welcome to spend the night if you want."

"Thanks. I think I will," she said, and wrapping the blanket tightly around her, rolled over and returned to sleep.

In the morning, the three of them vied for time in the single bathroom in calm domestic fashion, playing tag team with the shower.

"Have a great trip you two and come back safely. You both threaten the shit out of my cynicism, but I'll miss you," Dagmar said before departing to pack for a dreaded holiday visit home to Maryvale.

As the plane taxied to the terminal at the Newark Airport, Terp suddenly grabbed Cloud's arm. "It just dawned on me," she moaned, "that my mother will put us in separate bedrooms."

"I assumed she would," Cloud said. "As long as we're in her house, we should respect your mother's sensibilities."

"But I've gotten so used to curling up with you, I won't like sleeping apart," Terp said.

"Neither will I," he said, "but it's only for a couple of weeks. We'll manage."

Cloud's assumption proved correct. Penny had made up the downstairs den for him, far from the uncomfortably close guest bedroom adjacent to Terp's room upstairs.

Mary delivered immediate and unrestrained affection to her future brother-in-law, seeing him as strong and handsome. Penny, however, was not about to be rushed into embracing her daughter's fiancé. She was friendly but reticent. She needed time to assess this man.

At dinner, in response to Penny's pointed inquiries, Cloud spoke at length about his doctoral program in the history of Asian religions and his plans to become a college professor. Though she sought information about his time in the Army, Cloud said very little about it, dismissing his tour in Viet Nam as dull and routine administrative work. Terp remained silent, knowing that to say anything about the real story would discomfit him.

Close to midnight, when Terp and Cloud retired to their respective rooms, Penny dropped in on her older daughter. "Let's have a girl to girl talk," she said.

"OK, Mom, what do you want to talk about," said Terp, although she knew what was on her mother's mind.

"Well, honey, I sense that Cloud is holding something back, and I wonder if you might know about it."

"What makes you say that?" Terp responded, conscious that she had withheld a great deal from her mother over the years.

"When I asked about his military service, he was evasive. Your dad was never like that. He talked our ears off about the war."

"Oh, that. Well, he's kind of private about Viet Nam, but I managed to get him to open up about it. He was a Vietnamese linguist -intelligence analysis and stuff like that. I suppose it's natural that someone doing secret work would be tight-lipped," Terp explained.

"What rank was he? Was he an officer?" Penny wanted to know. "Your father was an officer."

"He was a captain."

Penny was impressed with this news. "Oh, that's quite an accomplishment for as young as he was then. Why didn't you tell me this before?"

"It didn't seem important," Terp said. "Anyway, there's more to the story, if you want to hear it."

"Sure I do," said Penny.

"Most of the time he was stationed in Saigon, and he received a Bronze Star for his work there. During the Tet Offensive, he was wounded and received a Purple Heart. After Tet he was transferred to the Mekong Delta. One day he went out on an airmobile operation and ended up rescuing a pilot from a burning helicopter and was shot by a sniper in the process. So he received another Purple Heart and a Bronze Star with V for valor. He doesn't like to talk about it because he thinks other men's wounds were far worse and many others were far braver than he. That's what he was holding back."

"Thank you for telling me this," Penny whispered. "It makes all the difference in my being able to embrace Cloud as my future son-in-law." But Penny was not yet ready to concede completely on Cloud's suitability. "I do have some other concerns, though."

"Such as," Terp said.

"For a while I was tempted to say that Cloud is too old for you. What is he -29? But then it dawned on me that you've been old all your life." Now Penny laughed. "Maybe you're too old for him."

"That's a strange thing to say, Mom."

"You know what I mean, Terp. You were always asking questions and doing things way beyond your years. What's the word for that?

Precocious. You were a precocious child, so I suppose it's only fitting that you would be a precocious bride."

"I'll be two years older than you were when you married Dad. What's really bugging you?" Terp asked.

"This is a sensitive subject, I know, but I need to talk with you about...money," said Penny. "You'll still have another year of college after you get married. I'm willing to pay your tuition for that year, recognizing it will be a strain for a poor graduate student like Cloud to provide you with that. I'd rather pay it than have you drop out."

"That's very generous of you, Mom, but it won't be necessary. We'll get by fine. And I won't drop out. In fact I'm planning to go on to graduate school, more specifically, to seminary. My goal is to become a minister."

"That's wonderful, Terp," Penny said feigning enthusiasm. "But how will you be able to afford graduate school on a teacher's salary?"

"When I turn twenty-one next May, I'll gain control of the trust fund Dad left for me. How much is that worth now?"

"Oh, I forgot about that," Penny said unconvincingly. "I'm not sure. It's close to two hundred thousand dollars, I think."

"Plenty to finance three years in seminary," Terp said dryly. "But lest you think Cloud is out to marry me for my money, he has a portfolio almost double my trust fund."

"Oh, I didn't think that for a minute," Penny said without conviction, and then added with a buoyant air, "but I guess I don't need to worry about my daughter living in genteel poverty."

"Not in any case," Terp replied. "College professors do quite well financially."

Breakfast was late the next morning, but when the four were at last gathered at the table, Penny acted noticeably more affectionate toward Cloud. It seemed as if she had fallen in motherly love with him overnight.

Cloud volunteered to do the breakfast dishes, and Terp immediately said she would help. Alone in the kitchen, Terp whispered, "Mom and I had a midnight chat about you. She now thinks you're a wonderful catch."

"I hope you didn't tell her how easy it was for you to reel me in," he said.

"I've kept secrets from my mother most of my life," she said. "She couldn't begin to comprehend the truth about either of us. By the way, I miss your body." She embraced him, her hands firmly fondling his buttocks. Mary stepped in and tiptoed out grinning.

Later that day, Cloud met the Rev. Argyle Watts, and the two men immediately liked one another. Terp's main concern was settling on a date for the wedding, but somehow Argyle and Cloud moved off course into a long conversation about Calvinism.

"The stupidest thing Calvin ever did was to sanction Servetus being burned at the stake," Argyle acknowledged. "The intellectually craven part was fastening Servetus' books around his waist to burn along with him. That one deed tarnished Calvin's legacy more than any of the weird twists of doctrine that certain among his followers devised."

"What do you think about the doctrine of total depravity?" Cloud asked.

"It's a bleak view of humankind," Argyle responded. "Three hundred years ago, Calvinists were exceedingly suspicious of human nature. They were sure that all people, including themselves, were unavoidably totally depraved. Burning Servetus with green wood to prolong his agony proved that about themselves. Like predestination, we tend to downplay that notion these days. It doesn't resonate well with optimistic Americans."

"Don't be too quick to abandon that one," Cloud said. "With all my aversions to hard and fast doctrines, it's one I think John Calvin was on track with. I believe we are all essentially flawed."

"Original sin rings easier in the ears of parishioners," Argyle said.

"But I don't like the tone it makes," Cloud responded. "I can't believe human beings are stained with sin because Adam and Eve, or any other early ***homo sapiens*** they mythically represent, disobeyed God. What's wrong with us has nothing to do with rebellion against God. It's not a punishment for sin. We're not screwed up because Adam was dumb enough to eat a piece of forbidden fruit that Eve slipped him. That story makes Adam into a schmuck, God into a scheming control freak, and the snake the truth teller."

"Why then are we, as you phrase it, screwed up?" Argyle asked.

"I wish I knew. The world is so complex that it's impossible for anyone to be completely good. A good deed in one place will result in suffering somewhere else. An evil deed can lead to unexpected blessings and inspire people to their noblest behavior. I think we need to start with the confession that we're all depraved, but it's not because some ancestor flaunted one of God's arbitrary regulations."

Argyle smiled. "What then is the answer to this problem of total depravity?"

"The one thing that makes any sense to me," Cloud said, "is the Judeo-Christian concept of grace. The only power that can cut through the thick and contorted knot of human stupidity, greed, and violence is the grace of God."

"I fully agree with your conclusion," Argyle said, "but not necessarily the route you took to get there."

Listening to this exchange reminded Terp of intense discourses on theological issues she had enjoyed with her pastor over the years. She was glad Cloud was doing the same, but she had another priority this day. She said, "As much as I find all this interesting, gentlemen - and I very much do- we need to return to the task at hand. Can we set a date for the wedding? How does Saturday, June thirtieth sound?"

Argyle looked at his calendar. "That date is open for me. We'll do it then. How about 2:30 in the afternoon?"

"Good," said Cloud. "That's settled. Now, about the Trinity..."

"Stop!" said Terp. "We have another item of business to take care of."

"She's right," said Argyle. "I told Terp on the phone that I won't do a wedding without pre-marital counseling. If you're going to be around till after New Year's Day, I propose we take care of that on this trip." They set dates for the counseling sessions.

"I guess my avidity for heterodox theological discussion is an example of my personal depravity," Cloud offered with a chuckle.

"If that's an example of your dark side, Cloud, you don't have much to worry about," Argyle said. "Most of the saints and prophets in this world have been obsessive monomaniacs with very unpleasant personalities."

"There's a lot more darkness in me than that," Cloud said. "Some day I'll tell you how total depravity showed its face in Viet Nam."

"But you didn't do those things, Cloud. You just saw them," Terp said, coming to his defense. "And they caused you great sorrow."

"I chose to be there. I was part of all that happened. I won't excuse myself like the Germans who shrugged off the Holocaust by claiming they were not Nazis and were only following orders. There is something about war that stains even the purest of heart, and I have never been anywhere close to pure."

"I suspect you're being too hard on yourself, Cloud," Argyle sighed.

"He's the kindest and gentlest man I've ever met," Terp said to Argyle. "And the simple way he lives and the way he shuns ostentation would please John Calvin's heart."

"Oh pshaw!" said Cloud, mocking his own modesty. Yet he blushed at her words.

The first pre-marital counseling session started on an awkward note. The source of that note was Argyle Watts. "The area I want to begin with is sex. This is the subject no one wants to talk about, least of all with a minister. And I confess it is a subject I am not comfortable with, but I feel obligated not to ignore it simply because I'm a bit of a prude. So my strategy is to deal with it first and then get on to more important matters.

"Back in the fifties, one assumed that couples who wanted to be married in the church had not engaged in sexual relations. Whether this was true is another question, but a minister could safely counsel with couples as if they knew nothing about sexual intercourse, and everyone went along with the...charade. Things are different today. Nearly all the wedding services I conduct these days are for people who are already living together or who have extensive intimate knowledge of one another.

"I recognize that the younger generation has freer views about sex than I. At times I wish I could be more liberal on this subject, but in the final analysis, I am rather old fashioned about sex, and I don't think that will ever change."

"You don't need to apologize for who you are," Cloud said. "There's nothing wrong in being faithful to what you believe."

"You should see the giggles and grimaces I get from young people today when I say what I believe about sex," Argyle said. "But what am I doing now? I'm talking with you two as if you were colleagues rather than young lovers at the peak of their sexual primes. I'm not in the habit of confessing my discomfort about sexuality with people I counsel. For some reason, with the two of you I feel the need to be more honest."

"I feel honored that you trust us with your inner life," Terp said. "And as a way of getting past the initial embarrassment, let me say that we don't need any counseling about sexual compatibility. But we would very much like to hear your wisdom about the place of sex in marriage as the years pass."

"Very well said," Argyle remarked. "I don't think I've ever heard a prospective bride express that thought so eloquently."

"Well, I'm an English major," said Terp, blushing at the compliment but not at the subject matter.

"My wisdom, huh? Let me see...How about this? As time passes, sex is seldom a problem in marriage. It is the absence of sexual relations that strains the marital bonds. Adultery, of course, tests this rule. Having sex with someone other than your spouse certainly damages a marriage. But adultery is not at heart a sexual sin; rather it is an attack upon the covenant that a man and woman make to one another in matrimony. Terrible things happen between partners when trust is wounded."

"My guess," said Cloud, "is that people eager to get married find it hard to conceive that they would ever be unfaithful. But time and bitter circumstances cause some individuals to change, and they find themselves behaving in ways they may not understand but that nevertheless seriously hurt their partners."

"I think," said Argyle, "that I may need to call upon the two of you to do this work for me in the future. I feel rather inadequate to the task right now."

"You're not at all inadequate!" interjected Terp. "This is a great conversation. It means a lot to us to receive your guidance."

"Alas, my dear, you don't need my wisdom on this particular subject. Let's shift to an area much more likely to cause problems in marriage -finances. More friction comes from differing expectations about spending money than from any other source. Some people are spenders and some are savers. When a lavish spender is married to a parsimonious saver, life with one another will be hell."

"Cloud is a saver," Terp said, "and I'm not wasteful, but I'm more apt to spend money on things I want."

"I'm not a slave to saving," Cloud explained, a bit defensively. "I'm not opposed to spending for needs or wants. But most of the things I want require little or no money. I have simple tastes. I've spent a great deal more on books and music over the last four years than I have on my wardrobe. I resonate with Erasmus, who said, 'When I get a little money I buy books, and if any is left I buy food and clothes.' He had his priorities straight."

Argyle was delighted to have hit upon a subject requiring his counseling skills. "You reacted with some emotion to Terp's statement about being a saver, Cloud. How do you feel about what she said?"

"Your question triggered an insight, Argyle. At times in my life I've been very generous with money. But I've been more inclined to spend it on other people than myself. I associate spending money with times of happiness and saving it with seasons of sadness. More of my life this past decade has been lived with pain than with pleasure. Until I met Terp, I didn't see much that I wanted to buy. Now there are hosts of things I could do with my money -our money- for our mutual enjoyment."

"Like what?" Terp asked.

"Like our apartment," he said. "If you want a bigger place or nicer furniture, I'm ready to move or buy new stuff."

"I like our place," Terp said. "It's perfect for a couple of students. I'd rather spend money on traveling to faraway places."

"Pack your bags, lover. We'll circumnavigate the globe."

She kissed his cheek. "What you need to know, Rev. Watts..."

"I think, Terp, it's time you started calling me Argyle."

"What you need to know, Argyle, is that Cloud and I both fall into what you would call the affluent category, and neither of us is prodigal by temperament. We won't have arguments about missing the rent payment in order to have Christmas presents."

"OK, let's move on to the subject of wills and estate planning."

The first session concluded shortly thereafter.

—o—

Argyle was reading at his desk when Terp and Cloud arrived for their second counseling session. As soon as they entered, he closed the book and set it aside, giving the couple his full attention.

"What are you reading?" Cloud asked with genuine curiosity.

"Elton Trueblood, ***The Humor of Christ***," Argyle answered. "He's a Quaker theologian. Are you familiar with him?"

"No," Cloud said, "but the title is intriguing. I've long thought Jesus was a bit of a trickster, so much smarter than the religious and secular authorities that he couldn't resist yanking their metaphorical chains."

"Trueblood treats Jesus more reverently than your image does," Argyle said. "Nevertheless, his aim is to puncture the common stereotype of Jesus as an overly serious merchant of gloom. I got a chuckle from Trueblood's contention that Jesus made an ironic joke when giving Simon the nickname Peter. Peter, as I'm sure you know, is equivalent to the nickname Rocky. But Peter was far from an emotional rock. He was more an emotional wreck. Although Trueblood did not use this example, calling Simon Rocky would be as cheeky as calling an ungainly obese person Twinkle Toes."

"Here we go again," said Terp with a sigh.

Discussion quickly refocused on the details of the wedding ceremony. Mary would be maid of honor. Lloyd would be best man. Argyle would not permit any secular music in the service. Terp and Cloud would write their own wedding vows, subject, of course, to approval by Argyle. He had once officiated at the wedding of a couple who had produced blatantly erotic vows, and he wanted to avoid repeating that embarrassment.

The only hitch concerned who, in the absence of her deceased father, would give Terp away. Terp made it clear she did not want to be given away by anyone, but she would like someone to escort her down the aisle. She suggested her mother, and Argyle thought that would be fine. Terp called Penny from Argyle's office, and Penny thought the idea was touching but preferred the traditional mother of the bride role.

"You've been like a father to me," Terp said to her pastor. "Will you walk down the aisle with me?"

A tear formed in Argyle's left eye. "I would be honored to do so," he said. "Of course this will create a complication in the order of worship. Let me think about how this would flow." A moment later he had a plan.

For the third session, Cloud and Terp came dressed in jeans and sweatshirts. As the visit exploring religious compatibility neared an end, Cloud said, "Argyle, we'd like to thank you with a gift."

"Oh no, it's not necessary. I don't accept honoraria for counseling with a member of the church," he said.

"We weren't thinking of money," said Terp. "We want to do something for your feet."

"Now you have me intrigued," the minister said.

"You'll have to trust us on this one," Cloud said. "Scoot you chair over here opposite us and take off your shoes and socks."

Argyle was somewhat abashed by this order, but he complied. From a large canvas bag Terp produced towels, which she and Cloud placed on their laps. She opened a thermos bottle and pulled out two hot, wet washcloths. Cloud lifted Argyle's feet into their respective laps and he and Terp gently washed the pastor's feet. Having completed the ritual ablution, they poured massage oil onto their hands and began rubbing his feet.

Argyle was nervous about the physical attention. What they were doing felt so good that surely it must be sinful. "I'm not certain this is proper," he said.

"Hush," said Terp. "Relax and enjoy our gift. A friend taught it to us, and we want to teach it to people we care about."

He did not protest further and allowed himself the luxury of lapsing into a meditative state. Thirty minutes later, the tension in Argyle Watts' body had been thoroughly eased to a degree he hadn't known for decades. Nevertheless, a vague feeling of guilt lingered as his superego confused the sensual pleasure of foot massage with what some might consider a perverse form of sexual activity.

"We have another gift and a request," Terp said. She placed the bottle of massage lotion in his hands. "Take this home and rub your wife's feet the way we've done for you. I'm sure Ruth will be pleased with your gift to her."

Argyle Watts was good at following instructions, and for some unexplainable reason, this assignment relieved entirely his sense of guilt about receiving tactile attention from Cloud and Terp. Therefore, he practiced reflexology on his wife that evening, and she liked it so much she insisted that foot rubs become a regular part of their television watching time. When Cloud and Terp returned to Arizona, they found a thank-you note from Ruth Watts in Terp's campus mailbox.

Before leaving New Jersey, however, Terp took Cloud to see Edison High School, the scene of many satisfying as well as painful and regret-filled experiences. The school was closed for the winter holiday, but Terp parked her mother's car in a field along Colton Road. Crossing to the school side, they found an unlatched gate that provided entry to the athletic field. As they had come dressed in sweat suits and running shoes, they ran a mile on the asphalt track, after which Cloud said, "I hope you can add this to your good memories of this place."

Terp grinned in reply.

CHAPTER FIVE

Dagmar visited Cloud in the third week of January 1973. Earlier that morning Terp had gone to class, and he was drying off from a shower when she knocked on the door. Cloud grabbed a pair of jeans and carried them with him across the room. Peering through the peephole and seeing it was Dagmar, he didn't bother to put them on.

"I want to talk with you without Terp being around," she said directly. Before saying anything else, however, she removed her sweater and stripped off her dress. Lounging on the couch in a provocative pose, Dagmar said, "I've fallen for you, Cloud, and I want you to know that any time you want me, I'm available." She ran her hands through her hair and then along the curves of her body.

Cloud sighed. "Well, Dagmar, maybe in another lifetime I might want you, but not in this one. Terp is more than enough for me. One tenth of the love Terp has shown me is enough to satisfy any mere mortal. After nearly five years of celibacy waiting for Terp to come along, I'm not going to do anything to jeopardize her love. I'm not interested in adultery."

"But you're not married yet, so it wouldn't be adultery," she said.

"We're married in every way that counts, clearly in a transcendent sense. The ceremony will only confirm that," he said.

"Did you really go five years without a sex partner?" she asked.

"Do you find that incredible?" he asked.

"I don't think I've gone five days without sex with someone or other since I was fifteen," Dagmar confessed. "In a way, though, I'm relieved you turned me down. If you had taken me up on my offer, I would have been furious with you for betraying Terp."

"But you were ready to betray her yourself," Cloud said.

"Don't expect me to be consistent," she said. "It's my nature to be seductive with attractive men, and you, Cloud, are irresistibly handsome, especially standing there in the buff." She paused waiting for Cloud to speak, but he said nothing. "Oh well, I guess I'd better get dressed and go," she whimpered.

The bedroom door opened and Terp stepped out. "Don't go yet. We need to talk first," she said.

It would be difficult to judge who was more startled, Cloud or Dagmar, for both jumped and gasped in dramatic fashion.

"I thought you were in class," Dagmar said.

"I did too," Cloud agreed.

"The prof is ill," Terp said. "The class was cancelled, so I came home. Cloud, you were in the shower when I got home. I went in the bedroom to switch books in my backpack and heard a knock at the door. I started to come out but then I heard Dagmar's voice, so, forgive me, I stayed in the room and eavesdropped. I heard everything."

"I should be the one begging forgiveness," Dagmar said. "I am so sorry, Terp. I told you before that I'm really screwed up. This proves it."

"Sit down, Dagmar. Cloud, come sit with us on the couch. I have something to say," Terp ordered. They complied. "Dagmar, I'm not surprised you're attracted to Cloud. What I can't understand is why he doesn't have a train of smitten women following him around all the time. And I believe you when you say you would have been mad at him if he had said yes to your offer."

"Nevertheless, I shouldn't have done it to my best friend," Dagmar said.

Cloud said, "I can't understand why Terp doesn't have a string of lovesick men mooning after her all the time. Yet it seems that neither of us has known that kind of attention in our lives. The world is so strange."

"Well, I've had that kind of attention," Dagmar asserted, "but the only one I really want is committed to someone else."

"You don't really want Cloud," Terp said. "He'd drive you crazy, and you know it. But I'm glad this happened. I learned something important today -about myself. The truth is, Cloud," she said, turning to face him, "if you and Dagmar ever had sex, I would be hurt, but it would not be the end of the world. It would not be enough to break my love for you."

"I don't think you need to worry about being hurt on that score," Dagmar said. "The man has an iron will."

Terp ignored this comment and continued, "I think you two need to find a way to be friends. You have a lot to give each other."

"I still don't have a sister. Dagmar, would you be my younger sister?" he asked.

"OK," she answered. "I'll settle for sister."

Terp said, "We've had this conversation before. Don't ***settle*** for anything, Dagmar. Take pleasure in whatever good is possible. Surely there are fulfilling aspects to savor in any kind of relationship."

"I don't freakin' know how to do that, but I'll try," Dagmar said mournfully. "Can I go now?"

They stood and Terp hugged Dagmar in sisterly fashion. Dagmar said, "Thank you, Terp." She looked at Cloud then back at Terp, mentally asking permission to hug Cloud too.

"Go ahead," Terp said. "Give him a hug." She did, and then she dressed and left the apartment.

When Dagmar had gone, Terp gave Cloud a hug that for the first time that morning caused him to become aroused.

"I heard you tell Dagmar that I am more than enough for you. Something about one tenth of me is enough to satisfy any mere mortal," she said. "Cloud that really turns me on."

They fell on the couch and without foreplay locked into unbridled, fast exploding sex. Both were quickly exhausted.

"Are you uncomfortable?" Cloud whispered in the aftermath of their passion. "Do you want me to move?"

"Don't you dare move!" she said. "Your body feels like part of mine."

Some minutes later he did move, however, sauntering into the kitchen to make a sandwich.

Just like a man, Terp thought, as she stretched out feeling smug and sated.

The Old One rested in an arbor at the north edge of the Anasazi College campus in Sedona. Since it was winter, and a cold wind stung its way between the red rock formations surrounding the school, no one intruded on the Old One's solitude. Had any students taken the opportunity to wander by, however, they would surely have noticed the Old One clad in a bright orange unisex neck-to-knee length ***kurta***. The thin cotton garment was much favored by Hindus in India but was unsuited to the cold January air in northern Arizona. Nevertheless, the Old One was quite comfortable, experiencing no discomfort due to the weather.

The attire was a matter of whimsy to the Old One, because the woman foremost in the Old One's mind happened to be Hindu. At that moment, Prasada Moksha was checking in at the Red White and Blue Motel thirty miles north in Flagstaff. The motel manager was also Hindu, and despite threats arising from doing so, he would soon fall in love with Prasada. But that was not the Old One's immediate concern.

Prasada Moksha had earned a PhD in political science from Harvard University eight months earlier and since then had been turned down repeatedly for college faculty positions. The interview she had scheduled with the experimental liberal arts college in Sedona seemed like her last hope for a position in her chosen field. Realistically, even here her prospects remained dim, for women of color were not in high demand for scarce professorships in 1973, particularly women who were not citizens of the United States.

Darshan Pratyaksha was on duty when Prasada entered the lobby. She had selected the Red White and Blue because its advertised room rate was the lowest in the area. With her Harvard stipend long gone, she needed to protect what little cash remained after eight months with no regular income. Darshan knew none of this, however. All he saw as she approached the registration desk was a beautiful young woman from his homeland.

After assigning her to the best room in the place, while nobly charging the lowest rate, he made small talk with her, reminiscing about India. Prasada, however, did not want to talk about India. She told Darshan she was going to Sedona the next day for an interview with an important academic institution, and he was impressed. In a bid to keep pace with her, he let it be known that his parents owned this and a large chain of motels throughout the Southwest, and he managed this one by himself.

"Because you are a distinguished PhD from Harvard," he told her, "I humbly request that you be my guest for dinner at a fine curry restaurant on Humphreys Street."

Prasada liked Darshan's breezy manner, but more because she had little money in her purse, she gratefully accepted his offer.

Over the vegetarian meal, Darshan said, "With my degree in hotel management, I expect one day to be running a big hotel in Hollywood. But my dream is to manage a hotel in Washington, D. C. where I would see to the needs of world leaders."

"I suspect that taking care of famous actors and actresses may be the better dream," she said. "Government leaders tend to be pretty boring people in real life."

"I defer to your wisdom," Darshan said.

Near the end of the meal, Darshan mentioned that he was Vaishya caste. Prasada had already guessed that, because his family owned motels and other businesses and staffed them with relatives. This meant, however, that he expected her to tell him the name of her caste, and this she dreaded.

Darshan steeled himself for her response. If she said Brahmin or Kshatriya, the priestly or ruling castes, he knew she would have nothing to do with him. Such a woman, even in America, would not look twice at a man from the merchant caste.

Prasada was happy for a few hours of companionship and a good meal. She had no expectations beyond this and felt that Darshan's generosity deserved an honest response. "I am Dalit," she said, watching his face closely for the expected flinch.

Darshan had decided he would not react when this lovely, literate, elegant woman told him she was from a higher caste. He would not show his disappointment. Thus when she revealed that she was an untouchable, the lowest of the low, he showed no emotion. This was worse news than he had imagined, but his quick mind produced a gracious response. "Well, this is America, and such distinctions mean little here."

"That's very kind of you to say," she said. "And thank you for dinner. I appreciate it very much. But now I think we should go back to the motel. I need to prepare for my interview tomorrow and get a good night's rest."

"Bapu was born into my caste," Darshan added defensively, "and he accepted all people as equal regardless of birth status."

"That's true," she conceded. "Mahatma Gandhi was born Vaishya and transcended its limitations. And apparently so have you. But what about the rest of your family?"

Darshan lowered his head and momentarily said nothing before changing the subject. "How does it happen that you have a name that means grace?" he asked with genuine curiosity. "Dalits are forbidden such exalted names and allowed only base ones."

"In America many things are possible," she replied. "It was by grace that I was able to come here and receive scholarships, so I renamed myself in this new land."

When she checked out the next morning, Darshan remained on duty, because the college student scheduled for the morning shift had not shown up. "I hope you get the position at Anasazi College," he said. "Then we'll be neighbors. I'd like that."

In truth, he had been brooding about her all night. She was everything he dreamed about in a woman, except the one small detail that she was an untouchable. His parents would never approve of a relationship with a Dalit. Even in America, many Hindus clung tenaciously to the prejudices of India. But she would probably not accept the job, and he would never see her again. So, what did it matter?

The interview began badly. The members of the search committee were white men with graduate degrees from universities of lesser prestige than the Ivy League. The committee chairperson seemed hostile, probing her motivation for immigrating to the United States. Although outwardly progressive in attitude, he was suspicious of foreigners who came to this country for advanced educations and then stayed.

"Would it not be more noble, do you think, for a foreign student to return to one's impoverished country so that it can benefit from the American education?" he asked.

"India suffers no shortage of political scientists," Prasada responded.

Another interviewer, who wanted to appear knowledgeable of Indian culture, asked, "Which is your caste?"

She said, "Dalit."

He said, "Never heard of it. What are they noted for?"

"Cleaning privies," she answered with more emotion than she had intended.

The conversation then settled into routine matters until the chairperson was ready to end the interview and thank her for her time. He had a standard rejection letter he would mail to her the next day. Then seemingly out of thin air, a thought came to him. This faculty includes no professors from Ivy League universities. This woman's degree from Harvard would add prestige to the Anasazi catalog and enhance recruiting efforts.

The Old One knew what motivated this man and provided the needed rationale for changing his mind. Another thought occurred to him that was not from the Old One but from the calculating cells of his own brain. Most likely she would accept a smaller compensation package than would a male. He could offer the low end of the range.

"Dr. Moksha, would you excuse us for a few minutes," he said. "I need to confer with my colleagues about some technical matters. There's a faculty lounge down the hall. I'll come for you when we're ready to continue the interview."

The other committee members were prepared to follow his lead, so it took little time to convince them to recommend Prasada for the political science position.

When she returned to the conference room, he said, "Here are the terms of the contract. If these are acceptable, Dr. Moksha, we would like to present your name to the President of the college, Dr. Magnus Bergen."

Prasada made a show of inspecting the document carefully, although even if it had provided compensation of room and board only, she would have accepted. "I didn't expect a response so quickly," she said. "But I have a good sense about this place. The open curriculum offers possibilities for profound educational experiences for bright undergraduates. I'd like to be part of this young institution.

The terms are satisfactory."

Though she felt chilly, Prasada took an exploratory walk around the school that would soon become her professional home. As a result she happened upon a deserted arbor at the north end of campus, where she found an Indian kurta draped over a low birch limb. This is an odd omen, she thought. The discovery of the discarded garment from her homeland made her feel welcome in this strange place.

She lifted it and shook it out. In doing so, she felt a distinct sense of elation. The reality of finally having a teaching post must be sinking in, she told herself in explanation of the sudden euphoria.

Despite the cold, she felt an urge to take off her clothes, don the kurta, and dance around the enclosed garden. Her superego, however, provided swift judgment that if she were seen doing such a thing, she would lose her job before she started.

Prasada sang to herself the entire winding thirty miles back to Flagstaff through Oak Creek Canyon. For a reason she did not entirely understand, she felt the need to stay at the Red White and Blue Motel that night and incidentally let Darshan Pratyaksha know that two weeks hence she would be teaching her first classes at Anasazi College.

He was delighted with the news and took her to dinner to celebrate.

Before going to bed that night, Prasada disrobed, slipped into the kurta, and danced around her motel room. She felt greater joy than she had known for many years.

On a sunny Saturday afternoon in February, Terp sought once again to master the art of floating. Cloud sat beside her as she lay supine on their bed and gently massaged the sides of her head. "Now don't frown. Just relax," he said. "And though this sounds contradictory, try to concentrate without concentrating."

"That's easier said than done," she replied. "It might help if I knew what it is that leaves the body when you float. Is it your soul or spirit or something else?"

"I don't know the answer to that," he said, "but I think of it as the energy that makes up consciousness being taken out for a ride. Of course it has to be put back for the person to be whole. At any rate, a tinge of distraction is needed to do it, combined with deep relaxation and artless concentration, all swirling together in your imagination."

"Actually, that's the best instruction you've given me so far. I'm beginning to understand," she said. "I just need to find the right mix of these techniques."

She began the yogic breathing and soon achieved a meditative state. As before, Cloud noticed that her brow furrowed and guessed she was concentrating with the left side of her brain rather than both hemispheres together. To help her along, he shifted to massaging the top of her skull. For a time it appeared this might tip the balance in favor of success, but when another ten minutes passed without result, Terp gave up.

"I wish I had the words to describe how I do it," Cloud said. "Something happens for which no language exists. Both sides of my brain are involved at the same time. There's a stimulation I don't know how to explain." He paused to let his mind wander freely and saw the image of a bird. "Have you ever seen a roadrunner fly?" he asked.

"I've seen them run on the ground," said Terp.

"Once I saw a roadrunner speed down a hill toward a cliff and spread its wings and glide on thermals into the valley below, almost like a ski-jumper. Floating is like that. Mentally you run down a slope off a cliff and spread the lobes of your brain like wings and sail out of your body and float into space."

"That's a wonderful metaphor, but maybe it'll never happen for me," she said.

"Would that be the end of the world?" he asked.

"Not at all. I think I'm being greedy again, wanting to float," she said. "So for now, I'm going to let go of trying."

The following Saturday, Cloud and Terp took Dagmar to New River to meet Adam and Evelyn. On the way, Terp encouraged Dagmar to confide in the pastors about her compulsive sexual behavior.

"I haven't been very good at confiding in anybody," Dagmar said. "It's not bloody likely I'll open up to a couple of preachers the first time I set eyes on them, even if they are stark naked."

"They may not be," Cloud said. "It can get rather chilly in the sanctuary this time of year, and their apartment is attached to the church."

No one was lolling about outside when they arrived on campus. The trio of visitors found Evelyn and Adam sitting on the carpet in their snug living room, playing Scrabble with their eleven year-old twins, Abram and Sarai. All four were naked.

"Come in, come in!" Adam said. "You must be Dagmar. Welcome."

"We can go in the study to chat," Evelyn said. "Terp and Cloud, why don't you fill in for us in the Scrabble game while Adam and I get to know Dagmar. But be prepared for a contest. These kids are very good at the game." The pastors escorted Dagmar to their pine-paneled office.

Terp and Cloud slipped out of their clothes and tossed them into one of the guest hampers along the front wall. "OK, let's see what letters I've got to work with," Cloud said, as he took Adam's place.

"It's my turn," said Sarai. She added x-y-l-o to the front of the word phone already on the board.

Evelyn closed the door to the study and said, "It's not necessary for guests to disrobe, Dagmar. We want you to be comfortable."

"I wouldn't be here it I weren't interested in nudism," Dagmar said while pulling her dress over her head and casually tossing it on the floor. "I've read some nudist magazines, as they say, for the articles. And frankly, for the pictures too." She sat in a rocking chair opposite the two pastors.

"Terp has told us you and she were roommates," Adam said, "but not much else. Tell us about your religious background."

"Well...uh...my parents are...members of the Fundamentalist Perfection Church," Dagmar said haltingly. Then she gained verbal momentum. "They wanted me to join when I was thirteen. My father ordered me to do it. You know, get dunked and commit myself to the plan of salvation through personal perfection. I refused. It was my first act of rebellion. Prior to that time I was as obedient to my father as my timid mother was -and is to this day. He gave me holy hell for refusing to be baptized, but I figured he was so far away from the plan of personal perfection himself that it would be hypocritical for me to pretend otherwise."

Words continued to rush out of her mouth. "He was furious, but I told him if he forced me to be baptized, I would tell the pastor what he'd been doing to me. He backed off then, but he didn't stop punishing me." Dagmar paused, surprised and chagrined that she had revealed so much so quickly to these strangers.

"What were you going to tell the pastor?" Evelyn asked.

Dagmar feared she had gone too far already and mentally searched for a way to get around the subject without telling any more secrets. From deep within, however, came a surge of desire to keep talking. She was bathed in a sensation of warm light probing into the dark places in her mind, evaporating stinging memories. "He was in the habit," she said, "of punishing me once or twice a week, for whatever infraction, real or imagined, he could find."

"How did he do it?" Evelyn asked gently.

Dagmar took a deep breath and slowly exhaled. "One time when I was about five, I was playing in the yard in my new Easter dress, and I got mud on it. He said I had ruined it and made me take it off and throw it in the trash. Then he pulled down my underpants and put me over his knees and spanked me. After that, he found reasons to pull down my pants and spank me on a regular basis. When my boobs developed and I started wearing a bra, he took that off too, before he spanked me. The spankings didn't stop till I was fifteen. That was my second rebellion. I stood up to him and said I'd fight back if he did it again. Physically. I said I'd kick him in the balls."

"It must have been humiliating," said Evelyn.

"I stopped wearing underclothes after that," Dagmar continued, "so no one could ever pull them off me again."

"Did your mother know about this?" Adam asked.

"She knew," Dagmar said with resentment quivering in her voice. "But she was obedient to my father, since God appointed him head of the family. He told her it was for my own good, and she accepted that hook, line, and sinker."

"Did he ever do anything else?" Evelyn asked.

"He never screwed me, if that's what you're asking. He kept his own pants zipped, but I could tell he got hard from spanking me. And he brushed his thumbs against my pubic region while he was sliding my pants down." Dagmar paused remembering a detail and added,

"He threatened me with violence, though. Just before I started at ASU, he told me the only reason they were letting me live in a dorm was that the long commute would eat into my study time but that I shouldn't get any ideas about personal freedom. He said, 'Don't get loose with boys while you're off on your own. If I ever find out you've had sex with anyone, those spankings I gave you when you were a kid will seem like gentle tickling. See, if you're already spoiled, there'd be no need for me to...hold back.' He gave me a creepy leer when he said that, but he never touched me again. Mom just stared at me with a strange, painful look in her eyes that I couldn't decipher."

"Have you ever had therapy to deal with the trauma?" Adam asked.

"Nope," Dagmar replied. "I've handled it my own way."

"Does that by any chance involve promiscuity?" Evelyn asked.

"You're smart," said Dagmar. "I started having sex with my father's younger brother soon after he quit spanking me. So I was already spoiled, but he didn't know it."

"In our particular ministry, we deal with a lot of different sexual issues," Evelyn explained. "We've heard stories very similar to yours before -too many times, sadly."

Dagmar said, "Terp wanted me to tell you. She's the only one I've ever confided in. I didn't intend to tell you, though. I don't know you at all, and I can't understand why I blabbed right away."

"You're not alone in that either," said Adam. "Perfect strangers come up to us in line at the grocery store and tell us their life stories. And Terp was right. Whether us or someone else, you need to find a safe place to talk about the abuse you suffered. And for what it's worth, Terp didn't say a word to us about your history."

"You don't need to reassure me on that point," Dagmar said. "I trust Terp more than any other person on this planet." Even after I betrayed her, she noted mentally. Then she smacked her hand to her forehead. "Oh wow! I just made a connection. My mom caught me having sex with my uncle once but she pretended like she never saw it. Never said a word to me then or later. I couldn't figure out why. That look she gave me when my father threatened me with not holding back...that's the reason she kept quiet! She was protecting me from what my father might do." She paled at the thought.

"I can recommend a therapist who specializes in sexual issues," said Evelyn.

"I'm not ready to try therapy," said Dagmar. "This conversation with you has about done me in."

"Let me give you her card anyhow, so you'll have it when you're ready," Evelyn responded. She handed Dagmar a business card bearing the name Edna Echo, PhD, Licensed Clinical Psychologist. "There's a sliding fee scale for NCC referrals."

"I have a question," Dagmar said. "Can I come to the church service here?"

"By all means," said Adam. "We were just about to invite you to stay over tonight and worship with us tomorrow morning."

"I didn't hear the two of you discussing it," Dagmar said.

"Oh, we do a lot of discussing without words," Evelyn said.

"That's just like Terp and Cloud," Dagmar said wistfully. "I wish I knew someone that well. But I'm surprised you'd let a sex maniac like me come to your church without laying down the law first."

"We have some simple rules of etiquette that everyone must follow," Adam said. "And we do a pretty good job at presenting what we believe about right and wrong, in our sermons. But we're not into judgment, Dagmar, and for the record, you're not a sex maniac. We're all flawed in some way. You have nothing to be ashamed of, only behavior to understand and come to terms with. If we thought you were dangerous, we would send you packing fast!"

"We've met with child molesters, wife beaters, rapists, and sado-masochists," Evelyn said, "and we refer them to competent professionals. We do not knowingly allow such people to worship with us. And it's not because we judge them to be beyond redemption. The simple fact is such people present dangers to others and themselves, and this is exactly the wrong environment in which to deal with their problems. You'll be safe here, Dagmar."

"I wasn't worried about my safety," she responded. "I figured you wouldn't trust me around all the husbands and teenage boys. I might seduce some of them."

"I won't say that's never happened," Adam said, "but we trust you to conduct yourself properly. If you don't, we'll face that in some appropriate way, but I'm not at all worried about your presence here at the NCC. I suspect it will be liberating for you."

Tears welled up in Dagmar's eyes. "I don't deserve your trust," she said. "Being trusted is a new experience for me, and I'm not sure I know how to handle it."

"Wipe your eyes," Evelyn said. "You'll handle it just fine."

When they returned to the living room, Cloud said, "You were right. These guys are whizzes. Abram and Sarai are wiping us out."

Evelyn said, "Dagmar, why don't you take over for Terp. I want to talk with her about assisting me with some special services." Dagmar settled down on the floor and took over Terp's letter tiles.

Terp followed Evelyn to the study. "I just want to remind you about helping me with healing services," Evelyn said.

"I know I promised," Terp said. "But I'd really like to beg off for a while. Maybe over the summer or sometime next fall. With two weddings, final exams, and a honeymoon, I can't afford to invest the necessary emotional energy in leading worship. And I know myself well enough to realize I'd jump in with all my heart and soul."

"It can wait," Evelyn said. "And you're right. Conducting a healing service requires a great deal of energy -physical, mental, and especially spiritual. You need to care for yourself a while longer. When you're ready, let me know."

Edna Echo's business card seemed to taunt Dagmar from the inside pocket of her purse. As much as she tried, she could not exorcise from her mind the compelling image of that small rectangle of cardstock. And so, despite firm intentions not to, on Monday morning Dagmar called the psychologist and made an appointment.

Although Edna did not reveal this to her new client at that first meeting, she had survived childhood sexual abuse much worse than Dagmar's. The two women quickly forged a strong bond of trust, and four weeks later, Edna introduced Dagmar to a group therapy session, where she discovered face-to-face that she was not alone in the world.

CHAPTER SIX

Cloud counted nine rings of the telephone before Narcissa picked up the receiver. She had been pouring cups of gourmet coffee for herself and a gentleman caller when the phone interrupted, and she was not inclined to answer. But the gentleman said it might be important and she should tend to it.

"Hi, Mother, it's Cloud. Do you have a minute for some important news?"

"This is not a convenient time. I have a guest. Can you be brief?" she said.

"I'll come to the point then. Terp and I have decided to have two wedding ceremonies, one in Arizona and one in New Jersey." He told her the dates and places. "We would like you to attend whichever one is more convenient for you. But before you answer, it's only fair to let you know that Dad will be Best Man at both services...in case that makes a difference to you. I hope it doesn't." He knew it would.

"Thank you for warning me, Cloud." He had given her the excuse she needed, and she accepted the gift. "I'm sorry to disappoint you, dear, but I don't think my fragile ego could take seeing my ex-husband with that new wife of his. It would be too painful for me, shattered as I am by his infidelity. I'm afraid my attendance is out of the question under those circumstances. I will, of course, send a wedding gift."

There had been no infidelity, Cloud knew. His parents' divorce had been final long before Lloyd started seeing Nissa. But he decided not to press the issue. "Your gift isn't necessary, Mother. Honestly, we have everything we need. I understand your feelings and respect them."

"While you're on the phone, Cloud, I have some news for you. I am...seeing...a distinguished widower, a Christian pastor to whom I was introduced by a Ladies' Patriotic Beauty Society client."

"Good for you," Cloud said, genuinely pleased. "What's his name and church?"

"The Reverend Cofflynn McCarthy, Commanding Pastor of the Arms for Jesus Ministries, Incorporated. He is sitting in my dining room as we speak."

"Sorry I called at such an inopportune time," Cloud said. "I'll let you get back to your gentleman caller."

"Goodbye, Cloud," Narcissa said and hung up.

The Reverend Cofflynn McCarthy was not, in fact, a widower, although he portrayed himself as one. His wife had left him during the Eisenhower administration due to lack of intimacy. The marriage went unconsummated for more than a decade, and she finally gave up and ran off with an encyclopedia salesman.

"Sexual intercourse is aptly named," he told Narcissa. "It is coarse and unseemly. The Apostle Paul described it as distasteful." Cofflynn was grateful that the Bible provided him cover for a dread fear of sex that had rendered him impotent.

In another arena of his life, however, he was far from impotent. Cofflynn held a massive gun collection, and it was this love of firearms that led him to hear the call of God to lead a powerful anti-Communist religious organization. The motto of Arms for Jesus Ministries, Incorporated was "Peace belongs to the strong," and members were allowed to bring weapons to Sunday worship. McCarthy himself occasionally entered the sanctuary with matched pearl-handled pistols tucked into his Wellington boots.

Razor sharp crossed sabers rested on the communion table in McCarthy's church, and the cross hanging above the chancel was made from a bazooka and an M-1 rifle. Services began with robust singing of "Onward Christian Soldiers." At an annual special observance of Epiphany, members passed a loaded pistol from hand to hand with the weapon holder chanting, "Peace belongs to the strong," and the recipient of the piece responding with, "We will be strong."

The first Sunday Narcissa worshiped at the Arms for Jesus, Incorporated chapel, McCarthy preached a sermon based on the second chapter of the Gospel of John, the account of the wedding at Cana, where Jesus turned water into wine.

"On the third day of the wedding feast," McCarthy intoned, "they ran out of wine. This was a major embarrassment to the groom. Wedding feasts back then went on for seven days, and in less than half that time, he would have to send the guests home thirsty. But Jesus saved him from his shame. And I'll get to that part in a moment.

"First we need to consider why they ran out of wine. The key to this entire passage -the key to understanding the scope of Jesus' miracle- is why the wine disappeared so fast. Did you know, friends, that the wine industry in Israel is controlled by the kibbutzes where the grapes are grown? Think about that for a moment. You know, of course, that a kibbutz is a collective farm. Is it dawning on you now? Collective is a fancy word for communist. The Communists in Israel control the wine industry today, just as they did in Jesus' day.

"The wine ran out at that wedding because the ancient proto-Communists in Israel knew the groom was a friend of Jesus and Jesus was present there. It was a plot to hurt Jesus, but Jesus got the last laugh. 'Hah!' Jesus said. 'If you and your incompetent thugs can't produce enough wine, I'll just turn ordinary water into the fruit of the vine.'

"With a snap of his fingers Jesus did something those bumbling Commies could never do. He made the best wine in the world."

Narcissa was entranced. She'd heard sermons on this text before. She seemed to remember something about Jesus' mother playing a role by encouraging Jesus to make the wine. Cofflynn McCarthy had a wonderful way with words. He could explain things so an average person could understand them. She was glad she had accepted his invitation to dinner.

Now, three weeks later, Cofflynn sat in Narcissa's dining room expounding on the crudity of sexual relations. "Ministers of the Lord do not think about such base subjects," he said. "We are much too occupied with holy matters to be troubled with the lusts of the common folk."

"You are such a devout man, Brother Cofflynn. I am much impressed," she said, mimicking his rhetorical style. This ability to parrot back speech patterns of people she was interested in was her greatest asset as a salesperson.

"Thank you, Sister Narcissa," he said. "Of course I don't mean to belittle you with my remarks. You have a son, I know, which means that you have experienced the pain of brutish penetration. It is a mark of your nobility that you bore that stain in order to bring a child into the world."

"That was my son on the phone just now," she said. "He's getting married in the spring."

"Congratulations," Cofflynn said.

"Oh, I'm not sure congratulations are in order. The young strumpet he's engaged to is something of a pinko, if you get my drift. I'm not thrilled with the match, but he refuses to listen to the sensible advice of his mother."

"A pity," Cofflynn said. "Parents try so hard to raise their children the right way, and yet the Communists in Hollywood so easily lure them into evil. My condolences, Sister Narcissa. I share your grief."

"Oh, Brother Cofflynn," she enthused. "We are such kindred spirits. Most men want nothing but sex, sex, sex. It is an honor to sit with a refined gentleman like you."

Cofflynn beamed. "Under the circumstances, I think -in private- we can dispense with addressing one another as sister and brother," he said conspiratorially.

Terp, Cloud, Evelyn, and Adam sat around an awning covered patio table next to the pool at the Natural Christian Church camp. The April afternoon was pleasantly warm, with a gentle breeze caressing their bare bodies.

"Last year," Terp said to Evelyn, "you mentioned Pacific Crossroads Theological Seminary. You said they teach liturgical dance there. Where is it?"

"Oh, didn't I tell you? It's in Hawaii -in Lahaina on the island of Maui. I have a current catalog for it. Would you like to borrow it?"

"Absolutely!" said Terp.

"I have it because I'm on our denomination's Candidates for Ministry Committee. We're such a small denomination that we don't have our own seminary. So we have a list of approved schools for our prospective ministers, and Pacific Crossroads is on the list," Evelyn explained. She ran to her office and returned shortly with the catalog. "I'd like it back eventually, but no hurry."

"Lahaina, huh?" Cloud said. "That'd be tough duty."

"Actually, the curriculum's pretty intense," Adam said, "but there's always a little time left over to enjoy Kaanapali Beach."

Terp became engrossed in the catalog and dropped out of the conversation.

"Adam, you asked me where I am in my search for what to believe about God," Cloud said. "Let me start with the Trinity, because that's been a sticking point for me for a long time. I now see the Trinity as a sublime model for understanding the expressive nature of God. I do not believe in three literal and distinct physical personages forming the Trinity, but I accept it as a metaphor for describing the multiple manifestations of God in the world.

"I'm drawn to Augustine's images of the Trinity. One of his metaphors has Father, Son, and Holy Spirit representing Memory, Understanding, and Will respectively. Another has them as Being, Truth, and Love. These concepts I can embrace."

"What about the divinity of Christ?" asked Evelyn.

"I see the divinity of Christ and the divinity of Jesus as separate issues," Cloud responded. "The New Testament presents different points of view about this. John described Jesus as one with God before his birth. Mark and Paul indicated he was adopted as God's Son after his birth. But being a Son of God doesn't necessarily mean divine. I don't have a definitive answer to this question about Jesus of Nazareth. But I believe something we experience as the Christ - something intimately connected with the life of Jesus- is part of the divine reality of God. But that doesn't mean God is restricted to engaging with humankind only through the Christ."

Adam glanced at Evelyn, and she winked back. "OK, Cloud. You win the argument. We're ready to baptize you this Sunday if you say the word."

"The word," Cloud said. Three of them laughed. Terp remained lost in the PCTS catalog and missed the entire exchange.

—o—

Evelyn's sermon prior to Cloud's baptism was based on Mark 14, verses 51 and 52. "Jesus was at the Garden of Gethsemane," Evelyn explained, "and guards came to arrest him and haul him away to trial. In the middle of this dramatic account, Mark adds a curious detail. A young man wrapped in a piece of linen cloth followed Jesus, and the soldiers grabbed him too. But he slipped out of the cloth and ran away naked.

"Why would Mark include this vignette in the narrative about Jesus' arrest and trial? What significance could this have? Some have suggested that the young man was Mark himself, and thus it is an autobiographical anecdote. Perhaps, even likely.

"But I see something greater in these two verses. So much in this gospel foreshadows life in the soon to be born Christian fellowships. In the early Church those to be baptized shed their clothes and stepped naked into the water. I can't help but think of Cloud Morgan when I read this passage. The young man described by Mark was set upon by soldiers, but he escaped, running away from them, saved by his nakedness. Through this ordeal he was prepared for baptism.

"Cloud knows something about the world of soldiers. He has experienced tragic loss as a result of war. There was a time in his life when Cloud ran away from God, too, but he has unclothed his doubts and has returned to embrace the Creator. And he has come to this place, safe in his nakedness and vulnerability, to receive the cleansing sacrament of baptism. Let us proceed to the font."

When the procession of members and guests reached the pool, Cloud jumped in, followed by Adam and Evelyn, who stood on either side of him. After a prayer, Cloud was asked the baptismal questions, and when he had answered affirmatively, he fell back into the pastors' linked arms and was immersed.

Adam placed a hand on Cloud's head and intoned, "Evan Cloud Morgan, I baptize you in the name of God the Creator, Christ the Healer, and Holy Spirit the Inspirer." Cloud didn't know if it was a trick of the sun's reflection or a spiritual manifestation, but he saw himself surrounded by white light when he rose from the water.

He looked at his beloved Terp and saw tears streaming down her face. Nissa was crying too, as was Dagmar, and to Cloud's surprise, Lloyd also had tears on his cheeks.

Afterward, Terp embraced him and before he could say a word, she whispered, "I saw the white light, Cloud. Don't let anyone tell you it wasn't there."

Not long after his baptism, Cloud visited Quinn at his apartment in Scottsdale to tell him about Terp and invite him to his wedding in New River. The paraplegic veteran, former tormentor of Cloud but now his good friend, was pleased at the invitation.

"It'll be a naturist wedding ceremony," Cloud explained. "The bride and groom and ministers will be naked, but you don't have to be. It's clothing optional."

"Let me give the nude part some thought," Quinn said. "But I'll be there one way or another. Will they let me swim in their pool?"

"Of course," said Cloud.

Darshan and Prasada began dating shortly after she started teaching at Anasazi College in February. She was careful not to become too emotionally involved, because she knew that his parents, when they found out, would never accept her. Nevertheless, she cherished Darshan's affection and planned to enjoy his companionship until the inevitable day when family pressure would end the affair.

Since his parents lived in Los Angeles, Darshan avoided telling them he was romantically involved with a Dalit woman. But by April he was hopelessly in love with Prasada and knew that sooner or later he had to face them with this news.

"I'll write to them," he proclaimed one evening over curry, "and tell them I am in love with a distinguished college professor. When I give them your name, they will investigate your background, and then they will learn you are Dalit, and they will race here in their new Mercedes and demand that I come to my senses and get rid of you."

"And then what will happen?" she asked.

"I will say no to them and they will fume and threaten. I'll say I am an American now, and there are no castes in America. They will say I bring shame upon the family. I will say Prasada has more class and grace in her little finger than anyone in my whole family. They will say that our caste may be created only from the thigh of God but Dalits are not from any part of God's body and are not human. Then they will race away in their new Mercedes devising ways to control the damage to the family reputation."

Prasada was touched by his defense of her and leaned across the table and kissed him. "Your scenario seems overly optimistic to me, but I will pray that it is so."

Darshan was partially correct in his description of his parents' reaction. They did commission an investigation of Prasada, and some of what they learned impressed them. But when they heard she was untouchable, they knew they had to act quickly for the sake of family honor. Darshan's father made inquiries about hiring a thug to threaten Prasada and scare her away from his son. But before he could engage the services of a suitable enforcer, a message blossomed in his mind, as if a guru had planted it there.

Violence will not demonstrate your superiority, the message said. You will be found out and the family shamed even more. Therefore, disown your son, and heap further embarrassment on him by providing him with a large financial gift as recompense for removing him from the family. This will prove your own wisdom and advanced spiritual evolution. (The Old One knew the difference between thoughts that could be integrated and accepted and thoughts that would be rejected as entirely alien.)

Darshan's father liked the idea of being spiritually advanced. He was approaching old age, and he fantasized about devoting himself to religious matters, becoming a sage, and leaving the details of business to his brothers, sons, and nephews.

Darshan's parents did race to Flagstaff in their new Mercedes and did try to convince Darshan to come to his senses. But when he told them he intended to marry Prasada (although he had not yet asked her), his father said something unexpected.

"The day you wed the Dalit woman, you are no longer part of this family. We must remove your name from all family records. Therefore, if you should ever have occasion to visit us, you will be received cordially as a guest but not as a son. On that day also one of your cousins will come here to take over management of this motel, and you will be cast out on your own."

"I understand, sir," Darshan said. "I will accept your decision and thank you for allowing me to visit you, even as a guest."

"One more thing," his father said. "As I approach my senior

years, I see the value of generosity of spirit. Thus I have decided, if you should go forward with marriage to the Dalit woman, I will present you with a monetary gift to compensate you for loss of family and employment."

"Thank you, Father. This is more than I had dreamed possible." Darshan embraced his father, who embraced him back.

"I hope this marriage does not come to pass," the father said, "but if it does, you know the consequences. I will do as I have said."

Prasada was amazed at Darshan's description of his father's decree. "He disowned you yet left the door open to still be a part of your family. That is a very generous thing. He maintains the family honor by pretending that you don't exist, while at the same time admitting you to his house."

"When shall we get married?" Darshan asked.

"You are presuming that I will marry you," Prasada said.

"But I love you, Prasada. I will give up my family and position for you. Please, will you marry me?"

Prasada's heart burst with affection for her merchant lover. "Yes, Darshan, I will marry you. I simply wanted a proper proposal."

They were unable to find a Hindu temple for the wedding service, and so Prasada Moksha and Darshan Pratyaksha said their vows before a Justice of the Peace in Flagstaff. Darshan's father sent him a check for $100,000, which the young man combined with his personal savings to leverage purchase of a financially faltering tourist resort in Sedona. The newlyweds would live on Prasada's teaching salary, while Darshan poured time and resources into making the resort profitable.

The naturist wedding of Cloud and Terp on a Wednesday evening in late May was an intimate affair. In addition to the bride and groom, the Best Man, the Maid of Honor, the two pastors, the organist, the wedding coordinator, and the photographer, a dozen other people gathered in the NCC sanctuary. Quinn's decision about clothing resulted in everyone present being nude.

Earlier in the week, at the wedding rehearsal, Cloud and Terp had met with Kwan-yin Burns, the wedding coordinator. Kwan-yin, who occasionally assisted Adam and Evelyn with worship on Sunday mornings and special occasions, was in her late-twenties, a high school speech teacher by profession. By ancestry she was American born Chinese, while her husband, Cochise Burns was the son of an Apache mother and a Scots father. Cochise was the official wedding photographer for the NCC church, and Cloud and Terp also conferred with him that evening.

"This will be an easy service to manage," Kwan-yin said. "There's not a lot for me to do, but I'll make sure the Best Man and Maid of Honor have the rings in their possession, see to the flowers, and so on." She walked them through the choreography of the ceremony, and Terp practiced walking down the aisle. She intended to do it in another way Wednesday evening but would not reveal that at the rehearsal.

"What sort of pictures do you want?" Cochise then asked.

"I prefer candid shots," Cloud said.

"Me too," said Terp. "I don't like staged wedding photos. Just shoot whatever happens as it happens. Of course, I would like a group picture of the wedding party. But there will be no ceremonial garter or stuff like that."

"No problem," said Cochise. "I'll use available light, so there won't be any annoying flashes." Cochise owned a studio in Phoenix and was internationally known for his vivid photographs of Arizona wildlife and scenery, with many credits in Arizona Highways magazine. Wedding work was a sideline exclusive to the NCC church.

When the rehearsal was finished, Cloud spoke to Kwan-yin. "You look familiar, but I've never met anyone with the name Kwan-yin. Where did you go to high school?"

"West High, class of 1964," Kwan-yin said.

"I was class of 1961," Cloud replied. "I remember a number of Chinese students in the student body but not with any Chinese forenames."

"Oh, in those days I went by Katy," Kwan-yin said and then laughed. "I was a bit embarrassed that my thoroughly American parents were so fascinated by the land of their grandparents that they named me after a Chinese goddess. In college I changed my outlook and proudly used my real name."

Mentally, Cloud saw the school auditorium and said, "You acted in school plays."

Kwan-yin replied, "In my freshman year I played Liat in the

school production of ***South Pacific***. Not that I was much of an actress. The role required no singing, and it wasn't a stretch for a Chinese girl to play a Vietnamese maiden."

"I was enamored of you -or your portrayal of Liat, that is," Cloud said. "I went to both performances. ***South Pacific*** just blew me away."

At seven thirty in the evening on the thirtieth of May, the service began. Adam and Evelyn, clad only in white stoles, Lloyd wearing a bow tie, and Cloud adorned simply with a large flower lei around his neck, walked to their appointed posts at the base of the chancel. When the organist began Pachelbel's "Canon in D" Dagmar entered the sanctuary and processed in stately manner to the foot of the chancel. She wore a single strand of pearls around her neck.

After a suitable passage of time, Terp appeared at the end of the aisle, wearing a tiara of daisies in her hair. As the peaceful strains of the canon progressed, Terp extended her arms to the front in a descending arc of invitation, forming a vee with her body. She stepped forward with graceful ballet movements, head high, pirouetting twice in her transit down the aisle. She danced into Cloud's extended left arm, as he turned with her to face Adam and Evelyn.

Evelyn prayed, and Adam read verses of scripture Cloud and Terp had selected. From the Song of Solomon he intoned, "You have ravished my heart, my sister, my bride, you have ravished my heart with a glance of your eyes." And from Isaiah he recited, "Who are these that fly like a cloud, and like doves to their windows?" Then he read John's account of the wedding at Cana, offering a brief meditation on savoring the good wine that ferments beyond the first passionate year of a marriage.

An anthem followed, sung by Nissa's friend Sandy and her family. Sandy's husband had a fine bass voice, while Sandy sang alto. Their fifteen year-old twins, a boy and a girl, sang respectively tenor and soprano. In four-part harmony the family performed "Ye Holy Angels Bright" complete with a soprano descant that caused Cloud's skin to tingle.

Soon came the time for their vows, which the bride and groom had jointly composed. In a clear, steady voice Cloud said, "Terp, I promise to be your husband, faithful to you always. I promise to be your shield and comforter, lover and friend, and to be kind to you in strength or weakness. I promise to be your gentle refuge whene'er your heart be vulnerable. Without reservation I give you my body, mind, heart, and spirit for as long as I draw the breath of life."

With equal strength of voice, Terp said, "Cloud, I promise..." and repeated the same vows he had made.

They exchanged unadorned gold bands. After the twins sang Noel Paul Stookey's recent, quickly become standard "Wedding Song," Evelyn said, "I now pronounce you husband and wife. You may kiss one another."

Cloud and Terp turned to kiss, but before doing so, Cloud lifted one end of his lei and placed it over Terp's head so they were yoked together by the fragrant blossoms. Their lips touched gently, and then by plan, they maneuvered the lei down their sides so that it circled their waists. As the recessional blared forth from the organ, they walked side-by-side, feeling the light tension of the flowers binding them together at the hips. In this manner they stepped into the warm, starlit night.

Nissa had put together a reception in the recreation room. When Cloud and Terp entered the hall, Terp saw Dagmar standing alone in the middle of the floor and spontaneously removed her tiara and tossed it to Dagmar. Cochise caught the action of Terp unpinning the flowers, the daisies in mid-air, and the blossoms coming to rest in Dagmar's outstretched hands.

As the evening progressed, Quinn wheeled himself to the edge of the pool and using his strong arms, propelled himself out of the chair and into the water. "This is great!" he yelled. Dagmar followed him outside and dove in beside him. They talked a long time while paddling around in the pool.

Abram and Sarai told the newlyweds they'd seen many weddings, but this was the most beautiful one ever. Evelyn said, "Terp your dance down the aisle was stunning. You definitely need to study liturgical dance."

"I've practically memorized the Pacific Crossroads catalog," Terp said. "I can't wait till I get there next year. That is, if they'll admit me."

"You don't have a thing to worry about on that score, young lady," Evelyn said. "They'll come after you, begging you to enroll. You'll be teaching them how to do it."

Two weeks later, Cochise and Kwan-yin stopped by the apartment to deliver the wedding photos to Terp and Cloud. Kwan-yin had arranged them in an album.

Cochise was full of himself. "Ordinarily, we don't deliver. Couples come to my studio and select what they want. But these are not ordinary. These are the best wedding shots I've ever done," he enthused. "This is some really good work. Thank you for allowing me to photograph your wedding."

"He's right," said Kwan-yin. "We wanted to come together to show them to you."

"Well then, let's see them," Terp said impatiently.

The first page contained an eight by ten standard landscape shot of the wedding party. Standing from left to right were Dagmar, Terp, Adam, Evelyn, Cloud, and Lloyd.

"Not a goofy smile in the lot," said Cloud.

The rest of the album was anything but standard. A dozen photographs documented Terp dancing down the aisle and several showed Cloud enraptured by his bride's choreography. Picture after picture captured the profound joy of the evening. The family anthem and the twins' duet were memorable images, but the kiss, and the lei-yoked recessional walk were more so. The expressions on Cloud's and Terp's faces as they said their vows reflected breathtaking inner certainty. In addition to Terp tossing her tiara to Dagmar, there were photos of Dagmar and Quinn in the pool, Nissa beaming at the beauty of it all as she served food, and dozens of other scenes of celebration.

"Wow," said Cloud. "I didn't expect you to shoot this many."

"I always shoot a lot, but usually most of them are unusable," Cochise said. "This collection is special, and we want you to have them all."

"Well then, we'll pay you more than the price you quoted," said Cloud.

"Nope," said Cochise. "This is our gift to the two of you."

"At least please stay for dinner," Terp said. "It's just soup and salad, but we have plenty and we'd like to share it with you."

"I never turn down food," Cochise said.

The four enjoyed sparkling dinner conversation.

CHAPTER SEVEN

From the east coasts of Georgia and Florida, extending south to Brazil and eastward across the Atlantic Ocean, over the continent of Africa, and descending down the southwest coast of India, much of the world this thirtieth day of June would witness the moon blocking the light of its star, creating for seven minutes, a total eclipse of the sun. But the sun would not be obscured in New Jersey. Nothing, it seemed, could darken the wedding of Cloud and Terp at Second Calvinist Church.

Unlike the service in New River, for the ceremony in Metuchen, Terp and Cloud obtained a wedding license for the pastor to sign. They also removed their wedding rings and entrusted them to Lloyd. Lloyd and Nissa were the only representatives of the groom's side present in New Jersey, and Nissa was the only one seated in a pew. Ruth Watts, however, chose to sit up front with Nissa, and the two had a splendid talk about the bride and groom and life in Arizona.

Ruth described precocious Terp's serious theological discussions with her husband around their kitchen table and the affection she and Argyle felt for the girl. Nissa spoke of Terp's unaffected ways and brightness of mind and how she was a perfect match for her stepson.

Ruth leaned over to Nissa and whispered conspiratorially, "Do you know about this reflexology business? Terp and Cloud demonstrated it to Argyle and he showed me. It's wonderful."

"Yes," Nissa said, "They showed us also. They learned it from Terp's college roommate. It's so relaxing."

"Well, I'll tell you it's revived my marriage," Ruth said. "Put touch back in it. It makes Argyle so relaxed he's capable of...of...intimacy once again. I'm indebted to those two."

"They seem to have a positive effect on lots of people," Nissa said. "Our pastors think they're soul-mates."

"Pastors?" queried Ruth.

"Co-pastors, husband and wife," said Nissa.

"What church do you belong to?" Ruth asked.

Nissa regretted this casual mention of her pastors. She would not lie but didn't want to complicate the day by saying anything about her congregation that might lead to questions about Cloud and Terp. A slip of the tongue about their wonderful naturist wedding would only hurt the feelings of Argyle Watts. "It's a small denomination, not well known," she said. "But look, the service is starting. I'll tell you about it later." Providentially the prelude had begun to bellow from the huge pipe organ. "I love the sound of pipes," she added. Now I've got breathing room to think about what to say to Ruth, she thought. Maybe she'll forget the question.

Several hundred guests sat in the sanctuary, ushered to their seats by former members of Second Calvinist's Youth Organization from the era when Terp had belonged to it. Among the guests were Penny's friends, Terp's friends from church, and teachers at Edison High School.

Argyle Watts led the groom's party to the chancel steps and once they were in place, he left them to join Terp in the bride's room. When the first notes of Jean Mouret's "Rondeau" sounded, Terp's friend Michelle, serving as a bridesmaid, stepped into the sanctuary and walked down the aisle toward the chancel. Terp's sister Mary, Maid of Honor, followed, and soon it was time for Terp to make her appearance.

She stepped into the sanctuary wearing a floor length, long-sleeved, high-neck, ivory gown. Since she wore no veil, the glow on her face was exposed to all assembled. As the music brightened the congregation stood to honor her. Terp processed down the aisle with graceful movements that seemed like dance though not consciously choreographed. Her right arm was linked in Argyle's left, as he escorted her to the chancel. When they reached Cloud, standing tall and handsome in his black tuxedo, Argyle placed Terp's arm in Cloud's and resumed his place in front of the wedding party.

Cloud thought Terp was as beautiful with her entire body covered with a wedding dress as she was naked. Of course, he thought she was beautiful in jeans and a sweatshirt too. Terp had similar thoughts about Cloud as she took in his formal attire.

The service was much like the one in New River, only on a larger scale. Music reverberated off the stone walls, magnifying the glorious sounds. A quartet sang "Ye Watchers and Ye Holy Ones" and a soprano sang Cesar Franck's "Panis Angelicus." Terp and Cloud exchanged the identical vows as in Arizona. Lloyd and Mary produced the same simple gold bands for the exchange of rings. Yet it all seemed new to Cloud and Terp, and each welled over with gratitude when Argyle pronounced them husband and wife. The traditional kiss was electric, and both smiled broadly as they recessed up the aisle. The professional photographer Penny had hired captured their riant faces in a shot they would treasure always.

At the reception, Ruth proved she had an excellent memory. "Before the service you were going to tell me about your church," she said to Nissa.

"It's called the Natural Christian Church," said Nissa. "We practice full immersion baptism." Nissa felt an intuitive urge to tell Ruth all about her church but felt constrained to protect the privacy of Terp and Cloud.

"Oh my!" said Ruth, imagining soaking wet clothes dripping all through the sanctuary. "That must require a lot of towels."

"Not too many," said Nissa. "We handle it efficiently."

At that moment, Lloyd joined his wife and said to Ruth, "What a wonderful service! Your husband is a fine pastor, and I'm so grateful he walked down the aisle with my daughter-in-law. It made my heart jump into my throat to see her take his left arm."

"That's very kind of you, Lloyd," Ruth said. "I never get tired of hearing people say nice things about Argyle. He ***is*** a fine pastor."

Lloyd and Nissa were then summoned to the head table, so there was no more talk about the NCC. As it happened, Ruth had lost interest in the subject after Nissa mentioned full immersion, and she said nothing about it to her husband. Had Nissa spoken about the nude part, however, Ruth's interest would have perked up.

The reception continued well into the evening, long after the bride and groom had departed for their hotel. Lloyd spent a great deal of time with Penny, listening to her retell Tom's stories of life in the Eighth Air Force. He knew the places in England she referred to and many of the people she named. Surprising to him was that he found the reminiscences more pleasant than painful.

The next day, Lloyd and Nissa took a commuter flight to Harrisburg to visit his parents, Evan and Elsie Morgan. Apart from Christmas cards and birthday phone calls, Lloyd had little contact with his parents for thirty years. It was time to change that. Nissa prodded Lloyd's parents into revealing stories about her husband's childhood, and they complied, pulling out old photo albums to illustrate their accounts. Lloyd found himself feeling affection for the little boy he had once been.

After this, they flew to London, so Lloyd could show Nissa where he had served during the war.

Three days elapsed before Cloud and Terp arrived in Sydney, Australia, and they were very tired from the long flights in cramped seats. After checking in to their hotel near Circular Quay, they slept for eighteen hours. They had a month ahead of them to explore and enjoy the world Down Under.

"I expected to get to Australia on R and R from Viet Nam," Cloud told Terp as they lounged in bed upon waking. "But then Tet happened, and the trip never materialized. I'm glad now that I waited to make the trip with you."

She snuggled against him. "I'm glad too. I wonder if we'll have any extrasensory experiences at the bottom of the globe?"

"Why would being south of the equator make any difference?" Cloud asked.

"I don't think it would," she replied. "Actually, I don't wonder about it so much as I have a premonition something extraordinary will happen here."

Following the priorities of a newlywed couple, they made love, showered and dressed, and ate a large breakfast in the hotel restaurant, and then went outside to hike the streets of Sydney. After wandering through the odd and fascinating flora of the Royal Botanic Gardens, the lovers ate a late lunch then resumed their exploration on foot.

Back at the hotel, they gave each other foot rubs, made love again, and dined in the hotel restaurant, where Cloud enjoyed a Foster's beer and Terp savored a local Chardonnay from the Mudgee region of New South Wales.

The next morning they hired a motorboat for a private escorted tour of Sydney Harbor. As they entered Watsons Bay, near the South Head, the pilot killed the motor. Before either passenger could enquire about the reason, the guide said, "You're blessed, mates. Look out there." Before them frolicked a pair of whales that had wandered into the harbor. "This happens rarely," said the guide. "People have lived here all their lives and never seen such a sight, and you two drop in from America and these Humpbacks swim right to you."

Cloud and Terp spent several days camping in the Blue Mountains and saw more kangaroos than they could count. In between tourist activities, they spent long leisurely hours enjoying one another in their hotel room.

It required two days of intermittent air travel to get to Alice Springs. From Sydney they flew to Adelaide and spent the night. The next morning they flew seven hundred miles in a small, single engine plane, much of the distance over empty desert. Alice Springs was an oasis in the sparsely populated center of the continent, and the honeymooners found little to do there except hike and absorb the arid aura of the place. The landscape reminded them of Arizona, except the vegetation was slightly odd compared with what they were used to.

The couple visited the School of the Air, which provided education to children living on remote Outback stations, and also the Royal Flying Doctor Service, which provided medical care for isolated families throughout the region.

One afternoon Cloud and Terp went for a walk in the dry bed of the Todd River. Along the way, they encountered a young Aboriginal girl, seven or eight years old -a member of the Arrernte Tribe- playing by herself in the sand. She was naked.

"G'day," the girl said.

"G'day yourself," Terp responded. "My name's Terp and this is my husband, Cloud. We're from America."

"Amoonguna," the girl said, pointing to herself.

The hair on the back of Cloud's neck stood on end and a sense of ***déjà vu*** flooded his memory. Terp experienced a similar feeling of having lived this moment before. Goosebumps rippled over her skin as a memory of the Old One opened in her mind.

With a flash of intuitive knowledge, Terp said to Amoonguna, "Did you dream about meeting us?"

"Yes," said the girl. "Not your names, just your faces."

"So, we've met before -in our minds," Cloud said.

"Where are your parents?" Terp asked.

"Mum works in Alice. Me old man drink too much. He's over there." She pointed to a tree on the bank two hundred yards away.

"Let's go visit him," Cloud said. "Come along, Amoonguna. We want to meet your father."

As they approached, they could see the drunk man passed out on the ground. Like his daughter, he was unclothed. Terp touched her husband's arm and said, "Cloud, we need to..."

"Yes," he said before she could finish the thought. They quickly stripped off their shirts and khaki shorts and undergarments, retaining only their socks and hiking boots. Amoonguna noted with approval their all-over tans.

"What's his name, Amoonguna?" Terp asked.

Amoonguna rattled off something they did not understand. "But they call him Jack," she added.

The odd trio quietly approached the Aboriginal man. "Jack?" said Cloud.

Jack stirred. "Whassit? Who you?"

"We're friends of your daughter," Terp said.

"That so?" Jack mumbled.

"We met in her dreams," Terp answered.

Jack sat up at this news, and in the process he noticed that these white people were naked. The fog in his brain began to clear and he made a rapid assessment of the situation. "You like to play with little girls, mate? OK. Fifty dollars, but bring her back tomorrow morning."

"No sir," said Cloud. "We like to protect little girls from being hurt."

Terp turned to Cloud and said, "Sit next to Jack and put your hands on his shoulders." Cloud complied, and Terp knelt beside Jack, placing her hands on his head. She closed her eyes and began to pray for healing for the Arrernte tribesman. Jack did not stir the entire time Terp prayed aloud. When at last she stopped and removed her hands from his head, Jack's face had changed.

For a long time Jack remained silent, and then said, "No more booze-up. I go get off the bottle."

Amoonguna could see that her father was no longer drunk. She looked with gratitude at Terp and said, "***He*** dreamed about you too."

"Maybe so," Terp said.

"Would it be OK if Amoonguna showed us around the area?" Cloud asked Jack.

"OK," Jack said. "You watch my little girl. She's a good girl."

Rather than put them back on, Terp and Cloud gathered their clothes into portable bundles. Amoonguna led them through the dry riverbed, digging up roots along the way, and then over the bank and into the desert. Presently they came to a small, unpainted concrete block house. "My place," she said with pride in her voice.

"You live in here?" Cloud asked.

Amoonguna frowned at Cloud's apparent lack of understanding about how normal people used houses and tersely explained, "Put ***things*** inside. Sleep outside."

The girl led them back to the river. "Maybe we see my friend," she said.

A quarter mile farther along, Cloud spotted someone in the distance, apparently meditating just outside the shade of a nearby coolabah tree. It seemed odd not to take advantage of any available shade, so they moved closer to investigate, and Terp noticed that the person had a large, triangular shaped head. "Oh my God!" she gasped.

"The Old One!" Cloud exclaimed.

They dropped their bundles and rushed reverently toward the creature, whose long white hair shimmered silver in the sunlight and who sat serenely cross-legged and naked on the sandy bank.

"Hello Terp. It's wonderful to see you again. Hello Cloud. At last we meet face-to-face. G'day Amoonguna," said the Old One genially.

Cloud and Terp fell to their knees, but Amoonguna remained

standing, happily at peace with the encounter. No words came from any of the human mouths.

"Your prayer for Jack was very powerful," the Old One said to Terp. "This time, I believe, he will have the strength to get help with his addiction. Thank you. And to you, Cloud, allow me to offer tardy condolences on the death of Xuan. It was not predestined, of course, but tragedy in that place was nearly inevitable. Please believe that she has found bliss." The Old One then turned to the child. "I don't think your father will beat you anymore, Amoonguna. Terp and Cloud have given him the strength to get better."

Amoonguna took hold of the Old One's left hand and kissed it. The Old One's arms then reached out, palms up, to Terp and Cloud, and without a word each placed a hand palm down on the Old One's hands. Warm euphoria cascaded through their bodies.

Then as if in prayer Cloud whispered, "Are we on the right path?"

The Old One smiled wistfully, mentally weighing how much to reveal and settled on, "The choices are many, and good and evil can be found on every path."

"That sounds like Zen." Cloud said.

"It is reality," the Old One replied.

"You told me the first time we met that I couldn't pronounce your name. Can I pronounce it now? Will you tell us what it is?" Terp asked.

"Not just now," said the Old One. "For the present I rather like being known to you as the Old One. By your standards it is an accurate appellation. Of course, Big Head is pleasantly apt as well, but on the whole I prefer Old One. Let us save the subject of names for another time. It is highly probable that some cold future day I will reveal my name to you and more. In the mean-time, a little mystery is good for everyone."

Cloud smiled broadly. "That means we will meet again."

The Old One nodded. "Our paths will cross many times, in mind if not in person."

"Are you an angel?" Terp asked.

"I would not use that word," the Old One said. "You have already ascertained, of course, that I am not God. And you know now from scanning my body with your eyes that I am much like both of you.

Think of me as a dear friend who travels a great deal and consequently whom you only see at odd intervals. Which reminds me, I especially enjoyed hearing "Ye Watchers and Ye Holy Ones" at your New Jersey wedding."

"Were you there?" Terp asked in astonishment. "We didn't see you."

"Not in the sanctuary but nearby," the Old One replied. "Alas, I had other responsibilities during your naturist service. However, I am sure it was a beautiful event. And speaking of responsibilities, please forgive me but I am needed elsewhere."

The Old One disappeared.

Still on his knees, Cloud instinctively scooped up a handful of sand from the place where the Old One's body had rested.

CHAPTER EIGHT

Terp and Cloud were famished by the time they returned to their hotel. They took an early dinner and retired to their room. After showering together, they cradled in one another's arms and debriefed at length their meeting with the Old One -without saying a word aloud.

Two days later they hired a car to drive to Uluru, the huge red stone known to the larger world as Ayers Rock. Uluru rises nearly a thousand feet above the plain and extends more than two miles across the land. Two thirds of the massive monolith is underground. A walk around it covers six miles. It is considered sacred by the Anangu people who live in the area, and their hearts break to see tourists climb to its summit and deposit cigarette butts and chewing gum wrappers there and urinate down its side.

Out of respect for the Anangu people, Cloud and Terp decided not to climb but to hike the circumference of Uluru. Their spirits were drawn continually to caves and erosion scars on the rock, as if these holes and imperfections revealed glimpses of the sacred inner character of the place. However, it was not emanations from the inanimate red object itself they perceived but the residual psychic energy of people and other sentient beings who had been gathering there for forty millennia.

Half way around, in the middle of the north face, they stopped for water and rest. Moving off the path, they stretched out on the ground facing Uluru. Terp pondered the rock, releasing her mind to absorb the view freely without conscious direction. She breathed deeply and held the air in her lungs for a few seconds before releasing it slowly. Suddenly, simply by wishing it, she popped out of her body and floated toward the rock.

Cloud looked into the face of his beloved and immediately knew she was gone. He lay still and entered into a well-learned pattern of breathing. A minute later he was out of his body floating after Terp. He couldn't see her but sensed her presence. She spoke to him telepathically.

"Wow!" she said. "The Old One's energy must have given me the needed boost."

"Do you think they'd mind if we went to the top this way?" he asked.

"If they knew, I think they'd be thrilled," she said.

"I'm quite sure they'll know," he said.

Soul beside soul they rose to the top of Uluru and followed its length. Then they moved half way down the north side and traced a path around to the east, south, and west, before returning to the north face.

"Let's go below," Cloud said. They descended to the plain and continued into the earth, following the edge of the rock as it turned and extended twice it's length beneath the desert floor. They circled under it and rose into the air above, flying over the summit again, and then back into their bodies, each of which twitched as they reentered.

"Whew!" said Terp.

"Well, it looks like it ***is*** your gift, after all," Cloud said.

"Now, dear husband," Terp said in a school teacher voice, "the next time I float, you've got to promise to stay in your body, so I can nestle in it the way you did mine."

"I promise," he said, "with eager anticipation of your next ecstatic excursion."

On the ride back to their room in Alice Springs, Terp smiled as she quietly hummed "Volare" -remembered from childhood as one of her dad's favorite songs. Now I, too, have wings, she thought, and to fly with Cloud this way is beyond ecstasy.

The following morning, Cloud ran a tub of hot water while Terp lounged in bed. He lowered his body into the tub and leaned back to savor the soaking warmth. After a few minutes the water cooled, and Cloud considered turning on the hot tap to replenish the heat. But he was so relaxed he did not want to move.

All at once he felt penetrating warmth enter his body, permeating every molecule of his physical being. The sensation was intense, beyond erotic, beyond a mystical sense of oneness with creation. He felt love so intense that it tested the endurance of his cells to contain it. More than feeling a general sense of love, Cloud felt fully known and loved, and it caused his body to tremble with sublime happiness. And when he sensed that his frame could hold no more and he must surely burst, the warmth evaporated and he was left with wrinkled skin in cool water. Cloud climbed out of the tub and mused on the experience as he dried off with a towel.

Terp awaited him on the bed with a smug grin on her face. "Well?"

"I don't have the words to describe it. Incredible. The love..." Cloud said. He lowered himself into Terp's open arms. "I have been ravished beyond my meager ability to comprehend ravishing."

"Excellent!" she said. "Now you can ravish ***me*** the old fashioned way."

He entered her, strongly erect, and she wrapped her legs over the top of his. They did not move but lay joined together marveling at the miracle of love in all its manifestations. An uncounted interval later, Cloud rolled over so that Terp was stretched out on top of him. He rejoiced in the weight of her body resting on his. Without conscious thought, he began to caress her hair.

"Sit up," she whispered and removed herself from their connection.

Facing him, she climbed into his lap and renewed their physical link. As they tarried in that position, arms wrapped around one another, luxuriating in pleasurable stillness, Terp sensed she could almost read Cloud's thoughts. When at last they uncoupled, neither had climaxed, but both felt as if they had done so magnificently.

In London, Lloyd rang up Dr. Clark Hyfrydol, his wartime

psychiatrist. Four years earlier, Lloyd had participated in a research project that Dr. Hyfrydol was conducting about the long-term effects of war-induced mental illness. Hyfrydol was delighted to hear from Lloyd and invited him to visit his place in Harley Street.

Lloyd and Nissa sat together on the couch in the therapist's office, not seeking professional advice but friendship. As Lloyd poured forth the account of his recent life, he inevitably came to the couple's long history with the Natural Christian Church. Clark Hyfrydol, an erstwhile Freudian, was always interested in stories that involved nudity.

"I've been known to peruse British Naturism magazine on occasion. Tell me, how does ritual nakedness affect one's sexual behavior?" Clark asked with a clinical voice.

"My sex life with Nissa is wonderful," said Lloyd straightforwardly. He looked at Nissa and she nodded with a smile. "But I don't think going to a naturist camp has any effect on that. Narcissa and I went to that same camp, and we hardly ever had sex."

"What then do you see as its value?" the doctor asked.

"Freedom," Lloyd said. "A sense of belonging to the earth. Relaxation. Elimination of shame. Feeling alive. I guess in that sense, it does contribute to a healthy sex life because naturism removes body hang-ups and anxiety."

Before leaving, Lloyd invited Clark to visit them in Arizona. "We have a large house with several guest rooms. You can stay as long as you like and wear as much or as little as you want. Your wife is invited too," he said, noting Clark's wedding ring.

"Unfortunately, my wife died three months ago. Cancer," the physician said.

"I'm so sorry," responded Lloyd and Nissa in unison.

"All the more reason to come to Arizona," Nissa said. "Get away from your memories for a while. It would be good to see the world from a different vantage point."

"If you really mean it," Clark said, "I would like to see the Old West. But if I come, will you promise that you'll show me around this naturist church of yours?"

"I am already making plans for it," Nissa said.

The next day, Nissa and Lloyd made a pilgrimage to Spielplatz, near St. Albans north of London. Despite its German name, Spielplatz opened in 1929 as the first naturist camp in England, home to visitors and year-round residents ever since.

Through connections with Adam and Evelyn, Cloud and Terp booked a week at a naturist Bed and Breakfast near Cairns, in the tropical north of Australia along the Pacific coast of Queensland. Cairns served as a tourist gateway to the Great Barrier Reef. In addition to breakfast, the resort provided guests with mid-day, evening, and picnic meals as requested, at additional cost.

A fully clothed Sydney Darwin, the co-proprietor, met them at the airport and transported them to his place. He was tall and wiry, mid-forties, with a receding hairline. "Welcome to the Queen's Paradise," he said as he drove them through the gate into the walled enclosure.

They were greeted at the front door by Alice Darwin, a plump woman with a plain, open face, about forty. Alice was naked. "Welcome, Mr. and Mrs. Morgan!" She turned to an equally naked teenager with Aboriginal features and said. "Koah, go fetch their luggage from the wagon."

The tall, muscular fifteen year-old scurried out to retrieve their things.

"That's my boy," Sydney said with a note of pride in his voice.

"Kuranda will show you to your room," Alice continued. "When you've had a chance to slip out of your underdaks and freshen up a bit, just come down to the dining room and I'll fix you a nice snack."

Kuranda was Koah's sixteen year-old sister -tall, slender, clearly part European, and wearing nothing but a smile.

When Cloud and Terp appeared in the dining room fifteen minutes later, without their underdaks or any other attire, Alice had lemonade and ginger snaps waiting for them. In the meantime, Sydney had doffed his clothing as well.

They sat around a circular teak table in view of a large watercolor print in a teak frame mounted into the red brick wall to the left of them. A picture window overlooked a covered veranda on the right. The brightly hued painting showed three nude women entering a tree-lined aquamarine stream.

"Who are they?" Cloud asked, pointing to the artwork.

"It's called 'Nymphs in the Glade' and it's by a famous Aussie artist," said Syd. "This is a copy, of course. We couldn't afford a Norman Lindsay original."

"Some of his paintings are too racy for my blood," added Alice. "This one, though, evokes the innocent spirit of our happy Queen's Paradise."

"Sydney, you said 'that's my boy' when Koah went to get our gear," said Terp. "Is he your son?"

"Fair dinkum he is, and Kuranda's my daughter," said Sydney.

"By his first wife," Alice explained. "She was Tjapukai. Died from the flu, poor thing, when the kids were four and five. Then he came around my door a year later holding Kuranda and Koah with snot all over their faces, and I lost my head and fell in love with him."

"She was a spinster school teacher," Sydney said. "Resigned to teaching math the rest of her life, with no man to crawl into bed with."

"Hush, Sydney," Alice said. "The science teacher fancied me."

"Too right, but he was married, looking for a sheila on the side," Sydney noted. "The fact is, I'm crazy about Alice, and she's crazy about Kuranda and Koah, and hasn't kicked me out of bed yet, so it's all dinky-di."

"So how did you get into the B and B business?" Cloud asked.

"Syd was working for wages, doing maintenance for hotels," Alice explained. "I said we ought to have a business of our own. 'What kind of business?' he said. Something that will lure the tourists in, I said. We looked around and found this property. With my savings, we made a down payment. It was a bit run down, but Syd fixed the place up, and we've been very successful from the start."

"How did the naturist part come into it?" Terp asked.

"Tourists love the chance to go about naked," Syd said. "We're never vacant in the dry, like now. The lull in the wet lets us go on holiday and do repairs. I learned to live without clothes from my first wife. Tribal people don't have much use for pants and dresses."

"What about you, Alice?" Terp asked.

"Syd talked me into it and I've never regretted stripping off. I haven't had a pair of knickers over my bum for ten years!"

"You should see the faces when she goes to town in the nuddy," teased Kuranda, walking by with a load of laundry.

"Mercy no!" said Alice. "I throw an old missionary frock over my head. It's hanging on a hook in the kitchen. Go have a look."

Cloud got up and peeked into the kitchen, and there it was -a large, shapeless cotton dress, blue with white polka dots.

"This being the tropics," she continued, "it's warm all year round. If we were in Melbourne, my bum would be frozen blue right now."

While Terp and Cloud were exploring Australia, Dagmar received baptism from Adam and Evelyn and joined the NCC congregation in New River. She continued to make progress in her therapy with Edna Echo, coming to terms with the lingering traumatic effects of childhood abuse.

"I see now that I had mixed motives for trying to seduce Cloud," she told Edna.

"Yes? How so?" Edna asked.

"The noble part was testing Cloud to see if he was good enough for Terp. I felt protective of her and suspicious of him. He seemed too good to be true. I needed to find out if he would betray her. The other part was...lust. I really wanted to screw him."

"And what was it about him that turned you on, as compared with the actors and athletes you've tended to become sexually involved with?" Edna probed.

"I don't know," Dagmar replied. "He radiates an innocent sophistication that I find really attractive. But he's also earnestly intellectual, and that turns me off."

"I see," said Edna.

At the time, Dagmar was dating Quinn Queensbury, and the subject turned to him. "He works out, so his arms and chest are pumped and rippled. I like that. Two of his legs are skinny and don't work, but his third leg works just fine. And he's truly gifted with his tongue." A wistful look spread across her face. "Just...gifted."

"I see. And what's going to happen when you dump this 'truly gifted' man for your next sexual conquest?" Edna asked bluntly.

"He's had his fun," Dagmar said. "He's been laid by an expert. What more could he possibly want with me?"

"A lot more, I should think," Edna said. "Companionship for starters."

"No way. Nobody wants me for companionship," Dagmar shot back. "Guys get turned off real fast by my sarcastic wit."

"I'm afraid, young lady," Edna said sweetly, "that is pure bullshit. I'll bet Quinn loves your caustic comments on the foibles of society."

"You're right about that one," Dagmar conceded. "He laughs like a loon when I go off on sanctimonious government officials. Wanna hear my Nixon impersonation?"

Edna ignored Dagmar's question. "What about knowing he can confide his deepest feelings in you? Is that something he would value? What about experiencing your love and respect? From what you've told me, I suspect Quinn loves ***you***, rather than your sex organs."

"Yeah, he'll be really hurt when I dump him," Dagmar said with a rueful tone in her voice.

Edna said, "Yes, but if you don't love him, the kindest thing you could do is dump him right now. Don't give him hope. That would be cruel."

"I'm not ready to do that yet," Dagmar said. "I like his sense of humor. I like the way he holds the door open for me at a restaurant, and that's not always easy for him to do. He's quite ingenious about opening doors from his wheelchair. And I told him some stuff from my childhood and he didn't bat an eye. He's the only man I've ever dated that I confided in about my childhood. Of course, he's had a lot of psychotherapy himself, so he's pretty cool about screwed up people."

"So you feel safe with him," Edna suggested.

"I guess I do," Dagmar replied.

"But you don't love him, even though you don't want to let go of him," the therapist continued.

"I'm afraid of the word love," Dagmar confessed. "I want him, but I know that sooner or later I'll want someone else. I always do."

"Yes," Edna noted, "if you let your past dictate your future."

"Nymphs in the Glade," the watercolor print displayed in the dining room at the Queen's Paradise appealed to Cloud. The trees and water setting and the confident and playful postures of the three nude women seemed artfully contrasted.

Syd found Cloud gazing at it one evening after the other guests had retired to their rooms and commented, "You seem to be fascinated by that painting. That artist, Norman Lindsay, caused a bit of a scandal before the First World War with an ink drawing called "The Crucified Venus."

"The title seems well suited for a scandal," replied Cloud.

"Too right," said Syd. "It showed a naked woman hanging on a cross with a monk on a ladder hammering in the nails while a crowd of churchmen stood below jeering. You could tell he was a monk by his robe and the whatchacallit bald spot on the back of his head."

"They call that a tonsure," said Cloud.

"Yeah, that's right. I knew there was a word for how they shave their heads," said Syd. "I heard that the Church tried to ban the 'Venus' when it was on display down in Melbourne, but the head of the Australian Society of Artists said he'd take down all the paintings if they got rid of that one. There was a principle of artistic expression involved. And Lindsay was a member of the society, so they had to stick up for one of their own."

"What do you think about depicting a naked woman on a cross?" Cloud asked.

"I dunno," said Syd. "I've no sympathy for the priggish antics of bishops and priests and certainly not for monks, but I do get a bit queasy about sacrilegious things. It makes my mind uneasy, so to say."

"Certain art is supposed to make us uneasy," said Cloud. "It's supposed to make us stop and think about some aspect of the world or the society we live in and to ask deep questions about it."

Syd strode to a large cabinet and pulled out a tome. "Here's a collection of Lindsay paintings. Have a look for yourself."

When Cloud opened to the print of "The Crucified Venus," he exhaled in response. After a time of silent observation he said, "I can see why the Church would find this at the very least unnerving and more likely blatantly offensive. But looking back at history, I can also see that the Church merited the criticism. Let's see, when was it drawn? Oh yes, here's the date, 1912. This is a feminist rebuke of the Church long before the advent of bra burning feminism. Lindsay is quite a prophetic artist."

"I don't know about prophetic artist," said Syd, "but I do know that Norman Lindsay had no use for pious prudes. He called them wowsers."

"An evocative word," said Cloud. "I see here in the preface that a major theme in Lindsay's work was woman as the Creatress. Very intriguing. Thanks for showing this to me, Syd."

"Glad to expand your mind with some Aussie culture," Syd said with a bow.

During their sojourn at the Queen's Paradise resort, Terp and Cloud took a catamaran excursion out to Michaelmas Cay on the Great Barrier Reef, where they snorkeled and played in the sand, feeling constrained all the while by the necessity of wearing bathing suits.

They also left their bodies in their room at the B and B and floated over the reef, flying along with the sea gulls, and diving under the water, trailing sea turtles through fields of brain coral. They dove into the sea and leapt out of it like a pair of laughing dolphins.

When they moaned in mock horror to Alice about their experience with dozens of noisy tourists on the catamaran and the tiny coral islet, she arranged for them to get away to a secluded location up the coast, north of Alexandria Bay, to a strip of fine white sand hidden between the rainforest and the blue sea.

Kuranda, with Koah along for fun, drove Terp and Cloud by jeep to this beach where they could sunbathe and play in the Coral Sea without bothering about swimsuits. Cloud and Terp bodysurfed and then spread out on the soft ivory strand to bask in the tropical winter sun.

Kuranda and Koah splashed in the waves and played tag across the sand and into the edges of the rainforest. The mixed-race siblings seemed to Cloud to be unaffected by the troubles of society. Whatever prejudice they may experience in the larger world could not intrude on their happiness here.

Cloud found himself whistling a sixties beach tune, "Turn Down Day," as the idyllic scene unfolded in serene syncopation.

Early afternoon, Kuranda brought a picnic basket from the jeep, and the four sat in the sand enjoying a naked lunch of Vegemite sandwiches Alice had made, tiny bananas, followed by store-bought sweet biscuits, and chased down with Alice's homemade tart lemonade. Neither Cloud nor Terp appreciated the pungent taste of Vegemite but were hungry enough not to care. The lemonade was cold and delicious.

"What do you plan to do when you finish school, Kuranda?" Terp asked.

"I dunno," the teenager replied. "Stay at Queen's Paradise. The work is OK, and it's safe. Nobody calls me dirty names there. Alice is good to me."

"Same for me," Koah said. "I like the place."

"Well, if you ever want to visit America," Terp said, "come stay with us."

"I don't think I'll ever leave Queensland," Kuranda said.

"But if you get the travel itch," Cloud said, "please write to us. We'd be delighted to put you up for a while."

At the end of the day, after returning to the B and B, Terp told Syd and Alice about their invitation to the teenagers to visit in Arizona.

"Well, they do have their passports, as we took them along on a business jaunt to New Guinea last year," Alice said. "But it's hard to pry them away from here. They love it so."

For entertainment while rearranging luggage on their last night at the Queens Paradise, Cloud switched on the radio.

"Remember 1962?" the ABC disc jockey asked. "You'll remember this international smash hit by Aussie yodeler Frank Ifield."

As the opening notes of "I Remember You" filled the room, Cloud scooped Terp's left hand from her suitcase. "This song has always reminded me of you," he said. "Dance with me a while and imagine us talking to the angels about each other." Their naked bodies merged and gently swayed to the nostalgic melody.

"I was only ten years old in 1962," Terp impishly whispered in his ear. "I didn't know you had a thing for little girls."

"No, no, only for you. I knew I would meet you someday," he said. "I've been ***saving*** this song eleven years for you to grow up so I could dance to it with you."

She nuzzled her face against his cheek. "Was I worth the wait?"

"Every aching minute of it," he replied and kissed the tip of her nose.

With faces chapped by wind, hair bleached by sun and salt water, and minds loaded with memories of ecstatic experiences, Cloud and Terp reluctantly said farewell to the Darwin family and returned to Sydney for their flight home.

On the trip back, they made a stopover in Honolulu and took an inter-island flight to Maui, where Terp met with the Dean and the Admissions Director of Pacific Crossroads Seminary. Terp's reputation had preceded her, via a letter from Evelyn Rarom, and the officials confirmed she would have a place in the entering class in September 1974. Evelyn had also informed them of Cloud's graduate work in Asian religion, and they encouraged him to consider teaching as an adjunct faculty member.

But all of this was more than a year away. A lot could happen in the coming months to alter their plans, Cloud thought. He considered the realistic possibility they might end up at the other end of the country, in Princeton, New Jersey. Terp was quietly confident, however, that Lahaina would be their home this time next year.

CHAPTER NINE

Once safely home from their honeymoon, returning to a daily routine and preparing for the resumption of studies in September, Terp and Cloud separately brooded about the same subject: the Old One's comment that Xuan's death had not been predestined. Without a word to the other, each pondered what would have happened to them if Xuan had lived.

All the scenarios Terp conjured were personally painful for her, while Cloud imagined himself torn between dreams of two elusively beautiful women and having to choose which dream was real.

While washing dinner dishes one evening, Cloud said, "Why so pensive, love?"

"I was about to ask you the same question," Terp replied.

"Something the Old One said has been nagging at me," he confessed.

"Me too," she said. "Xuan."

"Yes, Xuan," he said.

"If she had lived I would never have met you," Terp said, tears welling in her eyes. "But I don't want my joy to be derived from someone else's suffering."

"Maybe we would have met, and I would have been torn between the two of you," Cloud said. He took his wife by the hand. "Let's sit and reflect on this for a while." Side by side, they settled back on the couch, meditating silently.

It seemed as if the Old One had been waiting for them to arrive at this point, for the venerable creature placed an identical message in each of their brains: "The odds were always against Xuan surviving. If, perchance, she had lived through the war, a host of possibilities could have unfolded -as many as the two of you now face together. If Xuan had lived, what a peculiar trinity you would have made -three strange angels unloosed on the world." The Old One smiled at this prospect, but neither Cloud nor Terp could discern the upturned lips.

"You just received a message, didn't you?" Cloud said.

"Of course I did. The Old One again," Terp responded.

The image of a peculiar trinity did not raise any feelings of jealousy in Terp. She was incapable of feeling jealousy with respect to Cloud. They were now so closely woven together that such feelings about her husband would be directed against herself as well. That Xuan had been his first love had never been an issue before, because Xuan had died. But fantasizing about Xuan living and how that would have affected the unfolding of her life caused Terp psychic pain nevertheless.

She wondered what the Old One meant by a peculiar trinity. Certainly it indicated that Xuan also would have learned to float, she decided. But the three of us together? That would have made me the little sister in the relationship, she thought. Not nearly as satisfying as what I have now. But Xuan did not survive, so what purpose does this brooding serve? In a flash she saw it. A lightning bolt in her mind illuminated the answer. As deeply as she had already penetrated into Cloud's being, she was about to go deeper.

"Come sit on the bed, Cloud," she said. "The way you did in the motel near Uluru after I floated into your body in the tub."

Since it was a hot August evening, both were naked, and the memory of that event in Australia made him stiffen.

"Oh good. That's exactly what I want." Terp said, noting his physical response, whereupon she added an oral flourish to aid the process. When he was properly arranged on the bed, Terp straddled his lap, guiding his erection inside her. "Be completely still and stare into my eyes," she directed. "No swaying or thrusting."

For a few minutes, they peered deeply into each other. "Now,

Cloud," she whispered slowly, "I want you to think about Xuan. Bring to consciousness all the images of her that you can, even the most intimate ones. Close your eyes and remember her." She pressed her forehead gently against his and held him with her arms.

Cloud thought about the first time he saw Xuan, when the basket of figs was crushed by an Army truck, and the restaurants where they dined, and the temples they visited, the walks with her, caressing her hands, conversations, dancing, and making love. Then, as much as he tried to suppress it, he saw her head split apart by bullets. And Terp absorbed every image into her own memory. Thus Xuan became part of Terp as well as part of Cloud. Even the horrible vision of Xuan's death now resided in Terp's memory.

Terp massaged the sides of Cloud's head. "Open your eyes, dearest," she said. When he peered once more into her eyes, she said softly, "You have very good taste in women. I am so happy you loved Xuan, and I'm grateful you've shared her with me. I will treasure her memory always. Thank you, Cloud."

The next day, Cloud said, "Let's do that again. Only this time, I want you to conjure memories of your dad, so that even though I saw him only once, in the Edison Hotel, I will have your memories of him."

They went to the bedroom and sat facing each other, linked as before. With their foreheads together, she produced a torrent of images of Tom Person, which Cloud absorbed into his mind. Then, without prior discussion, Cloud filled Terp's brain with memories of Miss Listerbaum, including his visit to her deathbed. Terp then conjured her first meeting with the Old One, followed by Cloud projecting the scene of the first time he floated. Simultaneously they exchanged views of the New York City blackout, from their opposing perspectives. Weariness then descended upon them and they rested, cradling in one another's arms.

"And the two shall become one flesh," Terp said, breaking the silence with a quote from the gospel of Mark.

"I guess you're stuck with me, Terp." He said.

"***Au contraire,*** you're stuck ***in*** me, ***liebchen,*** but that's exactly where I want you to be," she said. "***Em yeu anh***, Cloud," she added in Vietnamese.

"***Anh yeu em***," he replied. "I guess, ***punkin***, that you picked up a little of the language yesterday, along with my memories of Xuan," Cloud quipped.

"And you must have absorbed something of my dad, because he was the only one who ever called me punkin," she purred.

They stretched out together and let their caresses grow in intensity.

As the weekend approached, Terp and Cloud made plans to go to church in New River. This raised the question of how much they should tell Evelyn and Adam about Amoonguna's dream, Terp healing her drunken father, and their meeting with the Old One. Each sensed they should not reveal everything but could identify no rational reason for their reticence. They had already told the pastors enough to have them locked away in an asylum, and they had been believed and even praised. So they had nothing to fear. Yet intuitively they knew some of what they had learned represented a sacred confidence.

"I think we should tell them about Amoonguna and her father," Terp said.

"Agreed," said Cloud. "And we should tell them about floating together, but not what happened in the bathtub."

"Yes," said Terp. "And about meeting the Old One in the river bed..."

"...but nothing about the Old One's physical appearance," said Cloud, finishing her thought.

"Exactly," Terp confirmed. "What about the sand?"

"I'll bring it along for them to feel," said Cloud.

"Let's not say anything about transferring memories into each other's brains," Terp suggested.

"Right," said Cloud.

Evelyn and Adam had been stunned by Cloud's earlier tales of floating and precognitions, and Terp's prescient dreams and meeting the Old One. Now, after hearing their honeymoon adventures, the pastors were flabbergasted.

Terp leaving her body? And healing an inebriated man? And both of them talking with the Old One face-to-face? Whatever next?

"I suspect there's more to the story," Evelyn said. "But you must have a good reason for editing your description, so I won't press for more information."

"Thank you for respecting our privacy, Evelyn," Terp said.

"But you ought to keep a record of everything you know about the Old One," Evelyn urged. "Including details like the Old One enjoying a nineteenth century hymn."

"That's a good idea," replied Terp. "I'll write down everything we can remember in a journal and keep it safely locked away."

"Here, Adam, feel this," Cloud said, handing him a vial of sand that he had scooped from the place the Old One had sat.

"It's warm. Did you leave it in the car in the sun?" Adam asked.

"Put it in your freezer for an hour and feel it again," Cloud said.

"You're going to tell me that it'll still be this warm, aren't you?" Adam said.

"Yep," said Cloud. "The Old One sat on this sand."

"As I suspected," said Adam. He believed Cloud, but did the test anyway for the joy of experiencing the result.

Once home from the weekend in New River, Terp filled a blank book with information about the Old One: all the conversations she and Cloud had had in person and through telepathy, notations about the Old One's garb -the purple robe and canvas robe- and a detailed description of the Old One's naked body. Cloud placed this and the vial of sand in his footlocker and put a strong lock on it. Eventually, Cloud would buy a large fire and waterproof safe, installed in Lloyd and Nissa's home, so the relics would be secure while Terp and Cloud were away at seminary. But for the present, the wooden box in their living room functioned as the repository for these items, and this would produce an unexpected development in their family.

The week before classes resumed at Arizona State, Terp joined Evelyn in conducting a healing service at the NCC camp. When all those desiring healing had gathered in the sanctuary, Terp and Evelyn read passages of scripture and offered prayers for the community. Then, one by one as they felt led by the Spirit, individuals came forward and sat in a chair on the chancel, with their backs to the congregation. Each petitioner quietly mentioned a specific concern -a difficult decision, a painful relationship, a bout of depression, an addiction. People came forward with spiritual confusions, persistent grief, and wounded psyches.

Evelyn anointed each one, making a sign of the cross in oil on their foreheads. Terp put her hands on the person's head and prayed. Evelyn then pronounced a blessing. They made no claims for permanent cures or miracles. Nevertheless, tears of relief or joy flowed freely, as worshipers gained clarity and strength to deal with their problems. A few experienced deep changes they identified as healing. All testified that Terp's presence added spiritual depth to the service. Evelyn was overjoyed with the partnership.

Firstlaugh Begay dialed Cloud's number, which he had obtained from Lloyd. "***Ya'at'eeh!***" he greeted his friend in Navajo. "Hey, you finally got a phone! Welcome to the twentieth century. That's what you white guys say to us up on the reservation. Anyway, we're in town for a couple of days, and I thought I'd call and say hello."

"***Ya'at'eeh*** yourself," responded Cloud. "Are you doing anything this evening?"

"Nothing special," Firstlaugh said.

"Well, I'd like to meet your wife," Cloud said, "and while we're at it, introduce you to my wife. Can you come over for dinner?"

"Married, huh? The last time we talked you were in the dumps about having nobody in your life. What time do you want us?" the Navajo said.

"About five. Same place as before."

"We've got Tzek with us. The baby. My son! Is that OK?"

"Absolutely!" said Cloud.

Thus the high school friends met each other's wives, and Terp got to hold nine month-old Tzekooh Hatsoh Begay. Terp and Cedar Cradle liked one another instantly.

"His name means Grand Canyon in Navajo," Firstlaugh explained. "We call him Tzek for short. My mother doesn't like it. She only calls him Tzekooh Hatsoh."

"I told Firstlaugh the next one will get a Lakota name," Cedar Cradle said.

"The Lakotas live somewhere in the Northern Plains, don't they?" Terp asked.

"Pine Ridge Reservation in South Dakota. I came down to do Indian rights organizing with the Navajo and fell in love with a war hero. I hate the war, but I love this warrior." She caressed the side of her husband's head. "My work has suffered, but my soul has blossomed," the Lakota woman added.

"Is Pine Ridge where that siege was?" Terp asked. "I read about it in the paper."

"Yep, at Wounded Knee," said Cedar Cradle. "That's where the U. S. Cavalry massacred my people in 1890. It's sacred ground. Last February, armed American Indian Movement reformers took control of the village for two and a half months, but the FBI reneged on an offer to negotiate, and in the end they all surrendered. We always do. Our grievances are real, but guns are not the answer. Our strongest power is spiritual."

After dinner, Firstlaugh and Cedar Cradle settled onto the couch, while Cloud and Terp pulled up chairs facing them.

"I'm really enjoying this conversation," Cedar Cradle said, "but it's time to nurse Tzek. I could go in the other room for modesty's sake. Or would it be OK to do it here?"

Terp and Cloud chuckled. "Preferably here," said Terp. "Modesty is overrated."

"Nursing in front of friends doesn't bother me," Cedar Cradle said, "but some people act really uncomfortable around bare nipples."

"Not us," said Cloud. "We're quite used to seeing women breastfeed with a whole lot more than nipples exposed."

Cedar Cradle unbuttoned her blouse, unsnapped her bra in the front and placed Tzek on her left breast. His eager sucking brought her remembrance of the joy with which he had been conceived, and she quietly crooned "Danny's Song" as he nursed.

"Do you volunteer in hospitals or something?" Firstlaugh asked.

"No," said Terp. "We spend time at a naturist camp."

"One of those places where people run around naked?" Cedar Cradle asked.

"Yes. It's connected with the Natural Christian Church," Cloud explained.

"Not everyone is naked all the time," Terp elaborated. "People can wear as much or as little as they like. Weather is more a factor than anything else in how much to put on or take off. But the unclothed human body is appreciated as normative."

"I went to a Catholic-Episcopalian boarding school," Cedar Cradle said, "and they were very strict about making us wear white-man's clothes all the time, and we hated it. Going to a church without ***any*** clothes seems so... egalitarian! It would blow their minds! So, I'm all for it. But Firstlaugh, being ***Dine***, is a little shy about his body."

"People come in all shapes and sizes, Firstlaugh," Terp said. "The great majority of people do not look like center folds or body builders."

"That doesn't bother me," Firstlaugh said. "I'm just as shy dressed as undressed."

"That's true," Cedar Cradle confirmed. She moved her son to her right breast. "And in fact, he has an excellent body to show off, if he wanted to." When Tzek was finished feeding, his mother said, "Since you go running around naked outside, I don't suppose you'd mind if I let these air out a little." She waved a hand across her breasts.

Terp said, "It's silly that men can go topless anywhere they want but women have to cover up. In the interest of female solidarity, I'll join you." Terp pulled off her shirt and undid her bra.

"***Brava***!" said Cedar Cradle. "Does that shock you, Firstlaugh?"

"Not a bit!" he said as he averted his eyes from Terp's chest.

"When I greet the Creator in prayer each morning," Cedar Cradle said, "I am as sky-clad as the moment of my birth. So is Firstlaugh when he opens the door and greets the sunrise. The nakedness is intentional for me but incidental for him."

"For years I've done my bedtime meditations with God in the nude," Terp said. "I wonder what it means that you pray in the morning and I do it at night?"

"Calvinists would tend to be grateful just to have made it through the day," said Cloud. "Indian spirituality seems more optimistic in that regard."

"Well, I'm grateful to the ***optimistic*** American Calvinists for sending me to Macalester College on a full scholarship," said Cedar Cradle in defense of Terp's church.

"Point well taken," said Cloud. "Now we want to do something for all three of you, something we like to do for our esteemed guests."

"Does it involve taking off our clothes?" Firstlaugh asked.

"No, but you have to take off your shoes," Cloud said.

Terp explained reflexology to them. "We'll demonstrate on Tzek first."

Cedar Cradle laid the baby on her lap. Cloud and Terp took off his booties. Terp held up a towel and said, "You need to pull up your skirt, Cedar Cradle. We don't want to get oil on it."

"Here, hold your son a minute," Cedar Cradle said to her husband. Rather than pull it up, she shimmied out of it. Terp placed the towel across Cedar Cradle's legs, and Firstlaugh put Tzek back in his mother's arms.

Cloud and Terp slipped out of their jeans, and Cloud removed his light blue polo shirt. "Cloud tends to get messy with the oil," Terp noted. Terp and Cedar Cradle were now clad only in sensible white underpants and Cloud in plain white boxers.

With Tzek's little feet on the towel, Terp and Cloud massaged them, and the baby soon fell into a contented sleep.

"I'm next," Cedar Cradle said. She put Tzek in Firstlaugh's lap. Terp and Cloud each placed a towel on their laps and took hold of one of Cedar Cradle's feet. They kneaded and massaged, and the Lakota woman groaned with pleasure. "You're going to love this, Firstlaugh," she said to her husband.

Before long it was his turn, and he placed his bare feet in his friends' laps. The Navajo man enjoyed the reflexology treatment immensely, and when they had finished, he was drowsy.

"Are you staying with your parents tonight?" Cloud asked.

"They moved to Fort Defiance," Firstlaugh said. "We're going to stay in a motel."

"Don't be silly," Terp said. "You'll stay here with us. We've got sleeping bags, and we can improvise a crib for Tzek."

"We have a portable crib in the pick-up," Cedar Cradle said.

"That settles it," Terp said. "Cloud and Firstlaugh, go get that crib and your things from the truck. Cedar Cradle and I will set up the sleeping arrangements."

Cloud put on jeans and loafers and the men went out to the parking lot.

"You still have your booger car, I see," Firstlaugh noted.

When they returned with the gear, they saw that two sleeping bags had been laid out on the living room floor. Terp and Cedar Cradle were in the bedroom changing sheets on the bed. The women were naked.

"OK, guys, time to doff your duds. ***Ha'diijaah,*** dear husband," Cedar Cradle said.

Cloud complied immediately but said, "We shouldn't pressure him if he's not comfortable with it. Suit yourself, Firstlaugh. Keep your pants on if you want."

Firstlaugh took some time stripping to his underwear, at which point he stopped undressing. The reason for his modesty was apparent to all through the cotton briefs. He had become partially erect.

"No worries, Firstlaugh," Terp said. "That's perfectly normal. After a while you'll see naked bodies in a different context, and that won't happen -unless, of course, you want it to."

The women took the crib into the bedroom and set it up.

"Oh, are you guys going to tend Tzek for us tonight?" Firstlaugh asked.

"That's a great idea," said Terp. "Let's move the crib into the living room."

"Are you sure you don't mind?" Cedar Cradle asked.

"I, for one, would ***love*** to do it," Terp said.

"I thought we were going to be in the sleeping bags," Firstlaugh said.

"We want you to have our bed," Cloud said.

Grateful for the break, Cedar Cradle said, "I'll pump a bottle of breast milk for his middle of the night feeding." She and Terp went into the bedroom for pumping and discussion of the feeding process. When they returned, they saw that Firstlaugh had taken off his briefs, but no one remarked about it.

The two couples talked for several more hours, but eventually weariness overcame them and they settled into their respective rooms. About three in the morning, a hungry Tzek awakened Terp. She warmed the bottle and held him in her arms, reveling in the task of feeding him.

Cloud woke and watched his wife with great affection. "Want any help?"

"When we have one of our own, you can help," she said. "But

tonight, Tzek is all mine." She rocked the baby gently in her arms, and he soon settled back to sleep. Terp also slept, dreaming of the infant she wanted to produce with Cloud.

Cloud had a more grandiose dream in which he saw them living in a large, rambling desert house with a pack of children running through it, playing noisy games. This was startlingly different from his solitary experience of childhood, and he found it pleasant to contemplate.

In the morning, Cedar Cradle said, "That was the best sleep I've had since Tzek was born. It was a wonderful gift. I'm grateful to both of you."

"The pleasure was mine as well," said Terp. "I loved feeding Tzek."

"When it's every night, the joyful feeling fades, but he's definitely worth the interruption of sleep," Cedar Cradle said.

"Holding him makes me want to have one of my own, but I need to get through school first," Terp said.

"When Terp finishes seminary," Cloud offered, "we'll make a bunch of babies."

"One at a time, buster," Terp said.

Cloud and Terp celebrated the first anniversary of their meeting in the drug store by making love. So relaxed and meditative was their coupling, however, that without intent the two popped out of their bodies simultaneously and floated to the ceiling with their souls wrapped together.

"Wow!" said Terp telepathically.

"Look at us down there," said Cloud.

Terp looked at their bodies linked on the bed. "Pretty erotic," she said.

"I think we're beautiful," Cloud said.

"Yes," said Terp. "Whene'er we're together, we are beautiful."

Having thus admired their bodies locked in love, they sailed through the ceiling and out into the evening air. Terp and Cloud had floated together before, but this time they were not simply together but inside each other's souls, and the experience was qualitatively different.

They explored the campus, observing students walking from place to place with hurried or leisurely gaits. In addition to seeing people, however, they heard things. Not conversations but silent groans of psychic pain, the rumble of doubts, hot anger, cold fear. They heard the brittle clang of certainty masking terror in some minds. A cacophony of psychic emanations flooded them. It seemed like a chaotic and unintentional chorus of prayer. Here and there amidst the silent noise, Cloud and Terp heard the sound of grace and peace. Audible amidst the babble of disordered minds came soft symphonic strains of love and hope.

The experience filled them with a profound sense of compassion for the fractured human community and a longing to contribute some part of their lives toward calming tortured minds and encouraging gracious ones. It also weighed heavily on their spirits, and they soon returned to their bodies to continue making love with a deeper sense of purpose and joy.

Terp's first Christmas in Arizona was a memorable occasion. On Christmas Eve, she said, "I want to go to church tonight, Cloud, but there's no midnight service at New River."

"How about College Avenue Calvinist at eleven o'clock?" he suggested.

"You have it all planned, don't you?"

"Let's just say I anticipated your wish."

Though the College Avenue sanctuary reflected airy, modern architecture, with comfortable cushioned pews, contrasting with the hard wood and heavily gothic appointments of Second Calvinist in Metuchen, the order of worship was reminiscent of what Terp remembered fondly from New Jersey, and she was grateful to be present for the service. There was, however, one major difference.

The processional was led by a choir of seven dancers, who glissaded and bowed gracefully to an exquisite arrangement of "O Holy Night" sung by the chancel choir. Terp sat rapt in awe of their sacred choreography. Long gowns flowed over the dancers' bodies and quivered with the movement of their limbs, adding a sense of flight to their progress toward the chancel. Each dancer held a lighted candle in her hands, and Terp held her breath, praying that no wick would fail as the women fell to their knees and rose again in effortless fluid motions as they continued through the sanctuary. Miraculously, every flame survived the wind generated by their genuflections and turns.

"Did you know beforehand that they did liturgical dance here?" Terp asked Cloud during the interval for seating latecomers.

"No," he said. "This was an unexpected blessing."

"It only confirms all the more my sense of call to be a dancing pastor," she whispered. "Even Calvinists, it seems, can dance in church." Terp's mouth formed into a wide and satisfied smile. "But probably not nude, the way Evelyn did in our apartment."

"Maybe someday they will," Cloud whispered back.

For Christmas, Cloud gave Terp an elegant woman's watch with a band of sterling silver set with four brightly hued but oddly shaped turquoise stones. One of the gemstones was roughly triangular, reminding Cloud of the Old One's face. The color matched the mysterious being's eyes. A Navajo artist who had a storefront studio in Tempe during the winter months had crafted the piece, and it had captured Cloud's heart. He imagined it on his wife's wrist as a fitting representation of her unique beauty.

Terp surprised Cloud with the man's version of the same watch, including among its four stones one that looked like a cloud.

CHAPTER TEN

Terp wrote to Argyle Watts in February 1974, asking how to come under the care of her denomination as she entered seminary and worked toward ordination. She told him she had applied to Princeton Theological Seminary and Pacific Crossroads. Application to the former she had made to satisfy a promise to her mother, although she did not mention this to her pastor. She did, however, tell him that Pacific Crossroads had an excellent liturgical dance curriculum, and this was a key element of her sense of call.

Argyle responded with the information she needed about the process and made an appointment for her to be interviewed in June by the Candidates for Ministry Committee of Witherspoon Presbytery in New Jersey. He wrote that he was very pleased with her application to Princeton but mildly dismayed by Pacific Crossroads. The Hawaiian seminary was fully accredited, he acknowledged, but it carried a reputation as eclectic, focusing too much attention on interfaith studies. Where Princeton was reliably solid, he added, Pacific Crossroads was unsystematically experimental.

The same day Terp received Argyle's correspondence about seminaries, a tragedy was unfolding in the antipodes at Cairns, Queensland. A guest at the Queen's Paradise was behaving suspiciously. He was an atypical boarder at the resort, because he was a single man. Most of the guests were couples or families with parents and children. The Darwins required the recommendation of a trustworthy former guest before accepting a single person, and this system had served them well. The occasional solos had proven to be delightful people. The majority were divorced men and women working on rebuilding positive esteem about themselves and acceptance of their bodies.

This man had obtained the needed recommendation from his cousin, who had visited the B and B several times with his wife and sons. Nevertheless, he seemed odd. He paced up and down the upstairs hall, as if spying on the other guests. He also watched the movements about the place of Syd and Alice, Koah and Kuranda.

One afternoon, when all the other guests were away pursuing various adventures, the man stayed alone in his room. Syd was in the kitchen repairing a leaky pipe in the sink while Alice provided him moral support. Koah was setting up the dining room for supper. Kuranda carried an armload of folded sheets from the laundry room to the upstairs linen closet.

Thinking that he and Kuranda were the only people in the house, the man called out to her as she carefully stowed the sheets on the shelf.

"What is it, sir?" she asked, walking to his open door.

His back was to her. "I need help with the bed," he said without turning around.

Kuranda approached him. "What's wrong with it?" she asked.

He faced her, revealing that he was sexually aroused. "You're not in it, my little creamy one," he said.

"No!" she yelled and started to run, but he grabbed her and pushed the door shut.

"I thought your job was to make guests happy," he snarled, shoving her on the bed. She screamed but the sound was quickly stifled by his huge hand across her mouth. She bit his hand and he slapped her harshly across the face with his other hand. "Shut up you black bitch!" he barked and savagely penetrated her.

At the foot of the stairs, Koah heard his sister's muffled scream and bolted to the room, leaping on the rapist, trying to pull the large man off Kuranda. The man elbowed Koah hard in the face, but the boy clung to him with all his might.

Seconds later Syd arrived, and with his wiry but strong arms -and Koah's assistance- threw the predator to the floor and tied his hands and feet with lamp cords. Alice then entered the room and saw immediately what had happened. She ran to Kuranda and cradled the girl in her arms.

"Koah, call the police, then bring mum's frock and my pants. I'll watch this bastard," Syd commanded. He put his foot on the rapist's neck and pressed firmly. He felt like standing on the man's windpipe with all his weight, but held his fury until the authorities arrived.

A week later, Cloud and Terp received an airmail letter from Alice, telling them about the assault on Kuranda. She wrote in part:

"The bastard's in gaol, but Kuranda is still afraid of him. She wants to go somewhere safe for a time. She remembers you fondly, talking about you often. Might your offer of a visit still stand? Syd and I have enough put by to cover her airfare, but nothing for room and board. Forgive me for being so forward. Ordinarily I would never impose on anyone this way, but this is no ordinary situation."

Cloud computed the time difference and determined that it was late morning in Cairns. He telephoned the Darwins. "Alice, this is Cloud Morgan," he said when she answered. "We got your letter, and yes, of course, Kuranda can stay with us as long as she likes. Don't worry about the room and board. We have plenty to share."

"Oh, thank you, Cloud. You're so kind," Alice said and then started to weep. "I had a bad feeling about that man. I told Syd we ought to refuse him, but he was recommended by a regular, and we didn't want to lose a regular."

"I'm so sorry, Alice," Cloud said. "But I wonder if Kuranda is in any shape to travel around the world alone. Can you send Koah with her?"

"We don't have the money to send both," she answered straightforwardly.

"No worry, Alice," Cloud responded. "I am personally inviting Koah to visit with us also, and I'll wire you the funds to pay for his ticket, plus a little pocket money for both of them while traveling." And so it was arranged.

Cloud and Terp met Kuranda and Koah at Sky Harbor Airport. It was fortunate that the teenagers carried one suitcase each, because only one piece of luggage fit in the trunk of Cloud's Volkswagen, and with four people in the small car, the other piece rested in Koah's lap from the airport to their apartment in Tempe.

Once safely home, Kuranda told Cloud and Terp that she wore clothing all the time now, as a shield against further assault.

"We will honor your concerns, Kuranda, and keep our clothes on, too," Terp said.

"Oh no, ma'am," Kuranda said. "I don't want to cause you any inconvenience."

Nevertheless, Cloud and Terp remained fully clad around the apartment that day and the next. Terp had called Evelyn the day before their Australian guests arrived, and the second day of their stay in Arizona, Evelyn and Adam came to visit them.

After introductions, Terp said to the three males, "We have some women's business to take care of. We'll be in the bedroom for a while and we'd appreciate privacy."

Terp, Evelyn, and Kuranda went into the bedroom and closed the door. There, the two women anointed the teenager's head with oil, placed their hands on the girl's head, and each in turn prayed fervently. A time of silent meditation followed, with Terp and Evelyn maintaining physical contact with Kuranda.

Kuranda's anxiety began to fade, and she smiled tentatively. After a while, she asked to be left alone, and Terp and Evelyn returned to the living room. Fifteen minutes passed, and Kurnada emerged from the bedroom naked. "I'm not afraid anymore," she announced, and proceeded heartily to hug Terp and Evelyn, then Cloud. She hesitated in front of Adam, for she did not know him, but she quickly decided that if he was Evelyn's husband, he was a good man, and she hugged him also. Lastly, she threw her arms around her brother, who was beaming at his sister's renewed spirit.

Before leaving, Adam invited the Aussies to visit the NCC camp, and they accepted. Kuranda and Koah spent the following weekend in New River and in comparison with the small apartment in Tempe, the siblings felt less constrained and more comfortable with the large acreage at their disposal. They volunteered to help out around the camp, doing tasks they were used to doing at home in Cairns. Thus they spent half their time with the Rarom family in New River and half with the Morgans in Tempe. The twins, Abram and Sarai, on the verge of becoming teenagers, developed an especially close bond with Koah, eagerly absorbing his tales of antipodes lore.

Evelyn spent a lot of time with Kuranda, and warned the traumatized girl that she would need more attention. "You may have flashbacks and bouts of depression and fits of rage. Don't try to deal with it by yourself. Find someone you trust to help you through the hard times."

"I trust you and the Morgans," Kuranda said.

"I'm so glad you do," said Evelyn. "But someday you'll return home to Australia, and you'll need to find reliable friends there. In the meantime, Terp and I would like to do some more women's business with you while you're here."

Kuranda wept at this news. "I was hoping for that," she said.

In the course of events, Terp and Evelyn conducted three more healing services with Kuranda, who gained greater emotional strength with each session of anointing, laying on of hands, and prayer. Her body had long since healed, and now the wounds to her psyche gave way to the restorative words, touch, and love of two remarkable women.

At the beginning of May, Kuranda and Koah boarded a plane for Australia. Their tears flowed abundantly at the airport as they said farewell to Terp, Cloud, Evelyn, Adam, Sarai, and Abram. They almost missed their flight because they couldn't stop hugging their American friends.

The first week in June, Terry Person Morgan was granted a Bachelor of Arts degree, ***Summa cum Laude*** and was inducted into Phi Beta Kappa. The highest honors came despite a slump in the first semester of her junior year when she had contemplated a suicide gesture and then met her future husband. Her subsequent work more than made up for the temporary inattention to academic matters.

Evan Cloud Morgan was conferred with the degree of Doctor of Philosophy. His dissertation received considerable praise among scholars in the Asian history community: ***The Urge Toward Syncretism Where Eastern and Western Cultures Intersect: A Study of the Cao Dai Religion***.

After commencement, Terp and Cloud happily accepted the invitation of Firstlaugh and Cedar Cradle to spend a week in Window Rock. The drive to the capital of the Navajo Nation took five hours.

Cloud noted that in Navajo eyes, his car became a blue booger as he crossed the line onto the reservation.

"***Whoshdee! Whoshdee!***" said Firstlaugh as he greeted them at the front door of his ranch style home. "Come in! Come in!"

The Begay house formed a rectangle of concrete block set on a north-south axis, with an octagonal stone room attached to the east side of its length. The front door that Terp and Cloud entered was on the south and led into the kitchen. The attached room, a modernized female hogan, also provided an entrance through French doors that opened to the east. This was the master bedroom, and it was by opening these double doors that Firstlaugh greeted each new day.

Terp delighted in playing with seventeen month-old Tzek the first evening they stayed in the Begay home. The next morning, Cedar Cradle delivered her son to the care of his grandparents, so she and Firstlaugh would be free to tour the reservation with Cloud and Terp. Their first stop was the two hundred feet high sandstone hill with a large hole in it that gave Window Rock its name.

"Its ceremonial name is ***Ni' 'Alnii gi***," explained Firstlaugh. "That means Center of the Earth."

Terp whispered to Cloud, "I'd like to float through that window some time."

"Me too," he whispered back.

From there Firstlaugh drove along a series of back roads to a deserted hogan near the base of a red, gold, purple, and blue butte. "My uncle used to live here," he said, "but his wife died inside so he moved out. No one wants to live in a place where someone died because of ghosts. ***Chiindi***! When it happens, some ***Dine*** destroy the hogans, but my uncle just left. This one's female, by the way. For family living. Male hogans are smaller, with pointed roofs, and they're used only for ceremonies."

"What a shame he abandoned her," said Cloud. "The setting is so beautiful here."

They entered the log and mud dwelling, and Terp said, "Well, I don't detect any evil spiritual presence here."

"And if there were, Terp would know," Cloud said.

"It doesn't bother me that a woman passed away here," Cedar Cradle said.

"Actually, I don't get spooked by this ghost business," offered Firstlaugh, "but most ***Dine*** do, so I respect their sensibilities."

"Can we climb that butte?" Terp asked.

"Sure," said Firstlaugh. "I know a good way to the top."

The four proceeded up the side of the multicolored rock formation. The view from the summit revealed a shimmering mixture of subtle and garish hues spread across the wide and high mesas.

"Ooh, this place is too sublime for clothes," said Terp. "Would you mind if I disrobed? Would that be a sacrilege or something in the eyes of the ***Dine***?"

"Nope!" Firstlaugh declared. "I knew you'd get around to that. Last one naked's a coyote!" While unbuttoning his shirt he began singing the new Ray Stevens novelty song "The Streak," gleefully chortling "boogety boogety" as he stripped.

In the natural course of undressing, they found they needed to remove their hiking boots in order to get their jeans off. When this ungainly task was done and they were all bare, Firstlaugh pulled from his backpack four pairs of moccasins for their temporary use. "The rocks and pebbles can hurt your feet," he said. "These will help."

"I don't remember you being a Boy Scout," Cloud said. "And yet you obviously prepared in advance for this spontaneous outburst of nudity."

Firstlaugh grinned and shouted, "***Adadiilzhish***! Let's dance!"

Terp was the first to dance, moving across the top of the hill with leaping ballet steps. Cedar Cradle followed with a side stepping Lakota round dance. Then Firstlaugh took up a Navajo sway dance. This left Cloud to admire the agility of the other three, until he began moving without conscious intention to an ancient Celtic midsummer rhythm. All of their movements were made to unvoiced music inside their heads, so there was no coordination to their choreography. Soon, however, melodic laughter arose among them, and this provided the soundtrack to their naturist gamboling.

When hunger nagged at them, they pulled on only their socks and boots and hiked down to the hogan. There they switched again into moccasins. Cedar Cradle spread a blanket on the earth for a picnic of fry bread, baked beans, strawberries, cherries, and peaches, chased by several canteens of spring water.

Terp then produced a bottle of massage oil from her backpack. “Time for foot rubs,” she announced.

The four friends took turns kneading and caressing one another’s feet. Each felt his or her particular accumulated tension melt away in response to the tactile attention. Eventually, they put their clothes on and headed back to Window Rock for the night.

The next day the foursome traveled to Canyon de Chelley, where Firstlaugh showed Cloud and Terp places where Navajos had hidden in the nineteenth century when Federal troops were rounding up his people for removal to New Mexico.

Terp said, “I can feel the spirit of the people who lived here then. Their prayers were powerful.”

“Don’t you think it’s the place that’s sacred?” asked Firstlaugh.

“I believe it’s the people,” said Terp. “I felt the same thing at Uluru in the Northern Territory. It’s the response of the people to the land and not the land itself that makes a place holy.”

“My people see it differently, “ Firstlaugh said, “but I like the way you say it too.”

The day before Cloud and Terp returned to Phoenix, the quartet made a return visit to the multi-colored butte. From their high vantage point, Cedar Cradle, Terp, Firstlaugh, and Cloud watched a female rain move from the west across the mesa below.

“I hope it reaches us here,” said Terp. “I love dancing in warm summer rains.”

“It’ll come here,” Firstlaugh said, “but it may not be as warm as you’d like it.”

“As long as it’s not chilly, I’ll revel in it,” Terp replied.

“I love the aroma that rises as the raindrops strike the dust,” said Cedar Cradle.

“Look north, past the edge of the storm, there’s a rainbow, and you can see both ends,” said Cloud. He pointed his right index finger at the colored arc. “Do you see it?”

“Absolutely beautiful,” said Terp.

“You’re not supposed to point at a rainbow with your finger,” Firstlaugh said.

“Why not?” asked Cloud.

"It's a Dine superstition," Firstlaugh explained. "If you point with your finger it will get sick and fall off."

"Yeah, the Dine use their elbows to point at rainbows," Cedar Cradle quipped.

"No we don't," responded Firstlaugh defensively. "The Navajo way is to take note of rainbows with your thumb."

"Sort of like trying to hitch a ride on a rainbow," said Cedar Cradle.

"What a wonderful image," said Terp with joy in her voice. "But Firstlaugh, do you ***really*** believe that your finger will fall off for pointing at a rainbow?"

"Of course I don't. I know it's silly," Firstlaugh replied. "It's like if you step on a crack in the sidewalk you break your mother's back. There is certainly no causal connection, but the two coincidental events may well have happened to someone at some point in antiquity. Nevertheless I do feel a certain neurotic urge to refrain from pointing in such circumstances."

"Go ahead and do it," Terp said. "Use your finger."

Firstlaugh hesitated. "It doesn't seem polite. You know, because we're on Dine land. When in Rome and all that."

"Polite or not, I dare you," Terp responded.

Firstlaugh turned his back on the rainbow and then raised his right forefinger over his shoulder in the general direction of the prismatic band. "Look, everyone! Over there," he said with a slight tremor in his voice. "There's a rainbow!"

Cedar Cradle quietly took his left hand and squeezed it gently.

The rain, too, was gentle when it arrived. The four friends held hands and danced in wide circles, whooping and laughing as the female shower tickled their skin.

Terp was sorry she mentioned visiting the Begays at Window Rock. The subject had started innocently enough. A Candidates for Ministry member asked if she had vacation plans, and she told the committee about Window Rock and Canyon de Chelley. That part was not problematic, but when she spoke about inspecting the hogan and the Navajo fear of ghosts, the door opened for deeper questioning.

"Well, what do ***you*** believe about ghosts?" asked a woman elder.

"I didn't detect the presence of any malevolent spirits near the deathbed of my friend's aunt," Terp said, and immediately wished she hadn't.

"So, you can detect the presence of evil spirits?" an acerbic minister asked, skepticism dripping from every word. "Are you one of those charismatic types?"

"Technically, yes," Terp explained. "In the sense that I believe I have been given certain spiritual gifts, but I'm no holy roller. Theologically I am decidedly liberal."

"Tell us more about your spiritual gifts," the woman elder said. She seemed genuinely interested, but Terp sensed that others around the table were ill at ease with the subject. The ethos of the Calvinist Church was deeply suspicious of mystical matters and antagonistic to anything that involved linking emotions to faith.

"People have told me I have a gift for...intercessory prayer," Terp said. She avoided the word healing, as she feared that subject would start an inquisition. "As for detecting evil spirits, my intention was simply to allay the anxieties of our hosts. I do not believe in ghosts that hang around hogans after someone dies."

"You said gifts plural. What others do you have?" the woman asked.

Terp paused and then plowed ahead. "I count mystical experience as a gift. At my baptism -at age fourteen- I was surrounded by a white light and felt powerfully loved."

A silence fraught with theological distaste reigned in the room for a time, and then a soft-spoken minister diffused the tension by asking, "Where have you attended church while away at college?"

Terp was not going to lie but hoped her initial truthful answer would be sufficient response. She did not plan to volunteer anything about the NCC because she knew there would be a hostile reaction to it. "I was heavily involved with the campus ministry program until my junior year, including leading worship services. Then I dropped out."

"Why did you quit?" the soft-spoken minister asked.

"To be honest," Terp responded, "I had difficulty with the campus pastor."

"What kind of difficulty?"

Terp paused again, recognizing that her next words would have significant impact on the rest of the interview and perhaps her future career. Whether for good or ill, she did not know. "He was a sexual predator," she said in a matter-of-fact tone.

The acerbic minister's face turned red. "That's a serious charge, young lady! Men have had their ministries ruined by such hysterical claims. On what basis do you make this allegation? Are you prepared to testify to that in the courts of the church?"

The other committee members stared at the piles of papers in front of them, and silence prevailed once more. Then Terp said, "Believe me or not as you choose. My statement is intended only for the people in this room. If you want to probe into the most humiliating episode of my life, I'm prepared to provide the sordid details. It's not a pretty story." No one looked at Terp or said a word. Half a minute passed, and Terp resumed speaking. "If my church involvement while away at college is not sufficient for this committee, then by all means do not endorse my candidacy. That's your choice, and I'll respect whatever you decide."

"No, no, no," said the acerbic minister, now on the defensive. "We don't mean to question your sincerity or your commitment to the church. Most students have sporadic church attendance records while away at school. Let's move on to other things."

What followed was a series of conventional questions and blandly comfortable answers, until only one hurdle remained for Terp, and that was her choice of seminary. Every member of the committee wanted her to go to Princeton, but she held her ground, arguing that liturgical dance was a vital element of her call to ministry. In the end, only because they saw her as the highly esteemed Argyle Watts' protégé, they grudgingly approved Terp's attendance at Pacific Crossroads Theological Seminary.

"However, young lady," the acerbic one said as a parting shot, "you can expect a thorough examination from us about Calvinist theology. We won't approve you for ordination unless you can demonstrate a competent knowledge of the essentials of our Reformed faith. We won't want to hear any New Age interfaith psychobabble."

"I welcome the challenge," Terp said.

When Terp returned to Arizona, she brought her sister Mary along for a visit. Mary had just finished her freshman year at Antioch College in

Ohio, where she was majoring in art. She aspired to be a painter, with oil on canvas her preferred medium.

By tacit agreement, Terp and Cloud said nothing to Mary about naturism or the Natural Christian Church, and they remained clothed around the apartment. It would only be a few weeks of slight inconvenience, which was more than compensated by the opportunity for Cloud to learn more about his wife's family.

Mary's bed consisted of a sleeping bag, which she laid out next to the footlocker in the living room. The morning after her second night in the fleece-lined sack on the floor, she said, "I'm not much of a camper, but there's something about that sleeping bag that makes me feel wonderful. I'm so relaxed, almost euphoric lying there."

Cloud and Terp exchanged knowing glances.

"The strange thing, however," Mary continued, "is that I had the same vivid dream two nights in a row. It was so clear in my mind both times."

"What was it about?" Terp asked.

"It was about your wedding," said Mary. "I saw you two in a ceremony, but it wasn't Rev. Watts who married you. There were two pastors, a man and a woman. Your dad was there, Cloud, but I wasn't Maid of Honor."

"Was there anything else unusual about the dream?" Cloud asked.

"Yeah. Everyone was naked," Mary said.

Terp turned to Cloud and said, "Go get it."

He went to the bedroom, returning shortly with their naturist wedding album and without preamble handed it to Mary.

Mary opened to the first photograph of the wedding party and gasped. "This is exactly what I dreamed!" She pointed to Adam and Evelyn and said, "These are the ministers. I remember their faces." As she leafed through the album she repeatedly said, "Wow!" and "Out of sight!" and "My God, how beautiful!" When she had viewed all the pictures, she said, "These are stunning, magnificent, expressive. I don't have the vocabulary to convey how great this work is. The photographer is a true artist whom I ***must*** meet." She realized that her first reaction had been as an artist, evaluating another's work. But then further questions began to fill her mind. These were her sister and brother-in-law, she thought. What's going on? "Tell me about this

other wedding none of us in New Jersey knew anything about," she said with a hearty let's gossip voice.

Terp told her younger sibling about the NCC, their friendship with Evelyn and Adam, and Cloud's involvement with the New River church as a teenager.

"I'm totally blown away," Mary said. "Very pleasantly so, I might add. Mom would ***never*** understand this, but I think it's beautiful."

"Well, you are an artist," Terp said, "so it's natural for you to think that way."

Mary peered deeply into Cloud's eyes, then into Terp's. "I have three things to say to you guys. First, you don't need to keep your clothes on around the house for my benefit." She began to remove her jeans as she continued to talk. "Second, I want you to take me to a service at your naturist church. I want to meet your pastor friends." She pulled her tee shirt over her head and tossed it aside. "Third," she said as she unsnapped her bra and let it fall to the floor, "you've got to let me paint you both -nude, of course."

As Mary slipped out of her panties, Cloud and Terp began to disrobe.

"With respect to meeting Adam and Evelyn," Cloud said, "we can easily arrange that, but not this weekend. The NCC is inaugurating a new church in Phoenix on Sunday, and we promised to help out. Our friend Kwan-yin Burns is the organizing pastor. You'll want to come with us, though, because Kwan-yin's husband Cochise is the wedding photographer."

"Out of sight!" exclaimed Mary. "I'll be there with bells on. I presume I won't need anything else."

"Bare flesh will be fine," said Terp with a chuckle. "And if you come wearing bells on your fingers and toes, we'll make you a choir accompanist."

"With bells on, I'd rather dance," said Mary.

"Me too," said Terp with a sigh. "Maybe in time we will."

"Terp has told me you're very talented with oil paints," Cloud continued. "As far as sitting for you is concerned, it's fine with me assuming it's OK with Terp."

"Mary asked me to pose nude two years ago," Terp said. "I told her someday."

"Apparently someday has arrived with a bonus model thrown in," he said.

Mary said, "I recall asking you when I walked in on you while you were doing nude yoga meditation. There was something sublime about your body and facial expression that I wanted to capture on canvas. Like you'd just heard from God. But I had no clue you were a budding naturist."

Terp smiled enigmatically.

CHAPTER ELEVEN

Denominational headquarters of the Natural Christian Church provided funds to lease a mansion in Phoenix, a block away from Central Avenue and south of Northern Avenue, for developing a new congregation. The six-bedroom home on two acres with mature citrus and palm trees had been entangled in a dispute over the owner's estate for years, and attorneys representing various family factions agreed that the income from the church would be received gladly by the heirs. The church promised to maintain the place, and if the congregation prospered, to sign a long-term lease.

A high privacy fence surrounded the property. The home featured a large recreation room with one side of an indoor/outdoor pool at its east end. This was ideal for baptisms, which could be conducted inside or out, according to the season.

Behind the privacy wall at the rear of the NCC grounds stood the Disciples' Angelic Fundamentalist Temple, which fronted on Central Avenue. The theological outlook of this neighboring congregation differed greatly from the Natural Christian Church of Phoenix.

DAFT was led by T. C. Smith, a self-ordained minister who began as a street evangelist and built up a church of two thousand members. Smith's preaching attracted crowds because he affirmed and validated their unexamined prejudices. The congregation had outgrown several buildings since its founding two decades earlier. In 1972 DAFT moved into a state of the art temple in the prestigious North Central corridor.

The pastor of the fledgling naturist congregation, Kwan-yin Burns, held a bachelor's degree in English from Occidental College and a master's in public speaking from ASU. For three years Adam and Evelyn Rarom had tutored her in theology, worship, Bible, and pastoral care. The previous Sunday she had been ordained in a special service at their church in New River and was now ready to lead worship for the first time at the experimental urban NCC congregation.

Membership recruitment for the new naturist church would be by personal invitation. Public advertising in the neighborhood, Kwan-yin feared, might produce negative and perhaps even wrathful responses from nearby churches like their neighbor, DAFT. In addition, the pastor and governing board planned to make strong efforts to screen out voyeurs and people with dangerous sexual proclivities.

From the beginning, the church presented a busy schedule. On Sunday morning, church school for children began at 9:30, followed by the worship service at 11:00, with a fellowship lunch after that. Small group discussions were held Tuesday nights. Kwan-yin led an adult Bible study Wednesday evenings. Thursday was reserved for an Alcoholics Anonymous meeting, and on Fridays, a sex addicts support group gathered at the church. Saturdays were reserved for weddings, retreats, and special activities. Clothing was optional for everything at the church except baptisms, for which full nudity was required.

Kwan-yin gathered a score of pioneers to launch the inaugural service. Among them were Cloud and Terp, and now Terp's sister Mary, Lloyd and Nissa, as well as Sandy and her husband Tim with twins, Kim and Mim, who served as four voice choir.

The new pastor also invited a Chinese couple and their three children. They were secular nudists and not particularly religious, but they had known Kwan-yin and Cochise for several years and came as a favor to their friend. Kwan-yin hoped that in time they would be inspired by the words and life of Jesus. Cochise invited his sister and brother-in-law and their two children. His twenty-one year-old brother Skye also attended, as did Dagmar and Quinn.

Through the efforts of Lloyd and Nissa, four more people were added to the congregation. Lloyd's business partner, Lowell Morgan and his wife Nora came along. Lowell and Nora were an African American couple who had enjoyed social nudity at the home of Lloyd and Nissa but nowhere else. Their presence that Sunday prompted Cloud to say, "Hey Dad, why didn't you tell me your business partner is a black man?"

"It didn't seem noteworthy," Lloyd replied.

"So, Morgan and Morgan Land Investments is a salt and pepper outfit. Cool!" Cloud said.

The other two were Tenny and Mandy Smith, the gay couple who rented the house Cloud had grown up in, which Lloyd now held as an investment property. It was coincidence that Tennyson Smith and Mandeville Smith, long-time partners, shared the same last name, but that coincidence allowed them a greater sense of being married, even though they could not legally wed.

Though it would not always be so, the entire congregation was nude this day.

Kwan-yin's first sermon focused on Matthew 6:25-31, with references to Genesis 1 added for emphasis. "Consider the lilies of the field," she began. "They are as naked as God created them, yet, as Jesus tells us, they are clothed by God in more glory than King Solomon with all his riches. Jesus also tells us not to be anxious about our bodies, what we shall wear. 'Why are you anxious about clothing?' Jesus asked his disciples, and by extension asks us.

"Margaret Mead said that clothes not only separate us from the bodies of other people, they separate us from our own bodies as well. You know what? I think that if everyone went naked, we'd have world peace overnight. Make all the generals and presidents and dictators negotiate without their clothes on and watch what happens.

"The answer to solving the problems of social violence, sexual perversions, and pornography is not puritanical repression. It is because of repression that these things flourish. The answer is healthy nudity and acceptance of our bodies as they are. The answer is respect for natural drives, not fear of them.

"Consider the lilies of the field. And then consider the antelope on the range, the chimpanzees in the jungle, and the dogs and cats in our homes. Pets with pants look silly. Humans are the only animals who wear clothes. Why? If your answer is protection from the elements, that's a good reason. If your answer is for decoration or to reflect one's personality, I think that's OK. You should see my closet at home. It's full of outfits that express my personality.

"To those who would answer by saying the human body is shameful or dirty and must be covered up, I say a resounding NO! Genesis says we are made in the image of God. Why would God create bodies that are inherently shameful?

"Consider the lilies of the field. Then consider your own face and arms and legs and breasts and buttocks and genitalia. You are created in the image of God. Do not be ashamed!"

The choir inaugurated a new hymn, written by Cloud for the occasion. He set his words to "Lancashire," a spirited tune by Victorian organist Henry Sweet, better known as "Lead On, O King Eternal." Skye Burns accompanied the family quartet on acoustic guitar, while Cochise beat an echoing rhythm on the tom-tom. Augmented by the voices of Kwan-yin and Mandy Smith, the expanded choir boldly sang:

We come to you, Creator, with reverence in our breasts.
We stand before you naked in search of holy quests.
We offer you our bodies as on our day of birth.
In faith we seek your guidance to do your will on Earth.

In mystic bright communion we sense your sacred frame,
And lay aside all garments and psychic shrouds of shame.
We dress in imitation of lily and of dove.
Our flesh invites your Spirit to color us in love.

We hide behind no covers, for you have made us free.
We offer our devotion and physiognomy.
O God we seek your wisdom, your goodness to embrace.
Please grant us now your pleasure, that we may know your grace.

Terp was surprised by the hymn, because Cloud had not told her about it. She found a way to surprise him, however, by sending a copy of it to Evelyn. The congregation at New River sang it the following

Sunday, and within a month it had been sung in every congregation of the denomination.

When Mary heard Skye play the guitar, an arc of electric energy left her body seeking connection with him. A similar energy rose from Skye aimed at her, and these emanations merged in midair, making a crackling sound. After the service they sat in the parlor and talked, oblivious to the food served on the flagstone patio.

Terp took Mary to an art equipment store, where she bought a large supply of canvas frames, brushes, paints, and sundry material.

"You bought enough to last all summer," said Terp.

"Actually, I want to ask you about that. Would it be OK if I stayed the whole summer? I have an idea for a painting of you and Cloud that'll take at least a month to complete, and after that, Skye Burns has agreed to pose for me," Mary said.

"You won't be surprised to learn that Cloud and I have already talked about it. He said to me on Sunday that you'd be staying till the end of August," Terp responded.

"Does that mean it's OK then?" Mary asked, adding, "Oh thank you! And if you need privacy from time to time, I could camp out at New River for a while."

"Here is fine. We'll try to model living simply," Terp said with a chuckle.

Mary had Terp and Cloud pose separately and side-by-side for several sets of pencil sketches. She then asked them to sit for longer periods while she worked in oils. As she applied paint to canvas, Cloud and Terp told Mary about their meeting during the New York City blackout in 1965, seeing each other at an anti-war rally in 1970, and their ultimate meeting in a Tempe drug store. Terp told her sister about the affair with Kirk Trilby that had triggered her trip to the place where she met Cloud.

"Wow!" said Mary. "You guys are full of unexpected news and wonders."

Terp laughed silently. You don't know a tenth of it, she thought.

Mary added, "By the way, Sis, I used to think it odd that you shunned lingerie and frilly things. Now I understand and even resonate with your desire for simplicity. Bare skin is more beautiful and in the end more erotic than lacy draping. Less is indeed more."

Everyone returned for the second week of worship at the Phoenix NCC, and additional people came also. Among the newcomers were husband and wife physicians Ed and Kay Lumen and their daughter Vala. Ed and Kay were Kwan-yin's family doctors, and for years they had been studying alternative medicine and psychic phenomena. Kwan-yin had spoken with them about the healing aspects of naturism, and they accepted her offer to investigate firsthand.

Sandy invited a divorced mother with two children. Quinn invited another paraplegic veteran and his next-door neighbors, a young Mexican couple with no children but one on the way. Tenny and Mandy invited the straight couple who lived across the street in Nissa's old house. Nissa had great fun telling the couple about many nude events that had occurred there. Mandy and Tenny also invited a lesbian couple they frequently double-dated with when social necessity called for male-female pairings. The Chinese couple invited another family of secular nudists.

Kwan-yin expected that some visitors would drop out before long but was encouraged at the auspicious launch of the new congregation. However, the problem of how to determine the suitability of all these new worshipers remained. The NCC lived with a tension between open acceptance of all people who wanted to participate and the practical need for screening out those few who presented dangers to the community. Not everyone was psychologically suited to a nudist lifestyle, and the needs of the community as a whole had to be protected from harmful individuals.

Everything in worship, in the educational program, in recreation, and in social activities was public, with no secret doctrines, no inner circles, and no hidden levels of attainment. The existence of the church was public information, yet discretion was necessary in publicity, due to hostility from some quarters of the religious community and its appeal to people with serious personality disorders.

Therefore, Kwan-yin insisted on interviewing every potential worshiper. After Ed and Kay joined the fellowship, she asked them to be part of a screening committee to examine prospects' motivations for participating in the life of the naturist congregation. A perfect and pure motivation was not required. Being curious about nudism was deemed acceptable. Admitting that the idea of running around naked was a little titillating did not disqualify anyone. This was seen as a mark of honesty. Some people expressed a deep-seated desire to go naked in everyday life. Several described feeling a deficit of nudity in their lives as one locked away in a dungeon might feel a deficit of sunlight.

Seeking to overcome a sense of oppression was seen as positive motivation. Even a tinge of exhibitionism was considered acceptable as long as it was not accompanied by overt sexual behavior. Occasionally someone mentioned an artistic sensibility that chafed at the restraints of clothing that blocked the essence of human identity.

The goal of the screening committee was to avoid violence prone individuals, sexual predators, and pedophiles. The system was not foolproof, especially with only one interview, so continual vigilance was required. Adam and Evelyn had taught Kwan-yin the signs to look for that could indicate trouble in paradise.

After lunch on the second Sunday at the new church, Cloud and Terp sat on the patio watching the children gambol unselfconsciously across the lawn. "They're so beautiful to see," he said.

"Do you find them erotic?" Terp asked.

"Certainly they're erotic," Cloud said. "And so are flowers, dolphins, wheat fields, coral reefs, and even cactus. The world is filled with erotic energy from many living things. But that doesn't mean I want to have sex with a dolphin, cactus, or child. My desire is to bask in awe of such beauty not scar it, and I find it hard to understand why anyone would want to violate children's bodies and destroy their natural innocence."

"Total depravity," said Terp. "We're all flawed, but some people's flaws make them want to hurt children by beating them or by having sex with them."

"Children are natural nudists," Cloud opined, "but society teaches them to be ashamed of their bodies, and perverse adults prey on them to satisfy twisted compulsions."

Terp said, "There must be a way to protect children from pedophiles and also from religious prudes. Both injure children, staining their bodies and minds."

The next Sunday, Terp and Cloud came early and found an empty bedroom to store their bodies in while they floated over the back wall to the DAFT Temple. Cloud wanted Terp to see and hear the pastor he had walked out on in 1957. T. C. Smith had a nine o'clock service they could attend out of their bodies and return in time for the eleven o'clock naturist service in the flesh.

Smith still preached the way he had in the 1950s. He opened the Bible at random and read a bit of text, then commented on it extemporaneously. He described this technique as using the Holy Ghost to explain God's word, though he now often aided the Spirit with prepared jokes. The Bible in his hand fell open to The Song of Solomon. Being near the middle of the book, the pages fell open to it with some regularity. This Sunday he read chapter four, verse nine: "Thou hast ravished my heart, my sister, my spouse." Smith grimaced. "Yuck!" he said. "Not everything in the Bible is pure and wholesome, brethren. Some of the stuff is about people God doesn't like. Like the pervert who wrote this. Like it says, anybody who'd marry his sister ought to be ravaged."

He leafed backward through the Bible and read from the opening chapter of Second Samuel. "Saul and Jonathan were lovely and pleasant," he pronounced. "Hmm, let's see where this is heading. 'Saul...clothed you in scarlet with other delights, who put on ornaments of gold upon your apparel.' Sounds like one of those tutti fruity fashion designers. They're all a bunch of three dollar bills, you know." T. C. pranced around the chancel mimicking an effeminate manner.

Returning to the text, he read, "How are the mighty fallen in battle!" It was an exclamation, but he read it as a question. "I'll tell you how! They were a bunch of pansies. They got beat up by real men. And the next verse proves it." He adopted a mock feminine voice and read, "I am distressed for thee, my brother Jonathan: very pleasant hast thou been unto me: thy love to me was wonderful, passing the love of women."

T. C. shuddered theatrically. "Children, put your hands over your ears for a minute. Folks, this passage is about a man who likes men better than women, if you know what I mean. And it got him killed. The meaning is clear. This tutti fruity stuff will get you killed, and God is the one who'll do it. God will smite any man who layeth down with another man."

He leafed forward through his Bible. "Let the Holy Ghost lead me to the New Testament, O God," he prayed. "We've had enough of Old Testament perverts this morning." His finger stopped at Matthew 9:32. "Behold they brought him to a dumb man possessed with a devil. And when the devil was cast out, the dumb spake: and the multitudes marvelled." Smith nodded with a sense of triumph. "Yea verily," he intoned. "Liberal, lying, devil-possessed preachers are everywhere. They look down on decent folk like you and me. But don't be deceived, folks. The multitudes often marvel when some dumb preacher speaks."

Cloud and Terp laughed. Had they been in their bodies, their outbursts would have been heard throughout the huge sanctuary. Since their laughter made no sound, however, no one took notice - except T. C. Smith. He didn't hear any sound, but he sensed someone had laughed and was spooked by it.

When they returned to their bodies, Cloud said, "Paraphrasing the Bhagavad-Gita, crude people often quote the letter of scripture while denying its inner truth."

After weeks of intense work, Mary unveiled her triptych of Cloud and Terp. She had painted three canvases, linked together with hinges. In the left panel was Cloud, lean and tan, absorbing the viewer with piercing, otherworldly eyes. His body was surrounded by a gold aura. In the right panel, equally tanned and slender, stood Terp, enchanting everyone with ancient, wisdom-drenched eyes. She, too, showed a gold aura circling her body.

In the large center panel Mary had painted the two of them merging, their features interchangeable and yet recognizable as male and female, distinguishable as Cloud and Terp. There were hints of feathers around their ears and on their breasts and in place of their pubic hair. The auras hugging their bodies in the side panels were bent away from their combining body, suggesting wings.

"You are indeed a gifted artist," Cloud said.

Mary beamed at the compliment from someone whose judgment she respected.

"It's disturbingly beautiful," said Terp. "I want to disappear into the painting. I've underestimated what goes on in my little sister's head."

"How did you know?" Cloud asked.

Mary said, "It's all in your eyes. You can't hide it."

Terp looked at Cloud and he nodded. She turned to Mary and said, "I think it's time to tell you what we didn't say before. When we talked about how we met, we left out certain pertinent facts."

"I had a feeling you were holding something back," Mary said, "but we all have our personal secrets."

"Well, you've splattered ours all over these canvases," said Cloud.

Terp told Mary about their psychic dreams, seeing auras, Cloud's out-of-body experiences, and their floating together like discorporate birds. She said nothing about the Old One. Still, Mary's mouth fell agape and her eyes dilated in wonder.

"Not only are our bodies nude in your paintings," Cloud said, "but our ***souls*** are naked too. Only a true artist could show that."

"And for that reason," Mary said, regaining her voice, "I can never exhibit this triptych. The finest thing I've ever done, and I can't show it to the public. I'm in awe of you both. This is my gift to you, with love."

"Thank you, Sis," said Terp. "We'll hold it in trust for you to reclaim in the future. You'll know when the time is right."

"If it will assuage your artist's need to have your work seen," Cloud added, "we can arrange a private showing for a few selected people." And so it was arranged for Adam, Evelyn, Kwan-yin, Cochise, and at Mary's request, Skye, to see the paintings.

Cochise was as impressed with Mary's painting as she was with his photography. The two of them had a wonderful time praising each other's work. Of course, Cochise, Kwan-yin, and Skye knew nothing about the extra-sensory experiences of Terp and Cloud, so they interpreted the paintings as mythical allegories rather than as a statement about the actual subjects.

Adam and Evelyn knew better, and silently marveled at Mary's perceptiveness. After Cochise, Kwan-yin and Skye left, Adam said to Cloud, "What have you said to Mary about her discernment?"

Cloud knew what Adam meant by his carefully worded question. "We told her about our out-of-body experiences," he said.

"Don't you think it's time you told your father about them?" Adam said.

"Right now, you, Evelyn, and Mary are the only ones who know about that," Cloud said. "And we only told Mary because of the paintings. And some details no one but Terp and I know."

"We can trust your dad," Terp said. "And Nissa too."

"OK," Cloud said.

Skye left town for a week, plying his craft as a folksinger in coffee houses and small clubs in Southern California. Upon his return, he collected Mary at the apartment.

"Don't wait up for me," Mary said as she headed out the door.

Skye took Mary to the lookout summit on South Mountain to see the lights of the Valley.

"Very nice," Mary said. "Now let's go to your place."

Skye drove directly to his studio apartment, and Mary stayed the night. Their coupling was not the first sexual experience for either of them.

The next morning, Mary returned to the apartment long enough to gather her painting supplies. "Skye's going to sit for me all day," she announced.

Terp was out at the time, and Cloud felt the urge to offer parental advice to his sister-in-law but could think of nothing sage to say. All the phrases that came to mind were echoes of his mother's words, which he would have ignored at Mary's age. "Let us know where you're going to be," he finally said, "so we won't have to call the Highway Patrol to search for you."

"Got the message," Mary acknowledged.

CHAPTER TWELVE

"Hey, Dad," Cloud said with a nervous twitch in his voice. "Do you remember when I had the measles?" Cloud and Terp sat opposite Lloyd and Nissa in the living room of the Tempe apartment.

"Sure I do," Lloyd responded. "I was worried you might die."

"I almost did," Cloud said. "And I had an out-of-body experience."

"I've read about those," Nissa said. "Did you see a tunnel of light?"

"No, but I floated up to the ceiling and watched my body lying on the bed."

"That must have been frightening," Lloyd said.

"Not at all. It was very pleasant," Cloud said. "After a while, though, I returned to my body."

"That must've been when your fever broke," Lloyd said. "It was a mystery to me. Your mother called and said you had a temperature of a hundred and five, but when I got home a few minutes later is was a hundred and one. What made you think of that?"

"Mary's artwork is the catalyst for telling you about it. We want to show you something she painted, but first we need to tell you a secret," Cloud said.

Lloyd and Nissa leaned forward attentively but said nothing.

"That wasn't the only time I floated out of my body." Cloud described floating escapades over the years, leaving out mention of the Old One. "Then I taught Terp to float, and we've done it dozens of times together," he concluded.

Lloyd sat in silence reflecting on this news.

"You know what? I believe you," Nissa said. "I always knew there was something out of the ordinary about you -about both of you. Cloud, you can look at me and I feel like you're reading my mind. And you too, Terp. It's like you know things mortals aren't supposed to know."

"I guess I've been too close to see it," Lloyd confessed. "I'm dumbfounded. But on second thought, it makes sense. I remember one Sunday at church in New River, you fell asleep during the sermon, and when you twitched, I said I wouldn't tell."

"I was out of my body, floating around the camp, and the twitch was when I returned," Cloud explained.

"I see that now. At the time I thought your sleep was odd. I can't tell you why. Just a sense of something not quite normal," Lloyd said.

"And now you'll see why we're telling you this," Terp said. She went to the bedroom and returned with the triptych.

"Mary knew nothing about our floating when she painted this," Cloud said.

Now it was Nissa's turn to be silent along with her husband. Neither had the words to respond with, but tears glistened in Lloyd's eyes while they fell generously from Nissa's.

"Beautiful," Lloyd at last mouthed. "So beautiful it makes me tremble for your lives. This is the kind of beauty the world won't allow to exist for very long. Be extremely careful who you show this to."

His own long repressed mystical experiences flooded his conscious mind, and he trembled in solidarity with his son. Lloyd knew more about such things than he had been willing to admit, but it seemed as if now the time had come to confess. "There's something I never told you Cloud...or you Nissa," Lloyd stammered, still reluctant to let the words pass his throat but bowing to the inevitable need for them to reach the open air. "Back when I was seventeen -that would have been 1937- I saw a vision."

Now Nissa, Terp, and Cloud leaned toward Lloyd in rapt attention.

Lloyd continued, "I was hiking in the woods west of the Susquehanna River, across from Harrisburg. I came to a wide clearing and saw a camera crew filming what I guessed was a World War I movie. There were planes in the sky above doing acrobatics and pretending to shoot at one another. I watched for a while until I saw a man fall out of one of the planes. It took me a couple of seconds to realize it was a stunt dummy, but it looked real.

"That wasn't the significant part, though. As I watched the dummy fall, I went into a sort of mystic state, something like being out of my body I suppose, and I found myself watching the scene from above as if I were in the airplane. I could clearly see the man falling -a human being, not a stunt dummy. I prayed his parachute would open, but it didn't.

"The whole thing really shook me up. When I returned to normal, I could see from the behavior of the film crew that it was a dummy, and then the dummy waved at me. I couldn't get the scene out of my mind. And, of course, you all know about my bombardier Tommy Olson falling out of my B-24 during the war."

"How did you interpret the vision?" Cloud asked.

"Before or after Tommy Olson?" Lloyd responded.

"Both," Cloud said.

"For a long time I didn't so much interpret it as simply accept it as one more weird experience. But I never forgot it. After I became a pilot, I took the vision to mean I should be vigilant to prevent anyone from falling out of my plane. I understood that dummy's wave as a warning. And, as you all know, I failed miserably at that task."

"I'm inclined to dispute that interpretation, but it raises the question about why you became a pilot in the first place," said Terp. "If this vision shook you up so much and was so memorable, why would you volunteer for the Air Corps?"

"I don't know," Lloyd said. "I was drawn to flying. It seemed like my destiny. I couldn't have prevented a man from falling from my plane unless I was a flyer."

"Did you ever have a sense that the one falling from the plane might be you?" Cloud asked.

"No," said Lloyd. "And even if it had been me, I would have preferred that to anyone else in my crew."

"I wonder what the significance of the dummy waving to you might be?" Terp said. "Could it mean the person falling from your plane would live?"

"Not a chance," Lloyd said forcefully.

"I had a nightmare once about jumping from a plane," Cloud said. "It came back to me just now. In the dream I popped out of my body before my parachute could open and my uncontrolled body slammed into the ground."

"When was that?" Lloyd asked.

"While I was stationed at Fort Benning. I was thinking about volunteering for airborne training, but before I could sign up, this dream showed me that it was not a prudent step for someone prone to out-of-body episodes to be routinely leaping out of airplanes. It's funny, though," Cloud continued, "ever since I was a kid, I've had an instinctual mistrust of parachutes, a fear that sometimes they fail to open."

"That's the way I've always felt," said Lloyd.

Terp said, "Cloud, I'll bet you subconsciously absorbed that sense of mistrust from your dad."

"Very likely," said Cloud.

The room fell silent for a while until Terp shifted from the particular situation while remaining with the general subject by saying, "Lloyd, I'd like to hear about any other paranormal experiences you may have had."

Lloyd recognized that the protective gates in his mind were now wide open, and he felt a wave of relief and many psychic pounds lighter. "Well, a year or so before the dummy incident, I was hiking west of Carlisle, and when I reached the top of a rise I stopped to look at the mountains further west. Then I went into sort of a trance and the green, tree-covered mountains changed to purple, and the trees disappeared, replaced by cactuses. In retrospect, I take that vision as confirmation that I belong out here amid the purple mountains' majesty."

"What else?" asked Nissa.

"I had a lot of dreams in my growing up years where I found myself out in public naked," Lloyd said.

Nissa, Terp, and Cloud laughed in unison.

"That was certainly prophetic!" Terp retorted.

"I know such dreams are common," continued Lloyd, "but the dreamer usually feels anxiety about being naked. I never did. I always felt perfectly at ease."

Nissa beamed with joy. "I knew you were special," she said and kissed his cheek.

Lloyd produced a wide grin and began to weep.

One Wednesday evening, Terp and Cloud led the Bible study at the naturist congregation in Phoenix. The class broke up at 7:30, and the couple decided to float over the wall to see what was going on at DAFT. Once there, they noticed a line of parents and children going into a building at the rear of the churchyard.

Inside was an open arena, covered with a large padded mat. Children were herded onto the mat, and T. C. Smith passed a hat among the adults, all of whom were trusted members of the DAFT Inner Circle. From the hat they drew slips of paper, each containing the name of a child. Members were thus assigned responsibility for the children whose names they had drawn. Occasionally the process would match a child with her or his own parent, and when this happened Smith said it was the will of God.

When the pairings were complete, Smith stepped forward and announced, "I have received grave reports from your parents that all you young ones gathered here have been disobedient. You must be punished!"

Participants were issued hemp fiber whips, and thus armed, they waded in and administered the ritual twenty lashes upon each child. Some produced pathetically mild swings, but other more enthusiastic parents gave blows that stung ferociously.

Afterward, Smith announced the name of the child who, in his estimation, had been especially bad since the last whipping ritual. That child would be indentured to the pastor for two days to learn humility in the Lord. This particular ritual took place only during the summer months when school was out. Sometimes the name he announced was a boy and sometimes a girl. Although no one ever commented on the phenomenon, those chosen were never older than ten or younger than six.

This day, when seven year-old Debbie was selected, she screamed, but her mortified mother dutifully delivered the girl to the pastor, and the group dispersed. Cloud and Terp followed Smith and Debbie to an apartment at the back of the manse -a place his wife Anjelina was not allowed to enter. She worried about what punishments might happen there but trusted and obeyed her husband as the Bible instructed her.

T. C. Smith led Debbie to a bedroom, where he flipped a switch in the wall, and bright lights flooded the room. "Take your clothes off," Smith gruffly instructed. "All of them."

"I don't want to," she said.

"I have to inspect your body for marks of purity," he explained in a now gentle tone. "God puts special marks on good children, and I need to find yours."

"No," she said with quivering voice.

"If you don't cooperate, I'll do it for you," Smith said, his words suddenly cold.

Debbie undressed.

"Lie down on the bed," he ordered. She complied. "On bad children," he continued, "Satan puts his marks, so I have to look for those too." He inspected her body, probing roughly with his fingers.

"Ow, that hurts!" she cried.

"Quit whining, and take your medicine," he snapped. "The Bible sayeth, 'Thou shalt not seethe a kid in his mother's milk.' You have to seethe in ***my*** milk!" With all the children he had thus far inspected, Smith had never yet found a mark of purity. On Debbie's body he identified a mole and several freckles as marks of Satan. He probed into her genital area and she cried in pain. "Shut up!" he yelled and slapped her face.

Cloud and Terp were furious. What could they do while out of their bodies? What would happen if they returned next door and called the police? How could they explain witnessing this? They did not want to leave Debbie, although they had no means of protecting her.

Smith unzipped his pants and pulled out his engorged penis. "This is the wand of God," he said. "If you want me to stop inspecting for marks of purity, you must kiss the wand and pet it nicely with your hand." Debbie obeyed her pastor, and he ejaculated on her body.

He then rubbed his semen over her chest. "This is the balm of Gilead," he explained. "It will dissolve the marks of Satan on you. But if you ever tell anybody about this, Satan will cause you to get leprosy and all your skin will rot off, and then your mother will give you to me permanently so I can try to cure you."

He left the room, locking her inside. Cloud and Terp followed him. After washing his hands in an adjacent bathroom, Smith stepped into a walk-in closet on the other side of the wall from the room where Debbie lay shaking in fear. Set in the wall was an eight-millimeter movie camera. He removed the film that had just captured his time with Debbie and put in a new reel.

As usual, he would wait until a few more rolls had been exposed before sending them to Mexico for developing. He opened the safe on the closet floor and stowed the film inside. Then, feeling a triumphant urge to fondle his organ, he strolled to the bathroom.

Inside the safe was a shelf with dozens of plastic reels of eight-millimeter film in yellow cardboard wrappers. Since he had access to indentured children only during the summer months, Smith filmed his work so that he could pleasurably review his accomplishments at leisure during the long school year.

Telepathically, Cloud said to Terp, "I wish we could get some of that film. Can you levitate a couple of those reels the way you did that angel in the Salisbury Cathedral?"

"I don't know," she said. "Will you add your concentration?"

"I'll try," he said.

Terp focused attention on two reels near the front of the shelf. One budged a tad, and then the other moved forward a quarter inch. Cloud added his perceptive strength to Terp's efforts, and the two boxes came forth from the shelf and drifted in air across the room. Now what to do with them?

Cloud rapidly scanned the area. "In the bathroom, there's a six-inch ventilation duct above the toilet," he reported. "And oddly, there's no screen on the outside end."

"The providence of God," Terp said.

"Spoken like a true Calvinist, but we don't have time for theology," he said.

They guided the reels into the bathroom, right above Smith, who stood in front of the toilet stroking his penis and meditating on new ways he would punish Debbie the next day. One reel slipped from their combined concentration and nearly hit Smith's head, but Terp exerted all the mental attention she could produce and it rose again.

Slowly they raised the reels to the level of the vent but seemed unable to make them move sideways into it. After long seconds of intense focus, Terp and Cloud maneuvered them through the opening then released control, letting them fall into the grass.

Smith strolled back to the closet and locked the safe, unaware that two reels of film were gone.

Cloud and Terp returned to Debbie's room and found her wrapped in a blanket, whimpering.

"I have a plan," Cloud said.

They floated outside and levitated the reels over the wall into the NCC churchyard. Then they returned to the bathroom and used all their concentrated strength to cause the toilet to overflow and the hot water pipe to crack open. For good measure, they set off the smoke alarm. No doubt their extraordinary psychic strength was augmented by fierce anger at what they had observed.

T. C. ran in and determined that a plumber was needed immediately. Before making that call, however, he phoned Debbie's mother, saying that Debbie had been very good and she could go home right away. The girl was cleaned up and gone before the plumber arrived.

After returning to their bodies, Terp and Cloud retrieved the reels and went home. Cloud put on white cotton gloves to examine the film. "I was fingerprinted when I went into the service," he said, "and I don't want to be identified by law enforcement when we send them this stuff. After all, we did steal it."

"Not only that," Terp said, "no one would believe how we did it. And we don't want the NCC to get any unwarranted publicity."

Using a lamp and a magnifying glass, Cloud learned the first reel showed Smith molesting a girl as he had done to Debbie. The second reel showed similar behavior with a boy. They decided to send the film to the Arizona Attorney General's Office and let that agency sort out the jurisdictional issues. Cloud carefully wiped the reels and cardboard wrappers, and still wearing gloves, wrote a note with his left hand. In big block letters he printed: "T C SMITH. DAFT TEMPLE. SAFE IN

APT BEHIND HOUSE."

"What return address should I use on the envelope?" he asked.

On impulse, Terp said, "How about Kirk Trilby?"

Cloud laughed. "Great idea! I'd like to see the expression on his face when Highway Patrol officers knock on his door." With neat small letters, Cloud placed the name and address of the predatory campus minister in the upper left hand corner of the large manila envelope, put the note and reels inside, sealed it using a wet sponge, then affixed postage by the same method. He dropped it in a mailbox near Trilby's office.

CHAPTER THIRTEEN

Sunday, August 4, 1974, Kwan-yin Burns officiated at her first baptism, and it proved to be memorable. Quinn Queensbury wheeled himself to the edge of the pool, and using the strength in his arms, propelled himself into the air, turning a somersault before splashing into the water. Kwan-yin jumped in beside him, followed by Dagmar, who assisted with the immersion after Quinn had answered the baptismal questions.

"We should all embrace the sacraments with such joy," Kwan-yin said.

The following Thursday, President Richard M. Nixon appeared on national television and said, "I shall resign the Presidency effective at noon tomorrow. Vice President Ford will be sworn in as President at that hour in this office."

Quinn missed the announcement, because he, Cloud, and a group of other Viet Nam veterans were raucously celebrating his forthcoming nuptials with off-key bellowing of "Dead Skunk," a current folk-rock hit by Loudon Wainwright III. Each vet imagined that the odiferous defunct polecat celebrated in the song represented one or another gung ho bastard who'd made their respective war experiences painful. Amid the cheer at Quinn's good fortune in love, bitter laughter greeted their side comments naming this general or that politician as responsible for the stench of war.

At the same hour, Dagmar was given a bridal shower by Terp, Evelyn, Kwan-yin, Nissa, and a few other women. In more subdued fashion, the women produced a gentle soprano and alto rendition of John Lennon's "Imagine." By consensus, where Lennon used the word brotherhood, they chose a feminist alternative. Thus they sang, "a sisterhood of man," then afterward in ribald fashion speculated on what such a male inclusive sorority might look like.

The next evening, at the wedding rehearsal, Cochise made a remark about President Ford, and Quinn said, "That's wishful thinking. You mean ***Vice*** President Ford."

Cochise brought the mentally distracted Quinn up to date. "While you were partying yesterday, Nixon resigned. Ford is now president."

"Whoopee!" said Quinn. "Hey Dag! Nixon gave us a fantastic wedding present."

On Saturday, August tenth, the Rev. Kwan-yin Burns performed her first marriage, uniting Quinn and Dagmar. Terp and Cloud were Matron of Honor and Best Man respectively. The parents of the bride and groom were noticeably absent, not because they refused to come to a nudist wedding but because they had not been invited.

Since both of their fathers were child abusers and both of their mothers were co-dependent enablers, Dagmar and Quinn decided not to tell them about their plans to marry. Each would make a phone call to their parents after the honeymoon to say they had eloped.

Three weeks after Cloud mailed the film to the Attorney General, a search warrant was served on Ten Commandments Smith, and after authorities removed the remaining reels of film from his safe, the DAFT pastor was arrested. The Arizona Republic ran the story on the front page, and local television news broadcasts led with dramatic descriptions of a police raid on a prominent religious leader accused of child molestation.

Included in the media reports was the fact that police had visited the Rev. Dr. Kirkegaard Trilby, Campus Minister at Arizona State University, because his name and address appeared on an item of evidence delivered to the Attorney General.

The Arizona Republic reported that a reliable police source said they could find no link between Trilby and Smith. An article in the newspaper about Trilby quoted the campus pastor as saying, "Some malicious person must have used my name as a prank. I enjoy an unblemished reputation in the university community, and I would never be mixed up with something as sordid as child molestation." It never occurred to him that he might have been considered a hero for providing the evidence against Smith.

In any case, the damage had been done. A score of former ASU coeds who had been seduced by Trilby read the article about him, and each was angered by it. Six of the women were so incensed they filed complaints against him with the national office of his denomination.

In an attempt to mitigate his position and spread the guilt around, T. C. Smith told authorities about the ritual whippings at the temple. This information was leaked to the media, and the names of the adults who allegedly participated were printed in the paper. The Arizona Republic also delved into Smith's background. "A copy of his birth certificate reveals that Thomas Charles Smith was born in Coolidge in 1929, but in 1954, the court granted his request to change his name to Ten Commandments Smith," an investigative reporter wrote.

DAFT members had been willing to give their pastor the benefit of the doubt on the charges of pedophilia. A man is innocent until proven guilty, they said. But when they learned he had lied to them by claiming he had been born on an Indian reservation and God had told his father to name him Ten Commandments, they fell over themselves lining up to testify against him when he came to trial. All sorts of odd behaviors they had overlooked in the past now seemed ominous.

In quick succession, DAFT collapsed and the church property was put on the market. Eventually, it was bought by the Arms for Jesus Ministries, Incorporated.

Mary turned Skye into twins on canvas. She painted two of him, side by side, connected at the hip, and nude except for headwear. One Skye wore a feathered war bonnet, and the other a plaid tam-o-shanter.

The mystical quality of her work impressed Skye, but he felt compelled nevertheless to say, "I've never worn either of those on my head."

“They’re symbolic of your Apache and Scots heritage,” said Mary.

“Yeah, I got that,” Skye said. “It’s a really good painting. But I need to find something to criticize you for to ease the pain of saying goodbye.”

“I know,” Mary sighed. “I’m going to miss you terribly when I go back to school. But neither of us is any good at making promises for the future. We both live in the present. The best I can say is I hope to come back to Arizona sometime but have no idea when. If you get any gigs in the East, please visit me if you can.”

The next day, Mary flew to New Jersey to prepare for her return to Antioch.

The weekend before Terp and Cloud departed for Pacific Crossroads Theological Seminary in Lahaina, Firstlaugh, Cedar Cradle and Tzek visited them in Tempe. The friends lolled about the apartment, most of the time without clothing, imbibing large quantities of home-squeezed limeade, nibbling cashews, walnuts, blueberries, and cherries, and speaking of things past as well as possibilities in the far future. An almost tangible atmosphere of mutual affection enveloped them.

Terp felt a tingling sensation at the back of her neck, and she looked at her husband and said, “Cloud I think we should...”

Before she finished her statement, Cloud sighed and said, “You’re right. They should see it, and then we’ll tell them.”

Terp went into the bedroom and emerged seconds later with the triptych. “My sister Mary painted this last month,” she said.

Firstlaugh and Cedar Cradle were impressed. That sentiment grew larger as Terp and Cloud unfolded what was now becoming a ritual recitation about their prescient dreams, visualizing auras, and out-of-body experiences.

Cedar Cradle said, “I’m so glad you told us about this, because I’ve had visions where I saw the two of you flying through the air. I was inclined to interpret them spiritually, but now I know they were not just fantasies.”

Firstlaugh said, “I left my body once. It was in Nam. I was leading a patrol and we got lost in thick jungle. I ordered a halt so I could figure out where we were, and while I was sweating over coordinates on the map, I whooshed out of my body and floated in the air above my men. For some strange reason, I wasn't astounded by the event, and on a hunch, I flew forward a couple hundred meters and saw an ambush waiting for us. I went back into my body and moved out in a different direction."

"How come you never said anything about this before?" Cloud asked.

"The same goes for you," Firstlaugh retorted. "Why did you wait till now to say anything about ***your*** experiences?"

They all laughed, and then Terp said, "Some things need to wait for the proper time. This is the perfect moment for us to share the secrets of our souls." She looked at Cloud, asking a question with her eyes.

"Go ahead," he said.

"We want to tell you about our most closely held experience," Terp said. She unveiled for them her childhood encounter with the Old One, described Cloud's mental relationship with the unusual being, and in quiet tones told about their joint meeting with the Old One in Australia.

Cedar Cradle and Firstlaugh seemed unsurprised by this news, as if they had suspected it all along. In reality, they had imagined nothing of the kind, but knew with certainty they would hear something profoundly spiritual from Terp and Cloud and were not disappointed. The four adults sat for an unmeasured interval in silent contemplation of Terp's words, lost in an unhurried realm of connectedness. The quiet ended when Tzek tugged on his mother's arm and said, "Foot time."

"Thanks to you two, Tzek has become a glutton for foot rubs," Cedar Cradle said.

"Perfect timing," said Terp. "Time to break out the lotion."

Cloud and Terp tended to Tzek's feet, putting the toddler to sleep in the process.

"Now it's the grown-ups turn," said Cloud.

They took turns massaging four pairs of feet.

"We'd like to add another dimension to our intimacy," Cedar Cradle said. "Terp, Cloud, come over here and stretch out on your sleeping bags."

With no questions asked, they did as she ordered. Firstlaugh settled beside Terp's head while Cedar Cradle sat cross-legged next to

Cloud's head.

"Now close your eyes and breathe slowly and deeply," Firstlaugh said. "But don't leave your bodies," he added as an afterthought.

Cedar Cradle began to massage Cloud's temples and forehead with gentle yet electric strokes, and Firstlaugh did the same for Terp. Expertly they traced the contours of their friends' faces -eyes, noses, lips, ears, chins, cheeks- and the tops of their heads with alternating pressure and caresses that transmitted deep joy as well as sensate pleasure.

"May we return the intimacy?" Cloud asked when the facial massages ended.

"Someday," Cedar Cradle said. "For today, this is our gift. First I'll need to teach you a few finger techniques and about pressure points, but I don't want to do that now."

"That's a powerful motivation for us to stay in touch," Terp said. "We'd love for you to come visit us in Hawaii. In the meantime, at least let us massage your faces without the special techniques. We'll stick to inexpert but heartfelt caressing."

"OK," Cedar Cradle responded. "Who could resist heartfelt caresses?" She and Firstlaugh positioned themselves to receive the tactile attention.

"I'll put some music on while we're doing it," Cloud said. Soon the evocative strains of Ferde Grofe's "Grand Canyon Suite" suffused the room as Cloud positioned himself beside Cedar Cradle and Terp beside Firstlaugh.

"My dad had a recording of this," Terp said wistfully. "On Sunday afternoons in winter, he sometimes played it on the stereo while stretching out on the living room couch. He said this kind of music was church for him. Hearing it always made me long to go back to Arizona, which in my childhood imagination was a very spiritual place. So Dad's comment about music and church seemed perfectly understandable to me, even after I started going to church in a formal way."

"Arizona, particularly the Grand Canyon, ***is*** a spiritual place," Cedar Cradle said. "But then, every place is spiritual for those who can perceive it. The prairies of South Dakota are sacred for me. I've never been to New Jersey, but I'll bet there are plenty of spots there that evoke a sense of profound awe or even holiness."

"Yes," said Terp. "Certainly the shore. But as much as I love the ocean, my young soul longed for the desert, which fortunately has now become my home."

In time the massage session ended and the four repositioned themselves on the sleeping bags to continue their anthropological, theological, psychological, sociological, and cosmological meanderings and speculations.

When Grofe's opus concluded, Cloud put Gershwin's "Rhapsody in Blue" on his stereo. "I've found this work an excellent catalyst for imaginative thinking," he said. "When I was a kid, this always conjured in my mind the sophisticated rhythms of New York City. For the sake of spiritual associations," he said, looking at Terp, "I would include suburban New Jersey in that memory. I yearned to experience the creative energy of the East Coast. Now I'm married to the epitome of that Eastern culture."

As the music sifted through them, and their minds gave voice to deep wonderings about their places in the universe, they casually tickled one another's feet and palms.

Thereafter, wherever these four might be, and regardless of previous associations, hearing strains from these two musical compositions would set off in each of them a wave of nostalgia for this one perfect and harmonious night.

The next morning, after the comic opera of four adults and a child negotiating toilet, sink, and shower in the apartment's tiny bathroom, the Begays and Morgans donned their Sunday best clothing and squeezed into Cloud's compact car for the trip into Phoenix to attend the NCC service. Once there they shed their finery, unceremoniously depositing their collective garments in the hamper assigned to Terp and Cloud.

At the beginning of summer, Cloud had surprised Terp with a hymn text sung by the choir in the inaugural service. On this last Sunday before they departed for seminary, Terp had a surprise for Cloud. For several weeks the choir had been rehearsing a special arrangement of the classic hymn "Holy, Holy, Holy!" The hymn text, based on the fourth chapter of Revelation, is laden with vivid imagery of angels, golden crowns, a glassy sea, and an early morning song ascending into heaven.

When the choir rose to sing the ethereal anthem, Terp stood, removed her glasses and casually handed them to Cloud, then moved to a spot at the base of the chancel. The organist initiated the piece with chimes, and as the voices of the singers filled the room, Terp danced, using her hands, arms, legs, feet, and face to depict adoration and darkness, sinfulness and glory, falling seraphim and rising songs.

Everyone in the sanctuary sat mesmerized, no one more firmly than Cloud. He began to weep quietly from the emotional beauty of the moment. Cedar Cradle reached over and touched his shoulder in wordless recognition of his response.

While preparing for the move to Lahaina, Terp went through the apartment in search of items to put into temporary storage at the home of Lloyd and Nissa. Standing on a dining room chair, she rummaged through the shelf in the bedroom closet and in a back corner found a grocery bag that had been folded over and stapled shut.

"Cloud, what's in this? Is it something important?" she asked over her shoulder as she held the bag behind her in the air.

Cloud looked up from his efforts to pack a suitcase as efficiently as possible and felt a wave of conflicting emotions as he saw what Terp had found. "Oh! I'd forgotten about those," he said. He felt a strong urge to protect the valuable contents of that paper bag and embarrassment as if his wife had discovered a guilty secret from his past. "Those are my dad's combat boots from World War II."

"Should we give them back to him?" she asked.

"No, he gave them to me a long time ago," he replied.

"Well, since you've never mentioned them to me, they must not be all that important," Terp said. "Should we pitch them?"

Panic struck at Cloud's brain. "Pitch them? We can't do that. Those boots are...are...meaningful to me."

"May I see them?" she asked.

"What?" he said in a mental fog. "Yes, of course. I haven't seen them since I packed them away in 1966."

She pulled at the fold, popping out the staples, and opened the bag. Inside was an old towel wrapped around a pair of brown leather paratrooper boots. She draped the towel over the back of the chair and climbed down with the boots in her left hand. "So, what's the story with these?"

"When I was a kid," Cloud confessed, "I snuck into the storage room and put them on and marched around the backyard, pretending to be a bomber pilot. They were way too big, of course, so I had to wear multiple pairs of socks. It thrilled me that my father had worn these in combat, and that made me want to be a soldier and emulate his bravery. But I never told him or anyone else that I used to wear his boots."

"Well, now you know what it's really like to be a soldier in wartime," Terp said. "You've earned the right to wear these openly. Here, try them on."

"No," said Cloud. "Not now. I think I've outgrown them. But after all that's happened, it feels like a sacrilege to get rid of them. Put them in that carton over there with the other memorabilia and heirlooms and we'll stow them in Dad's new storage room."

II

SACRED DANCE IN PARADISE

I am satisfied
I see, dance, laugh, sing.
Walt Whitman

I would believe only in a God that knows how to dance.
Friedrich Nietzsche

The dancer at the court of Paradise...laughs and plucks
the minds of the wise from their cold meditations.
Rabindranath Tagore

CHAPTER FOURTEEN

Lahaina in the 1970s sat on the growing edge of the tourist boom. Hotels built along Kaanapali Beach in the sixties were gaining popularity as alternatives to the crowded scene in Waikiki. Yet the town retained a portion of its nineteenth century charm.

The seminary occupied a fifty year-old wood frame building on Lahainaluna Road two blocks up from its intersection with Front Street. Standing on the second floor lanai that ran the length of the street side of the building, students could see the breakers in Auau Channel. Originally, the edifice had been a general store but since then had gone through three renovative incarnations. Before the building was leased for use by the seminary ten years earlier, it had been a hotel.

Pacific Crossroads was an innovative theological school. The faculty represented the religious spectrum from liberal to exceedingly liberal. Its mission was to educate future Protestant ministers in progressive thinking about the Church and the Christian faith. The interface between Christianity and other world religions formed an important element of the curriculum. The arts were also central to the aims of the seminary.

The institution was unaffiliated with any denomination, although its professors represented most mainline Protestant bodies. They were, for the most part, scholars who had been frustrated with the constraints on theological inquiry they had experienced in other schools and were thus happy to pursue their intellectual labors in paradise, exploring without hindrance the implications of sundry modes of religious thought.

Terp and Cloud rented a cozy, breeze-receptive apartment three blocks away. Cloud had been offered an adjunct faculty position, so he was busy preparing lectures for a class on Buddhism and another on Christianity in Southeast Asia. Terp registered for courses in Bible, systematic theology, Church history, Hebrew, and the social gospel. Liturgical dance would have to wait until she had completed certain basic requirements.

"Hey, man, I'm broke," the street punk said to his pal. "Let's go roll a fag and pick up some scratch." They left the snug warmth of a working class tavern at the edge of downtown Chicago and walked against the January wind toward a gay bar four blocks away. The recessed doorway of a closed shop next to the bar provided them a sentry position from which to assess their prey.

"The next fairy that walks out that door is gonna bankroll us for a week," the second punk said. He pulled his collar close to his neck and settled in to wait for the pounce.

Inside the establishment, Theo Gynt sat in a booth with an attractive young man, but was not enjoying the prospect of going to bed with him. He was, in fact, experiencing great guilt. I should be home with Keefe right now, not flirting with a sweet young thing in a bar, he thought. I have to get out of here. Theo stood and put on his overcoat and hat. As he walked toward the exit, a strange thought entered his mind.

Several miles away in Hyde Park, the Old One sat on a frozen patch of ground, looking like a beggar. The venerable creature wore a torn flannel shirt and threadbare jeans, with a large red bandana in place of a hat. People walking by turned the other way to avoid looking at the pitiable person. The Old One paid them no attention and instead concentrated on Theo Gynt.

Theo had been Cloud's best friend in college. They went separate ways after graduation, Cloud into the Army and Theo to seminary in Chicago. In 1968, Theo was awarded a Master of Divinity degree, qualifying him for ordination in the Scandinavian Protestant Church to which he belonged. However, his homosexuality disqualified him from the ministerial office. Unable to be ordained, he went to work for an organization that provided encouragement and spiritual support to recovering drug addicts.

The thought that saturated his brain was more like a silent command than an idea he had originated, Theo decided. Return to the booth and tell the young man about your soul-mate waiting for you at home! This is silly, Theo thought. Yet he obeyed the silent voice. The resultant conversation took longer than he anticipated, because his booth companion was touched by his explanation and spent some minutes affirming Theo's desire for fidelity. As a result, another man preceded him out the door of the bar.

The punks charged at that man, unaware of their strategic error, for he was an off-duty police officer. As they reached out to attack him, he pulled a revolver from under his coat. Three seconds later, his partner (in the precinct and in his bed) stepped out of the bar and immediately understood the situation. Now recognizing their mistake, both would-be assailants chose that moment to soil themselves.

Theo never knew that the Old One had saved him from a mugging, but he quickly realized that returning to explain his situation to the young man had been providential, for as he exited the bar, the gay policemen were holding the thugs against the wall. "These big bad boys thought they'd beat somebody up," said the first officer to Theo.

"Yeah," said the second officer, "we think it would be nice of them to go inside and tell everyone they'll never try it again. Wanna meet our friends, guys?"

Both punks trembled with fear.

"Go on, get the hell out of here," the first officer said to their captives. "And if you ever come around here again, we'll play ping pong with ***your*** balls."

Theo returned home with his mind at peace. "Keefe, I stopped at a new bar tonight," he confessed to his partner.

"You don't need to say any more," Keefe said. "I know how difficult it is to forswear all others."

"I was ready to leave, but something made me stop and explain to the man I'd been flirting with that I needed to go home to be with the man I love. If I'd gone out two minutes earlier, I would have been mugged."

"I guess confession is good for the body as well as the soul," Keefe said.

"Let's get out of here," Theo said. "Let's go somewhere warm and start over."

"Moving won't solve the temptation problem," Keefe said.

"I know," agreed Theo, "but I'm tired of the cold and the constant threats of violence. I'm serious. Let's move to Phoenix."

"They have plenty of gay bashers there too," said Keefe. "But if that's what you want to do, I'll go with you."

In her second semester, Terp was allowed to take a course dealing with the arts in religion, which included a section on dance. It was all lecture and reading, however. No actual dancing occurred. Nevertheless, she gloried in her studies.

She also enjoyed leisurely hours at the beach with Cloud, despite the necessity for bathing suits due to the heavy concentration of tourists. For freedom's sake, Terp and Cloud periodically shed their bodies and explored the region from the depths of Maalaea Bay to the ten thousand feet summit of Haleakala Crater.

The T. C. Smith trial was sensational news all across Arizona. Lloyd sent newspaper clippings to Cloud. His accompanying note commended Cloud for having the good sense to walk out on a T. C. Smith service in 1957. Although they had never mentioned the subject, Lloyd had an intuitive suspicion that his son and daughter-in-law were in some way responsible for Smith's arrest. The verdict was guilty on forty counts, and he was sentenced to consecutive ten-year terms on each count.

Information about a certain ecclesiastical trial reached Cloud and Terp by means of the Northern Reformed Congregational Church Bulletin, which Terp found on the periodical shelf in the library. The cover article concerned a denominational sex scandal. The Reverend Doctor Kirkegaard Trilby had been tried in the denomination's disciplinary court and found guilty of twelve counts of adultery and nine counts of sexual intimidation. Since churches have no authority to incarcerate or fine wayward clergy, the only recourse the denomination had was defrocking Trilby. His ordination was revoked and he was expelled from the church. A footnote to the article reported that Trilby had moved to Utah where he opened a marriage counseling practice.

"Despite the emotional pain involved, if I'd known about it, I would have testified at that trial," Terp asserted.

"In a way you did," Cloud said. "You got it started by suggesting I use his address on the envelope of Smith films."

"And his arrogance did the rest," she said.

Penny Person was a trim forty-seven year-old in March 1975. She had been a widow nine years and was now feeling that her life was empty. Terp was married and living in Hawaii. Mary was away at college in Ohio. She was therefore receptive to a dinner invitation from an old friend of her late husband.

Randall Owen had been navigator on the crew in which Tom Person had been bombardier. The Owens and Persons got together periodically until the Owens moved out west in 1960. Thereafter they faithfully exchanged Christmas cards. The holiday mailings continued to include Penny after Tom died. The previous Christmas, Penny received a card from Randall with news that his wife had died of breast cancer ten months earlier.

"Penny, this is Randall Owen. I'm in New York on business and wonder if you might be able to join me for dinner tonight."

"That's very thoughtful of you, Randall," she said. "Where are you staying?"

"At the Ritz-Carlton on Central Park South. I can have a driver pick you up."

Randall's timing was perfect. Penny was ready to get out of the house for some spontaneous fun. "What time shall I be ready?" she asked.

"I can have the car at your door at six-thirty."

The car turned out to be a limousine. Randall met her in the hotel lobby. He was tall and tan, with gray streaks in his hair but no paunch on his fifty-two year-old frame.

"Penny, you look great," he said. "Do you mind if we eat at the hotel? I've made a reservation."

"Not at all," she said. In truth, she would have been happy to eat at a fast food restaurant if it meant an evening in the city with a handsome gentleman.

Over soup Randall said, "I need to be honest about the limo and the luxury hotel. I haven't become a wealthy business tycoon. I manage a resort in Hawaii, and we have a trade-out agreement with the Ritz management. My room, meals and limousine service are complimentary, and we provide a similar courtesy to Ritz-Carlton execs when they get away to Oahu."

Penny was impressed with Randall's straightforward manner. Their conversation was relaxed and laden with mutual assumptions about the state of the world. Over wine, Randall said, "There's a club in mid-town with a swing band that plays music from the forties. Would you like to go dancing?"

"I'd love to, Randall, but to be honest, it's been so long since I've enjoyed good conversation with a gentleman that I'd rather find a quiet nook and talk for a while first."

"Your wish is my command," he said. "We can move to the bar...or to my suite."

"Your suite would be quieter," she said.

They never made it to that mid-town club. Instead, they spent the night in Randall's room, enjoying gentle, nurturing sexual relations. The following evening, Penny fixed dinner for Randall at her home. They danced to big band records in the living room. After flirtatious swinging to Benny Goodman's "***Bewitched,***" abetted by Helen Forrest's captivating vocal, they rushed to the bedroom and made love.

Neither was sleepy, so they talked of intimate things as they lay together in bed.

"I've gotten used to having the house to myself," Penny said. "The closets I used to share with Tom are now completely filled with my things. And with the girls gone, I've become very casual about what I wear around the house. ***Very*** casual. I clean the bathrooms and do my vacuuming in the nude. When I'm done, I jump in the shower."

"I'd like to see that," Randall said.

"Which part?" she asked.

"Any of it," he said.

"OK," she said and jumped out of bed. She ran into the master bathroom and turned on the shower. "Would you care to join me?"

He would and did.

Before returning to Hawaii, Randall asked Penny to visit his resort on the North Shore of Oahu. She accepted the invitation and made plans to combine it with seeing Terp and Cloud on Maui.

In April, when Penny arrived in Honolulu, Randall met her at the airport with a lei. She spent three days at the resort. At certain times of day when most guests were at the beach or shopping, Randall put up a "Closed for Maintenance" sign in front of the entrance to the enclosed pool, so he and Penny could skinny dip. They didn't need the sign for the sauna and whirlpool bath in his private suite. Penny found the whole experience scandalously delicious. They also enjoyed romping around Sunset Beach, discreetly clad in bathing suits. Penny wasn't entirely demure, however, for she bought a bikini in the resort gift shop -the first one she had ever owned.

Terp was pleased at the prospect of Penny's visit. For a long time she had wanted to build a new relationship with her mom, adult to adult. If circumstances develop favorably, she thought, we'll tell Mom about some of our extrasensory experiences. That'll blow her mind!

Cloud and Terp greeted Penny at the Kahului Airport and drove her south across the neck of the island to Papawai Point then northwest along the coast to Lahaina. Terp noticed that something was different about her mother. Penny was glowing.

Over dinner at the Pioneer Inn, Penny told her daughter and son-in-law about Randall Owen.

"How exciting," Terp said. "I'm so happy for you. Are you in love with him?"

"I don't know," Penny answered. "It was love at first sight with your father, but now I think I should take romance at a more leisurely pace. I certainly don't want to invest my heart in the relationship if he's just having a fling. In the meantime, I'm enjoying life fully for the first time in years."

"Let's invite him over, so Cloud and I can check him out for you," Terp said.

"Talk about role reversal," Penny said. "You sound like my parents."

At her daughter's urging, when they arrived at the apartment, Penny telephoned Randall and invited him to Maui.

"I can get away three days from now," he said. "I have business I could take care of with the Kaanapali Beach up the road from Lahaina."

Terp and Penny spent the next three days learning things about one another that they had never previously shared. In carefully edited format, Terp told her mother that she had dreams about Cloud before they met and Cloud had similar dreams about her.

Cloud revealed his childhood out-of-body experiences, and Penny expressed deep interest and no shock. Terp then took the plunge and told her mother that she and Cloud routinely left their bodies to explore the countryside.

To this all Penny could say was, "Holy smokes!" In light of her new and candid relationship with Terp and Cloud, she felt like revealing some of her own secrets. She did not, however, have many. "I shouldn't be telling you this," she said, "but Randall and I went skinny dipping in the pool at his resort -several times. He has an all-over tan. I guess that's pretty common in a tropical paradise."

Terp smiled broadly. "I don't know how common it is, but Cloud and I have all-over tans too."

"You don't!" said Penny, genuinely surprised.

"We do," said Cloud. "But we didn't acquire them in Hawaii. We're part of a naturist group in the Phoenix area. We haven't yet connected with naturists here, so mostly we go naked just around the apartment."

"Well, I'm sorry to cramp your style," Penny responded with a chuckle.

"It's no problem, Penny," Cloud said. "Terp and I are not easily cramped. But we certainly don't want people to be uncomfortable around us, so we dress according to the sensibilities of our houseguests. Truth be told, we wear clothes more often than we shed them -at least during daylight hours."

"Mary would be shocked by all this," Penny said.

"I don't think so, Mom," Terp responded. "She's an artist, and she's painted nude models in art class at school. And what do you think happened when Mary spent all last summer with us?"

"Don't tell me the three of you ran around naked together!"

"The three of us and our friends," Terp said. "Mary went with us to a naturist church camp."

"Church?" Penny said.

Cloud explained the Natural Christian Church.

"Well, I can see being naked by yourself, or with your spouse...or with a lover," Penny said, "but I have a hard time with the idea of being naked around strangers."

"They're not strangers, Mom," said Terp. "They're dear friends."

"I won't pass judgment," Penny said. "I do my housework in the nude and love the feeling of freedom I get from it. So I understand why people would want to run around without their clothes."

"Aha!" said Terp. "I see now that Mary and I inherited our naturist instincts from you. But I'd like to change the subject if you don't mind."

Penny did mind, because she was thoroughly enjoying the conversation, but she made no protest.

"We have a ritual gift for you," Terp continued. "We've given it to other family members and friends, including Argyle Watts. Have you ever heard of reflexology?"

Penny had not, but when she learned what it was, the prospect of a foot massage greatly appealed to her.

"Usually we take off our clothes to do this, because the oil stains the fabric," Cloud explained. "We can put on old trunks or something if you'd be more comfortable that way. You don't need to disrobe, although I'd recommend you hike your sun dress up to your knees."

"It won't bother me a bit if you two parade around in your completely tan birthday suits," Penny said. "But I'll keep my pants on, if you don't mind."

"Mom, we don't mind at all. We never pressure people into taking off their clothes if they're uncomfortable with social nudity. That's not what naturism is about," Terp said in preacherly fashion.

Cloud brought in the massage lotion and towels, then he and Terp disrobed.

"OK, Mom, put your feet in our laps," Terp instructed.

"Were you naked when you did this for Rev. Watts?" Penny asked.

"No," said Cloud. "We wore old jeans and sweatshirts."

"I remember that day!" Penny exclaimed. "I thought it was odd you were going to visit the minister dressed that way." She pulled her dress up to her knees, thought better of it, and said, "Give me a minute." She slipped out of the dress. "I'll keep my bra and panties on all the same."

The recent return of sex into her life had made Penny more sensitive to non-sexual touch also, and she reveled in the expert foot massage. "I didn't want it to stop," she confessed when it was over. "I suppose you do this for each other all the time."

"We do it a lot," said Terp.

"It must be a great blessing to your marriage," Penny said.

"Our marriage is more blessed than anything else I can imagine," said Cloud. "Penny, I am head over heels in love with your daughter, and for some strange reason, she seems to love me too."

"I can't think of any better words a mother could hear from a son-in-law," she responded. "I'm very happy you came into our family."

"Sit back and relax, Penny, while Terp and I clean up," said Cloud.

"I'll use the bathroom while you're doing that," Penny said, "and then we can continue our talk. I want to hear more about this nudist church."

Cloud and Terp washed their hands in the kitchen sink.

When Penny returned from the bathroom, her undergarments were missing. "I haven't been very good about keeping my pants on lately," she said.

By the time Randall knocked on their front door two days later, Cloud and Terp had given Penny three more foot massages, and Penny had twice practiced the art on her daughter and son-in-law. Penny didn't look her age anyway, but the week she had spent on Oahu and Maui had erased even more years from her face and body.

Randall's knock was an hour earlier than they were expecting, and no one in the apartment was wearing clothes at the time.

"Why don't you answer the door naked, Penny," Cloud said. "And enjoy the look on his face."

"Alright," she responded. Penny looked through the peephole to make sure it was Randall standing on the other side and then opened the door. "Come in, Randall," she said. "I want you to meet Terp and Cloud." Penny did enjoy the look on her beau's face.

"My, don't you look beautiful, Penny," he said and kissed her on the cheek.

Cloud said, "To quote the English mystical poet William Blake, when he and his wife Catherine found themselves in a similar situation, 'Come in! It's only Adam and Eve, you know!'"

Randall wasted no time in proving that his tan was every bit as extensive as Cloud's and Terp's.

That evening, Penny said, "You've got to show Randall your reflexology."

They did.

Penny spent the night with Randall at the Kaanapali Beach Hotel. During a moonlight stroll along the sand, he serenaded her with a romantic island favorite, "I'll Remember You."

"Kui Lee was dying of cancer when he wrote this song a few years back," Randall said. "I'm only sick with love for you, Penny, and I'll never forget this moment."

When he took her back to the apartment the next day she bubbled with news for her family. "He told me he's in love with me," she said.

"From my observations of him yesterday, I believe it," Terp said. "You and Randall make a good pair. Of course, the question is, do you love him?"

"Yes, I do," Penny confessed, "but I don't want to rush into marriage. I'm kind of attached to New Jersey, and he's just as attached to Hawaii."

On April 30, 1975, Communist North Vietnamese troops entered Saigon with tanks and infantry, and the Republic collapsed. Cloud watched the news reports of the chaotic evacuation with rising anger. "If you want to know what total depravity is, this is it!" he growled to Terp. "The behavior of all of the belligerents -North and South, American and Vietnamese- is reprehensible. And the people are shafted from all sides. Nothing can heal this debacle except the throbbing grace of God."

As the marriage of Dagmar and Quinn reached three quarters of a year, life was good for the couple. Quinn continued as a vocational counselor for the State of Arizona, deriving great satisfaction from his efforts to encourage people to get beyond their impairments and build confidence in their abilities. He was especially skilled at working with disabled veterans, for he spoke their language and had traveled their roads.

Making the most of her degree as a drama major and her physical attributes, Dagmar appeared steadily in dozens of local television commercials, mostly in small parts but occasionally as a featured speaker. She didn't make a lot of money doing commercials but became known as a reliable professional.

In March, the owner of a travel trailer dealership liked her looks and voice and picked her to play an enthusiastic trailer owner in an ad. She appeared in a short skirt behind the wheel of an open convertible pulling an aerodynamic silver trailer.

"It's light and easy to tow," she said with her head over her left shoulder, "and there's plenty of snuggle room inside."

The commercial was an instant hit, and within a month, she became the dealership's exclusive spokeswoman, appearing in TV commercials, newspaper ads, and representing the company at conventions and special events. Soon everyone in town knew her trademark greeting. "Hi! I'm Dagmar, and I want to get you into a Sleekbody trailer." This gig paid well.

CHAPTER FIFTEEN

Synchronous events had occurred many times in Cloud's life, when improbable coincidences brought him together with significant people. Thus he was not surprised to see Gunnar and Irene Bishop set their towels beside him and Terp on Kaanapali Beach one sunny June day. Though Gunnar's hair was now short and his beard gone, Cloud knew him at once by his penetrating eyes.

"Hi Gunnar. Hi Irene," Cloud said, as if he had last spoken with them yesterday rather than eight years past. Gunnar had been a seminarian and a conscientious objector in 1966 when he and Cloud met. Cloud was studying at the Defense Language Institute in Monterey, California at the time. Irene was Gunnar's fiancée in those days, but looking at the matching bands on their ring fingers, Cloud judged they were now married. Motivated by loneliness more than anything else, Cloud had briefly been infatuated with Irene, but he never told her about his feelings.

Gunnar flinched and shouted, "Cloud Morgan! How the hell did you get here?"

Irene was calmer about the chance meeting. "Hi, Cloud. How are you?"

"Terp, these are friends from my year in California. Gunnar,

Irene, this is my wife Terp," Cloud said.

After introductory small talk, Gunnar said, "The last I knew, you were off to Nam. I see that you made it home OK."

"Physically OK," Cloud said, "but mentally wounded. Watching the Communists cruise into Saigon with their tanks five weeks ago brought back a load of painful memories."

"Yeah, they looked like a bunch of cocky bastards," said Gunnar. "I was against the war, but I have no affection for Ho Chi Minh's minions. They're sure to wreck the economy of the country."

"Where are you staying?" Terp asked. She had a fleeting thought about inviting them to their place, but her intuition suggested that might be premature.

"The Sheraton," Irene said. "And you?"

"We live here," said Cloud, "at least for the next two years. Terp's a student at Pacific Crossroads Seminary in Lahaina, and I'm teaching a few courses there."

"Cloud Morgan the atheist teaching in seminary," Gunnar said. "The world has indeed turned upside down."

"Meeting Terp caused me to believe in God," said Cloud.

"So, how did you get to be a seminary professor?" Irene asked.

"I'm only an adjunct," Cloud said.

"He has a PhD in Asian history, specializing in Asian religion," said Terp.

"Cao Dai?" asked Gunnar.

"Good memory," said Cloud. "My dissertation focused on the Cao Dai religion."

Gunnar invited Cloud and Terp to dinner at the hotel, where they continued their conversation.

"Are you still a Socialist?" Cloud asked Irene.

"I gave up that pipe dream years ago," she answered. "Are you still a Republican?"

"Nope," said Cloud. "I've moved to the left of the Republican Party but have resisted registering as a Democrat. Independent suits me better."

"Your work for an ad agency sounds interesting, Gunnar. Tell us about it," said Terp.

"He's a senior vice president," said Irene proudly. "He's their resident whiz kid, and they pay him big money for his smarts."

"Mostly what I do is devise effective ways to use psychological motivators to sell things to people. Most people are cattle, and advertising is a means to corral them and fleece them of their money," Gunnar explained, mixing metaphors in a matter-of-fact voice.

"That sounds pretty cynical," said Cloud.

"I like to think it's realistic. I can't be responsible for the stupidity of others."

"Hmm," said Cloud.

"And how do you occupy your time, Irene?" Terp asked.

"Mostly I spend the money Gunnar pulls down from the agency. After throwing off the yoke of socialist poverty, I'm finally enjoying myself."

Cloud sought a neutral response. "You two look happy. Apparently married life suits you," he said.

They nodded in agreement.

The couples went for an evening stroll along the beach, and in due course, the men walked far ahead of the women.

"We've been married eight years," Gunnar confided to Cloud, "and what they say about the seven year itch is true. Irene really gets on my nerves sometimes, but I've compensated with a little secretary on the side."

"Are you having an affair?" Cloud asked.

"Something like that. My secretary takes care of all my needs -***all*** of them. Irene doesn't know, of course. I don't want to rock the boat at home."

"Then you're not in love with your secretary?"

"Of course not!" Gunnar said. "But I love how she loves me. It's one of the perks of being a highly compensated ad executive."

A hundred yards back, Irene said to Terp, "Gunnar is a good man, but he's not very affectionate, and I'm a real needy person. I don't want to hurt him, because he's good to me and provides an elegant lifestyle, but I've had to turn elsewhere to get my physical needs met."

"Hmm," said Terp.

"Don't believe any stereotypes about interior decorators," Irene continued. "My decorator knows how to please me very well. And Gunnar thinks he's gay, so it's a perfect setup." Irene chuckled to herself.

When they returned to the Sheraton, Terp and Cloud said farewell to Irene and Gunnar. No one mentioned getting together again. On the drive down to Lahaina, Terp and Cloud reported on their separate conversations with the Bishops.

Terp said, "I'm sorry to say that Gunnar reminds me of a line from Shelley. 'The tongue that's bought to speak.' And Irene reminds me of the next line in that couplet. 'The heart that's paid to feel.' When we first met on the beach this afternoon, I thought we might be introducing reflexology to some new folks tonight."

"No such luck," said Cloud with disappointment in his voice. "I feel sorry for them both. But if you're not tired of me, I'll rub your feet -or anything else you want massaged."

"I'm not tired of ***you***," Terp said. "My body eagerly awaits your touch."

Firstlaugh Begay had been working on a Master of Science degree in educational administration for two years, and in early June, he received the graduate degree from the University of New Mexico. The same week, Cedar Cradle gained a diploma in massage therapy, after completing five hundred hours of formal training in anatomy, physiology, ethics, therapeutic philosophy, and Swedish and other massage methods. To celebrate, they decided to go to Maui to visit Terp and Cloud. His Grandparents would care for Tzek.

When Firstlaugh telephoned to say they would be coming to the islands, Cloud told him they wouldn't need sleeping bags. "If you want something more luxurious than a mattress on our living room floor, or want extended privacy, there are luxury hotels in the area, but we believe camping out with us will be much more congenial."

"Your floor sounds plenty luxurious to me," Firstlaugh said. "There's no place we'd rather stay."

The Morgans met the Begays at the Kahului Airport with delighted hugs, warm kisses, and welcoming leis. Once inside the Lahaina apartment, everything but the leis came off.

"We're so glad you're here," said Terp. "We've missed you

terribly. What's happening in Arizona?"

Cloud served limeade over chipped ice, and the friends stretched out on cushions on the rug to catch up on life.

"I had a vision last summer about a major news event in Arizona," said Cedar Cradle. "In the Navajo Times there was a picture of that creepy minister T. C. Smith. He was on trial for child molestation. Anyway, as soon as I looked at his face I went into a trance and saw you two flying around in his bedroom, and you lifted a little naked girl from his bed and spirited her away, and Smith sat on his floor, which was covered with water flooding in from under the door, and a whole bunch of movie reels rained down on his head."

Cloud and Terp looked at each other with expressions of sublime joy, which quickly led to laughter.

"So, you guys ***did*** have something to do with that case," Firstlaugh asserted. "As soon as Cedar Cradle told me about her vision, I knew you were involved."

"Well, your details are a little surreal, but that about sums it up," Terp said. She and Cloud took turns telling them about Smith molesting Debbie, the film reels they levitated outside, and focusing their energy to cause the plumbing problems.

Cloud said, "The last time we were together, Cedar Cradle, you talked about the four of us going to a deeper level of intimacy. Your vision accomplished that."

"You're right, Cloud," she replied. "I was referring to facial massage at the time, but looking into your lives from a distance is, ironically, a very intimate experience."

"Speaking of facial massage," Terp said, "you promised to teach us how to do it."

"Well, I can't officially teach you, but informally among close friends, I'll show you some techniques. And we can practice on one another. I have no worry that either of you would misuse this."

The bed in the furnished apartment Cloud and Terp rented was not a mattress and box springs resting on a frame. Instead, it consisted of two queen size mattresses one on top of the other resting directly on the floor. They suspected it had something to do with the eccentricities of the previous tenants, but in any case, the odd arrangement came in handy when guests arrived. Cloud moved the top mattress into the living room for Firstlaugh and Cedar Cradle to use.

All four settled onto this mattress for Cedar Cradle's lesson. She massaged Cloud's head and face, explaining to Terp what she was doing as she went along. Then she did the same for Terp so Cloud could watch and learn. Afterward, Terp practiced on Firstlaugh and Cloud practiced on Cedar Cradle.

"You're really good after one lesson," Firstlaugh said to Terp.

"So is Cloud," Cedar Cradle said.

Foot rubs followed all around. Following Terp's explicit instructions, everyone was careful not to get oil on the mattress.

"It's odd," Cloud said in a philosophically reflective voice. "We go from head to foot but skip everything in the middle. I wonder what that means?"

"If you'd like, sometime while we're here, I'll give you both body massages," said Cedar Cradle.

"We'd like," said Terp.

They lay on the mattress talking of esoteric and extrasensory things until three in the morning, when Cloud and Terp retired to their bedroom. Each one had experienced paranormal events over the years, and this commonality drew them closer together.

The two couples slept late the following morning, and after brunch went to the beach, where they played in sand and waves all afternoon. Cloud and Firstlaugh entertained their wives singing a duet of "White Silver Sands," which they had listened to on the cafeteria juke box the first time they ate lunch together their freshman year in high school. The song immediately took on new associations as the four frolicked on the white sands of Maui.

Though they had rinsed off in the outdoor shower next to the hotel pool, the Morgans and Begays nevertheless managed to track a significant quantity of sand into the apartment when they returned.

"It's a good thing you have tile and hardwood flooring," said Cedar Cradle. "It would be a real pain to get all this sand out of a carpet."

"It's an integral part of life here," said Cloud. "Hawaiian homes are built and furnished accordingly. Island architecture is influenced by four realities -sand, wind, rain, and insects."

After showering and removing amazing quantities of tenacious sand from their bodies and hair, they donned clothing for an evening out. Cedar Cradle stood an inch shorter that Terp, and her figure was a little fuller, but she fit nicely in one of Terp's flower pattern Hawaiian dresses. Terp wore a similar outfit with a different color scheme, while the gentlemen put on white Bermuda shorts and loose fitting aloha shirts. With arms linked they strolled to the Pioneer Inn for dinner.

They were early to bed that night, for the next morning they rose well before dawn to make the circuitous drive to the summit of Haleakala. There the Begays and the Morgans, wrapped in blankets and shivering nonetheless, waited in the frigid dark nearly two miles above sea level to greet the sunrise.

When the sun at last appeared in spectacular shades of red and gold, they joked of taking off their clothes and dancing around the top of the volcano as they had done on the multicolored butte on the Navajo Reservation. That it was cold out did not weigh heavily against dancing naked on Haleakala, for they were willing to freeze their nipples and bums, however briefly, for the sake of the experience. The forty other people at the summit, however, including a National Park ranger, settled the matter for them. They did not dance at all, but huddled together for warmth and ogled the new day, as Firstlaugh greeted the dawn with the Navajo sunrise prayer, "Today I will live well."

After lunch, the two couples took naps on the living room mattress. When all were again awake, the conversation turned to out-of-body experiences. Cedar Cradle was the only one who had never left her body. Firstlaugh had done it once, under extraordinary circumstances, but he had no idea if he could do it again.

They decided to try to float together. Cloud and Terp provided instructions. When they were ready for the experiment, Cedar Cradle and Firstlaugh lay on their backs and began breathing as told. Five minutes later, Cloud and Terp saw that Firstlaugh was gone.

"Why don't you go with him, Cloud," Terp said. "I'll stay here with Cedar Cradle. She may not make it out today."

Cloud stretched back and quickly left his body. He perceived his friend hovering near the ceiling looking down at the four bodies below, two of which were not occupied.

"How does it feel?" Cloud asked telepathically.

"It's great!" the Navajo said. He looked lovingly at his wife. "It looks like Cedar Cradle is having a hard time with it, though."

"She's in good hands with Terp," Cloud said. "We should give them some space. Let's explore the channel."

The two men floated out to the water, where they sailed through wave crests, dived below the surface and flew up into the air, in and out, over and under that fascinating region where sea and sky meet.

They had no idea how long they'd been floating, but eventually Cloud said, "We'd better get back and see what the women are up to."

"Don't bother," Terp said. "We're right here with you."

"We just got here," Cedar Cradle communicated. "Let's not go home so soon."

Silent laughter rippled through the waves, and Firstlaugh later swore that he saw waves undulate in response to their mirthful rejoicing. In the timelessness of the event, Cedar Cradle, Cloud, Firstlaugh, and Terp floated over and under the water for what they determined later to be two hours.

They napped again after returning to their bodies, ate a light supper upon rising, then took turns massaging faces. For the reflexology sessions, Cedar Cradle and Terp did Firstlaugh's feet, then Cloud's feet, and Firstlaugh and Cloud rubbed Cedar Cradle's feet then Terp's.

At sunrise the next morning, Cloud rolled out of bed and stepped into the living room, where he encountered Cedar Cradle straddled across Firstlaugh's midsection, the two joined in intercourse. She was gently rocking back and forth.

"Pardon me," Cloud said and turned to retreat into the bedroom.

"Wait!" Firstlaugh said. "It's OK. This was bound to happen sooner or later."

They remained linked and Cedar Cradle continued her slow movements.

Terp then emerged from the bedroom. "What are you guys...oops!" she said.

CHAPTER SIXTEEN

Cedar Cradle said, "Come over here and make love with one another. There's been too much sexual tension in this place the last couple of days, and we all need to release it." Firstlaugh cupped his hands over his wife's breasts, and Cedar Cradle bent forward and kissed her husband with great passion.

Cloud reclined on the other side of the mattress, his head near Firstlaugh's right foot, and Terp settled onto his erection. Already aroused by the scene they had entered upon, they quickly approached the heights of sexual pleasure. The movements and exclamations of both couples intensified until all four reached orgasm within seconds of one another.

After tending to the damp residues of lovemaking, Terp and Cedar Cradle went about making breakfast, while Cloud and Firstlaugh set the table. As they broke their fasts with whole-wheat toast, blueberries, yogurt, cranberry juice, and coffee, they talked about what had happened a few minutes earlier.

"Now we don't have to tiptoe around the subject of the pent-up sexual energy among us," Cedar Cradle said. "At a normal sensate level, sex is pretty powerful, but when you add extrasensory activities and spiritual experiences it can become over-powering."

Terp said, "We've studied the erotic energy present in most worship services. It subtly but strongly influences the behavior of worshipers."

"When four people care for one another as we do," Cedar Cradle said, "and sit around naked and do incredibly intimate things that involve physical touch and leaving their bodies, sooner or later something sexual is bound to happen."

"Nothing like this has ever happened before with any of the other people who've stayed with us -couples or single," Cloud said.

"Have you floated with any of them?" Cedar Cradle asked.

"No. We've had deep philosophical discussions and talked about our experiences and felt intense affection for one another, but you're the only people we've actually ***done*** extrasensory things with," Cloud said.

"If we want to go deeper together in a psychic way, we have to acknowledge the sexual element and deal with it so it doesn't hinder our spiritual adventures," Cedar Cradle continued.

"Sex is inherently spiritual," Cloud said.

"Yes, but Cedar Cradle is right," Firstlaugh said. "I've felt immense and mutual erotic energy among all four of us in the past couple of days."

"That's true," Terp said. "I've certainly sensed it...and felt it."

"I have too," Cloud confessed, "but I'm passionately in love with Terp, and we're committed to one another exclusively."

"I'm passionately in love with Firstlaugh," Cedar Cradle said, "but that doesn't eliminate the attraction I feel for you, Cloud. But unless we're prepared, intentions can be trumped by spontaneous opportunities. We need to come to some understanding about this."

"Didn't we just do that by having sex in the same bed?" Cloud asked.

"It was a first step," said Cedar Cradle. "Pretty soon we're going to engage in whole body massage. Ordinarily that's done in a controlled environment. The therapist is fully clothed, the client's body is covered with a sheet, and touch is restricted to non-genital areas. There is a client-therapist relationship that prevails.

"But this is far from ordinary. We're all naked, and we love each other, and it's easy to imagine any one of us in an unguarded moment of attraction crossing a personal boundary without meaning any harm. So we need to agree up front what the limits are," Cedar Cradle said.

"There's so much mutual affection here and so much physical contact," Firstlaugh said, "that sexual arousal is almost inevitable."

"There's nothing shameful in that," Terp said. "I think that's OK. As long as we expect it to happen from time to time, we don't have to be afraid of it."

"Of course," said Firstlaugh, "but we do need to have an understanding of how we handle it."

"Arousal is one thing. Intercourse is another entirely," said Cloud.

"I think that's our first basic agreement," Cedar Cradle said. "No matter what else may happen -if I may be clinical about it- genital to genital contact is acceptable only between spouses."

"That was easy," Terp said. "And I would add the same applies for hand to genital contact, at least below the waist. Inadvertent brushing of chests is bound to happen."

All agreed.

What else?" asked Terp.

"How about kissing and hugging?" said Firstlaugh.

"Let's see," said Terp. "I think any kind of hugging is OK among the four of us, even face to face, as long as it's hugging and not groping." The other three nodded assent. "And kissing above the neck is good and welcome as long as no one's tongue is involved." They agreed with this proposal also.

"This sounds legalistic, like we're writing a checklist," said Cloud. "Why don't we identify the elements of intimacy we would each invite before deciding where the boundaries are. We may not need a long list of thou-shalt-nots."

"OK," said Cedar Cradle. "A number of times when the four of us have been together on the mattress I've had the urge to reach out and caress each of you. But I held back out of a sense of propriety. I didn't want my tactile affection to be misunderstood. And yet I would welcome such caresses from any of you, if you felt so inclined. And in that context, I give you all permission to spontaneously touch my body whenever you want -preferably gently."

"You mentioned the mattress, but that sounds more like ***blanket*** approval to me," Cloud said.

Cedar Cradle groaned at the pun.

"Pardon my husband, Cedar Cradle," said Terp snidely and then continued in a confessional voice. "But this is important. I too have ached to reach out and touch your face or side or hip when you've spoken of some deep experience. And I've felt the same about you, Firstlaugh. So I give the same permission as Cedar Cradle."

"Me too," said Cloud and Firstlaugh simultaneously.

"The thing is," added Terp, "I'm perfectly at ease about you, Firstlaugh, and you, Cedar Cradle, touching me. I trust you both completely to honor my body and soul." The other three decided this was a good summary of how they felt as well.

"Well, then, let's put that trust to the test," said Cedar Cradle, "as a way of further dissipating the sexual tension. For me, the issue of bodily contact is intent. If anybody but Firstaugh touched me in pursuit of turning me on or for sexual gratification, I would object strongly, very likely involving a physical connection with my fist. But if either of you affectionately caressed me, almost anywhere on my body, I can't believe that you would be attempting to initiate sexual activity."

"Nevertheless," said Cloud, "you can't entirely eliminate erotic feelings from the kinds of affection we experience among one another. Feelings don't force inappropriate actions but they can certainly lead to them."

"You're right, Cloud," Cedar Cradle responded, "but to me, the key is the honorableness of a person's intentions. As long as you're expressing genuine love but not pressing for unwanted sex, we share equal control in the relationship."

"That's all good, but the real danger comes if inappropriate sex is ***wanted***," said Terp. "I can easily imagine that in a moment of intense intimacy -physical, intellectual, or spiritual- my erotic curiosity could carry me away."

"You're not alone in your erotic curiosity. That's why the boundaries we agreed to are so important," said Firstlaugh.

"As I said, let's test those boundaries," Cedar Cradle continued. She went to the mattress and assumed a supine position with her arms and legs apart. "I invite both of you, Cloud and Terp, to satisfy your curiosity by caressing me -anywhere you think appropriate."

"Keeping in mind the strength of your fists," said Cloud with a laugh.

"Exactly," said Cedar Cradle.

Terp sat cross-legged with Cedar Cradle's head in her lap, massaging her friend's skull. "Will you let me brush your hair sometime?" she asked. "It's so beautiful."

"Absolutely!" enthused Cedar Cradle, "and I'll do yours. That's something the guys won't understand, but I love having my hair brushed."

Cloud sat at Cedar Cradle's side tracing a line with his right index finger along her left hip and side, skipping up to her neck, and then following the shape of her chin, nose, and forehead. "You have a uniquely beautiful face," he said.

"And beautiful breasts, too," said Terp. "Much more...bountiful than mine."

"I rather admire the graceful and youthful curves of yours, Terp," Cedar Cradle said. "I think mine are too full."

Neither Firstlaugh nor Cloud commented on this verbal exchange.

"Well, definitely no boundary issues here," said Cedar Cradle a few minutes later. "Who's next?"

In turn, Firstlaugh, Terp, and Cloud assumed the supine position, allowing their non-spouses to caress their bodies.

When they had finished, Terp said, "I feel electricity all through my body, and I love you all so much. I need to hug everyone."

They stood and engaged in affectionate hugging and kissing of cheeks.

Cedar Cradle said, "Well, there's still plenty of sexual energy in the room. It's time for action."

Cedar Cradle escorted her husband to the mattress and climbed into her husband's lap, quickly sinking onto his rising organ, and Terp did the same with Cloud. The couples faced their mates, locked together, with no one in any hurry to end the erotic enjoyment.

Terp reached across and stroked Cedar Cradle's back. "If you float while linked this way, your souls are intertwined, and your powers are magnified."

"Let's do it," said Firstlaugh, and soon the two sets of connected souls were floating toward the top of Haleakala, where they danced in spirit around the rim of the volcano and then dove down to the floor of its ancient valley.

As they hovered over the collapsed land, Terp said, "I feel the presence of massive power beneath us, but it seems to be in a state of passive equilibrium."

"That's reassuring," said Cedar Cradle. "I wouldn't want to discover what a volcanic eruption would do to disembodied souls."

"It would be a fascinating experience," said Cloud with enthusiasm. "I accidentally floated through the engine of a speeding car once and nothing happened."

"Fascinating for us," said Firstlaugh, "but not for the people below."

"Good point," said Cloud.

Most of the remainder of the Begays' visit was spent with all four in their bodies, building sand castles on the beach, snorkeling, body surfing, hiking in secluded valleys, and giving and receiving massages. With the sexual issues acknowledged and addressed, each was free to relax and enjoy the fullest pleasure from the tactile attention, and no boundaries were breached.

They did, however, float together one more time. As four individuals, they sailed across Alalakeiki Channel to the nearby island of Kahoolawe, which was used by the military for bombing practice. There they hovered in a bomb crater and prayed for the strength to be peacemakers in a violent world. They did not pray that tyrants would see the error of their ways and suddenly become nice, nor did they pray for God to smite their enemies. Each simply prayed for the courage to approach the wounded world with irenic heart and healing spirit.

The couples parted amidst prolonged hugs.

On a hot evening in July, Narcissa and her beau Cofflynn McCarthy went for a walk to explore the grounds of the new church property Arms for Jesus, Incorporated had bought from the now defunct DAFT organization. They strolled side by side with a foot of space between them, and though she would have liked to hold hands, he thought it was an unseemly custom.

"This is just what we need to grow the congregation, Narcissa," Cofflynn said expansively. "We will be so successful, I predict within a year the Soviets will add this place to their primary strategic targets in America. But I'm not afraid. Let them try to attack us with their impotent missiles. The shield of Christ will protect us. That's what I call the American nuclear arsenal, because Christ inspired us to create it."

They stood near the back wall and surveyed the massive sanctuary. Though the thermometer registered 102, Cofflynn was clad in a black suit, with white shirt and tie and spit-shined black military style shoes. He was sweating profusely but declined Narcissa's suggestion that he loosen his tie.

Narcissa wore a long sleeved white cotton blouse that buttoned at the neck and an ankle-length black wool skirt. Cofflynn favored this uniform look that represented a distinct contrast to her usual wardrobe, which tended toward revealing cuts and bright colors. Though she liked pleasing him, the expense for these new old-fashioned garments aggravated her.

At that moment, Narcissa had trouble concentrating on the Soviet missile targets her gentleman cited, because her mind flooded with memories of her time at the naturist church in New River years before. She remembered the place fondly, particularly her baptism, but her reverie was doused in fear that Cofflynn would find out about her past and end the relationship.

Luckily, he had never asked where she had been baptized and prayed he never would. As long as she was with him, she thought, she was situated next to power and by extension powerful herself. If he deposed her, however, she would be bereft of authority.

"Communists will stop at nothing to destroy Christianity," Cofflynn continued. "Their latest dirty trick is duping publishers into issuing Bibles with ***red*** covers. It's a subliminal message to equate the Bible with Chairman Mao's ***Little Red Book***."

"My Bible has Jesus' words printed in red," Narcissa moaned. "I had no idea that was a Communist plot!"

Cofflynn sputtered in protest. "No, no, dear lady! ***That*** red is to remind people his precious blood was shed to save God's elect. It's exactly the same color as the stripe in the American flag. Surely you recognize the distinction between the different reds."

"Yes, of course," Narcissa responded quickly. But she didn't really see the distinction at all.

Eight feet away from them, on the other side of the wall, stood Narcissa's ex-husband Lloyd and his wife Nissa. In total contrast to the overdressed couple, they were naked, and Nissa was nestled in her husband's arms, offering thanks to God that his life and hers were joined together.

"I love you so much, Nissa," Lloyd whispered in her ear.

"Everyone's gone home except Kwan-yin and Cochise, and they're inside straightening up," Nissa said in a low voice. "Let's make love."

They lowered themselves to the grass and began caressing each other, stifling their groans of pleasure, lest there be anybody on the other side of the wall. Their coupling was splendid, and they could not entirely suppress all their noises in the midst of mutual climaxing.

"Did you hear anything, Narcissa?" Cofflynn asked.

"No my dear," she answered. Nevertheless, she imagined hearing a familiar voice quietly expressing sexual release, and the thought of it sent a stab of regret through her well-covered body.

CHAPTER SEVENTEEN

Australia was much closer for Terp and Cloud, beginning their journey from Honolulu rather than Newark as they had on their honeymoon. In August, they boarded a Boeing 747 operated by Qantas and flew to Sydney, where they made connections on a domestic flight to Cairns, for a stay at the Queen's Paradise. Syd and Alice insisted on providing lodging and all meals at no cost, out of gratefulness for their care of Kuranda and Koah a year and a half earlier.

Kuranda threw her arms around Terp and then Cloud, ecstatic to see them again. Koah offered a more subdued handshake but was exceedingly pleased by the visit of the Americans.

"How are Abram and Sarai?" Koah asked.

"We haven't seen them in over a year," said Cloud. "We've been living in Hawaii."

"Kuranda told us about your healing powers," Alice said to Terp. "We were wondering if you might lay hands on her again -a bit of a refresher."

"Of course," said Terp.

"And there are a couple of other people who've heard about you and would like some prayer if you don't mind. I hate to burden you on your holiday, of course, so I can always tell them it doesn't fit into your travel schedule," Alice continued.

"How many people?" Terp asked.

"Not more than a dozen, I think," Alice said.

"Sounds like a full fledged healing service to me," Cloud said. "I'll bet you can get some anointing oil from a local Anglican Church."

And so arrangements were made and the word went out among friends of the Queen's Paradise Naturist Bed and Breakfast that Terp Morgan, the woman who healed Kuranda, would be conducting an anointing service at the resort three days hence.

On the day of the service, at Terp's request, Cloud floated out of his body and nested in her physical body, from which location he prayed for strength for her. Thus, when she entered the dining room, which had been arranged into a chapel, she was physically and spiritually fortified for the energy draining work. She was not prepared, however, for the thirty-six people who sat naked in folding chairs anxious for her hands to be laid upon their heads.

"A few more than I expected," Alice said apologetically. "I didn't think I could turn them away."

Cloud read a portion of the fifth chapter of the Gospel of John, about the healing qualities of a pool at Bethesda whenever its waters were stirred up. Jesus asked a chronic invalid there if he ***wanted*** to be healed. "You need to bring your own motivations and intentions to this service," he told the group. "Whatever happens here will be done ***with*** you not ***to*** you." He then led the ***ad hoc*** congregation in singing the naturists' hymn he had written for the new congregation in Phoenix.

"We come to you, Creator, with reverence in our breasts. We stand before you naked in search of holy quests," reverberated off the walls as they sang with brio.

Terp's face glowed as she said, "The poet W. H. Auden described healing as 'not a science, but the intuitive art of wooing nature.' Our bodies, including our minds, are organically part of nature, and all nature is drenched in the presence of God. Together, let us entice healing through prayers -verbal and tactile- as alluring to God as we intuitively know how to make them."

One by one, people came forward to tell Terp about their wounds, their sorrows, their failures, their fears, and their addictions. She anointed them all with oil, making the sign of the cross on their foreheads, and then placing her right palm on their heads, prayed for them individually.

The response to the service was overwhelmingly positive. People lingered about the place, hugging Terp and talking with her about the great burdens she had lifted from their hearts and souls.

Terp repeatedly explained that she had not healed anyone. "The relief you feel now will not last forever. It will provide temporary strength or courage or patience to get you on the road toward healing. You have to walk that road yourselves. And whatever benefit you have gained through my hands and prayers came from God, not me. I am not a holy person."

No one believed her protestations, however.

"Hail to Saint Terp!" a woman shouted, and the congregation soon took up the chant. "Hail Saint Terp! Hail Saint Terp! Hail Saint Terp!"

Searching her mind for something to distract the temporary congregation from idolizing her, Terp hit upon an idea. She turned to her husband and said, "Cloud, we should get..."

"I'll be right back with it," he said. "Set up chairs for Syd and Alice. We'll demonstrate with them." A few minutes later he returned with a large bottle of massage oil and a pile of towels from the linen closet.

"Please gather round, everyone," Terp announced. "We're going to demonstrate something that will bring you good health. Make a circle here so you can see."

Cloud took Syd's left foot in his lap and began a reflexology workout, while Terp did the same for Alice's left foot.

"Watch what we're doing, now," Cloud said, "because you're going to select partners and do the same thing to each other."

Syd and Alice delighted in the pleasant and relaxing tactile attention. Soon Terp and Cloud switched to their right feet and continued kneading.

"We have a slight problem," Cloud said. "There's not enough massage lotion in this bottle for everyone. We'll have to find a substitute."

"That's not a problem," Alice proclaimed. "Kuranda, go to the kitchen and fetch that big bottle of vegetable oil."

The teenager quickly returned with a half-liter container. While foot-rubbing partners were arranging their chairs, Cloud distributed towels and Kuranda decanted oil into paper cups. Soon all the folks were having a merry time rubbing feet and chattering away about how good it felt. Occasionally someone would run a fingernail up the length of a foot, eliciting startled whoops.

Most of the towels ended up on the tile floor rather than in laps. A significant quantity of the vegetable oil seeped onto surfaces other than feet and hands, as people applied the lubricant liberally.

"We need more oil over here," a middle-aged man roared good-naturedly. Syd filled another cup and presented it to him. Rather than apply it to his wife's feet, however, he poured it down the back of the redheaded man sitting next to him. "I always thought you were a slippery bastard, Blue," he said.

Blue laughed and called for more oil too, which he disposed of in his neighbor's lap. Soon people were pouring oil all over backs and breasts and heads. The glee that filled the room served to confirm the belief of nearly everyone present that something healing and holy had happened through the presence of Terp Morgan.

Two years after Lloyd and Nissa extended him an invitation to visit Arizona, Dr. Clark Hyfrydol accepted. The occasion that motivated him to travel from London to Phoenix was his sixtieth birthday. Lloyd met him at Sky Harbor Airport and whisked him to their home in Paradise Valley.

Since the couple had discussed their practice of naturism with the psychiatrist in his office in Harley Street, and he had expressed interest in investigating the phenomenon, Nissa felt no need to dress for his arrival. She was in the kitchen when Lloyd escorted Clark through the foyer into the dining room. As she hurried out to greet him, she removed the apron she was wearing before taking his hand.

"Dr. Hyfrydol, welcome to our home. You must be tired from the long journey. Please sit down and stretch your legs. Can I get you something to drink?" she said.

Hyfrydol was six feet two, and his legs had been very cramped during flights across the Atlantic Ocean and the American continent.

"Thank you, Nissa," the doctor said. "Under the circumstances, please call me Clark. I would appreciate the chance to stretch my calves a bit. You wouldn't by chance have a dark ale?"

Lloyd carried the luggage to a guest bedroom, while a grinning Clark followed with a bottle of Newcastle Brown Ale in hand.

"You have your own private bath," Lloyd explained. "And this door leads directly outside to the patio and tennis court. Here's a key, because if you venture out this way you won't be able to get back into the house without banging on a window to get our attention." Lloyd handed Clark a key attached to an elastic wristband. "Most of our guests don't have pockets to put a key in," he said.

"Thank you, Lloyd. This is a most pleasant room. I know I shall enjoy staying here," said Clark.

"We eat early, around six, but you've got another hour before we sit down to dinner," Lloyd said. "It's a bit warm out, but a quiet stroll around the property might ease the jet lag. There's no schedule here, other than the dinner bell. And...uh...dinner is informal. Wear as much or as little as you wish. Just because Nissa and I may be nude around the house doesn't obligate you in any way. We want you to be comfortable."

Lloyd left Clark alone and went to the master bedroom to undress. Clark finished his ale, took off his tie, and slipping the key around his right wrist, went outside to loosen his muscles. He paced in leisurely fashion along the flagstone path through the desert landscaping. Soon he was drenched in sweat. Returning to his room, Clark undressed to get a quick shower. He thought better of the plan, however, and checking to see that the key was still securely on his wrist, stepped outside naked. After three barefoot steps on sun-baked stones, he returned to the room to slip on a pair of loafers before venturing out again.

The constrained and orderly psychiatrist felt a sense of liberating ardor surge through his limbs. Perspiration flowed from his forehead, armpits, and chest as he walked briskly about the property, and it felt wonderful. He was sufficiently prudent, though, not to overdo his first nude exposure to the Arizona summer sun. Returning to his room, he jumped into the shower and stepped out a few minutes later refreshed and hungry.

When in Rome, he thought, and picked up his empty bottle and stepped naked into the hallway. He found Nissa in the kitchen. "Would it be possible to get another one of these?" Clark asked, extending the bottle toward her.

"Absolutely," Nissa said. She pulled another Newcastle from the refrigerator. "Lloyd's in the living room looking through some snapshots from the war. You can join him if you like or you can stay here and keep me company while I get dinner ready."

"Options, options," said Clark. "You two are so accommodating. If I were less secure, I would worry there was a tacit agenda and I might make the wrong choice."

"The only wrong choice you can make here is to do something you don't want to do," said Nissa. "Would you like a glass?"

"The bottle's fine, thanks. One less thing to wash," said Clark. "I think I shall do both. I'll chat with you for a bit then get out of your way and look at photos with Lloyd."

Lloyd was quietly whistling the "Colonel Bogey March" when Clark entered the living room.

"During the war, British soldiers sang a verse about Nazi testicles to that tune," Clark noted with a chuckle. "As a Freudian, I found it a fascinating phenomenon."

"Hitler has only got one ball," Lloyd merrily sang.

"That's it! A patient taught me a multinational variation," Clark added. "It goes this way: Hitler has only got one ball. Duce has two but very small. Quisling is now a gelding, just like old Tojo with no balls at all."

"Pity the Axis," Lloyd said. "But that's the best explanation I've heard yet of what motivated their cruel and raging behavior."

Dinner was green salad, baked salmon, and mixed vegetables with fresh blueberries and frozen yogurt for dessert. They retired to the living room after the meal, where Lloyd and Nissa gave Clark a reflexology workout. Soon thereafter, he retired to his room and slept soundly.

The next day, Lloyd and Nissa drove Clark around the Valley to see the sights. That evening, Adam and Evelyn as well as Kwan-yin and Cochise came to dinner to talk to the psychiatrist about the Natural Christian Church and respond to his professional questions about social nakedness and nude worship. Thus briefed, the following

Sunday he attended the service at the NCC in Phoenix.

This is not the Church of England, Clark thought, but it's orderly and traditional Protestant worship. He acquired a Cheshire cat grin while imagining an Anglican high-church service with naked priests officiating. In his mind he could hear the measured tones of a BBC News reporter: ***Druids have invaded the Anglican Church. The Archbishop of Canterbury announced today that additional Pagan practices have been approved for all services of worship. Bare skin will replace clerical vestments.***

During the fellowship time that followed, Dagmar and Quinn latched onto the distinguished visitor, engaging him in conversation about the English theater and about post-traumatic stress treatment of veterans. Hyfrydol was pleased to talk to Quinn about his research project with combat induced mental illness.

Noticing a regular visitor to the church sidling toward the clothing bins next to the exit, Dagmar said, "Oh, doctor, there's someone you have to meet." She ran to stop Edna Echo before she could get dressed and leave, lugging the therapist by the arm to where Clark was standing.

"Dr. Hyfrydol, this is Dr. Echo," Dagmar said. "Dr. Echo specializes in sexual disorders and has been a Godsend to me."

Though Clark was fifteen years her senior, Edna felt an immediate attraction to the lean, gray haired psychiatrist. Edna justified her attendance at the NCC as an adjunct to her practice, gaining insights into sexuality that would help her with clients. She brought all her analytical skills to observation of the healthy interactions of naked males and females in this place. She was nude simply because everyone else was, and in the context of a religious service with so many people around her, she felt safe.

What she avoided acknowledging to herself was that social nudity satisfied a longing she had known prior to the time her father began to abuse her sexually but which she had suppressed since escaping his exploitation. She wanted to be sensually free but would not allow herself that indulgence because it interfered with her cold objectivity on behalf of patients. Nevertheless, Edna was not only comfortable conversing with Clark, slinging professional jargon with abandon, but she felt erotic stirrings looking at his white body with new layers of sun reddened skin.

The two therapists settled onto a couch to continue their conversation.

"Would you two like some salad or sandwiches?" Nissa asked.

"That would be lovely," Clark said. "Here, Edna, let me get you something to nibble on." He stood up. "What would you like?"

Edna felt a pulse of magnetic energy move through her body. She was quite adept at stifling such feelings, but in this case she let it continue. Don't let your past dictate your future, Edna my dear, she said to herself. "Whatever looks good to you will be fine with me," she said.

Clark soon returned with glasses of lemonade and a selection of cheeses, fruits, raw vegetables, and crackers. "I hope you don't mind sharing from one plate," he said apologetically. "I couldn't manage the drinks and two plates at the same time."

Ordinarily, she would have considered such an arrangement the lead-in to an indecent proposal. But Clark seemed so genuine, almost boyish, in his offer, she could not resist. As she picked strawberries from the plate, and bits of cheese and broccoli spears, and put them in her mouth, a sense of conspiratorial communion with this Englishman grew in her mind. The only word that came to her adequately describing the feeling was delicious. Both the food and her enjoyment of Clark were delicious.

After lunch, Clark and Edna strolled around the grounds, comparing therapeutic modalities. From time to time, one or the other would inadvertently sway a bit to one side and their legs or hips would brush against each other fleetingly. Each felt electricity when this happened.

When Edna took leave to visit the rest room, Nissa sidled up to Clark and said, "We have a place for one more at dinner tonight. Would you mind if I invited Edna?"

Clark did not mind, and Nissa extended the invitation. Edna, despite a natural inclination to control the evolution of such events, accepted. After dinner, Edna and Clark took a walk in the moonlight that included a spontaneous and unabashedly erotic episode of kissing while seated on a bench surrounded by jumping cactuses.

"We can't go back into the house with you aroused this way," Edna said to Clark.

"You look rather flushed yourself, my dear," he said. "We can go through my room," he suggested, displaying the key around his wrist. "That will give us time to...to calm down."

They entered his room from the outside, but neither he nor Edna calmed down. Instead, uncharacteristic of both, they made passionate love. Being essentially careful people, they followed the sexual episode by showering together to dissolve any evidence of their activity and returning outside to dry off in the warm night air before joining Nissa and Lloyd in the living room.

Terp and Cloud returned to Alice Springs intent on finding Amoonguna, and this proved providentially easy. Before they had an opportunity to hike the dry bed of the Todd River in search of her house, they strolled along Railway Terrace in the center of town, and Terp spotted the words Calvinist Mission Society stenciled in black on the door of a clean but modest and weatherworn office. Since Terp was under care of the American Calvinist Church, she was naturally curious about their Australian cousins. More than merely curious, she thought. Terp experienced a strong intuitive urge to drop in and chat.

The Calvinist Mission Society of Alice Springs was an outreach ministry of the Australian Calvinist Church that provided social service care mainly to Aboriginal people but also to any others who were in need.

Terp ventured inside and without preamble said to the prim, gray haired woman behind the counter, "Would you by any chance know of a young Aboriginal girl named Amoonguna?"

"I know her quite well," said the woman. "How do you happen to know her?"

"We met her two years ago, when we were here on our honeymoon," said Cloud.

"She took us to see her father, who at the time was in bad shape," added Terp.

"Crikey! Are you two the mysterious Americans who sobered up her old man?" the missionary asked. "That's a famous story around here."

"I guess we are," said Terp. "How are they doing now?"

The prim Calvinist produced a mysterious and knowing grin.

"They're all bonza. The old man's clean and sober. He's one of our clients here at the mission. And Amoonguna is doing well," said the missionary. She stood and reached out to shake hands with the Americans. "And my name's Geneva Andrews."

"Terp Morgan, and this is my husband, Cloud. It's good to meet you, Geneva."

"What brings you back to Alice?" Geneva asked conversationally.

"We were visiting friends in Cairns," said Cloud, "and thought we'd pop over to check on Amoonguna."

"That's quite a pop," said Geneva.

"Actually, we're going to do some hiking about the Red Center also," said Terp. "We love this area. It reminds us of home. We're from Arizona."

"But we're living in Hawaii for the present. Terp's going to seminary in Lahaina," Cloud added.

Terp told Geneva about seeking ordination in the American Calvinist Church.

"The Mission Society has an internship program for seminarians to complete their field education credits," Geneva said. "We're always looking for divinity students willing to spend a few months in the Outback. For some reason, not many are drawn to ministry in what they dismissively call the Ghastly Blank."

"I haven't done my field ed work yet," said Terp. "I'd be very interested in learning more about your program." Terp left with a folder full of information about the Mission Society, an application form, and a feeling this opportunity was predestined.

Amoonguna was pleased to see Terp and Cloud walking out of the river toward her but was not surprised. She knew all along that her American friends would return.

"Have you seen the Old Once since we were here last?" asked Cloud.

"Only in here," Amoonguna said, putting a finger to her head.

Cloud and Terp were disappointed, for they had been harboring unspoken hopes they might again encounter the Old One on this trip.

The following day Terp and Cloud revisited Uluru, once more hiking its perimeter and savoring the supersensual spirit of transcendence surrounding the monolith. This time they stayed in their bodies. Then they set off for two days of hiking at Kata Tjuta, twenty miles west of Uluru.

Named the Olgas by Europeans, Kata Tjuta -the Place of Many Heads, according to the Anangu people- is a field of thirty-six large granite and gneiss stones, small only in comparison with Uluru. The range of red and gold domed rocks encompasses twelve square miles, forming steep-sided valleys.

Few tourists visited the place in those days, and once they had reached the third narrow valley, Cloud and Terp were alone. At times they climbed up long forty-five degree slopes and felt the oxygen burn in their legs. The wintry August temperature was in the high thirties that morning, so Cloud and Terp dressed warmly against the chilly air. By mid-afternoon the thermometer registered seventy degrees, and they were quite warm from physical exertion. They stripped off everything but socks, hiking boots, and hats, shrugged into their backpacks and continued their trek, communing naked with the ancient iron oxide stained sandstone and golden granite towers.

Late in the day the couple moved out of the boulders and into the broad central valley, but even here, they had to negotiate around rough-edged rocks amid the muted green brush, while also crunching across loose gravel. They found a sandstone outcrop that offered protection from the wind for their overnight camp.

Curled up in a double sleeping bag that night, they nestled together for warmth while gazing at the Southern Cross in the clear sky overhead. The patterns of the stars were strange to these natives of the Northern Hemisphere but no less enchanting. Wrapped in each other's arms, Terp and Cloud lost their individual identities in contemplation of the mysterious universe, experiencing profound solitude in the center of a vast empty continent and yet fully connected with the cosmos.

When she drifted off to sleep, Terp dreamed that Cedar Cradle was pregnant, having conceived while in Lahaina. Cloud dreamed that Cedar Cradle would give birth to a girl in the spring and that he and Terp had been present during the act of her conception. When they got back to Alice Springs, Terp wrote a letter to Cedar Cradle and Firstlaugh describing their nocturnal visions.

CHAPTER EIGHTEEN

From Alice, they chartered a flight to Darwin. On Christmas Eve 1974, Cyclone Tracy passed north of Darwin across the western tip of Bathurst Island. If it had continued this course, all would have been well. However, the storm turned around and at midnight Christmas morning crossed over Darwin, raging with one-hundred-thirty miles per hour winds for seven hours. Homes and businesses disintegrated from Tracy's force. Sixty-five people died and many hundreds were injured. Seventy percent of the city's homes were wrecked beyond repair, and Darwin was cut off from the rest of the country as its communications network disappeared. More than half of Darwin's population evacuated the city either voluntarily or by government order. For the next six months, as the reconstruction efforts progressed, special permits were required to get to Darwin.

The rebuilding of the capital of the Top End of Australia was years away from completion when Cloud and Terp arrived there in August. Surveying the remnants of chaotic destruction provided ample evidence of the force of nature. Yet a determination to start again and rise above disaster that they saw in the faces of the people of Darwin fed their spirits with a sense of hope for humankind. In later years when their lives were beset by storms of a different nature, they would gain courage from remembering the spirit of Northern Territorians in the face of great tragedy.

When they returned to Lahaina, they found a letter from Cedar Cradle in the bundle of mail held for them at the Post Office. She wrote:

Dearest Terp and Cloud,

I am indeed pregnant, and we know for certain that you witnessed the conception, because the only times we made love in Lahaina you were with us. I am certain that Cloud is right that I'm carrying a daughter, and I know that she will be strongly drawn to the two of you, her spiritual parents. Firstlaugh says to tell you he dreamed your firstborn will be a girl.

No prediction of when.

Love,

Cedar Cradle

Clark Hyfrydol returned to London in a state of pleasant agitation. He found it difficult to focus needed attention on his practice. He was, he confessed to himself, in love with Edna Echo. Being a decisive man, Clark quickly dealt with the existential ambiguity of his life by ringing up Edna and telling her his feelings.

The American sex therapist responded in an equally decisive manner, saying, "I've always wanted to visit England. If I showed up on your doorstep, could you put me up for a couple of weeks?"

During her stay in London, Edna helped Clark close his practice and lease his flat. He would be spending the winter in sunny Phoenix, and beyond that had no particular residential plans. Evolving in his mind, however, was a notion to research and write about experimental nude therapy.

Clad in a black leotard and white tights, Isadora Coryphee stood motionless and silent in front of her new class. Five students had signed up for her sacred dance practicum, four of them female. All had some previous formal instruction in dance, ranging from limited ballroom to extensive Polynesian. No one had greater comprehensive experience, however, than Terp.

After a sufficiently dramatic interval, Isadora's lips began to move and sound poured from her mouth. "Congregations in the primitive Christian Church of the first and second centuries were exposed to far more letters, gospels, and other pious writings than we know today as the official twenty-seven books of the New Testament. I shall begin this practicum in sacred dance with words from the Acts of John, an inspiring second century work that was not, alas, included in the canon.

"These words are excerpted from the 'Round Dance of the Cross' that Jesus led for his disciples at the Last Supper. The disciples formed a circle and Jesus sang, 'Grace dances. I would pipe. Dance all of you!' The disciples responded, 'Amen.' Jesus sang, 'The Whole on High takes part in our dancing. Whoever dances not, knows not what comes to pass. You who dance, perceive what I do.' The disciples sang, 'Amen.'

"I believe that God takes part in our dancing. Jesus Christ is the piper whose sublime tunes direct our movements. In ***Much Ado About Nothing*** Shakespeare suggestively wrote, 'dance out the answer.' Therefore, dance all of you, and you will glimpse the mystery of what is to come. 'Dance is the hidden language of the soul,' according to the wisdom of Martha Graham. She also said, 'The body is a sacred garment.' In this course we will use our sacred garments to explore and express deep mysteries of faith and to speak through movement and thus reveal our souls wordlessly to God."

To assess levels of skill, Isadora arranged for each student to dance individually. Terp went last, and Isadora's eyes grew wide to see Terp's mastery of the art. As the weeks passed, Terp loosed a torrent of creativity, developing choreographies to dozens of hymns and sacred music pieces, and then dancing them exquisitely alone and with partners. Four weeks into the semester, Isadora invited Terp to be her unpaid co-instructor.

Each Friday that semester, the Reverends Bill and Cathy Blake flew over from Honolulu to teach a course in the history, theology, and polity of the Natural Christian Church. They were co-pastors of the NCC congregation on Oahu and made the flight for the sake of Malama Kohana, a member of their congregation who was studying for the ministry. She was the only NCC member enrolled at the seminary at that time, however Cloud, also a member of that denomination, registered for the class for his personal edification. Ten other people signed up for various reasons ranging from ecumenical interests to simple curiosity. It was widely known that the course featured slides of naturist services, and this may have been a motivator for some of the registrants.

The Blakes were founding members of the NCC, serving as part of a pastoral team at the Malibu congregation before shifting to Honolulu to start a new congregation a year later.

Bill was an introverted intellectual from an aristocratic family that disowned him when he joined company with nudists. More outgoing than her husband, Cathy grew up hungry for ideas and knowledge of the wider world. Her roots were in a working class, anti-intellectual family. To her father, any man with his nose in a book was effeminate, and women were wasting their time with anything beyond cookbooks. Cathy's rebellion from her family of origin led her straight into the arms of the shy and liberally educated Bill Blake.

"There is a general gestalt in human societies as to how people will behave," Bill intoned the first day of class. "Particular behaviors may vary between densely populated places like Tokyo and New York City and sparsely populated rural regions. Nevertheless, societies have norms of acceptable behavior. The average person can articulate, if asked, those behaviors that reflect politeness and those that are considered offensive or boorish.

"This holds true whether the people in a particular society are fully dressed or naked. People in naturist settings maintain the gestalt of acceptable behavior, and if anything, act with greater consideration and deference than in clothed society. Princeton Professor of Psychology Howard C. Warren studied German naturists in the 1930s and noted that where an entire group goes without clothing, the naked body no longer arouses curiosity, nor does social nudity generate eroticism. Naturist gatherings are not, in bare reality, havens for sex maniacs. Writing in the March 1933 issue of Psychological Review, Dr. Warren concluded that social taboos against exposure of certain body parts are not fundamental human traits and can be readily broken with no harmful results."

As the semester unfolded, Cathy and Bill described the history, governing rules, worship practices, and distinctive theology of the Natural Christian Church. Having been present at the creation of the denomination, they shared personal anecdotes that added flesh to the skeleton of facts and figures.

"We started in 1953 with five congregations in four states," Cathy reported. "They were New River in Arizona, San Diego and Malibu in California, Las Vegas in Nevada, and Santa Fe in New Mexico. The following year, we added churches in Boulder, Colorado, St. George, Utah, and Honolulu in the Territory of Hawaii. Today we have twenty congregations in nine states plus one each in British Columbia and Baja California. All but the one in Honolulu are in western North America. We have engaged in some tentative conversations about merging with a naturist denomination headquartered in Florida. They have churches throughout the Southeast, but nothing promising has developed yet.

"These are plain facts. But the work that led to our founding was far from plain. There were great arguments about structure, requirements for ordination, sacramental theology, and requirements for membership."

"One of the original five had been an independent church started the previous year by Korean War veteran Petrus Dort," Bill said. "This became the San Diego NCC, and Dort is still there as pastor. But in the early discussions about the shape of the new denomination, Petrus was an outspoken advocate of conservative theology and local church control. 'You shall not have pseudo bishops usurping the God-given right of congregations to set strict doctrinal standards for admission to their fellowship,' he bellowed on the floor of our first organizational meeting."

"Meanwhile," Cathy said, "Adam Rarom in Arizona was arguing for mutual accountability in matters of worship practice but more flexibility in theological requirements. Rarom was socially conservative but theologically liberal. Dort wanted a literal interpretation of the Apostles' Creed as foundational for the denomination, while Rarom argued that agreement with the creed as metaphorically true should be acceptable for membership. Adam's camp won out eventually, because the practical effect of Dort's position would have been to empty out our pews.

"What developed was -and is today- a denomination with checks and balances, so that ministers don't make all the decisions, and within broad limits, congregations can decide whom to call as pastors, but they can't summarily fire them without approval from the denomination. Most of our congregations are led by husband and wife co-pastors, but San Diego with Petrus Dort and Phoenix with Kwan-yin Burns are notable exceptions."

"The central distinctive of the NCC is immersion baptism while naked," Bill said. "This follows the practice of the primitive Christian church in the first and second centuries. For a decade and a half, this was an absolute requirement for anyone who wanted to join the church, including those who had been previously baptized by sprinkling or immersion while wearing clothing.

"Then came the Morgan case. Evelyn Rarom brought the matter of Lloyd Morgan to the National Assembly of the church. Lloyd, by the way, is Cloud's father, so I imagine he can add some personal details to our presentation."

"I'm very interested in hearing about it from the denominational perspective," said Cloud. "What I remember is my dad insisting to Adam and Evelyn that he had already been baptized in the name of the Father, Son, and Holy Spirit, and he didn't believe the sacrament administered to him as an infant was in any way defective. He very much wanted to join the church but refused to be baptized a second time, because he was convinced that God was satisfied with what happened the first time. He and Evelyn had long conversations about the subject. He was stubborn and she was patient and creative."

"The National Assembly approved a reform of our baptismal theology," Bill continued. "We now offer a Renewal of Baptism rite. We still require the naked immersion, but those who have been baptized previously can affirm what had been done before, and the pastor prays without re-pronouncing the baptismal formula. There was a remarkably peaceful debate about it. All the other pastors had encountered similar situations in their parishes, even Dort, so the Morgan Reform, as it is now called, was enacted unanimously. We gained more than a hundred new members almost immediately as a result of this action."

At the end of the first session, Malama asked, "Will there be any written assignments?"

"Thanks for reminding me," said Bill. "At midterm, each student will submit a ten page paper arguing a positive case for social nudity and a five page paper taking the contrary position, citing specific Bible passages in defense of both papers."

"Why twice as much in favor?" asked a young woman.

"Because the Natural Christian Church obviously supports the practice of social nudity," explained Cathy. "But we want you to be able to identify pros and cons. I suspect you'll be able to find more biblical references affirming nakedness and fewer negative ones than you might have expected."

"Cloud and I will be way ahead of the rest of you on the ten-pager," Malama quipped. "I've got plenty of research material, and I'd be glad to share it." Malama Kohana was twenty-three, a warmly compassionate native Hawaiian woman. Native, however, did not mean pure Hawaiian ancestry, because her family tree included Japanese, Chinese, Norwegian, and English forebears as well as Polynesian.

"One more thing for your calendars," Cathy said. "The first weekend in December we'll have an optional retreat at the NCC church in Honolulu. All members of the class and your spouses and children are invited. But it's not required. In lieu of the retreat you may write a journal detailing your meditations and reflections on the subject matter of this course."

"How long does the journal have to be?" asked a young man.

"A minimum of ten pages," said Cathy.

"What if we want to go but can't afford the airfare?" asked another.

"You could swim," said Bill. "Aside from that, an anonymous grant will cover transportation costs for anyone who needs help." The grant came from Cloud and Terp.

Terp and Malama were resting in the student lounge before a hymnology class, when their classmate Pound Starr joined them. Pound was a lapsed member of the Strict Constructionist Anabaptist Federation, and he seemed to invest most of his energy demonstrating against the narrowness of his former denomination.

"Have you ladies ever wondered why so many of the nineteenth century hymns are about coming?" he said as he plopped into a stuffed chair.

"As in Advent?" Terp asked out of politeness rather than interest.

"No, as in orgasm," said Pound. "I wonder what Sigmund Freud would have made of all that Victorian sexual repression? I think it bubbled out in the hymns. Take 'Just As I Am' for example. 'O Lamb of God, I come, I come!' Clearly that's about sexual gratification with a sheep, don't you think?"

"I think you need help, Pound," said Terp. "Charlotte Elliott wrote that hymn, and she may have been repressed, but I seriously doubt she was lusting after a wooly animal."

"Well then, consider 'It Came Upon the Midnight Clear.' Didn't you ever wonder what ***it*** was that got off in a public place that night? And surely you can see that 'O Come All Ye Faithful' is a carol about group sex. And with pedophile elements in it, because it describes coming while looking at a naked baby -'now in flesh appearing.' Am I right?"

Terp decided to ignore Pound's iconoclastic provocation while taking the subject seriously. "It is true that much of the passionate language in Victorian hymnody lends itself to erotic re-interpretation in these post Freudian days. But you'll search in vain for deliberate double entendres."

Pound was disappointed at the calm response to his words. "Well if you say so. I guess that means I'd better keep quiet in class about my theory of sacred masturbation and ejaculation motifs in Christian hymnody."

"Oh please, Pound, don't let us get in the way of your big chance to make a fool of yourself," Malama said. "Nevertheless, as much as I hate to encourage you, sexual energy is often channeled into religion, and the same language and imagery tend to be chosen to describe both carnal and spiritual euphoria."

"You guys are no fun at all," Pound said with self-mocking inflection. "Where can I find someone around here to shock and disgust?"

"In case you hadn't noticed, you've enrolled in a very tolerant seminary," said Terp. "Try your former denomination. Surely they'd provide the desired gag response."

"They'd go berserk," said Pound. "As addicted as I am to seeking attention, I'm not crazy enough to mention worship and sex in the same ***sentence*** in that crowd. Probably not in the same ***paragraph***."

Pound's countenance suddenly turned grave. "I can see my father now, if I had said something like that in his hearing. He'd be shaking with rage, trying to hold himself back from thrashing me -damned if he committed violence and damned if he didn't physically punish my blasphemy. I don't know which side of him would win out.

"They're fundamentalist pacifists, you know, living in an alien world. The other fundies hate them and the liberals don't trust them. They're locked in a doctrinal box. They create neat and orderly lives, all peaceful on the outside but ***seething*** with anger on the inside. Pacifists can be fierce when challenged, you know. Fundamentalist pacifists can be downright violent. No one in my former denomination could even remotely conceive that my comments were an attempt, however feeble, at ironic humor."

"It looks like you kept some of that anger when you left them," said Malama.

"Yeah," Pound confessed. "I'm haunted by rage, and I can't seem to let it go."

CHAPTER NINETEEN

Randall Owen and Penny Person conducted a long-distance courtship. Penny's phone bills were up tenfold. A constant stream of cards and letters flew back and forth between New Jersey and Hawaii. Randall made two business trips to New York after Penny's visit to Hawaii, staying at her home both times.

In October he returned to the Ritz-Carlton to negotiate a long-term honeymoon package deal with a consortium of travel agencies.

"Penny, I can't get out of the city," he told her over the phone. "Can you come to my suite tonight?"

In response to her yes, he dispatched the limousine with a key to his room. When he returned after the marathon bargaining session, he found Penny resting in an easy chair, wearing a meditative smile and nothing else.

"Let me get a quick shower, sweetheart," Randall said, "and then I'd like to have a serious talk about an important matter."

"What's wrong?" asked Penny.

"Nothing is wrong," he said. "Why don't you join me in the shower, and we can begin the conversation there."

Once under the hot spray, Penny took the cake of soap from

Randall's hand and began lathering his chest. "OK, buster, what's on your mind?"

"We've been avoiding a certain subject for months now, and I think it's time to bring it out into the open."

"Marriage," she said.

"Yes, marriage," he confirmed. "Penny, I love you, and you've told me dozens of times you love me. The only thing that stands between us is the continental United States and half the Pacific Ocean. Both of these are smaller than my love for you. I will give up my position in Hawaii and move to the East Coast if that's what it takes to get you to say yes." He got down on his knees in the tub, holding on to her hips to avoid slipping. Looking up into a spray of water, he said, "Penny, will you marry me?"

She joined him on her knees, feeling the water cascade through her hair. Touching his face with her hands, she said, "Yes, Randall, I'll marry you. And since you've mentioned moving, I'm getting a strong yen to relocate to a more tropical climate. Would you have any real estate suggestions for me?"

Penny was a cultural Protestant who did not attend church, and Randall was a lapsed Catholic. Neither had a church affiliation but both believed that social propriety called for a wedding to be officiated by a member of the clergy. Neither could articulate why they felt this way, but they were of one mind that a justice of the peace would not do. Penny called Terp to seek her assistance. "We want to get married in Hawaii," Penny told her daughter. "Do you know any ministers?"

"I know a lot of ministers," she said. "I would recommend Bill and Cathy Blake, co-pastors of the NCC church in Honolulu. You'll have to go to some pre-marital counseling sessions, though."

"So, you're recommending that your ***mother*** should get married in a nudist ceremony?"

"That's right, Mom!" said Terp. "And I guarantee you'll both treasure the experience the rest of your lives."

"Hold on a second," Penny said into the phone. "Randall, how would you feel about a nudist wedding?"

Randall bent over to speak into the receiver in Penny's hand. "Bless you, Terp."

The next call Penny made was to the Blakes. They set a date for a meeting in Honolulu the following week. In the meantime, Penny made arrangements to store most of the family heirlooms and items she wanted to keep, ship her car and personal effects to Honolulu, engage an estate auction firm, and put her house on the market. Much to Penny's amazement, both her of daughters applauded what she was doing.

The counseling sessions went smoothly and the wedding ceremony was set for Saturday, November first. This was Cloud's thirty-second birthday and a convenient time for Mary to get away from Antioch for a long weekend.

Randall, in particular, liked Bill and Cathy immensely and asked Penny to think about the two of them becoming members of the congregation some time in the future. He had been baptized, but she had not, so a decision to join would affect them differently.

Cathy and Bill engaged Penny and Randall in a conversation regarding their beliefs about the nature of God and humankind. This was an illuminating experience for Penny, because no one had ever asked her what she really believed. Bill, Cathy, and Randall all listened intently to what she had to say.

"Well," she began, "I believe in God. But I don't think the Christian Church has a monopoly on God's love or salvation. And looking at it from the outside, all the fights that different religions have over fine points of dogma and such look pretty silly to me. The God I believe in simply loves the world and doesn't pick and choose people to save or send to hell on the basis of what they profess. I mean, think about it guys. If God only saves those people who are lucky enough to believe the one right thing out of millions of possibilities, there's no hope for the vast majority of us. God must love fools and idiots as much as sages, because there are certainly a lot of the former and damn few of the latter."

"Well said!" Bill exclaimed. "That's profound."

"I should think a preacher wouldn't want to hear something like that," Penny said.

"On the contrary," said Cathy. "For someone who has shunned the practice of religion all her life, you have a deep sense of God. I have great respect for your words."

"I haven't recovered from all my Church induced guilt, not yet, anyway," said Randall. "But I'm working on it, and I think Penny's onto something important."

Penny glowed in this affirmation of her conceptual universe. She had spent most of her life assuming she had no depth of mind. A conventional façade had been her defense against the critics of the world. She had always been gloriously normal. But now she was selling her home, moving to an island in the Pacific, on the verge of getting married stark naked, and if that weren't strange enough, thinking deep thoughts about God. And all this felt to her like a kind of redemption of her heretofore prosaic life.

Penny wanted to treat her daughters equally in their roles in the wedding, so she named Mary Maid of Honor and Terp Matron of Honor. Randall invited his twenty-five year-old son Edsel to be Best Man and Cloud to stand with him in an unnamed capacity. Bill and Cathy co-officiated. There were no other guests. Thus the only person in the sanctuary who was not a member of the wedding party was the photographer Cathy Blake recommended and Terp strongly insisted that Penny engage.

"You've got to have photographs," Terp said, "so we can sit down someday and compare pictures of our naturist weddings."

So it was that Penny Person married Randall Owen surrounded by all their naked children and settled down to the mundane realities of life in paradise.

Edsel Owen was a computer wizard who worked for a small company in Seattle. He was experimenting with individual computers, which seemed a wild extravagance to his father. Apart from his work, which he loved to talk about with considerable passion, Edsel was generally inarticulate and socially inept.

Mary found him fascinating, thinking he had an intelligent face and nice body. When, at the wedding reception, he confessed to her he was a virgin, she felt immediately compelled to remedy that situation. Something in Mary's artistic sensibility made her enormously curious about people, especially men, and for an odd assortment of these men from time to time over the years, that curiosity extended to their sexuality. Mary thought of herself as selective rather than promiscuous but certainly not chaste.

Mary led Edsel to her room at the naturist camp and initiated him into the realm of sexual intercourse. He fumbled with the condom and she had to help him. Not bad, Mary thought, although a bit premature. As they lay together afterward, he rambled on in minute detail about computer languages and programming code, and she decided that her curiosity had been fully slaked with this one encounter. Edsel later wrote her a letter professing his deep love, and she replied as gently as she could that she had moved on.

"In the published minutes of the National Assembly of the Natural Christian Church," Bill Blake pronounced in his best professorial voice, "the subject for today's lecture is officially referred to as the Substance and Normative Etiquette Debates. The denomination made decisions about a series of controversial matters in the late 1960s. Interestingly, secular nudist organizations were also grappling with the same issues."

"However, many people tend to be uncomfortable with stuffy officialese," Cathy Blake added. "Most Natural Christian pastors -and members who know about the debates- refer to these controversies as the Vice Capades."

"It all started in 1965," Bill continued, "when the congregation in Las Vegas petitioned the Assembly to ban alcoholic beverages at all church camps. They had been dry from the start, but new members, who had transferred from naturist churches in other parts of the country were accustomed to bringing beer and wine with them on weekends, and they were challenging the Las Vegas rules."

"About half of our churches banned alcohol from their campuses, except for communion wine," Cathy said. "The biggest objection to the Nevada prohibition proposal came, surprisingly enough, from Utah. The St. George congregation strongly supported the availability of beer and wine at church camps. In this case, they were motivated by the anti-alcohol culture all around them. Apparently they did not believe that running around naked sufficiently distinguished them from the rest of Utah."

Bill took up the narrative from there. "The 1965 National Assembly responded in typical ecclesiastical fashion by appointing a committee to study the matter. And before they could report back to the next Assembly with their recommendation, the California churches jointly came forward with a petition to ban coffee, tea, and caffeinated colas as detrimental to the healthy lifestyle of naturists. Herbal teas were exempted."

"The vote on the California matter was overwhelmingly no. The delegates would not even permit a study committee," Cathy said. "But they debated for two days on the committee recommendation for local option about alcohol. A strong bloc wanted a national ban.

"The historic link between proponents of naturism and the temperance movement in early twentieth century America was still evident in the NCC. It's not that the anti-saloon crusaders had naturist sympathies. I suspect Carrie Nation and her supporters would have been scandalized by the thought of people running around naked. But many pioneers of the nudist movement also advocated abstinence from alcohol for health reasons.

"Ultimately, local option was approved by a vote of slightly more than fifty percent. As a consequence, several churches lost members when their congregations exercised local option by approving alcoholic beverages at their camps."

"The following year, 1967, California came back to the Assembly with another petition, this one to ban all tobacco products at NCC facilities," said Bill. "This time a study committee was narrowly approved."

"Their recommendation was to concur with the California tobacco petition," said Cathy. "And as it happened, the 1968 Assembly was in such turmoil over another issue that the tobacco ban was approved by a wide margin just to get it settled so the participants could launch into the red hot debate about accepting deviants."

Students who had been nodding suddenly perked up.

"I thought that word might generate some interest," Cathy commented. "The word deviant was actually used by some folks at the Assembly. But a more accurate word would be hippie. During 1967 and 1968, many of our churches saw an influx of new members who were enamored of the hippie and the back to nature movements and consequently attracted to us because of our practice of nudity in daily life. To the rather staid ethos of Natural Christianity these folks brought ideas about flower power, getting high, living off the land, and free love."

"Of course, the older mostly conservative members were appalled by these newcomers," said Bill. "From its inception in the early 1950s, the NCC was racially integrated without any stress or conflict. Now suddenly in the late sixties, members and some pastors were calling for the exclusion of certain people based on their counter-cultural views and behaviors. The arguments for barring hippies were deeply felt and persuasive for many at that Assembly. These so called deviants were threatening a settled and secure way of life."

"At most church camps, those who were attracted to the hippie movement only talked about it. They did not do drugs or engage in sexual relations in public areas. They just talked," Cathy said. "This proved to be their salvation. The Assembly voted by a sixty-forty margin to remain fully inclusive to anyone who wanted to be part of a congregation, as long as they ***acted*** in conformity to church rules of ethical behavior. Though not specified, most understood this to include full acceptance of homosexuals."

"This meant that congregations were able to focus on preventing the ***real*** deviants from access to the church," Bill continued. "Screening for pedophiles and sex abusers continued. Married people had to be accompanied by their spouses. Less than a decade later, some of our most committed and reliable current members came into the denomination as a result of the hippie movement."

"Just a reminder," Cathy interjected. "There will be no class next Friday, as some of us will fly to Honolulu for a clothes-free retreat. Those not attending will, of course, be busy writing journals containing their thoughts about the social and personal value of people running around starkers."

The retreat at the Honolulu NCC center turned out to be a small event. In addition to Cloud, Terp, and Malama, two other class members attended: Ben, a young man in his mid-twenties and Amy, a woman in her mid-thirties. Both were members of the Universal Salvation Church, and both shed their clothing without reservation.

During a time of personal reflection in a prayer circle, Ben and Amy separately revealed they had grown up in chaotic homes with alcoholic parents. After the session, Terp suggested a healing and anointing service to Bill and Cathy, who readily agreed. That evening the seven retreatants (including Bill and Cathy) gathered in the half-lit sanctuary for more prayer, laying on of hands, and anointing with oil, led by Terp. The experience was especially powerful for Ben and Amy, who experienced breakthroughs in their efforts to come to terms with their pasts.

The seminarians, whom Cathy introduced as ***kahunapule*** in training, joined the congregation for Sunday worship. Cathy and Bill entered the sanctuary wearing purple leis, befitting the liturgical season of Advent. Rather than traditional stoles, the clergy couple wore fresh leis of varying colors in accordance with the church calendar.

"***Aloha! Kakou ka ohana 'o Ke Akua!***" Cathy proclaimed.

"Welcome! We are -all of us- the family of God!" Bill repeated in English.

"***Kakou po'e hele wale na Ke Akua, na pono 'uhane,***" Cathy continued.

"We are a congregation of naturists for God and for spiritual well-being," Bill translated.

After the invocation and prayer of confession, the choir sang "***Ho'ola Nani***" which Terp immediately recognized as her much loved "Fairest Lord Jesus." Following the scripture readings, a ***kama'aina*** man stepped forward to sing a baritone solo of "Mary's Boy Child."

Congregants and seminarians alike were pleasantly surprised when the choir rose to sing the Pete Seeger folk song "Turn Turn Turn" for the offertory. The surprise came not from the song, a congregational favorite, but because Terp handed her glasses to her husband and danced to the piece, spinning, leaping, and lifting her arms triumphantly throughout the sanctuary.

Bill and Cathy asked Terp to stand with them to greet worshipers after the service. "Your dance gave me a lump in my throat," Cathy said to her before an onrush of people filed by telling Terp the same thing.

A man in his seventies took Terp's hand and said, "My dear, your dance would have been sublime if you had been wearing a costume, but to see you dancing in nothing but the garment God gave you was a spiritual experience deeper than any I have ever known. God bless you."

For the second semester of her middler year, Terp enrolled in Reformation history, process theology, kinetic worship, and dance therapy, while continuing with Biblical Greek.

Kinetic worship dealt with various ways of invoking all the human senses in praise and worship. Isadora taught this course, beginning the first class by saying, "Sage, smoke, and incense can be fragrant offerings to God. The mingled scents of perfume, cologne, deodorants, talcum powder, and aftershave in the sanctuary on a Sunday morning can be a fragrant offering to God as well. But so, too, is human sweat from exercise or hard work."

To Terp, all movement in worship was choreography. The way parishioners selected and sidled into their pews, the processional of the choir, opening the Bible to read from it, breaking the loaf of bread at Communion, and everything else that involved human muscles she considered a form of dance. She was pleased, therefore, when Professor Coryphee told the class the same thing.

"Pay attention to how you move your arms and legs when leading worship," Isadora said. "Don't pull the lid off the communion tray and set it down somewhere on the table. Lift it intentionally and set it down it deliberately. This does not make an idol out of a tray, it demonstrates that you are mindful of what you are about, which is leading the congregation in holy business. The visual aspect of worship is every bit as important as the aural. Yet most pastors spend far more time worrying about the music program than about the one thing they have greatest control over -their own movements."

Most of what she heard in the kinetic worship class Terp already knew at some level, but this was not the case with process theology, which was entirely new to her. As the semester progressed, Terp fell in love with Whitehead's God. That is, she became enamored of Alfred North Whitehead's concept of the nature of God that formed the basis for process theology.

Process thought seeks to integrate science and theology. Humans commonly think of themselves as having two parts, body and soul. Whitehead envisioned God as having two natures. God is, in part, eternal and unchanging, but also growing and continuously changing. It is this second aspect of God that interacts with the universe.

From the first process theology lecture, Terp was intrigued not only by the subject matter but also by Professor Ogden Cobbhart, who habitually ran a hand through his thin white hair, much as some people repeatedly fiddle with their eyeglasses.

"God is immanent with the world, feeling, suffering with, and loving humankind as our lives unfold," Dr. Cobbhart intoned. "Each moment of existence brings new shape to life, new possibilities, thus

God grows along with creation, by absorbing all that is new into the being of God. What theological implications do you see in this model?"

Terp raised her hand. "If this is true about God," she speculated, "then God must be dependent, at least in part, on us, because what people do affects God's feelings."

"Quite so, Terp," he said. "In a sense, humans, along with all other sentient beings determine the content of God's divine life -at least, as you say, in part. There is much more to the universe than human beings."

"So, let me explore the consequences of this," Terp continued. "If God is even in some small way dependent on our actions, then what becomes of predestination and God's plan for our lives and all that stuff?"

"God, in the Whiteheadian understanding of things, does not predestine lives or coerce events, but rather suggests, influences, and ***lures*** people toward alignment with God's will," Cobbhart explained.

"What, in this context, is God's will?" asked Malama Kohana.

"In any given moment, each entity faces an array of possible next moments. Humans can make choices in this regard. I could decide to stop speaking. I could walk out the door. I could kick you in the shins. I could change the subject. Each of those possible futures will create its own set of consequences and new range of possible next moments. God's will for me, as an entity, is simply the best possible future choice for the next instant of my life. God desires the best possible existence for each of us. Of course, humans collectively have made a whole lot of bad choices, and this has an impact on the future choices of any given individual. Therefore the best possible next moment for a particular person will be influenced and in some ways limited by the actual life lived up to that new moment."

"So," said Terp, "if I smoked two packs of cigarettes a day for twenty years, and this damaged my heart, the range of possible next moments for me would be limited because of what I had already done. God's will -the best possible next moment for me- would not and could not include, say, my getting up and running a marathon."

"Exactly!" said the professor. "The weight of the past has tremendous impact on the possible futures available to us. Much of that weight for humans, however, comes from feelings and attitudes about what has happened to us in life. Bad experiences have a way of paralyzing some people and causing them to self-limit future possibilities. But God offers us continually new opportunities to change our minds about past suffering and mistakes. Despite the massive accumulation of bad choices or painful experiences, God's will is always for the best eventuality from whatever is possible. Sometimes that best doesn't look so good to us, however. That's where prayer and discernment come in.

"With respect to the smoker," Cobbhart continued, "the best possible future may involve acknowledging physical realities, medical intervention, or putting affairs in order in anticipation of a premature death. In the case of, let's say, a victim of incest, the best possible future may develop from letting go of self-loathing or making a wise decision about a potential romantic relationship. There are far more options available to these hypothetical people, of course, from minute to minute, day to day, and year to year. In any case, the more one knows about and consciously acknowledges one's past, the better equipped one is to alter positively the future direction that past is pushing toward."

A student in the back of the room raised his hand. "What would you say to our evangelical colleagues, who would see this as completely unbiblical? They claim God had a plan for Jesus to save the world and has a specific plan for each of our lives."

"I would ask them to reconsider their contentions about pre-set plans," Ogden replied. "What are the passages that support that argument? Process theologians argue their view of God is more biblical than what passes for orthodoxy. In process thought, God is dynamically involved in the ebb and flow of human history. The First Testament account of God changing God's mind in response to Abraham's pleas, for example, illustrates process thinking.

"There are many process indicators in the gospels. Look at John's account of the wedding at Cana. Jesus attended a wedding party at which the supply of wine was exhausted. What would be God's will in such a circumstance?"

"The best possible future," several students responded in unison.

"Precisely," the professor said. "Jesus directed a servant to take purification rite water to the steward and pass it off as wine. By that point in the celebration, the steward's taste buds no doubt would have been dulled, so it is not hard to conceive of God using that opportunity to influence the steward's perception of the clear water as fine wine. And surely at that particular moment more wine was not in the best interests of the guests. Thus the best possible future would be for the guests to switch their consumption to water and yet enjoy it as if it were wine. That's the miracle in this pericope."

Malama raised her hand and was recognized. "Going back to God's will, would that extend to other creatures, such as dolphins or the now extinct Neanderthals?"

"Interesting question," said the professor. "How would you answer that, Terp?"

"I think God's will must interact with all creatures capable of choice," she said. The mention of Neanderthals reminded her of the Old One, which led to an intuitive flash, and she added, "So the process of human entities opening to the best possible future must also encompass evolution parallel to or even extending from Homo sapiens."

"A novel thought," Ogden said. "I see no reason to reject that possibility."

That evening over dinner, Terp said to Cloud, "I caught a glimpse today of your passion for the integration of science and religion."

Apart from a publicly eloquent devotion to process theology, Ogden Cobbhart was a shy man in his late forties, tall, thin, and deeply tanned. The former Maine Yankee's darkly wrinkled face was framed dramatically by shoulder length silvery hair. He had been married four times to women who had pursued the craggily handsome professor, but all four had divorced him when they discovered they couldn't pry him away from his first love, the queen of the sciences -theology. His life was absorbed into the intellectual realm, where he lived most of the time, except for certain physical routines.

Ogden was in the habit of greeting each morning in the nude with a series of yoga positions. Then he fixed a concoction in his blender and without bothering to dress, sat in a wicker chair on his lanai sipping the drink. This morning cocktail consisted of fresh papaya, mango, pineapple, banana, coconut milk, and ginger root, with dashes of gingko biloba and ginseng. Once blended, he added half a bottle of island-brewed Primo Beer.

With breakfast consumed, he then spent an hour on the lanai writing theology, working on his ***magnum opus,*** titled ***Eternal Becoming: Process Theology, Ecology, and Living Simply***. He had been writing the book for a decade and was getting close to halfway finished. His goal was to demonstrate ways to increase the riches of the human mind while protecting the planet. Having produced a few more profound thoughts by means of fountain pen applied to paper, he showered, dressed, and walked to the seminary in pursuit of bracing intellectual encounters with faculty and students.

On Sunday, Ogden dutifully attended the eleven o'clock service at the Universal Salvation Church but as a professional courtesy refrained from commenting on the pastor's sermon and never stayed for the fellowship time. Each night before bed, he squeezed half a lime into a jigger of rum and downed it in one swallow.

That spring semester, Cloud taught two classes in Asian religions, and in lieu of payment from the seminary, he enrolled for academic credit in a course in pastoral care and counseling and also in a spiritual exercises practicum. The practicum included guided meditation, fasting, various kinds of prayer, yoga, and free association reading of scripture and religious texts.

The initial lecture of the pastoral care course did not begin the way he expected. Evangeline Beecher England had chaired the Pastoral Care Department at Pacific Crossroads from its founding. Born at the turn of the twentieth century, her septuagenarian aristocratic bearing was accented by an intelligent face, warm brown eyes, and crowned by short gray hair. EBE, as she was called by faculty and students alike, although not to her face, carried a reputation for being an accomplished and exacting scholar.

She had published a dozen professional books, her most recent being ***Narcissistic Pastors and the Congregations Who Love Them***. The second part of the title was not to her liking. That part of her working title had been ***Congregations Enabling Them***. However, sales of the text had spread beyond academia, so she found no cause to condemn her editor for making the title more appealing to the general public. Indeed, she once remarked to a colleague that since the ranks of the clergy held such a large percentage of full-blown narcissists, she was gratified that her work had reached the attention of frustrated and suffering parishioners.

Once Cloud and the other students had settled into their seats, Evangeline Beecher England rose from her chair, regally walked to a spot in front of her desk, and began to lecture without notes. "The first commandment for pastoral care of a congregation is pastor heal thyself. Everything else in parish ministry depends upon that. Pastors must be emotionally strong and mentally vigorous. As a member of the clergy, maintaining your physical, mental, spiritual, and emotional health is your top priority."

Everyone in the class sat up a little straighter.

"In this course, we will ***not*** concern ourselves with the counseling techniques you are eager to learn, as disappointing as I suspect that prospect may be to you," the professor continued. "Techniques are for actors. Ministry requires ***authenticity***. Rather, you will be called upon to dig deeply into yourselves and name your dysfunctions, recognize your shadows, face your fears, and confess your inadequacies. Said another way, you will be expected to expose your psychic wounds to cleansing sunlight and healing air. I expect nothing less than courageous honesty from each of you.

"It is critical for pastors to maintain a non-anxious presence in their congregations. Given the prevalence of dysfunction and tragedy in the lives of many church members, it is exceedingly difficult for pastors who have not dealt with their own ***excrement*** to fulfill this requirement. This course will be a starting point to help you function as your authentic selves unburdened of your own anxiety and that projected upon you by parishioners...as well as by colleagues in your ecclesiastical structure.

"If anyone here is not prepared to endure personal embarrassment in order to confirm and to fulfill your perceived call to ministry, I advise you to visit the registrar this very afternoon and ***drop out***. There is no penalty, I assure you, for opting out now, because I will allow you to register at a later time, presumably when you are better prepared to face these necessary risks for fruitful ordained service.

"Now, all who are ready to remain and to begin mucking out the clutter and gunk hidden in your brain cells, I bid you gird your minds for an adventure in self-awareness!"

"Wow!" Cloud half whispered to himself and those in the desks immediately around him.

"Please share your commentary with the class, Dr. Morgan," EBE said to Cloud.

"Yes, professor. What I said was 'wow!' Although the meaning of such an expression may be subject to various interpretations, I meant it as an affirmation. I would unpack the sense of it as an appreciation of your words and gratitude that the time spent with you promises to be most productive. I would broadly paraphrase the wow as this is going to be very cool!"

EBE betrayed the hint of a smile. "Very well, Dr. Morgan. Cool perhaps, depending on your interpretation of that idiom, but certainly not pleasant. Let me remind all of you that everyone here has attained at least a bachelor's degree and several, like Cloud Morgan, have earned graduate degrees. Collectively you are bright achievers. You constitute a socially elite group. But you are not as smart as you think you are, and I would be very surprised if we do not soon uncover among you expressions of emotional immaturity, dysfunctional mental processes, neuroses, obsessions, and perhaps even an array of personal demons. I give you fair warning: If you have suffered any significant trauma in your life, the effects of it will show in our work together. Please make an appointment to speak with me privately if your personal history involves violence, sexual abuse, or substance addiction."

Cloud immediately thought of his experiences in Viet Nam and wondered if he would be pressed to confess the worst of his memories in front of his classmates. He found the thought simultaneously threatening and liberating.

EBE continued. "The dark secret of institutional religion is that too many pastors, priests, ministers, rabbis, or whatever title they may be given, are emotionally unfit for spiritual leadership among real people. An unfortunately large number of clergy seek the center of attention as a means for satisfying their own needs, essentially forcing congregations to care for ***them*** rather than being pastors for the people. This course aims to initiate healing processes for prospective pastors ***before*** they can inflict their neediness on unsuspecting congregations."

"Welcome to humility 101," Cloud whispered to the student on his right.

At the end of the class, he made an appointment with Dr. England to discuss his physical and emotional wounds from his time in Viet Nam. In the event, he told her more than he thought he would ever tell anyone about mutilations he had seen, atrocities he had witnessed, and the systemic obstacles he encountered that precluded investigations of these war crimes. He confessed his personal guilt about quietly acquiescing to the institutional indifference that effectively covered up gross evil. The most difficult part was describing events without revealing to his professor that he was out of his body during many of them. He left her office feeling that EBE was an extraordinary listener and quite knowledgeable of the psychic consequences of war.

Cloud had felt good about himself since meeting Terp. She had brought him significant healing, and he thought he had been able to lay aside the traumatic effects of the war because of her. But he had withheld from her some of his most painful war memories. As a result of confessing his psychic wounds to Evangeline, he felt healthier and stronger and decided that if she wanted to hear it, he would tell Terp all he had revealed to EBE. Terp did want to hear it, and with this telling, he did not have to withhold the matter of being out-of-body. Afterward, they held each other and wept.

Cedar Cradle gave birth to a daughter in March. They named her Wakhan Lahaina Begay. Wakhan is a Lakota word encompassing the concepts of energy, mystery, sacredness, and creation. Lahaina, of course, was the place where she had been conceived. Cedar Cradle maintained a deep sense of assurance that Wakhan would grow up to be a spiritual healer.

In April, a troupe of Thai dancers itinerated through Hawaii on their way to an international arts festival in Los Angeles. Through faculty connections with a seminary in Chiang Mai, the Thai performers agreed to dance at Pacific Crossroads. Isadora Coryphee suggested adding seminary dancers to the program to create a visual exchange of stylized movements. A consensus soon grew that the local offering should be a hula.

Only two students were sufficiently adept at this art. Malama had grown up with the sacred dance, and Terp had learned Polynesian movements as a child, performing a New Jersey variation on the hula. They selected recordings of a sacred hula drum chant, "***Ke Akua I***

Ka Uwalo I Ka La'I E" segueing into "***Ke Kali Nei Au***," a haunting wedding song.

Terp and Malama put together costumes and set about rehearsing in the campus dance studio. After running through several variations, Malama, reverting to pidgin for emphasis, said, "Mo bettah nekkid!"

Terp walked to the door and locked it. They quickly shed their costumes and danced with greater energy and élan. While the two were lost in the emotion of their dance, Isadora used her key to enter the studio.

"Are you planning to dance that way for the concert?" she inquired.

"Alas, no," said Terp, "although it would be a memorable performance."

"It's better this way," said Malama, "but we have costumes. See?" She pointed to the bikini tops and skirts on the floor.

"All my life I have yearned to dance naked," Isadora said with a sigh, "But I have never found the right occasion or appropriate audience for it."

"Take off your clothes and join us," said Terp. "We'll be your audience."

As Isadora disrobed, she thought it odd that unlike herself, Terp and Malama had no tan lines. Then she remembered their Natural Christian Church connections. "There is yet another observer," she said, looking toward heaven. In the fullness of time, Isadora Coryphee would now dance naked before God and glory in every movement.

The concert was a great success. The Thai women moved their hands and fingers at sharp angles with exacting stylized gestures, their intricate movements beautiful to behold. Malama and Terp were also beautiful as they gyrated hips and made waves in the air with flowing movements of hands and arms. Though they received high praise for their performance, both women knew their most deeply satisfying, freely offered, and best executed hulas had been danced in rehearsal, seen only by Isadora Coryphee and God, neither of whom would ever mention this fact to the seminary community.

Terp and Cloud returned to Australia in June for Terp's internship with the Calvinist Mission Society. Geneva Andrews met them at the

Alice Springs Airport and took them to a small apartment that would be their home for two and a half months.

"I'm sorry it's not much to look at," Geneva apologized.

"We're used to living very simply," said Cloud. "This is more than adequate."

"A true Calvinist," Geneva said. "Shunning ostentation."

"In that respect yes," said Terp, "but don't get him started on doctrine or theology. Apart from his carefully nuanced expression of total depravity, his Calvinist credentials are seriously suspect."

"But I'm not a member of the ACC," Cloud protested, "so my conformity to classic Calvinist doctrine is irrelevant."

"No worries, Terp," Geneva said. "You're the intern here, not him. But I truly hope the three of us can get into some rip-roaring theological arguments in the time you're here. After a long day dealing with abject poverty and pain, there's no better relief than speculating about God's mischief while guzzling a few beers."

"I look forward to that," Cloud said. We'll have to show Geneva the relief of reflexology, he thought to himself.

Terp read his mind. "Give it a couple of weeks," she whispered to him.

The next day, Geneva took Terp out into the bush in the mission's jeep. "I'll introduce you to some of the families we work with," she said. "Some of these are very sad situations. It tears at my heart."

"Is this only social work, or can we pray with people and talk about God?"

"We do both, my dear, out of desperate need. And I'm anxious to see you in action. I've heard how your hands on Amoonguna's old man sobered him up in a flash."

"Somewhat exaggerated," Terp said. "But he did come around pretty fast."

Geneva downshifted expertly and steered the jeep around a huge rut in the dirt track. "The story going around is that he was passed out naked and drunk in the sand, and you stripped off and walked right up and confronted him. You and Cloud held him up and prayed, and he came to right away. He hasn't had a drink since."

"Do you believe that story?" Terp asked.

"I do," Geneva said.

"And what do you think about it?" Terp asked.

"I presume you want to know what I think about the stripping off part," Geneva said. "Here in the bush most of the folks don't care much about clothing. I've seen everything there is to see, and I got over my shock at nudity a long time ago."

"Well, we did take off our clothes," Terp confirmed. "It was an instinctual thing."

"I'll let you in on a secret, Terp," Geneva said. "Sometimes when I'm out here in the mallee working with youngsters running around like Adam and Eve, I strip off too. They feel more comfortable that way, seeing the old white missionary starkers. But nobody at the society head office knows about that, so I trust you'll keep it to yourself."

"You know I will, Geneva," said Terp.

Cloud spent the day hiking around town, exploring for interesting places. He bought a few books on local history, and stretched out with one of them mid-afternoon, waiting for Terp and Geneva to return. His feet ached from hours of walking on sidewalks and he daydreamed about Terp massaging his feet that evening. Of course, she'll be tired from an extroverted day in the bush, he thought. I should do her feet.

In the event, he ate sandwiches with Terp and Geneva at Geneva's favorite pub. Neither he nor Terp was accustomed to drinking more than an occasional glass of beer or wine, so after two beers each, they were both feeling the effects of the alcohol.

"My feet don't ache anymore," Cloud announced, apropos of nothing they had been talking about. "Two stubbies have done wonders for my soles."

"I know the perfect cure for aching feet," said Geneva. "Aching anything, actually. It's called reflexology. Have you heard of it?"

"Cloud was wondering yesterday how long it would be before we introduced ***you*** to it," Terp said, laughing.

"I'm way ahead of you on that one," the Australian missionary said. "Living alone out here, I'm quite good at taking care of my own needs."

"In that case," said Cloud, "please allow us to take care of your needs for a change. Let us rub your feet. I've done my own feet, too, but it feels immeasurably more relaxing when someone else does it to me."

"Look at him," Geneva said to Terp. "Put a couple of Fourexes in him and he's ready to make love to an old lady's feet."

"You're not so old, Geneva," said Terp.

"I'm Fifty-five," she said proudly.

"Old lady or not," Cloud said, "the foot-rub offer is still on the table."

"Some other night," Geneva said. "You put temptation before me, but like a good Calvinist, I'm a pro at delayed gratification."

On a free day, Terp and Cloud borrowed Geneva's jeep and followed an unsealed track eighty miles west to the quartzite-lined cliffs of Glen Helen Gorge at the headwaters of the Finke River. Geologists have reckoned that at four hundred million years, the Finke is the oldest existing river on the planet. Water flows its entire length only during rare floods but some isolated spots retain water year-round.

After a day of hiking and exploring the area, Cloud and Terp skinny-dipped in a Finke River billabong, shivering in mystical consciousness not from the cool water but from naked contact with primeval elements.

"I feel like I've risen from the mud," said Cloud. "As if I were newly born from the primeval ooze encasing my feet."

"Of a piece with all creation," echoed Terp. "The sense of eternal connection is especially intense here. Or is it just us -a couple of mad mystics out to uncover the cosmos in a billabong?"

"It's us alright," said Cloud, "but this spot is clearly evocative. It feels like being in a place where the mind of the universe is exposed."

"Like you, I feel newly born here and yet exceedingly ancient at the same time," said Terp.

"That's exactly what I was about to say," said Cloud.

Their laughter echoed off the stone walls of the gorge.

CHAPTER TWENTY

Three weeks into her internship, Terp encountered a life changing experience.

The telephone rang in the CMS office, and Geneva immediately lifted the receiver to her ear.

"Geneva, this is Johnny." Johnny was the dispatcher at the Royal Flying Doctor Service. "I hear you've got a chaplain-in-training with you this winter. We have a situation out at Nicker Flat Station, and we'd like to borrow her for the day."

"What happened, Johnny?" Geneva asked.

"Bad accident. It looks like the younger boy is dead and his dad's in a bad way."

Geneva turned to Terp. "Are you up for some pastoral care on a station? A ten year old boy's been killed and his dad's injured?"

"How do I get there?" Terp asked.

"By air. You'll go with a Flying Doctor." She picked up the receiver again. "Johnny, we're on our way to the airport."

An hour and a half later, the Beechcraft Super King Air turboprop skidded to a stop on a rough landing strip two hundred miles northwest of Alice Springs. A boy about thirteen met the doctor and Terp and took them by Land Rover two miles over a bumpy track to the house. Along the way the boy said efficiently, "Dad was mounting a brumby and it bucked him off. He fell hard and got knocked out. Jim tried to get the brumby away and it kicked him in the head. Dad's got a broken leg, all bent back. Jim's dead."

The physician went immediately to the injured man, and Terp threw her arms around the grieving woman. "I'm so sorry," Terp whispered in her ear.

The woman, who had maintained the presence of mind to radio for assistance and stay in charge until help arrived, now began to sob. "He was only ten," she wailed. "Poor Jim. I don't know what I'll ever do without him!"

Terp held the woman tightly and allowed her to mourn. She felt a shudder rise from the mother's breast. "Where is he now?" Terp asked after an interval of silence.

"In his room," the mother said. "Let me show you." She led Terp down a narrow hall to a small bedroom, where Jim was laid out on top of a quilt. A large blue bulge showed prominently on the left side of his forehead. Someone had shut Jim's eyes.

Terp placed her hand on the swollen area. It was cool to the touch. "Come sit and let's pray," Terp said to Jim's mother. They sat beside Jim's body on the bed. With one hand on Jim's forehead and the other grasping his mother's hand, Terp began to pray for God's presence in the midst of tragedy, for courage, for strength, for healing the wounds of grief. Words poured from Terp's mouth and she made no effort to edit them. As she prayed, she felt warmth return to the boy's face.

She stopped in mid-sentence and placed both hands on the child's cheeks. His eyes blinked open.

"Where's Mum?" he said. "What happened? The brumby..."

"Stay with him, ma'am. I'll get the doctor," said Terp. She went flying down the hall.

The physician examined Jim carefully. "Apart from a nasty bruise on his forehead, Karen, I can't find anything wrong with the boy," he said. "I see no sign of brain damage. His pupils are normal size."

"Oh, Karen," Terp said. "I'm sorry. I never asked your name."

"He was dead," his mother said, ignoring Terp's remark. "I've seen dead people out here. No breath. No pulse." Karen turned and pointed at Terp. "She did it! Jim was dead but she prayed and he came back to life."

"He was already alive," said Terp. "His breath may have been imperceptible and his pulse faint, but I'm sure he was alive."

Karen threw her arms around Terp. "Bless you miracle maker. Oh, bless you!"

On the return flight, the doctor agreed with Terp's description of events. "Probably Karen was too agitated to detect any pulse," he said, "but you'll never convince her of that. Every family in this region by now knows that an American saint brought Jim back from the grave. Of course, you ought not discount your prayer entirely. You may have brought him out of a trauma induced coma."

The news of Terp's miracle preceded her return to Alice Springs. Geneva and Cloud were waiting at the airport. So was a stringer for the Adelaide Advertiser.

"Stuff a duck!" said Geneva. "What'll you do next? By the by, there's a reporter waiting to see you."

"I don't want to talk to any reporter," Terp said.

"If you don't," said Geneva, "the story will be wilder than you can imagine."

Terp told the reporter the bare facts and rejected the claim that she had brought the boy back from death. Within two days the miracle story had been printed in papers all over the country, and Alice Darwin called from Cairns to say she wasn't the least surprised that Terp had done such a thing.

"But I didn't do it!" Terp wailed to her husband later that day. "Why won't anybody believe me?"

"Because believing in miracles is more powerful. It gives them hope," said Cloud. "And I'm not convinced you had nothing to do with Jim's recovery. I've witnessed the healing power in your touch and prayers."

"Maybe I shouldn't touch anybody anymore," she said.

"You know better than that, Terp," Cloud said quietly. "You have a gift, and like it or not, you must use it."

"I'm happy to do that," said Terp. "I just don't want the publicity that goes along with it. I want to be left alone."

"So did Jesus," Cloud noted.

Eventually life in the Northern Territory quieted down for Terp. She fell into a routine of assessing the needs of families in crisis two days a week and traveling into the bush to visit families three days a week. On Sundays she led a chapel service in the store front office of the CMS. Most of the dozen or so worshipers were clients of the ministry.

At the beginning of August, Cloud at last prevailed on Geneva to come to their apartment for dinner and a reflexology treatment. When the meal was finished, they rearranged the chairs so that Geneva faced Cloud and Terp with a foot in each of their laps.

"This feels vaguely sinful," Geneva said.

"That's what my pastor in New Jersey said when we did his feet," Terp noted.

"If we sin, let us sin boldly," said Cloud, paraphrasing Martin Luther.

Geneva recognized the allusion and laughed. Soon she settled back and enjoyed the massage. "Too right, Cloud. This is much better than doing it to myself." After another silent interval had passed, Geneva said, "Terp, did you say anything to Cloud about...my old lady costume out in tribal lands?"

"No," said Terp. "You asked me to keep it confidential."

"Thank you, dear. I should have known you would," Geneva said.

"Do you want me to tell him?" Terp asked.

"I suppose since I brought it up, I ought to be the one to do that," Geneva said.

Cloud remained silent during this exchange. He had long since learned that he did not need to ask for information. For some reason he did not fully understand, people confided all manner of things in him and Terp. What was it about the two of them that led friends and colleagues to reveal the most intimate details of their lives? Why did even casual acquaintances and sometimes strangers trust them with their greatest vulnerabilities?

"On our first day out in the bush," Geneva said to Cloud, "Terp and I talked about the healing intervention you two did with Amoonguna's father. I told her the word around town was that you stripped off your clothes before laying hands on him and praying."

"That's true," Cloud said.

"Then I told her that sometimes when I visit groups of children and young families in the bush, if they're naked, I take off my clothes too, to build trust and solidarity with them. But the good Calvinists in the head office would not approve."

"Your secret's safe with me," Cloud said.

"I know it is," replied Geneva. "But I was thinking that before you leave, you should go out visiting with Terp and me some afternoon. So I want to give you advance warning that your wife and I may take off our clothes under certain circumstances. Be prepared for a shock."

"The only shocking thing," Cloud said, "is that we're getting massage oil all over our jeans when you're perfectly comfortable with nudity." He set her foot aside long enough to remove his pants, then resumed massaging Geneva's right foot.

"You're not upset with me, are you Cloud?" Geneva asked.

"No, of course not," he said. "I'm teasing you."

"We're almost done anyway," said Terp.

"Oh, it goes by so quickly," said Geneva.

"What ever happened to the vague sense of sin?" Cloud asked.

"Long forgotten," said Geneva.

"Well, if you feel the need to atone," Cloud said, "maybe I could prevail on you to help me rub Terp's feet."

"I'd love to," Geneva said, "but not in this dress."

"You don't need the dress," said Terp.

When Terp lifted her feet into Cloud's and Geneva's laps, all three were naked, and they continued in that state when Cloud's turn came to entrust his feet to the hands of the two women.

As his feet were massaged, Cloud continued meditating about people trusting him and Terp. What were the odds that so many people would quickly shed their clothing in their presence? Why did this phenomenon recur with unlikely people? Then again, who was he to judge likelihood? Cloud believed the baring of souls and bodies that had become a theme in their lives was not coincidental. Something is happening in the world, he thought, and its unfolding is certainly intriguing.

Ensconced in a library two hundred miles away, the Old One paused to note Cloud's thought and smiled. Something was indeed unfolding, an evolving enterprise that was proving much more probable ever since Cloud and Terp demonstrated that they possessed the inherent ability to exchange memories with one another.

Before returning to Hawaii, Cloud and Terp spent a little time with the Darwins in Cairns. By popular demand, Terp and Cloud led another prayer and anointing service, followed by a rowdy group reflexology session.

The big news this visit was that Kuranda had a boyfriend. His name was Nguyen van Nuoc, and he was half Vietnamese and half Cameroonian. His father, whom he never met, had served in the French Army during the war and had abandoned Nuoc's mother when his unit returned to France. Shunned by her family and neighbors for bearing a mixed race bastard, Nuoc's mother turned to prostitution for a livelihood, entrusting much of his care to a series of co-workers while she was engaged with clients.

When the Communists prevailed in 1975, Nuoc, now a young adult, found the new regime even more intolerant of biracial sons of prostitutes than the defeated Republicans. He managed to escape in a small boat and eventually reached Australia, where he was accepted as a refugee. Nuoc loved the water, and so he was delighted to find employment in Cairns cleaning marine equipment and tourist boats.

Kuranda was helping Nuoc learn English. For a few days, Cloud enjoyed conversing with Nuoc in Vietnamese, and this in turn helped Nuoc understand some nuances of the English language that Kuranda had not been able to explain.

"How do you describe Nuoc's ancestry?" asked Terp. "His father was French by culture but African by birth. So he's not Eurasian. Is there such a word as Africasian?"

"I don't think so," said Cloud. "And I'm wondering how to describe any children they might have. If Kuranda -half European and half Aborigine- has children by Nuoc -half African and half Asian- they would possess the genetic inheritance of four continents. Quite a powerful combination."

The first semester of her senior year in seminary seemed to fly by for Terp. For the holidays, Cloud and Terp flew to Phoenix, spending Christmas with Lloyd and Nissa. On Friday night they all attended the eleven o'clock Christmas Eve service at the Phoenix NCC. Worship concluded in candlelight, while the congregation sang "Silent Night." Standing in a circle, they passed the flame from one candle to another. Kwan-yin said, "Please be careful. Hot wax on bare skin hurts." The naked, singing pilgrims then marched into the chilly night and gathered around the stable and manger the youth group had constructed on the flagstone porch. Meditating on Jesus' birth in such primitive conditions caused them all to feel gratefully warm in comparison with what they imagined Mary and Jesus must have felt.

"The grace of the newly born Jesus Christ be with you all!" Kwan-yin proclaimed when the singing stopped. "Merry Christmas everyone!"

Back inside, Lloyd introduced Cloud to Clark Hyfrydol.

"Clark has done a great deal of research into war induced mental illness," Lloyd said, "and now he's researching the therapeutic effects of naturism."

"A lot of the naturists around here are combat vets," Cloud offered. "Why don't you convene a group of them and see what they have to say?"

"That's a wonderful idea," said Clark.

After talking through the logistical difficulties, Lloyd, Clark, and Cloud made plans for a gathering of naturist war veterans at Lloyd's house on Sunday afternoon. Cloud and Terp were planning to fly to Gallup on Monday to visit the Begays in Window Rock. Cloud called Firstlaugh and prevailed on him to fly to Phoenix Sunday morning and return with him and Terp the next day.

The gathering included two World War II veterans. Lloyd had served in the Army Air Force, and his business partner Lowell had been a truck driver assigned to the predominantly black Red Ball Express in France.

Cloud had been an Army officer and Firstlaugh a Marine officer in Viet Nam. Quinn and another paraplegic friend, Bill, who attended the NCC in Phoenix, had been Army enlisted men in that war. Mandy and Tenny Smith, Lloyd's tenants in the Villa Verde house, had met while stationed at the Navy base at Nha Be, South Viet Nam.

All of them reported favorably on their naturist practice, and in varying degrees affirmed that it helped them process anger, shame, fear, and other negative feelings associated with their wartime experiences.

Clark found plenty to follow up on with these men. He would spend more time with Lowell, exploring the effects of segregation and racism in a war zone. Firstlaugh would provide a wealth of information about the Enemy Way ceremony and how Navajo spirituality helps combat veterans re-integrate with civilian life. Mandy and Tenny had a great deal to reveal about hidden homosexuality in the military. Quinn and Bill would provide Clark with a bonanza of data about the treatment of paralyzed veterans in America. Bill's sexual functioning had been affected by his injuries, and he had received treatment from a sex surrogate, who taught him how to achieve orgasms from non-genital erogenous parts of his body. The brain is the biggest sex organ in the human body, the therapist had told him. Clark was very interested in learning more about this also.

As time passed, Clark seemed to find more reasons to extend his stay in the United States. The next day, he went to the Federal Building in Phoenix and applied for permanent residency status.

During winter months, Window Rock frequently reports the lowest temperatures in the state. The thermometer registered well below freezing when Cloud, Terp, and Firstlaugh arrived there. Nevertheless, Cedar Cradle welcomed them with her naked body, for the Begay home was snug and balmy inside. "***Ya'at'eeh,***" she greeted them. "***Whoshdee! Whoshdee!*** See, I'm learning more Navajo! But come inside quick before the wind behind you freezes my nipples."

Four year-old Tzek was accustomed to seeing his parents nude around the house, so he was not surprised when Terp and Cloud quickly disrobed in the kitchen.

"Let me see Wakhan," Terp said as soon as the warming hugs and kisses were out of the way.

"I'll show you!" said Tzek. The naked boy led Terp and Cloud to the nursery.

Terp held the nine month-old girl in her arms, grinning with pleasure from the feel of the baby against her breast.

"Ooh!" said Cedar Cradle, "It's milk time. Let's go pile into bed and catch up on things while I feed Wakhan."

"I'll make hot chocolate and join you in a couple of minutes," said Firstlaugh.

The others paraded into the cedar-paneled master bedroom. Cedar Cradle sat with her back against the headboard and put Wakhan to a breast. Terp sat beside Cedar Cradle, and Tzek bounced into her lap, snuggling in with his back against her chest. Terp began to massage the top of Tzek's head, and Cloud sat at his wife's feet and rubbed Tzek's feet. The boy knew he had made the right decision to climb into Aunt Terp's lap.

Firstlaugh entered the room with a tray containing five mugs of steamy hot chocolate. "These will need a few minutes to cool down," he said. He put the tray on a bedside stand and sat next to his wife and daughter. As Wakhan nursed, Firstlaugh gently stroked his daughter's back.

"Ooh, that makes her suck harder," said Cedar Cradle.

"Is that good or bad?" asked Cloud.

"Good, I think," said Cedar Cradle.

With the nursing completed, Terp took Wakhan for the burping, while Cedar Cradle distributed the mugs. They sipped the warm, stimulating beverages and talked of matters trivial and intimate.

"I went off the pill last month," said Terp.

"How wonderful!" said Cedar Cradle. "Let us know the minute you're pregnant."

"You two will be the first to get the news," Cloud said.

"OK," announced Cedar Cradle, "you guys are in charge of the kids for a while. Terp and I have some serious playing to do." She placed a chair next to the bed and sat in it. Without a word exchanged between the women, Terp selected a brush from Cedar Cradle's dresser and began to pull it slowly through Cedar Cradle's long black hair.

Tzek said, "I rub Uncle Cloud's feet."

Cloud settled into the place Terp had previously occupied and made pleasurable noises as Tzek used his little fingers to tickle and lightly knead his feet. Firstlaugh stretched out with Wakhan resting on his chest, his arms wrapped lovingly around the baby as she slept.

After a time, Terp and Cedar Cradle traded places, and Cedar Cradle brushed Terp's fine brunette tresses.

"This is ***hozho***," Firstlaugh said. "Living in beauty and harmony."

"This room is so fragrant and warm, like the breath and hearts of our hosts," added Cloud. "***Hozho*** this certainly is. I am overcome with affection for all of you here."

"We call our home ***Ohoneedza,*** Ideal Place," Cedar Cradle said.

"You seem to have adapted well to the ***Dine*** ethos," Terp said to Cedar Cradle. "I don't even know what your Lakota maiden name is. Do you miss Lakota country? The name Pine Ridge evokes such wonderful images."

"I miss the people," Cedar Cradle answered solemnly, "but not the poverty of the place. Pine Ridge is the second largest reservation in the country, second only to Navajo, but lacking the resources that many much smaller reservations have. And for the record, my maiden name was Voiturier."

"That sounds French," said Terp.

Cedar Cradle chuckled. "Well, a couple of centuries back, a lot of lonely French trappers married Lakota women, so there's a significant amount of European DNA in the Lakota gene pool. And a few names also."

That night, Cloud and Firstlaugh carried a double bed mattress from the storage room and placed it on the floor in the master bedroom, next to the Begay's bed. Cedar Cradle and Terp put sheets, covers, and pillows on it.

The next day was sunny but very cold. Snow lay in patches across the landscape. After depositing the children with grandma and grandpa, the Begays and the Morgans set out for the old hogan they had visited the last time Cloud and Terp stayed in Window Rock. After stashing their picnic supplies inside the place, they set out to climb the multicolored butte where they had danced naked in much warmer weather.

"Wowee, it's cold up here!" Cloud shouted when they reached the summit. A sharp wind cut across the top of the mountain.

"No wimping out, Cloud," said Firstlaugh. "Remember Haleakala. No other people are around here to inhibit us."

They quickly stripped and Firstlaugh handed out moccasins. Each one laughed against the freezing gusts as they danced across the top of the butte. The cold bit into their skin, and much sooner than in the summer, they ended their freeform movements and dressed. All the way down to the hogan they laughed about their frigid adventure.

Inside the earth and log home once more, Firstlaugh kindled a fire. Ravenously hungry, the four stuffed themselves with chicken sandwiches and potato salad and drank hot coffee from a large thermos bottle.

Late in the afternoon, they returned home to Window Rock. Before retrieving the children, the friends stripped again and indulged in whole body massages all around. Their bodies and hair were redolent of smoke from the hogan fire, and now the scent of massage lotion added a layer of fragrance to each of them.

Cloud nestled his face against Terp's neck. "I love the odor of smoke on your skin and hair," he said.

"Smoke and oil smell great," Cedar Cradle said, "but the truth is, we're all a little gamy. Everybody into the shower before we visit the grandparents!"

They showered in pairs, splashing much water on the tiled floor. After toweling off, the women engaged in prolonged skin grooming and mutual hair brushing. The men talked about Clark Hyfrydol's research projects until it was time to get dressed and go.

That evening, Cloud and Terp treated the three generations of Begays to dinner at a Chinese restaurant in Gallup. Grandpa and Grandma favored Cantonese cuisine, although Wakhan preferred breast milk over the bits of steamed rice Cedar Cradle offered her.

CHAPTER TWENTY-ONE

New Year's Day, with Tzek and Wakhan safely in the care of their grandparents, Cedar Cradle, Cloud, Firstlaugh and Terp lay together in bed and made preparations to leave their bodies. Soon they were floating over mesas and gullies, enjoying from above the subtle hues of the land.

They passed over two boys herding sheep and sensed unease among the animals as they hovered near them. They continued their explorations, sailing through columns of smoke rising from dozens of hogans.

Approaching one homestead, they saw a skinny child, about three, sitting in the rutted track of a dirt road. No one was near her. Less than a mile away, an intoxicated man in a pick-up truck rumbled down this road faster than prudent for prevailing conditions. All four floating people instantly recognized that the driver would not see the little girl.

"Everyone concentrate on lifting her out of the road," Terp said.

Terp and Cloud had experience levitating objects while out of their bodies, but never a living thing, and certainly not anything as heavy as this child. All four focused attention exclusively on moving the child. Nothing happened for what seemed like an eternity. The truck rounded a bend and bore down on the spot where the girl sat.

Slowly, the child's body rose two inches above the ground, then three more. A few seconds later, she floated sideways out of the path of the oncoming truck.

"Let's move her over to that hogan," Cloud said.

Gently they lowered her to the ground in front of the entrance to the dwelling and then passed through the walls to see if anyone was home. The little girl's mother was passed out drunk on the floor.

"We can't lay hands on her," Terp said, "but we can pray."

"Let's float inside her body and pray from there," Cloud suggested.

The four souls entered into the space occupied by the inebriated woman's body, and immediately the woman awoke from her stupor. Her mind was clear. Terp directed an image of the daughter into the woman's mind, and she rose, opened the door, and scooped her little girl into her arms.

Another image entered the mother's mind: a truck crushing her child into the dirt. She shuddered. A sense of remorse drenched in grace cascaded through her brain and into every cell of her body.

"Mommy's gonna throw 'way the bottles, little one," she said to the girl. "Tomorrow I go to the clinic for help."

At Terp's urging, on the way home, they navigated to the weathered stone that gave Window Rock its name. "For a long time, I've wanted to float through the window in this rock," Terp said. "Would it dishonor the ***Dine*** if I did that?"

"I don't see how it would dishonor anyone," Firstlaugh said. "Let's all do it."

The four souls sailed through the hole in the rock then looped up around and through it again, over and over as if they were on an amusement park ride. Soon satisfied with their whimsy, they pneumatically moseyed home to ***Ohoneedza***.

The next day was a time for farewells. "***Hagoonee,***" said Firstlaugh, offering the Navajo word said at partings.

Responding with the same expression in English, Cloud said, "Well, okay then."

"We'll be back this summer," said Terp to Tzek, who was weeping at their leave-taking. "That's not such a long time."

—o—

In her last semester of seminary, Terp enrolled in the pastoral care course taught by Evangeline Beecher England that Cloud had found personally transforming the previous year. EBE challenged Terp to dig up and examine her feelings about her father's premature death. This proved to be more emotionally wrenching than she had anticipated, for she discovered that her pain from fatherly abandonment and her anger at God had not dissipated, as she thought, but rather had been shuttered in rarely accessed brain synapses. She also began to recognize how much she still missed her dad.

Although she blushed when she said it, Terp then surprised herself by voluntarily telling her classmates about her sense of shame at not being asked to the senior prom. This prompted a stirring discussion about episodes of loneliness and rejection that each of the students had experienced at various times, and the professor was very pleased with what she described as a productive conversation.

Terp also had a private talk with Dr. England about her experience with the campus pastor at ASU. This trauma, unlike her father's death, had not lingered in her psyche, and she was able to speak of it with objective anger.

"I think my healing was helped because I never felt any guilt or shame over having sex ***per se***. The pain was over the lies and betrayal and feeling duped," Terp said.

"An astute insight," EBE replied.

Later in the course, EBE delivered a lecture on sexual abuse among clergy. "This is a hidden epidemic," she explained. "Unfortunately, the incidence of sexual misadventure in the church is rather high, and nearly always, the perpetrator is quietly whisked away to some other parish rather than defrocked. Let me clarify that what I am addressing here is the serial abuser, the sexual predator. There are also those unhappy clergypersons who improperly and unseasonably fall in love with someone not their spouse and foolishly pursue love affairs. These situations are more often matters of temporary insanity rather than abuse and require a more gracious standard of evaluation."

Without mentioning her own involvement, Terp told the class about Kirk Trilby's trial and being stripped of his ordination, and EBE added that this was an exception that she hoped would one day become the norm for such cases.

—o—

On a balmy Lahaina afternoon in mid-January, Terp and Cloud were engaged in unhurried lovemaking. On this occasion they opted for the missionary position, with Cloud on top.

"I love the ***hozho*** of slow passion," Terp whispered in his ear.

They lay still, savoring the feelings of their physical connectedness.

"Let's float," said Cloud softly.

Soon their souls were intertwined and hovering near the ceiling.

"Let's make our bodies move," said Terp.

Cloud concentrated on animating Terp's hips, while Terp focused attention on Cloud's pelvis. Then other parts of their bodies began to undulate, and the two souls watched as their bodies reached simultaneous orgasm without them. Immediately they returned to their bodies and invested all their mental energy on the army of sperm cells set loose in Terp's vagina in search of an egg. No doubt influenced by their encouragement, one tiny tailed creature succeeded. Terp was certain she was pregnant, but she waited for medical confirmation before calling Cedar Cradle with the news.

On his second day in office, January 22, 1977, President Jimmy Carter pardoned all the Viet Nam War era draft evaders. Cloud cheered, and for the first time in his life, wrote a letter of thanks to the President of the United States. On a whim, he included his service number in the letter to signal to the staff person who read the president's correspondence that the writer was a veteran who heartily approved of this act of grace as well as justice.

Someone on the president's staff did a bit of homework, for the return letter Cloud received noted Cloud's Purple Hearts and Bronze Stars. Hand written at the bottom of the letter was a note from Jimmy Carter expressing thanks for Cloud's service and for his generosity of spirit in support of the pardons.

Ogden Cobbhart rarely entertained faculty colleagues in his home and had never asked a student to visit. Yet in April, with the end of another school year on the horizon, he felt an impulse to invite an adjunct professor and a graduating senior student to dinner. This unprecedented prospect seemed intuitively right to the introverted scholar and he followed through on it. Cloud and Terp accepted immediately.

After a leisurely vegetarian meal, they retired to the lanai for conversation, Cloud and Ogden with bottles of Primo and Terp, being three months pregnant, with a glass of limeade.

"Tell me about this Natural Christian Church you belong to," Ogden said to Cloud. "I'm intrigued by the ecologically friendly possibilities of such a manner of life."

Cloud told stories about the NCC, weaving in his theological quest with the denomination.

"Splendid!" said Ogden. "This would make an interesting excursus in my book. But what about you, Terp? You're a Calvinist. What do you make of naturist theology and practice?"

"I'm a rather progressive Calvinist," she replied. "And I have been thoroughly enriched by association with my husband's church."

"My interest is not entirely academic," Ogden confessed. He told them about his nude morning exercise and writing routine. "I have a housekeeper who comes in once a week. She has observed me writing on the lanai many times. She calls me ***Polopeka hele wale***."

"Professor who goes around naked," Cloud translated. "Very appropriate."

"But I don't go around very far," Ogden responded. "Only around the lanai."

Terp said, "In the spirit of process theology, professor, what's the best possible future choice for us in the next moment? What would God be luring us toward as becoming entities?"

"Ah, so many possibilities," said Ogden. "In the context of our discourse, I suppose it would be for each of us to remove our clothing and continue this conversation in a natural state."

"I was hoping you would say that," said Terp. The three disrobed and resumed their verbal interweaving of process theology and naturism, concurrently enjoying the warm evening breeze that tickled their bodies.

Half an hour later Cloud said, "I have another suggestion for a best possible future this evening. Ogden, are you familiar with reflexology?"

"My second wife introduced it to me," the professor said. "But a long time has passed since I have enjoyed the practice."

"Your wait is over," Terp said. "Do you have any massage oil in the house?"

"No, but I seem to remember that vegetable oil will do in a pinch," Ogden replied.

Soon oil and towels were procured and seating arranged on the lanai. "One more thing," Ogden said. He went inside and returned two minutes later with a boom box and a cassette tape. "Let's have a musical accompaniment."

As the professor reclined with one foot in Cloud's lap and the other in Terp's, the insistent opening of Grieg's Piano Concerto in A Minor filled the air. "Surely this celestial sublimity is the best possible choice this moment for this very content entity," Ogden sighed.

As the concerto continued, Ogden and Terp massaged Cloud's feet, and then the two men took care of Terp's feet.

When the last echoes of the concerto faded, Terp said, "I think the baby enjoyed the music and massage as much as I did."

Oblivious to Terp's remark, Ogden said, "I think I shall spend my Sundays in Honolulu this summer, researching possible connections between Natural Christian practice and process theology. There must be another chapter or two in all this for my book."

In the months leading up to graduation from seminary, Terp sought permission from her Candidates for Ministry Committee in New Jersey to begin searching for a call as pastor of a congregation. She gave particular attention to churches in Arizona and New Mexico, sending her resume to pastoral search committees throughout the Southwest.

The second week in May, she received a telephone call from the chair of the search committee of the First Calvinist Church in Prescott, Arizona. After a brief preliminary conversation, he invited Terp to preach in a neutral pulpit in the Phoenix area, to be followed by an extensive interview with all the committee members. The visit was set for the first weekend in June.

First Calvinist was a relatively small church of a hundred and fifty members. Its sanctuary was situated a block from the town square of the mile high territorial capital of Arizona. The congregation was typically Calvinist in that its members were mainly teachers, lawyers, physicians, nurses, business managers, and other professionals. With regard to church doctrine, most members leaned decidedly to the left, but when it came to matters of economics, they tended to be conservative.

As a matter of prudent stewardship and as a statement of goodwill, First Calvinist shared its sanctuary with a small Jewish congregation. Beth Shalom Synagogue, connected with the Reformulationist denomination founded after World War II, held services Friday evenings, so there was no conflict over use of the sanctuary. First Calvinist was the only Christian church in Yavapai County with a kosher kitchen.

Beth Shalom had only a dozen families on its rolls and for a long time had difficulty attracting a rabbi. In 1976, however, the congregation contracted for the services of a woman rabbi, Darla Nabi. Her husband Yonah owned a printing company in Phoenix that published a popular shop and swap newspaper. The Nabis had a summer home a few miles outside of Prescott, so it was a convenient arrangement for all.

At the end of May, Terp received a Master of Divinity degree from Pacific Crossroads Theological Seminary, graduating first in her class. As part of the commencement service, Terp, whose pregnancy was now showing, danced a stunning solo as the choir sang the classic hymn "Come, Labor On."

Later, at the graduation party, Terp and Malama produced comic choreography for two currently popular religious parody songs, "Drop Kick Me Jesus" and "Mercedes Benz." Students and faculty howled at Malama launching Terp through heavenly goalposts and Malama begging God for the gift a Mercedes Benz while Terp buzzed around her in a make-believe Porsche. And then they danced to a solemn arrangement of "***Aloha Oe***" and the laughter turned to nostalgia-laden tears.

Preaching in a neutral pulpit and the face-to-face interview went well. Pending approval by her presbytery in New Jersey, the search committee invited Terp to appear before the Prescott congregation for election as pastor. She accepted.

Terp did not have an opportunity to meet the rabbi with whom she would be sharing the sanctuary but looked forward to that happening for a personal reason. Although Terp said nothing about this to the search committee, she knew that Rabbi Nabi had been her husband's date at their high school prom. Cloud and Darla Zadok grew up in the same neighborhood, and in 1961, Cloud took Darla to the West High School prom. It had been their only date, much to Cloud's disappointment.

Terp stood in the pulpit of Second Calvinist Church of Metuchen, but she wasn't there to preach to the congregation that had nurtured her in the faith. Second Church was host to the June presbytery meeting, at which Terp would be examined for ordination. If she passed the oral exam, the church in Prescott would be permitted to call her as their pastor. The Presbytery of Arizona would ordain her upon Witherspoon's approval.

Witherspoon Presbytery, however, had a history of saying no. It hadn't happened often, but on occasion, a candidate for ordination was judged to be too conservative or too liberal by a majority of the members, and ordination was denied. In recent years, new ministers coming into the presbytery tended to be more conservative than those of past eras. Thus Terp faced a significant risk of being deemed too liberal.

Terp read her written Statement of Faith to the assembled ministers and elders. "I believe in the God who cut through the twisted web of human sin with a word of grace and an act of love. Both that grace and that love were incarnate in Jesus Christ. I believe that God weeps when we weep and laughs when we laugh."

She stepped out of the pulpit and turned sideways so her pregnant state was visible to all. "I believe that when the child in my womb moves inside me, God dances for joy. And not only for me but for every mother who is in love with the new life she carries within her."

Walking back to the pulpit, she continued, "I have seen the Holy Spirit enter into a room full of contentious people and convince them to make peace. I have seen the power of prayer to release tortured people from the guilt or envy or fear that bound them." Terp continued with her statement, covering what she believed about the Bible, the church, and the sacraments.

When she finished, the oral examination began. Anyone present could ask her anything about her beliefs and her life. The fact that she had attended a liberal seminary guaranteed that questions from conservatives would be rigorous and pointed.

Argyle Watts had given Terp one piece of advice about this ordeal. "People who ask questions will have their own agendas. Some of these people are not popular with their colleagues. Don't try to provide the answer a questioner wants to hear. Someone else will want to hear a different answer, and you'll get all balled up trying to please everybody. Just say what you believe and let the chips fall where they may."

The acerbic minister who had challenged Terp when she first met with the care committee stood and spoke. "Scripture is quite clear that Mary, the mother of Jesus, was a virgin when she became pregnant by the Holy Spirit. Yet some in our denomination have fallen into the error of denying the literal nature of the virgin birth. What do you believe about this critical doctrine, Terp?"

She drew a deep breath and said, "First, I don't believe scripture is completely clear on this matter. There is a discrepancy between what the first chapter of Matthew reports about a virgin conceiving and the seventh chapter of Isaiah, which Matthew references, that says a young woman -not necessarily a virgin- shall conceive. Historically, we have here issues of preferred translation as well as interpretive agendas. I must confess that this is not an important doctrine for me. My faith in the resurrecting power of the Christ does not depend upon the virginity of Jesus' mother. If incontrovertible scientific proof were presented this afternoon that Mary was not a virgin, it would have no effect whatsoever on my Christian faith. On the other hand, since this is not a critical issue for me personally, I have no cause to challenge the doctrine, and I accept it as a traditional creed of the Church."

Following up on Terp's response, the acerbic minister continued, "So with the impertinence of youth you dispute the Bible's clarity. How do you justify that?"

"Just because some people insist the Bible is perfectly clear about one subject or another, that doesn't make it so, certainly not for everyone. From my intense reading of it, the Bible speaks with differing, even contradictory voices about many things -forms of worship, slavery, divorce, female leadership, and sexuality among them. Some prefer to rationalize or explain away ambiguous, contradictory, or barbaric passages. I choose to embrace them with a holy skepticism. I'd rather dwell in God's deep mystery than the shallow trenches of human dogma. Those entrusted with ordination have a responsibility to their parishioners to take these contrasting biblical voices into account before making absolute pronouncements about the whole book."

The minister began to speak, challenging her doctrinal view, but three other people were waiting to interrogate Terp, and the moderator cut him off and recognized the next one.

"Tell us what you believe about the atoning sacrifice that Christ made on the cross so that those who believe in him may be saved from hell."

Terp stepped closer to the microphone and paused. This was an area of theology she was not clear about in her own mind. She was not comfortable with the blood atonement views common among conservative Protestants. But she could not offer a concise explanation of what she truly believed about this subject. In order to provide some kind of answer, she began to describe the various theories of Christ's atonement that had developed over the centuries. As she recited information, she compared and contrasted the differing views. In her nervousness, she provided more and more details.

As she spoke, many elders present, who knew little about historic theories of the atonement, responded favorably first to this model then to that one. By the time Terp realized she should shut up and take the next question, many people in the sanctuary were not sure what they believed about the meaning of the cross.

The acerbic minister rose and said, "Mr. Moderator, I submit that the candidate has not answered the question."

"Sit down, John," the moderator said. "You've had a turn." An elder was recognized.

"I was in Australia last July on vacation," the elder said, "and I read a story in the paper about an American seminarian named Morgan who went out to a remote station with the Flying Doctors. Was that you, Terp?"

"Yes, it was," she said, "but those reports in the papers were exaggerated. My prayer did not bring that boy back to life. His mother only thought he was dead."

A loud murmur passed through the assembly.

"Will you please explain what this is all about?" the moderator asked.

Terp told the story with simplicity and humility, and by the time she finished, many in the sanctuary were dabbing at tears or stifling lumps in their throats.

The moderator recognized Argyle Watts. "I move the examination be arrested," he said. A dozen voices shouted, "Second." The motion passed resoundingly.

Terp along with Cloud, who had been sitting with Argyle, were excused from the room so the assembly could deliberate on her readiness for ordination. The couple passed an uneasy hour waiting in Argyle's office with no word from the meeting. Terp fretted that the archconservatives would carry the day and she would not be approved.

A few minutes later Argyle came in, wearing a non-committal expression on his face. "They're ready for you now," he said quietly.

"What happened?" she asked.

"A bloc of conservative clergy argued hard against you. But the elders were so touched by your episode in the Outback and the humble way you told the story, that in the end you were approved by a wide margin." He now allowed himself a wide grin and swept his protégé into a proper hug.

Tears of relief poured down Terp's face. When she entered the sanctuary, the assembled commissioners rose to their feet and applauded. More tears flowed from her eyes as she stepped into the pulpit and said, "Thank you. From the depths of my soul, thank you, and God bless you all.

III

ZARA

A waking eye, a prying mind,
A heart that stirs, is hard to bind.
Charles Lamb

In what distant deeps or skies
Burnt the fire of thine eyes?
William Blake

Many come to bring their clothes to church rather than themselves.
Thomas Fuller

CHAPTER TWENTY-TWO

First Calvinist Church unanimously elected Terp pastor. She and Cloud went searching for a place to live and found a furnished two-story Territorial house two blocks east of downtown. It had four bedrooms, two ancient bathrooms with huge porcelain tubs but no showers, and a large, sunny room in the southwest corner downstairs that a previous resident had used as an artist's studio. Also downstairs were a formal dining room, a parlor, and a library with built-in floor to ceiling bookcases. The large kitchen lacked modern appliances but featured an adjacent walk-in pantry. A covered porch extended across the eastern front of the place. Attached to the back of the garage was a servant's apartment with bathroom and kitchenette.

The owner, who lived in Phoenix, was temperamentally opposed to borrowing money to renovate the house and was thus having difficulty renting it. This was unsurprising since the kitchen and bathroom facilities had not been upgraded since the 1930s. As a result, the terms were modest. Though it was larger than their needs, Terp developed an immediate attachment to the mansion and had an intuitive sense that all the space would be well used before too long. Cloud was not one to question Terp's intuition, so they signed a year's lease.

—o—

Cloud caught Darla by surprise. She had heard that the Calvinists had elected a woman pastor and was looking forward to meeting her. Darla had not, however, gathered any information about the new pastor's husband. The encounter happened mid-afternoon Friday, while the rabbi was checking to see that the sanctuary had been properly arranged for the evening service.

"Hello Darla," Cloud said.

Darla had been concentrating on her task and was unaware anyone else was in the room. Thus she was doubly startled. "Cloud! What are you doing here?"

"I'd like to introduce you to my wife," he said matter-of-factly. "Terp, this is Darla. Darla, Terp."

"I'm the new pastor," Terp said, taking the rabbi's outstretched hand.

"If you're anything like your husband," Darla said, "I look forward to a wonderful relationship between church and synagogue."

"I'm glad you reached your goal, Darla," Cloud said. "Congratulations! We'd like to hear you preach. Would it be alright if we attended services tonight?"

"It would be more than alright. I'd love to introduce the new pastor and her husband to my congregation. And by the way, Cloud," Darla said, "I don't care if you mention the prom. These folks don't care about such things. In fact, I think they'd find it charming that their rabbi once had a crush on a ***goy***."

"I thought I was the one with the crush on you," Cloud said.

"It's obvious that it was mutual," said Terp with a bemused smile.

"What about your novel, Darla?" Cloud asked. "I imagine with the press of rabbinical studies it would be hard to find time to write it."

"So true," said Darla. "And at least for now, I've lost interest in the things I wanted to satirize in a novel. I have other and higher priorities to keep me busy."

Over the next month, Terp and Darla developed a mutually admiring collegial relationship as well as a caring personal friendship. Such was their bond that Cloud, despite having known Darla for more than half his life, was peripheral in this human constellation.

Sunday evening July thirty-first was the time set for Terp's ordination. Terp invited Argyle Watts to preach, and he gratefully accepted. He and Ruth arrived in Phoenix Saturday afternoon. Lloyd and Nissa picked them up at the airport and delivered them to the house in Prescott. Firstlaugh and Cedar Cradle drove down to Prescott that night. Less than two weeks into their lease, therefore, every bedroom in the house that Cloud thought would be too big was occupied, at least temporarily.

Penny and Randall flew in from Honolulu, and Mary, who had graduated from Antioch and was living in Greenwich Village, arrived from New York. Penny and Randall stayed in the servant's apartment, while Mary slept on an air mattress on the floor of the studio.

As a result of the odd mixture of people gathered in the house, Cloud dubbed the place Strange Haven, and the name stuck. An unusual tension permeated the atmosphere in Strange Haven that weekend. Everyone in the place, except Argyle and Ruth, practiced naturism, but since no one wanted to create any problems for Terp, they all kept their clothes on. This generated a tide of frustration that erupted from time to time in sniping remarks and over-reactions to inconveniences such as waiting for access to a bathroom.

On Sunday, a caravan of NCC friends arrived for the ordination. Adam and Evelyn brought Kwan-yin, Cochise, and Skye. Cochise offered to photograph the service and Terp gratefully accepted. Mary and Skye had not seen each other for three years but resumed their friendship as if the intervening separation had been only a few days.

Darla and her husband Yonah attended also.

The sanctuary overflowed with members of the congregation and visitors, and the chancel was crowded with representatives of the Presbytery of Arizona, who were officiating at the ordination. Argyle sat as a corresponding member with the local denominational leaders. Ruth was thus on her own, but Nissa quickly invited Ruth to sit next to her.

According to custom, Terp sat in the front pew with her family. After a stirring sermon by Argyle Watts, Terp was called forward to answer the ordination questions. Following her affirmative responses, she knelt on the chancel steps, and the moderator invited all Christian ministers to come forward for the laying on of hands. Ordinarily, in the American Calvinist Church, only ministers of that denomination were invited to participate in this part of the service. But the moderator for Terp's ordination was a committed ecumenist, and on the spur of the moment, he extended the invitation to all ministers regardless of denominational affiliation.

A dozen Calvinist ministers gathered around Terp, placing their hands on her head and shoulders. Adam, Evelyn, and Kwan-yin came forward also. The moderator opened his mouth to pray and his eyes fell on Darla. "Rabbi," he said, "My prayer for Terp is one that Jews and Christians can affirm together. Given the special relationship between your congregation and this one, we would be honored if you would join the other clergy here." He left it open for Darla to decide if she would lay hands on Terp or simply stand with the others.

Darla came forward, squeezed in between Adam and Argyle, and placed her hand on the side of Terp's head.

As the moderator prayed, Cochise circled unobtrusively, noiselessly taking a series of photographs. He found one angle at which Terp's head was visible and made several quick shots. When the moderator concluded his prayer, the mass of clergy separated, revealing Terp lifting her head. Her eyes glowed with spiritual energy. Cochise captured this moment as well.

At the end of the service, the Reverend Terp Morgan stepped forward to pronounce the benediction. Her words were simple but her voice was powerful, and all assembled in the sanctuary knew they had been blessed by the prayer of this woman.

During the reception, Cedar Cradle sidled up to Terp and whispered, "I saw the gold aura around your head."

Terp gave Argyle a prolonged hug, thanking him profusely all the while her arms were wrapped around his body. "I owe this day to you," she said.

"I think you owe it to God," he said. "But I am so grateful to have been a part of this occasion. Would you mind sending me a photo of it when you get the chance?"

"Yes, of course," promised Terp.

Lloyd and Nissa took Argyle and Ruth to their home that night, because they had an early flight from Sky Harbor the next morning.

Skye did not return to Phoenix but elected to stay the night at Strange Haven. He and Mary shared the bedroom recently occupied by Argyle and Ruth. Randall and Penny moved into the main house, taking over the fourth bedroom. The tension from the night before disappeared with the clothing everyone shed.

Terp spread old blankets on the floor of the studio and the four couples held a reflexology party before going off to their respective rooms. Even so, there was a bedroom available, because Firstlaugh and Cedar Cradle joined Cloud and Terp in their king size bed, where they put their hands on Terp's belly to feel the baby kick.

Cofflynn invited Narcissa to sit beside him on the chancel for the Sunday morning service. During his sermon, he introduced her to the congregation as the ideal model of virtuous womanhood. He said nothing of marriage, however, either to Narcissa in private or to the congregation.

"Sister Narcissa," he announced, "is well known to some of you in the Arms for Jesus organization. I want you all to know how impressed I have been with her Christian modesty and self-control. I intend to have her sit with me during sacred worship as a reminder to all women present that holy chastity is a worthy and achievable goal."

Narcissa soon became a celebrity within the anti-communist community in Central Arizona, and she loved this spotlight that Cofflynn had created for her. She came to depend on the praise of ordinary church members as well as high officials in the network of patriotic organizations. Some observers might conclude she was addicted to this attention, but Narcissa had no doubts she was entitled to public approbation.

Every once in a while in the middle of the night, she experienced a terrible dream in which she sat naked in her chancel chair while Cofflynn announced a long litany of her past indiscretions. She awoke from this nightmare feeling rage against the unidentified villain who had stooped so low as to expose her and threaten her rightful place of honor in the community.

Lloyd and Nissa had a delightful talk with Argyle and Ruth on the drive to Paradise Valley, a great deal of which was in praise of Cloud and Terp. Once home, Argyle joined Lloyd in the living room for a nightcap, while Ruth and Nissa retreated to the kitchen for a private conversation.

"At the wedding in Metuchen, we were talking about your

church," Ruth said, "but we were interrupted. I seem to remember something about total immersion baptism, but I have the sense there was something else important you didn't get a chance to tell me."

Despite previous misgivings, Nissa had an intuitive sense she could confide in Ruth without threatening Terp's position with the American Calvinist Church. "Something very important, actually. Members of the Natural Christian Church worship in the nude."

"Really?" Ruth said. This was something she had not anticipated. "Even the minister?"

"Everybody -most of the time. The services are officially clothing optional, and once in a while a newcomer will stay dressed. But that's rare," Nissa answered. "In cold weather people wear sweats and the like."

"I must admit this is a novel concept for me. I'm not a prude, but it seems a bit naughty to sit in church in the all together."

"God knows what we look like without our clothes," Nissa said. "Would you like to see some of our literature? I can give you a pamphlet to take home with you."

"Alright," said Ruth conspiratorially. "By the way, have Terp and Cloud attended your church?"

"Yes," said Nissa without elaboration.

"I think I'll not mention this to Argyle," Ruth said with a note of wistfulness. "At least not right away."

Early in August, Cloud was offered a tenure-track position as assistant professor of history at Anasazi College in Sedona. This meant a round trip commute of one hundred twenty miles the four days each week he would be expected to be on campus, but Cloud was not daunted by time on the road. His only hesitation related to the temporary circumstance that he might be at the school when Terp went into labor and would miss the delivery. Terp assured him that when the time came she would be in labor many hours, and he would have plenty of time to get to the hospital from Sedona.

With both of them working, they now needed two cars, so they went shopping and came home with a dark blue Volvo station wagon.

"It's plain, boxy, and utilitarian but much safer and roomier for a growing family than the VW," said Terp, who would be the car's primary driver.

This proved to be a summer of transitions, because Firstlaugh was invited to be Director of the Native American Educational Outreach Program at Northern Arizona University in Flagstaff. NAU was Firstlaugh's alma mater, although the institution had been Arizona State College at Flagstaff when he enrolled there in 1961. The Begay family moved to Flagstaff. As a result, the Begays and the Morgans lived much closer than they had in the past and thus were able to spend more time together.

Cochise mailed Terp a thick packet of photos from her ordination service. They were all good, but among them were two stellar pictures. Knowing that others would want copies of these two, Cochise generously included five prints of each. The first special photograph showed Terp from the back, with her head bowed and covered with hands. A mysterious radiance showed around the outlines of the hands.

The second noteworthy photo was of Terp raising her head as the clergy who had laid hands on her stepped aside. Her eyes shone with wild intensity, and a bright aura surrounded her head.

Cochise included a note, which said, "None of these have been retouched. This is what the film actually recorded."

Terp remembered her promise to send an ordination photo to Argyle. "I think I'll send him one of these other ones," she said to Cloud.

"He would want both of these," said Cloud, pointing to the shots with multiple prints.

"But they are so intimate, and...misleading," Terp said. "They make me look like some kind of holy person. I don't want anybody thinking I'm trying to come off as a saint or something."

"I will admit these are similar to the painting Mary did of you and me. They're not for everybody's eyes," Cloud said. "But Argyle should see them. You can trust him with these images."

Terp conceded the point and mailed the two photographs to Argyle Watts, with a note that said Cloud had encouraged her to send these particular shots.

When Argyle looked at the photos, he understood both Terp's reluctance and Cloud's desire for him to see them. As Cloud had predicted, Argyle decided to file them away in his desk drawer, although he did show them to Ruth first.

Five faculty members stopped by Cloud's office to welcome him his first day at the school. College President Magnus Bergen visited, soon followed by assistant professor of political science Prasada Pratyaksha, and associate professor of religion Mito Picaron. Picaron was a Yaqui Indian and a former Catholic priest married to a former nun. Later in the day, Emily Congo, associate professor of women's studies and black history visited with her husband, Bookman Donne, professor of English.

So, Cloud mused to himself, the first colleagues to extend friendship to the new guy are a white man of Norwegian ancestry, an East Indian woman, a Mexican Indian man, and a black married couple. He liked the eclectic mix and was therefore in an optimistic mood when he arrived home late that day.

Anasazi College rose from the ferment of 1960s idealism. The hallmark of the institution was interdisciplinary learning. The guiding assumption was that every subject, whether practical or theoretical, was related to everything else, and the faculty worked hard at integrating their specialties with those of their colleagues. No specific courses were mandated for graduation, and students were encouraged to explore their personal interests by arranging independent studies with faculty members of their choice. The baseline requirement was that students must study with a minimum of fourteen different professors over four years to qualify for a bachelor's degree.

Because of his long experience as a hiker, Cloud was immediately tapped by President Bergen to head the new wilderness ecology program, which combined classroom study of environmental issues with field explorations of the natural world. The fact that his academic expertise was Asian history was another matter. He would also offer courses and independent studies in this area.

Hearkening back to an epiphany he experienced as an undergraduate, where he saw in a vision the inter-relatedness of all learning, Cloud had no difficulty understanding the relevance of nature walks to the caste structure of India or the population of endangered species in Oak Creek Canyon to the Analects of Confucius.

Bergen gave Cloud autonomy to develop the program any way he liked, although the president suggested Cloud could benefit from coordination with Bookman Donne and Emily Congo, who jointly led the mountaineering program.

Cloud need not have worried about being away from home when Terp went into labor. They were curled up together on a Thursday night, catching up on the events of their respective days when the first contractions came.

"It's time to pack up a few things for a visit to the hospital," Terp said calmly.

With unhurried motions, they gathered what they would need and walked out to the station wagon.

Cloud stayed with Terp in the labor room through the long night. For the first few hours they chatted and played word games to pass the time. They tried to outdo one another with atrocious puns but had to stop because the laughter interfered with Terp's breathing.

Approaching four in the morning, Terp's contractions increased markedly but she was not sufficiently dilated for delivery. Two more hours passed before she was wheeled into the delivery room. Cloud stood by Terp's side, cradling her sweat-drenched head with his hands. Precisely at sunrise on October seventh, the baby's head emerged. A moment passed before the doctor announced, "It's a girl!"

Two days later, Cloud drove to the hospital to bring Terp and their daughter, Zara Person Morgan, home. Terp sat in a wheelchair with Zara in her arms as Cloud maneuvered them down the corridor and out to the entrance and into their car.

Nissa greeted them at the back door when they arrived at Strange Haven. She would stay with Terp for a few weeks to help with Zara's care.

"I never had a baby of my own," Nissa said. "I wanted children in the worst way, but Onan was incapable, and by the time I married Lloyd, I was past my prime."

"I suspect, Nissa," said Cloud, "that you will have an eager outlet for your maternal instincts with your granddaughter Zara."

"Oh, I like the sound of that," Nissa said. "I know I'm not a blood relation, but would it be OK if she called me grandma when she gets older?"

"You are one of Zara's grandmothers in every way that counts," said Terp. "Love is thicker than blood. We have no step relatives in this house."

The congregation granted Terp four weeks maternity leave, and Cloud volunteered to fill the pulpit during that time. The elders were pleased that they would not incur any expenses for supply preachers, and the members liked his preaching well enough, particularly his in-depth historical narratives. Still, they missed Terp's more personal and engaging style.

Following the service the second time that Cloud preached, a parishioner shook his hand and said, "That was a really interesting sermon, but very intellectual. It made me think too hard."

"If the sermon made you think," Cloud replied, "I take that as a high compliment. That's what sermons are supposed to do."

"Well yeah, you're pretty good with words, but my poor brain is overheated," the man said with a chuckle. "I have to go home now and watch cartoons or something to cool it down."

Revealing a British accent, the man next in the greeting line quipped, "Maybe what you need is a cold shower. Apparently all that Ancient Near East fertility goddess information in the sermon has affected more than your brain."

All three men laughed and the parishioner with the hot brain moved on.

"We haven't formally met. I'm John Wickham," said the Englishman as he grasped Cloud's outstretched hand.

"I know who you are," said Cloud brightly. "You teach anthropology at Prescott College. I'd like to get together with you sometime to compare impressions about the existential realities of life in academia."

"Wonderful idea," said John. "For the moment, however, others are waiting patiently to greet you. Fine sermon. You know your stuff."

Reflecting on the overheated brain comment later that afternoon, Cloud decided that he should work on making his sermons more accessible to the average person in the pew. But then again, he mused, he would be filling in for Terp only on rare occasions, so learning homiletics was probably not a good use of his time. A vivid image of something he had seen right after graduating from high school emerged into consciousness. On the way to Tuba City, he had driven by a large rock that looked like a pulpit, and in a vision he saw himself preaching there. At the time he had considered the idea absurd. But now he had done it more than once.

"Well, I guess I can cross that off my list of unfulfilled visions," he said.

Mary called Terp late in October with a proposition. She was ensconced in a loft in Greenwich Village, trying to make a living as a painter, but the life of a starving artist was not as romantic as reported. In reality, she had a comfortable income from her father's trust fund but was lonely. She offered to be a live-in nanny for Zara in exchange for room and board and the use of the studio for painting.

Terp loved the idea. Doing full-time ministry and caring for Zara would be complicated, even with Cloud's flexible schedule, so having her sister in the house would be a blessing. Mary moved into Strange Haven the day before Terp returned to work.

With three adults tending to Zara's needs, each had time to attend to their callings. Mary set up a crib in the warm and sunny studio and painted while Zara slept. She delighted in the clothing optional ethos of Strange Haven and did most of her artwork in the nude. Zara became a favorite model.

The Board of Elders of First Calvinist Church set Sunday November twenty-seventh as the date for Zara's baptism. Terp preached a sermon that day in which she described the sacramental practices of the early Christian church. "In those days," she said, "people desiring membership in the church stepped forward naked and after baptism by immersion were clothed in white robes."

When the time came for Zara to receive the sacrament, Cloud brought his naked daughter to the font. Mary, Lloyd, and Nissa stood beside him. An elder read the baptismal questions, which Terp and Cloud answered on behalf of Zara. Then Terp took her daughter in her arms and announced, "Zara Person Morgan, I baptize you in the name of the Father..." She poured a handful of water over the baby's head "...and the Son..." She scooped up more water and let it flow over her daughter. "...and the Holy Spirit." A third liberal application of water followed.

Terp placed her hand on Zara's head and prayed for God's blessing in the child's life. She then anointed the child with oil, making the sign of the cross with her finger on Zara's forehead. During the entire rite, Zara calmly cooed with pleasure. Mary handed Cloud a towel to dry Zara, and Nissa brought forth the white gown.

Cedar Cradle said, "I saw a violet aura around Zara's body during the baptism."

"You see auras around everyone, Cedar Cradle," said Cloud.

"Well, everybody has one," Cedar Cradle said, "but not violet. That's a sign of intellect and psychic power."

Tzek said, "I want Aunt Terp to pour water on me too!"

"Maybe someday she will," Firstlaugh said.

By the end of the day, it was clear that most members of the congregation loved the naked baptism, but a few were scandalized by it. Hortense Bowdler, the matriarch of the congregation, huffed and puffed in indignation. "We can't allow such a precedent here. What's going to happen when some teenager demands to be sprinkled with no clothes on?" she said to one of the elders.

"Probably a record attendance that day," quipped the elder.

Mrs. Bowdler did not appreciate the humor.

With all the publicity Narcissa was receiving, it seemed inevitable that someone would say something to Cofflynn about her past. It was not her past, however, but her present that caught up with her. The husband of one of Narcissa's patriotic beauty supply clients told McCarthy about the see-thru panties with a strategically placed American flag that Narcissa had sold to his wife. He didn't report this to get Narcissa in trouble but rather to boast a little about the extent of his wife's patriotism.

Cofflynn blanched with embarrassment but from years of practice held his face in stoic stillness, saying nothing to the parishioner. Later when he and Narcissa were alone, he flew into a rage.

"How dare you sell such filth!" he yelled. "I am loath to ask this but am compelled to do so by circumstance. Do you place such vile garments on yourself?"

"There's nothing vile about the American flag, Cofflynn," Narcissa shot back.

"But placing it on unmentionables that touch shameful parts of the body is a sacrilege." Recalling his Grandmother Le Fay's oft-repeated dictum, he added, "The freedom our flag stands for has nothing to do with sex!"

"For the record," Narcissa said, "I have never worn those kind of panties myself, but they're a popular item, and I make a 50% commission on them. That's American capitalism in action."

"But this is scandalous!" Cofflynn continued. "Sister Narcissa I order you to divest yourself of this Ladies' Patriotic Beauty Society business immediately! I must never again be embarrassed by stories of you purveying...sex paraphernalia."

"But Cofflynn, it's currently my only source of income," she said.

"You don't need an income, my dear. I shall provide for your needs. You will depend on my generosity," he said.

As much as she loved the limelight Cofflynn made possible for her, she knew that becoming financially dependent on him would take away the last shred of independence she enjoyed. "Let me pray about it," she said.

"Pray, then," he said, "but I am certain God wants you to give up selling whores' garments to decent women."

Now that his suspicions had been aroused, Cofflynn's innate paranoia led him to engage a private detective to look into Narcissa's background. Two weeks later he had a thick dossier on his desk that outlined Narcissa's involvement with the Arizona Past Lives Association and a spin-off group called the Northern Arizona Trans-Solar Alien Service Society. The former organization was thought to dabble in the occult, the report noted, and the latter was suspected of practicing bizarre sexual rituals.

The detective, who had worked fast so he could carve out time for an extra-marital affair, decided he'd gathered enough to satisfy his client and justify his large fee. "There's plenty of red meat here for the carnivorous preacher," he mused as he typed his report. Thus he failed to delve further into Narcissa's past, depriving Cofflynn of any intelligence about Narcissa's foray into naturism.

Cofflynn telephoned Narcissa. "I have two acronyms to share with you, my dear," he said smoothly. He paused for dramatic effect then spoke, "APLA and NAT-SASS."

Narcissa went cold inside. "How did you..."

"Good-bye, Narcissa. I had such high hopes for you, but you have betrayed my generosity and trust. If you ever set foot on my church property again, I shall personally...see to...your...everlasting fate."

"But Cofflynn, let me expl..."

The line went dead.

The following Sunday, Cofflynn explained Narcissa's absence from her seat of honor on the chancel in a way everyone present could understand. "Sister Narcissa broke down and confessed to me recently that she had a youthful fling with satanic rituals. She has long since renounced the vile practices but is filled with remorse at withholding this vital information from me, and more importantly, from the congregation. She said she needs time away from church to atone for her malignant misadventures. She is, at present, too ashamed to show her face. I do not know when she will return to our fellowship, if ever."

CHAPTER TWENTY-THREE

Cloud had dutifully called his mother to tell her about Zara's birth on October seventh. Narcissa congratulated her son but seemed uninterested in the event. In fact she was not as indifferent as she sounded. She cringed when Cloud used the word grandmother, for this was an epithet she did not wish to be associated with, but he could not see this through the telephone wire. As a consequence of this awkward phone conversation, Cloud did not invite his mother to Zara's baptism.

After Cofflynn banished Narcissa, she went into depression. Days passed in which she neither showered nor dressed. She sat naked in her living room and drank Bourbon. Occasionally she would switch on the television and watch game shows as a distraction from her misery. Mostly, however, Narcissa wallowed in self-pity.

Halfway through December, she sat drunk on her sofa at two in the morning, brooding about all the unfairness she had endured in life, and the notion entered her mind that Cloud had deprived her of seeing her granddaughter. This was the final insult from an ungrateful son who clearly took after his father.

"I'll bet that kid's surrounded by Lloyd and that hussy he's married to," she mumbled to herself, not recognizing how slurred her words were. "They just shove me aside like a piece of junk."

Narcissa got so steamed up that she looked up Cloud's number in her address book and clumsily but accurately dialed it.

The ringing woke Cloud out of a sound sleep. "Hullo," he muttered into the receiver. He looked at the clock and realized that it must be an emergency call. Perhaps one of Terp's parishioners. Ministers often receive calls in the middle of the night when someone is dying or some tragic event has occurred.

"Cloud, thish your mother," Narcissa said forcefully but not crisply.

"What's happened, Mother? Are you alright?"

"No, I'm not awright," she said. "I wanna see my granchile right now!"

Cloud put his hand over the mouthpiece and turned to Terp. "It's my mother," he whispered. "She sounds drunk, and she wants to see Zara."

"Invite her up Saturday," Terp said. "Maybe this will soften her heart."

"Mother," said Cloud, "why don't you drive up on Saturday. We can have lunch together and you can play with Zara."

"I'll have to check my book," said Narcissa. She had no book with her. "Yes, I can do that. I'll shee you there around 'leven."

She arrived on time and sober, and having overthrown Cofflynn McCarthy's fashion mandates, sporting a frilly red hostess gown, jade earrings, a three strand pearl necklace, gold bracelets on each wrist, and zirconium rings on both middle fingers.

Cloud and Terp were dressed alike, wearing blue jeans and gray sweatshirts. They escorted Narcissa to the parlor, where Zara was lying in a portable crib.

"Well, here she is," Terp said. "Isn't she beautiful?"

"Why indeed she is," said Narcissa with a sugary voice. "She reminds me of baby pictures of myself." She pushed a finger into Zara's stomach. "Hi there, little one. I'm your mommy Narcissa."

"Waaaa," cried the baby.

"Feeding time," Terp said. "Have a chair, Narcissa, and we can talk while I tend to Zara." Terp pulled off her sweatshirt and picked up the baby. Sitting on the couch, Terp placed Zara on her left breast.

"What's new in your life, Mother?" Cloud asked.

"Oh, the same old thing. The beauty business is doing very well. Patriotism never goes out of style."

Cloud noted mentally that she made no mention of her gentleman caller and felt intuitively he should not ask about Cofflynn. The conversation wandered instead into comparisons between the weather in Phoenix and Prescott. Zara, having switched breasts, had her fill of milk. Burping in pleasant satisfaction, she promptly fell asleep, and Terp put her back in the crib.

Narcissa sniffed at a cushion on the couch and grimaced. "I haven't seen this style of furnishings since before the Second World War," she said. "I presume you have a plan to redecorate."

"The house is leased, and the furniture came with it," Cloud said.

"Well, aren't you going to show me the rest of the house?" Narcissa asked.

"Why don't you do that, Cloud, while I see about lunch," Terp said. She wheeled the crib into the kitchen.

Cloud showed his mother the kitchen and pantry, then doubled back through the dining room and into the library. From there they went to the studio.

"Terp's sister Mary is staying with us as a nanny," Cloud explained. "She's an artist, so she uses this room for a studio. He opened the door. "Mary, meet my mother."

Mary was standing naked in front of an easel with a large canvas on it. "Hello Mrs. Morgan. It's nice to meet you." She lifted her right hand in the air. "I'd shake hands with you, but I've got oil paint all over mine."

"Lunch in a few minutes, if you're close to a stopping place," Cloud said to Mary. "Otherwise you'll have to fend for yourself."

"I'll clean up and be right there," she said.

Terp set out a meal of tuna salad, a selection of cheeses, and mixed fruit slices. Mary sat at the table without clothes, Terp topless, Cloud in sweatshirt and jeans, and Narcissa fully dressed and bejeweled.

"I see you're rather casual about attire around here," Narcissa said.

"I remember when you used to be rather casual too, Mother," Cloud said.

"Those days are gone forever," Narcissa said with a cheerless sigh.

"They don't have to be," said Terp. "We have friends much older than you who still enjoy running around naked."

Narcissa felt insulted to be reminded of her age but said nothing.

Mary cleared away the remains of lunch.

"I suppose I had better be going soon," said Narcissa.

"Would you like a foot massage before you get on the road?" Terp asked. "It'll make you mellow for your tangle with traffic."

"That's a great idea, Mother. Come into the studio for a reflexology session."

The prospect of a massage appealed greatly to Narcissa, but she mentally calculated that accepting would leave her beholden to Cloud and Terp in some way. It never occurred to her that Terp and Cloud saw this as a gift with no strings. "Thank you, anyway," she said. "But I really must be going. I have a busy schedule ahead of me."

All the way back to Phoenix, Narcissa brooded about the conspiracy in her family to deprive her of love and affection. Lloyd was no doubt the ringleader, she thought.

After vetoing Terp's request to start a liturgical dance choir, the Board of Elders approved a seemingly less controversial consolation prize of allowing Terp to conduct Wednesday evening healing services beginning January 4, 1978. As she had done in New River and Cairns, these services included scripture readings, prayer, and anointing with oil. A core group quickly became regulars, frequently inviting friends from outside the congregation who were suffering in various ways.

Hortense Bowdler was distressed by this development and communicated her displeasure to dozens of parishioners, although not directly to Terp. "Popish practices don't belong in Calvinist churches," she said repeatedly to everyone she met.

Mrs. Bowdler gained little support for her position, however, until Terp gave her the ammunition she needed. One Wednesday, Terp invited Cedar Cradle to offer prayers for anxious people while massaging their necks and shoulders.

Although she personally found the massages offensive, Hortense knew she would get no traction from complaining about them. But Terp had provided her a huge opening by inviting a non-Christian to pray in church. This was an issue she could gain headway with. "Our ultra-liberal minister has gone too far by having a pagan Indian pray within the sanctified space of our church," she reported to every member of the Board of Elders. "This heresy must be stopped!"

"How do you know she's a pagan?" one elder asked.

"I have it on good authority from someone who was there that the Indian announced to everyone that she followed the Lakota spiritual path. Not only that, she burned sage to make smoke and fanned it in people's faces. That sounds disgustingly pagan to me," Hortense said.

As a result, Cedar Cradle became the major topic of discussion at the next Board of Elders meeting.

"I hate to admit it," said one elder, "but Mrs. Bowdler has a point. We can't allow non-Christians to pray in Calvinist church services."

"Why not?" asked Terp. "The moderator of the presbytery invited Rabbi Nabi to lay hands on me at my ordination. She's certainly not Christian."

"Yes, Pastor Terp," said another elder, "but Judaism is a recognized religion, and they're our ancestors in the faith."

"Cedar Cradle is my dearest friend, and Darla and I have become very close over the last six months, and the fact is," said Terp, "regardless of her official church affiliation, Cedar Cradle's religious beliefs are closer to Christianity than Darla's. Cedar Cradle honors the healing power of the Christ."

"What about this smoke business?" an elder asked.

"Many Christian churches use incense in worship. This is no different from that," Terp explained.

"But our tradition doesn't do that, does it?" the elder asked. "Didn't we dispense with all that priestly business in the Protestant Reformation?"

"We have an acolyte who lights the Christ candle every Sunday morning. That candle is scented and makes smoke. Betty, your daughter is an acolyte. Should we discontinue the acolytes?"

"No," said Betty. "My daughter loves lighting the candle at the beginning of the service. She says it makes her feel closer to God."

"Pastor Terp is right, and we need to back her up about the healing services," said the elder who had spoken first. "But for the sake of peace in the church, we need to have a policy that from now on only baptized members of a Protestant church are allowed to participate in worship at First Calvinist. That'll keep Mrs. Bowdler quiet."

"That's a good plan," said another elder.

"I disagree," said Terp. "It will only embolden Hortense to find more things to complain about. And what will happen when it's our turn to host the community Thanksgiving service? Will I have to inform Rabbi Nabi and Father Jones and Elder Stake from the Mormon Church that they're not allowed to offer prayers?"

"OK," said the first elder. "Let's make it only baptized Christians."

"Are you including Mormons in that category?" asked Terp.

"I'm not sure," the elder said.

"And what about Quakers?"

"Well, of course Quakers are included," the elder said confidently." They're a respected Christian denomination."

"Quakers don't practice the sacraments," said Terp, "so they aren't baptized."

"You're making this more complicated than it needs to be, Pastor Terp," the elder said. "We have to do ***something*** to get Mrs. Bowdler off our backs."

Betty said, "I make a motion that we reaffirm the Wednesday evening services as an experimental ministry of First Calvinist, but we also commit to make no changes in our traditional Sunday morning services."

"Second," said the first elder.

"Discussion?" asked Terp in her role as moderator of the board.

The chair of the worship committee said, "How long will that be with no changes on Sunday morning? My committee has been studying some things, like the choir processing in once in a while and different ways of doing communion."

"I withdraw my motion," said Betty.

"I make a motion that we thank Mrs. Bowdler for her concern about the healing service and assure her that in the future only people known to be Christian will take part in leading it," said the first elder. "That ought to placate her for a while."

"Second," said another elder.

The board members debated this motion for half an hour and then passed it by a six to three vote.

"I am furious," Terp barked to Cloud later that evening. "They say they support my ministry but they cow tow to that...that narrow-minded...bitch!"

"They're not as strong as you, Terp," said Cloud, "and they'll have to live with Hortense Bowdler for a long time after your tenure here has ended."

"Do you think they're right?" she asked.

"No," said Cloud. "But most people try to avoid conflict. It's your job to help the elders find the courage to face problems head-on. You have three strong elders already. Work on building up any of the others who show potential for growth."

At the next Anasazi faculty meeting, Cloud discovered that his colleagues were more divided than the Board of First Calvinist Church, and less constrained by any religious impulse toward decorous speech. At issue was the creation of a gender studies program.

"I'd like to appoint Emily Congo and Prasada Pratyaksha to develop and co-direct a curriculum that explores gender identity and sexual orientation," said Magnus Bergen.

"With all due respect," said Mito Picaron, "we have too many specialized programs now. Rather than integrating our studies according to our educational mission, we continue to spin out finer and finer specializations."

"Gender studies will attract additional students," Magnus said.

"Certainly," said Mito, "if we want to attract young people who are confused about their sexual urges. We could develop a program in foot fetishes too, and draw a splendid batch of compulsives who'd integrate math and history with their toes."

"I'm not opposed to establishing the program," said the mathematics professor, "but it ought to be directed by someone other than radical feminists with their anti-male agenda. A male scientist is needed for objective balance."

"Feminists they may be," said the professor of sociology with a note of scorn, "but they're both married women, so they must not hate ***all*** men."

"I resent the personal attacks on the integrity of my wife and Prasada," said Bookman Donne.

"The issue is most assuredly not their integrity," said the math professor, "but the agenda they would bring to such a discipline. Gender studies requires scientific dispassion that these women professors, however well-intentioned and however accomplished they may be in their specific fields, would find a difficult task."

"With all due respect," Bookman said, "my esteemed mathematics colleague has spoken what we in the English department would place in the genre of bullshit."

"Let me remind you all," said Magnus, "that personal attacks have no place in our community of scholars. This is an experimental college, and most of our students have come here because of our openness to new areas of inquiry. Every member of the faculty would place himself or herself -however tentatively- in the progressive camp."

"It has been well documented," said the professor of geology, "that a significant plurality among the students matriculated at Anasazi have come here, at least in part, because they believe Sedona to be the physical locus of so-called spiritual energy. In this they display gross ignorance, yet their tuition pays our salaries, and we in turn have the obligation to help them grow out of their primitive mythology."

Emily Congo turned to Cloud, who was sitting to her right, and whispered, "Welcome to Vortex U."

"I think I do a decent job of transforming them from superstitious innocents into disillusioned existentialists," said the professor of philosophy.

"So good that I'm treating half of them for clinical depression," quipped the psychology professor.

"Let me remind you the subject at hand is gender studies," said Magnus Bergen.

"The real subject," Cloud said, "is whether we trust the judgment of our president. No one is always right about everything, so our advice is important. But it's his job to evaluate leadership, and I propose we let him do that."

By voice vote, the faculty approved the president's proposal. By unspoken agreement, they recognized that the newest professor, Cloud Morgan, had aligned himself with the Congo-Donne faction.

Rex Fisher's female co-host on the Arizona Afternoon television talk show resigned, Rex informed the viewing audience, because she wanted to devote more time to her family. The reason she gave to the station manager for her decision to quit was frustration with Rex's repeated sexual overtures.

"Just tell him no and forget about it," the manager said.

"I've told him no at least fifty times and he hasn't got the message."

"Well, my dear, Rex gets more fan mail than anyone at the station, so if you can't handle his playfulness, I won't stand in the way of your departure," the manager said.

In March, Dagmar Solbrent was tapped as Rex's fifth female co-host of Arizona Afternoon. Though she took Queensbury as her last name when she married Quinn, she used her maiden name professionally.

The first three weeks on the job, Rex behaved himself and did not proposition Dagmar. At the beginning of the fourth week, however, he let himself into Dagmar's dressing room thirty minutes before airtime. At that moment, Dagmar was clad in bra and panties, contemplating which among the five outfits for the week she should wear for this day's broadcast.

Prior to marrying Quinn, Dagmar had not been in the habit of wearing undergarments, but Edna Echo had urged her to get beyond associating underwear with her father's abuse, and she had come to treasure the gentle and loving way her husband helped her out of them. Being a naturist, Dagmar was not shy about her body, but she did not appreciate the unannounced intrusion.

"Don't you know how to knock, Rex?" she said.

"Stars don't have to knock," he said. "I just stopped by to ask a question."

"Yes?" said Dagmar impatiently.

"Did you have to put out for that Sleekbody guy?"

Dagmar's first impulse was to slap Rex, but her quick intellect led her to a different response. "Sure," she said casually, "and we filmed it.

Would you like to watch the movie?"

Dagmar's response had been made so artfully that Rex believed her. "I'm always up for a stag film," he said. "Why don't you slip it to me some time."

"It's at home. I'll see that you get it soon," she said. "Now if you'll excuse me, I have work to do." She ushered him out and locked the door.

Dagmar mailed a reel of film to Rex's home. His wife handed him the package when he walked in the door.

"What's this?" she asked. "It's addressed in green letters."

"Oh, probably some promo from somebody who wants free publicity," he said coolly. He recognized the color of Dagmar's fountain pen ink.

"It's odd they would send it to your home address," she said. "Open it. I'm curious."

Rex's hands trembled slightly as he ripped open the envelope. The sixteen-millimeter reel bore a label with "Dagmar's Picnic" hand-printed on it. "Oh, a gag gift from my new co-host," he joked.

A postcard fell from the wrapping. Printed on the back was: "Rex, dear, here's the private movie you asked to see. D."

"Let me in on the gag," his wife said.

Reluctantly, Rex fed the film into the projector in his den. He dreaded his wife's reaction to the pornographic images that would soon appear on the screen. Then it occurred to him that he wouldn't be in the movie. He could dismiss the whole thing as a sick joke.

A scene flickered before them. The Sleekbody dealer stood on a secluded porch and embraced Dagmar. He then stepped to the right, leaned over and took the outstretched hand of Quinn Queensbury.

Oooh, thought Rex, it's a threesome with her husband. Damn! I wish my wife would go away so I could watch this alone. I wonder how long it will be before they start taking off their clothes?

Next, the wife of the trailer dealer stepped into view and greeted Dagmar and Quinn. She was an attractive woman in her late forties, a few years younger than her husband.

Even better, Rex thought.

The film continued with scenes of a picnic table laden with food, the two couples eating, Frisbee tossing on the lawn, Quinn playing with a Chihuahua in his lap, and a concluding shot of Quinn with an American flag flying from his wheelchair. The dealer stepped into view wearing his American Legion cap and saluted the flag.

Dagmar invited Rex into her dressing room the next day.

"Very funny," he said to her.

"Well, you asked me if I put out for him that day you barged in here ogling my underwear. I thought the film was erotic, not funny," Dagmar said.

"I wasn't ogling. I was appreciating fine flesh. One of the perks of this job is checking out the curves of my co-hosts. And since they keep changing, I never get bored with the same old bodies. Anyway, there's nothing erotic about saluting the flag," Rex responded.

"Uh oh!" Dagmar said. "Did the label have the title in quotation marks or underlined?" she asked.

"Quotes," Rex said.

"I'm sorry, Rex. I sent you the wrong reel. I'll get you the one you want tomorrow," she said.

"Don't mail it to my house! I don't want my wife to see it. Just slip it to me here at the station," he instructed. "Maybe you and I can make a film someday. I have a very photogenic pecker."

She ignored his directions, however, and mailed the reel to Mr. And Mrs. Rex Fisher at his home address. His wife met him at the door holding the reel -which was smaller than the previous one- in her hand. "This came addressed to both of us, so I went ahead and opened it. Why would your co-host be sending you such things?"

"Have you looked at it?" Rex asked.

"No, I didn't look at it," she answered truthfully.

Rex breathed a sigh of relief. "It's just more of the same picnic stuff," he said. "She told me she would be sending it along. No need to waste time with it. It's sure to be as boring as the first one."

"Oh, it's not at all boring," his wife said.

"I thought you said you didn't look at it," Rex said.

"I didn't ***look*** at it," she said. "It's not film. It's a tape recording."

Rex turned pale.

"Apparently it was made in Dagmar's dressing room the day after the picnic movie arrived," she continued.

He said nothing.

"I've put up with your philandering for years, Rex. No more. Those days are over. One more episode and this tape goes to every station in town."

"Give me that!" he yelled and wrenched the reel out of her hand.

"Take it, Rex," she said calmly. "I made a copy and gave it to my lawyer."

"Your brother?" he asked.

"My brother," she said. "Convenient isn't it?"

Rex slumped into a chair, put his head in his hands, and wept.

Thereafter, Rex was the perfect gentleman around Dagmar, and as the months passed, the flow of fan mail for Dagmar steadily grew, eventually surpassing that of her co-host. After she interviewed her husband for a Memorial Day program, her popularity skyrocketed.

CHAPTER TWENTY-FOUR

They knew Zara was unusual. At six months she began saying words, such as dada and mama. At six months and one week, her vocabulary had progressed to include more than fifty nouns. At six and a half months, she added verbs and adjectives to her vocabulary and began speaking in complete sentences. They were simple sentences, to be sure. "Zara hungry." "Zara sleepy." "Zara want bath." "Mary fix bottle."

As the weeks passed, her mastery of language increased geometrically. "Zara see daddy kiss mommy." "Zara want daddy kiss." "I want mommy's milk." "Change my diaper." "Rub my feet, please."

One evening in early June, when classes at the college were out for the summer, Cloud and Terp invited Darla and Yonah to dinner. Mary was away visiting Skye, so Cloud tended to Zara and chatted with Yonah, while Terp prepared the meal with assistance from Darla.

Zara said, "Daddy, I'm hungry."

Yonah was startled by the declaration from an infant.

"She's a little advanced," said Cloud. He carried his daughter to the kitchen, with Yonah following. "We'll watch the pots and pans for a while, so Zara can have her supper," Cloud said to Terp.

Terp and Darla went to the parlor, where Terp unbuttoned her blouse, unsnapped her bra, and put Zara to her right breast. When Zara finished nursing on both sides, Terp put her down for a nap. "She should sleep through dinner," she said to Darla. Terp buttoned up and the women traded places with the men.

After supper, the two couples returned to the parlor to talk at leisure about personal dynamics in their respective congregations. Darla had a matriarch very much like Hortense Bowdler. The clergywomen swapped stories about their problem parishioners, laughing therapeutically in the process.

Zara's portable crib was at the end of the sofa, and the laughter woke her. "Mommy laughs," Zara said. "She tells funny story."

"My stars!" said Darla. "That's amazing. I've never heard an infant speak like that at eight months."

Zara rolled over and sat up. "OK guys, time for foot rubs!" she said. "Me first!"

"What's that all about?" Yonah asked.

"We'll show you," said Cloud. "Follow us." He led them to the studio, where they had set up a reflexology area in one corner.

Terp, wearing mid-thigh khaki shorts, sat in a wicker chair and placed Zara supine along her legs, the baby's feet extending past her mother's knees. Cloud, also in khaki shorts, draped a towel over his legs and proceeded to massage his daughter's feet with an oily lotion.

"I like foot rubs," Zara announced.

Presently, Cloud said, "OK, who's next?"

"Oh no," said Yonah. "We couldn't ask you to do that for us."

"What's the name of the ancient rabbi who said God will hold us accountable for all the good pleasures we refused?" Cloud asked.

"He's right, Yonah," said his wife the rabbi. "We should accept their hospitality."

"Get your shoes and socks off, Yonah, and put your right foot up here," Cloud said. "And hike up your pant legs."

Yonah complied. Terp moved her chair around, pulled a towel across her knees, and lifted Yonah's left foot onto the towel. Soon he was deeply relaxed, savoring the wonderful sensations.

Then it was Darla's turn. As she was wearing Capri pants, no hiking up was needed. She, too, thoroughly enjoyed the tactile attention.

"I feel like we should somehow return the favor," Yonah said.

"You can do that, some time when you're dressed for it," Terp said.

"Where do you get the oil?" Darla asked.

Terp told her the name of the shop.

"Why don't you come to our cabin for dinner Sunday night? Dress casually and we'll rub your feet," Darla proposed.

Mary took care of Zara on Sunday. Cloud and Terp found the Nabi's cabin in the forest community of Walker. Although the word cabin seemed to fit the rough exterior of the house, it did not adequately convey the elegant luxury of the interior. The two-story home was tastefully decorated in Danish modern furniture, with Afghan carpets used as area rugs over portions of the hardwood floors.

After the meal, Yonah said, "We cleared an area in the living room for foot massages. Don't worry about oil on the floor." Yonah was dressed in red sweat pants and a faded souvenir tee shirt from a Simon and Garfunkel concert, while Darla wore cut-off jeans and a sleeveless gray sweatshirt. Based on the jiggling in front, Cloud deduced she was not wearing a bra.

Cloud and Terp came prepared for the evening to unfold in any number of possible ways. If the conversation should evolve in an authentic way toward naturism, they would talk about it openly, and even demonstrate it if the spirit moved in that direction. But they would not initiate the subject. They did not want to offend the sensibilities of these friends, especially since Darla and Terp were clergy colleagues sharing the same sanctuary. For the occasion, Terp wore a white cotton halter with short plaid culottes, and Cloud was clad in a purple polo shirt and khaki shorts.

Cloud went first, putting one foot in Yonah's lap and the other in Darla's. After a few minutes, Cloud said, "You guys are pretty good for never having done this before."

"We've been practicing on each other," Darla said.

Soon it was Terp's turn, and when they finished with her feet, it took very little toe twisting to convince the Nabis to let Cloud and Terp do their feet again. The evening ended without the subject of naturism arising and with no one removing any garments. The couples exchanged warm hugs on the porch before Cloud and Terp wended their way to town in the Volvo.

—o—

Near the end of June, Terp said, "Now that we have all this space, I think we should get a pet, and I vote for a puppy."

Mary and Cloud voted for a kitten. In the end, they compromised and brought home from the animal shelter a black and white Australian shepherd, a shorthaired white cat with black markings, and a shorthaired black cat with white markings, all three males. Terp named the dog Preacher, Cloud named the black cat Poet, and Mary named the white cat Painter. All proved to be affectionate creatures, although Poet became a skittish introvert whenever strangers visited.

As the summer ticked away, it became evident that the animals favored one human over all the others. Zara understood their languages, and they obeyed her instructions. Even the cats obeyed when Zara ordered them down from someone's lap, for example, or to come snuggle with her on the quilt on the floor. On more than one occasion, Zara fell asleep on the quilt with Preacher, Poet, and Painter wrapped in a circle around her.

The pets also favored Tzek and Wakhan over any of the adults, when the Begays came to visit. One Saturday evening, with Zara, Wakhan, and Tzek in the bathtub together, Preacher jumped up on the toilet and leaped into the tub with the children. Terp was in her room rehearsing her sermon at the time, so she did not hear the splash and shrieks and was spared the extensive cleanup that Mary and Cedar Cradle faced. Firstlaugh and Cloud were summoned to bring extra towels.

Before they arrived, however, Zara told Preacher to be still, and he obeyed. Thus it was easier for Firstlaugh to dry the dog than for any of the other adults to tend to their assigned children.

Later that night, after Terp had rehearsed thoroughly and the children were asleep, Cloud asked Mary to watch over things while the two couples went out for a while. The four went to the master bedroom and lay together on the large bed. Soon they were out of their bodies and floating around the house. Preacher barked and the cats hissed as they sailed overhead on their way to downtown Prescott. They hovered over the Whiskey Row area, observing the Saturday night crowd.

Drifting into a bar for a time, they formed a halo around the bartender's head and listened in as patrons unloaded their cares on the man behind the counter. The saloon-keeper provided sage advice. Most of his wise counsel consisted of phrases such as, "I know what you mean" and "what a bummer" and the best one of all, "hmmmmm?"

For a reason the bartender did not understand, during a brief period of time this night the customers seemed to be revealing more intimate problems to him and with greater honesty. They also seemed more relieved than usual with his verbal assurances.

As soon as the floaters left, life returned to normal in the bar and the tales of woe reflected a lesser level of insight.

They zoomed along Gurley Street for a time, levitating cigarettes out of teenagers' mouths, feeling like adolescents themselves engaging in practical jokes. "Even if only one of them is startled enough to quit smoking, it was worth the energy," Terp said.

The pets barked and hissed again when they came back into the house.

"Hush!" said Mary. "It's just the four strange angels returning to Strange Haven."

They reentered their bodies, tended to their teeth brushing and so forth, then climbed into bed and went to sleep.

The next morning, the Begay family attended First Calvinist Church, and Cedar Cradle deliberately sat in the back pew on the left where Hortense Bowdler always held court. During the time for parishioners to stand and greet one another, Cedar Cradle took Mrs. Bowdler's hand, looked into her eyes, and said, "The peace of Christ be with you."

"And also with you," the matriarch said ritually, but she averted her eyes when she spoke the words.

A letter from Alice Darwin arrived at the Morgan home in mid-July. Kuranda had married Nuoc in a quiet ceremony at the Queen's Paradise in February, and on July fourth, Kuranda gave birth to a daughter, Terp Alice Nguyen. Mother and child were doing well, and father was very proud. Alice was deeply touched by Kuranda's choice of a middle name for the baby and hoped Terp would be pleased, too, at having a child named after her.

Terp wept with joy at the affirmation. "The blood of four

continents flows in a child bearing my name," she said to Cloud. "What an honor!"

"What would the word for little Terp be?" asked Cloud. "Aboafricangloasian?"

"How about citizen of the world?" said Terp.

"I like that," Cloud responded.

Terp's terms of call included four weeks of vacation, and the Board of Elders made it clear that her maternity leave the previous fall did not count against this holiday time. The Morgan family began their holiday from First Calvinist the day after Alice's letter arrived. Cloud, Terp, Zara, Mary, Preacher, Poet, and Painter piled into the station wagon along with extensive luggage and gear. The days of simple living were over. Their destination was Paradise Valley, where the entourage would reside with Lloyd and Nissa for a few weeks. Nissa played grandma with abandon, and Lloyd took a turn as well.

The NCC was celebrating its twenty-fifth anniversary as a denomination that month. Adam, Evelyn, and Kwan-yin would lead a special joint service of the New River and Phoenix congregations, and Cloud and Terp were invited to participate in the weekend festivities at the camp.

Saturday evening, Terp and Evelyn led a healing and anointing service, which attracted an overflow crowd of fairly healthy people who were simply seeking a moment of transcendent bliss amid the busyness of their lives. No one was disappointed, as evidenced by the smiles and hugs afterward.

The next morning, Cloud taught the adult Sunday school class, providing a history of the denomination. "The Natural Christian Church began in a garden tended by Adam and Evelyn," he said. "They were naked and not ashamed -and they stayed that way! Scores of people came to this peaceful garden in the early years of the atomic age, and to other gardens throughout the great western states of North America." Having thus captured the attention of everyone in the room, Cloud delivered a ***tour de force*** lecture on the evolution of the church. When he finished, the class erupted in applause and cheers.

Cloud held Zara in his lap during the eleven o'clock service. Terp, Skye, Mary, Lloyd, Nissa, and Cochise filled the rest of the pew. During the pastoral prayer, Cloud fell into a trance and saw a vision of Cathedral Rock. This did not seem unusual, because he had gazed often at the colorful twin-spired formation near Sedona. Then eleven women appeared on the highest point of the left spire. They were dancing around the full moon, clothed only with rays of the sun and garlands of stars in their hair. He could see that they were all pregnant, and he perceived that they carried twelve babies among them.

Zara squirmed in his lap, bringing him out of his reverie in time to hear Kwan-yin pray for God's blessings upon all the children gathered in the sanctuary that day and upon all the children who had no sanctuaries to be safe in.

At dawn three days later, Cloud, Terp, Mary, and Lloyd began an ascent of Camelback Mountain. Nissa stayed home, preferring baby and pet sitting duty. As the morning temperature had not yet risen into the nineties, the climbers reached the summit without difficulty. Neither Terp nor Mary had been at the top of the hump before, and both enthused about the panoramic view of the Valley of the Sun.

After a few minutes of gazing, however, Mary turned to Cloud and said, "If I intuit your thoughts correctly, you and my sister have been conversing mentally about what fun it would be to float from this spot."

"You know us too well," said Cloud.

"Well, why don't you go ahead and do it. Lloyd and I will watch over your bodies in case any others show up," Mary said.

"There's a party of climbers about a quarter mile back," Terp said. "But still, Cloud, let's do it."

Once free of their bodies, Terp and Cloud sailed across to the camel's head. While hovering there, an inspiration rose between them, leading them to a quick return to the hump. Simultaneously, they nestled into Mary, radiating familial love throughout her body.

Mary jumped and moaned, "Oh! Oh my God! Oh my God!"

"What's wrong?" Lloyd shouted. "Are you alright?"

Before he could assess the situation, however, Cloud and Terp left Mary and nestled into his body, and he too responded with ecstatic exclamations in response to the sense of love permeating his anatomy. Terp and Cloud then reentered their bodies.

Upon leaving the summit, they passed a group of hikers who glanced at them quizzically. "Is the view really that spectacular?" one of them asked.

"Absolutely," said Lloyd with a wide smile.

Debriefing during their descent, Mary said, "What I felt up there was similar to the mystical sensation I sometimes get in the act of artistic creation, but this was way more intense."

When they reached home, Nissa wanted to hear about the outing. While Lloyd talked about the wonderful view, Terp and Cloud excused themselves. Two minutes later, they returned without their bodies and nestled into Nissa. Lloyd and Mary laughed when Nissa whooped for joy. As the loving sensation faded from Nissa, they all turned to Zara in her highchair and watched as the infant's face glowed with delight and she started giggling uncontrollably.

Back in Prescott with a week of vacation left, Terp and Cloud hosted an evening party at Strange Haven. The invitations noted in bold print that guests should dress in comfortable old clothes. Among the twelve adults present, only four did not know this meant a reflexology session would be part of the fun.

Those in the know, besides Terp and Cloud, were Mary and Skye, Firstlaugh and Cedar Cradle, and Darla and Yonah. Prasada and Darshan Pratyaksha had no idea why they were instructed to dress this way, and neither did Emily Congo and Bookman Donne, but they all complied.

The particular configuration of couples at Strange Haven that night created a field of energy that animated everyone. The eclectic mix of religions, races, professions, and temperaments led to spirited conversations among the entire group, atrocious puns from a few, and great laughter by all. They ate brownies, homemade ice cream, strawberries, orange slices, and rhubarb pie in varying quantities. Those who came knowing only a few people left feeling bonds of friendship with everyone.

After the sweets settled in their stomachs, they assembled in the studio, where Mary organized them into six unrelated pairs for the giving and receiving of foot rubs. Shoes and socks flew into a pile, and the partners stretched out before one another. Emily, Bookman, Prasada, Darshan, Darla, and Yonah received first. Then they reciprocated.

The conversation continued during the massages, getting a bit ribald at times. The laughter continued as well. As a consequence of the relaxed atmosphere, there were numerous oil spills on clothing, the blankets they sat on, and the floor. No one cared.

While Mary tended to Darshan's feet, she told him about her work as an artist. "This is my studio," she said. "The closet over there is filled with my canvases."

When Darshan began working on Mary's feet, he said, "Would you do me the honor of showing me some of your paintings before we leave tonight?"

"Sure," said Mary. "I can mount a show in about five minutes."

Though everyone else was mellow from the reflexology sessions, Mary was excited because of Darshan's interest in her work. She had an intuitive sense something important was about to happen. After washing her hands, she set about arranging a dozen selected paintings around the room.

Darshan wasn't the only one who wanted to see what Mary had done. Yonah was taken by a painting of Mingus Mountain. "Is this for sale?" he asked.

"They're all for sale," Mary said, "but I don't know how to market them."

"That's where I can help," said Darshan. "I have a gift shop at my resort, and I could display your paintings and take care of sales for a modest commission. I can help with pricing too."

"Before Darshan makes you rich," Yonah said, "I offer you three hundred dollars for this landscape."

"Sold," said Mary.

Emily was intrigued with a nude study of a dark skinned young woman of indeterminate race. "What can you tell me about the model for this one?" she asked. "I'm really drawn to it. She's a woman of color, obviously, but I can't discern which color. There's even a hint of European about her."

"She's a composite of a number of women I've known," said Mary. "Their features merged in my imagination as I was painting, and Eve emerged."

"Is that what you call her?" Emily asked. "What a wonderful name!" She turned to her husband. "Oh, Bookman, what do you think?"

"It's a stunning piece, and you already know the perfect place to hang it in our home," he said.

"How much are you asking for it, Mary?"

"Gee, I don't know," Mary replied.

"Five hundred dollars," said Darshan. "I could sell it for a thousand in my shop, but we're among friends here."

Soon Mary had two checks totaling eight hundred dollars in hand and two fewer paintings in her closet. Darshan identified seven of the remaining pieces to display at the resort, with an understanding that as they sold, Mary would provide additional works.

Around midnight, when the Nabis, the Pratyakshas, and the Congo-Donnes said their goodnights, Terp gave them towels to protect their car seats from the massage oil deposited in their garments. All three couples were pleased, for different reasons, with the oil paints Mary had deposited on canvas.

As soon as they were gone, the remaining six stripped and tossed their clothes into a wicker basket, which Mary carried to the laundry room. She then checked on Zara and Wakhan, asleep in their cribs, and Tzek, asleep on the twin bed in the nursery. Seeing all was well, she trundled off to bed, fully awake and basking in the affirmation of her art she had heard this night. Skye was waiting for her, and she fell into his arms.

Classes resumed at Anasazi College in September. Cloud taught courses in ancient and modern Asian history and worked independently with three students who were pursuing interests in Shinto, the atomic blasts over Hiroshima and Nagasaki, and Taoism. For the wilderness ecology program he had been assigned by Magnus Bergen, he took interested students on day hikes through Oak Creek Canyon.

He tried to avoid the politics of academia as much as possible, but once a week or so a faculty member would take him aside and try to enlist his support for one issue or another. In response to the continuous campus intrigue, Cloud developed a passive-aggressive strategy, listening politely to anything anyone wanted to tell him about but not following up on what he had heard.

Shortly after Zara's first birthday, she greeted Cloud with a startling announcement when he arrived home one evening. "Daddy, I'm potty trained!"

"Congratulations Zara! That's pretty fast, isn't it?" he said.

"It's amazing, really," said Mary. "She wanted to know why older children don't wear diapers, and I explained about the muscle control. She said, 'I can do that' and did."

"No more diapers for me," Zara said.

"You're such a joy," Cloud said, taking his daughter in his arms. "Let's dance a little before dinner. He put a Curtis Lee recording of "Pretty Little Angel Eyes" on the stereo and bounded around the room holding Zara close to his chest.

Terp walked in, exhausted from a day of hospital calls, taking communion to parishioners in nursing homes, and fending off complaints from Hortense Bowdler about a presbytery in New York that ordained a woman who used to be a man.

"Before we debrief the day," Cloud said to his wife, "Zara has an announcement."

Terp was very impressed with the news, but felt a pang of guilt at not being around for these developments in her daughter's life. Mary had been first to see Zara walk also. Zara didn't seem to mind, however. She received a great deal of attention from three adults all the time, plus Grandma and Grandpa and Aunt Cedar Cradle and Uncle Firstlaugh whenever they visited. She had no doubts about her mother's love.

"It's not ***my*** responsibility what they do on the other side of the country," Terp unloaded at the dinner table. "But Hortense wants to make it my problem. She's going to complain to the Board of Elders that I'm not leading the charge against Niagara Falls Presbytery."

"She won't get very far with them," Cloud said.

"I know," Terp sighed. "It's just a pain to deal with her constant unhappiness."

"Maybe Mr. Bowdler doesn't rub her feet often enough," Cloud suggested.

"I'll bet it's more than her feet that never gets rubbed," Mary quipped.

"Let's give Mrs. Bowdler a foot rub," said Zara.

Mary laughed, but Cloud and Terp exchanged anxious looks. It was only a matter of time, they recognized simultaneously, before Zara would repeat something in church that would complicate Terp's life as a pastor and perhaps make her position untenable. They would have to talk with their daughter about family privacy. But it seemed absurd to have such an abstract conversation with a one year-old.

As life unfolded, however, Zara did not reveal any family intimacies in church. In fact, she talked very little outside her home. Even as a toddler, she had an intuitive sense that her home life, which she dearly loved, was a private matter not to be shared with the wider world.

It would be Terp's intentional words in church that brought on the complications.

CHAPTER TWENTY-FIVE

The forty-two-foot boat that Tran Huu Den huddled in was perilously close to sinking in the South China Sea. The combined weight of the seventy-five people aboard the craft was responsible for this tenuous situation. Yet they all prayed it would carry them to freedom from the repressive government of Viet Nam. These boat people had set out from Vung Tau on a clear March day in 1979. But the motor failed, and they had been drifting for three days and were now out of drinking water. Though the passengers were unaware of it, their escape boat was stalled in the middle of a powerful triangle.

Ten miles away to the north, an odd looking being sat naked in the sand under a palm tree on a tiny spit of a tropical island. The Old One was aware of the plight of Den and the other passengers and was concentrating on possible ways to save them. The Old One had a particular interest in Den, however. Twelve years earlier the Old One had saved Den's life by distracting him from a booby trap. Now he was a young man of nineteen and in desperate need of help once again.

To the west, a crew of six well-armed men sped toward the overcrowded boat. They were not intent on helping the freedom seekers, however. Their goal was to rob them of anything of value, throw all but the young girls overboard, rape the girls, and then throw them overboard too.

Cruising to the east of the boat people was a fifteen-hundred-ton refitted freighter that had been chartered by a consortium of Christian peace organizations. The sole purpose of this ship was to locate and pluck boat people from the sea and take them to refugee camps in neighboring countries. This day the rescuers were discouraged, because they had found no one, and the captain had just given the order to turn northeast and steam for Manila. Suddenly a strange voice spoke inside his head, countermanding his decision. Go west! The captain shook his head to clear the fog from his brain and ignored the voice. It came again: Go west! The third time it happened, the captain gave orders to change course.

The pirates were anxious to get to the foundering boat before it went down. If they didn't get there in time any gold and jewelry the runaways might be carrying would sink to the bottom of the sea, and all their efforts would have come to naught. The motorboat moved at top speed across the waves. So fixed were the thieves' eyes on their intended prize that they failed to see the freighter looming ahead of them in the mist.

Den stood, nearly losing his balance, and waved a large piece of saffron cloth a monk had given him as a good luck gift. Crewmembers from both approaching vessels spotted it. The freighter sounded its horn, and the pirates saw with dismay that they must prepare for a bigger fight or run away.

Fleeing seemed the better option, and the pilot of the motorboat, unmindful of the speed at which they were traveling, turned the wheel sharply and the vessel began to tip. He then overcorrected which knocked his partners from their seats. Paying no attention to what was ahead of him, the pilot turned to see if any of them had gone overboard. As a result of his inattention, the motorboat grazed off the side of the freighter and flipped over, sending the pirates and all their weapons into the depths.

The boat people were delivered to a refugee camp in Malaysia, which became Den's home for the next six months.

After ten consecutive months of Dagmar's fan mail surpassing that of her Arizona Afternoon co-host Rex Fisher, Rex was feeling the need to do something dramatic to regain his dominance. He was musing about what tricks of the trade he might pull off as he meandered to his regular monthly meeting with the station manager.

The manager leaned forward in his plush chair and stared directly at Rex. "I'll get right to the crux of the matter, Rex. Your Q Score has fallen a couple of points, which by itself is not a big deal. But Dagmar's has risen considerably. And last month, her fan mail more than doubled yours. The team is out of balance."

Rex slumped into his chair as a wave of depression washed over him.

"Your assignment," the manager continued, "which you have no choice but to accept, is to endear yourself to your audience and to your co-host. I don't care how you do it. Grovel if you have to. Just make yourself more likeable."

"But I ***am*** likeable," whined Rex. "Viewers have loved me for years."

"Well now they're getting a little tired of you," the manager said. "It happens in a lot of relationships. You need to do something to spice up your image. Find a way to garner some favorable publicity."

After he left the station, Rex visited a favorite bar in search of inspiration and instead dulled his mind when he became roaring drunk. As soon as he had clumsily negotiated his car out of the parking lot to continue on his way home, he was stopped by a Scottsdale police officer, whereupon he was arrested and taken to jail.

The headline in the local section of the Arizona Republic the next day announced his DUI arrest. Subsequent stories reported his excessively high blood alcohol level and the five-day jail sentence he received. Rex was summarily fired. A week later, his wife acted on her oft-repeated threat and sued him for divorce. Within the year he filed for bankruptcy protection.

The station decided to let Dagmar work solo for a while, to see if the viewing numbers would hold without a co-host. They did not remain at the previous level but rather the audience grew.

Life had been fairly peaceful at First Calvinist since the Board informed Hortense Bowdler that they were not interested in picking fights with other churches in their own presbytery, much less presbyteries on the other side of the country. Mrs. Bowdler's complaints seemed to go into remission. Therefore, Terp intended to do her part to continue the era of good feeling by avoiding controversial subjects.

In the spring she preached a series of sermons on the Hebrew prophets. While preparing for the subject, she repeatedly encountered scriptural connections between nakedness and prophecy. This may stir up a hornet's nest, she thought, but if I have any integrity, I've got to address this phenomenon in at least one sermon.

Her final sermon in the series was based on First Samuel 19, the narrative about King Saul's attempts to snatch David from the protection of the prophet Samuel. "Saul approached Samuel with violent intent," Terp said from the pulpit, "but the Spirit of God came over him, and his behavior changed dramatically. The scripture says, 'And Saul too stripped off his clothes and also prophesied in front of Samuel and lay naked all day and all night long.'

"There is something about uncovering oneself -making oneself vulnerable if you will- that's conducive to recognizing and telling the truth. The biblical prophets stripped off their garments as a way of seeking the truth of God. They responded to the presence of the holy by removing their clothing. Have you ever felt like doing that? As I noted at Zara's baptism, the earliest Christians approached that sacrament naked. Surely these practices are interrelated.

"Baring one's soul, baring one's mind, and baring one's body all lead to the same result -greater honesty. I think there is a natural human desire to be completely honest with God, with ourselves, and with one another. When Micah started out to prophesy about the coming doom to Judah, he declared, 'I will go stripped and naked.' Walt Whitman wrote, 'I will go to the bank by the wood and become undisguised and naked, I am mad for it to be in contact with me.' Undisguised and naked is what the prophets were. And God was not offended by their nakedness. God treasured these speakers of the truth. Their words and their ***actions*** are preserved in the Bible for us to ponder today."

The sermon brought a vigorous response from members of the congregation. Most appreciated Terp's straightforward approach to a sensitive subject. The majority responded favorably, but the feelings among those who were negative about it were strong. What quickly became known as "the naked sermon" generated more discussion than anything she had spoken from the pulpit in nearly two years.

It became a topic of conversation in the Beth Shalom congregation as well. Darla met with Terp to talk about the Jewish response to her interpretation of Hebrew scripture.

"Several of my members have asked me to get a copy of it so they can read what all the fuss is about," the rabbi said.

"No problem," said Terp. "Copies are circulating around my congregation and other churches in the presbytery. I'm surprised at all the reaction. It's not that big a deal."

"In the minds of people who have been taught by church leaders that the human body is shameful or dirty, it's a very big deal when a pastor relates nudity directly with religion in a positive way. Most people connect nudity with sexual activity," Darla said. "Church and synagogue both have major taboos about sex."

"Well, sex happens when people are naked," said Terp, "but it's not the only thing that happens. But the kinkiest sex happens when people are dressed in various... outfits."

"What makes you so interested in this subject?" Darla asked.

"Pastoral confidence?" asked Terp.

"Yes," said Darla.

"Cloud is not a Calvinist. He's a member of the Natural Christian Church, where they worship in the nude."

"I think I've heard of them," Darla said. "There was a couple on my block when I was a kid who belonged to it."

"Onan and Nissa Verrall," said Terp.

"Yes, they're the ones."

"Onan is dead," Terp explained, "and Nissa is now married to my father-in-law. Cloud and his parents started going to that church in the late fifties."

"Unreal!" Darla exclaimed. "That means I went to the prom with a nudist. So, how do you feel about your husband's church?"

"I have attended services there and led worship myself. More of my closest friends are associated with the NCC than with the Calvinist Church," Terp said.

"This is a lot for me to absorb," said Darla. "I respond better to the printed word. It's an occupational hazard. Do you have any written material about this naturist church?"

Terp went to a file cabinet and pulled out a pamphlet. "You may keep this if you like. And with respect to pastoral confidence, it's OK to share what I've told you with Yonah if you deem it appropriate - and the booklet too."

"Ooh," said Darla leafing through the pages, "pictures too!"

"I know what you're thinking, Darla," said Terp. "You won't find any photos of your prom date in there -or his wife either."

Darla laughed. "Am I that transparent?"

"No, just human," said Terp.

"By the way," said Darla, "I've studied a great deal about the Holocaust. The Nazis made a point of stripping the Jews naked before gassing them. That's a perverse and unholy association with nudity."

"The Nazis had warped ideas about a lot of things," Terp said. "There was a flourishing naturist movement in Germany before Hitler came to power. In 1933 the Nazis banned it as part of their ***Gleichschaltung*** program to synchronize German society with Nazi ideology. Their edict said, 'One of the greatest dangers for German culture and morality is the so-called naked culture movement. It takes away women's natural shame.' The Nazis preferred women to be ashamed of their bodies."

"All the better to control them," Darla said. "Of course, men have a long history of trying to control women. It's certainly true in my tradition."

"As a woman rabbi, I guess you would know that first hand," said Terp. "Christian tradition doesn't have much to brag about in that regard, either. But in my experience, men who are naturists tend to be less concerned about controlling other people -female or male."

"I look forward to reading this booklet," Darla said, "and looking at the pictures too."

"I think Nissa's in one of the shots of a worship service -from the back," Terp said.

"I've already seen a naked picture of Nissa," Darla said. "When I was a teenager, my brother showed me a nudist magazine that was floating around the neighborhood, and she was in it. It didn't offend me then and it doesn't now. But that doesn't mean that I plan to run around naked myself. I'm a bit more modest than that."

That wasn't the only thing floating around your old

neighborhood, Terp thought. My husband was doing that without his body. However, Terp refrained from mentioning this to Darla.

The next afternoon, one of Terp's parishioners called and said he wanted to see her about a matter of concern. She agreed to meet with him in her office later that day. Wake Dolmen was a moderately reserved man married to an outgoing woman named Aimee. They had three children aged ten, twelve, and fourteen.

"Thanks for your time, Pastor. I know how busy you must be," Wake said when he arrived at the church.

"No problem at all," Terp replied. "Time with parishioners is first priority. How are things going with your business?"

"We're scratching out a living chiseling dead people," Wake said jauntily.

"You must really enjoy that line, as often as you say it," Terp said.

Wake and Aimee owned a company called Carved in Stone that produced granite and marble grave markers, monuments, and statues, mainly for cemeteries and parks.

"I suppose it's time to retire the line," Wake said. "Especially since I don't actually do the chiseling any more. We employ several artisans for that. But I still carve the occasional angel with my own hands. I finished one last year that's so beautiful I can't bear to sell it. It's elegant and somber. I have this feeling that I should keep it to watch over my own family."

"Is that why you came today?" Terp asked. "A family concern?"

"In a way, but not about anyone's health. We're all well, thankfully," Wake said with a tinge of nervousness. "I wanted to have a private conversation with you about the implications of your sermon."

Terp considered asking which sermon, because she had preached a lot of them, but she knew what he was referring to. She had no idea, however, whether he had come to praise or condemn her words.

"I interpret your sermon as approving of public nudity," he continued.

Terp was wary of responding to this leading statement. "There is nothing inherently shameful about the human body," she said carefully, "and nudity ***per se*** is not incompatible with the Christian faith."

"I'm worried about a situation, Pastor, and your sermon has opened the door for me to talk about it." Wake paused to gather courage before revealing his news, and then plunged ahead. "Aimee and I and the kids are social nudists. We're regulars at the Sol Identity Naturist Camp near Cordes Junction. But sometimes I have a recurring nightmare that you and the Board of Elders found out and condemned us in front of the whole congregation and threw us out of the church."

"Why would I do that? I have no intention of condemning you," Terp said with a gentle voice, "and I doubt the elders would either, although I can't speak for them. But let me assure you that your involvement with family nudism is not grounds for removal from membership in the Calvinist Church. There's nothing at all immoral, illegal, or unbiblical about it."

"That's good to hear," Wake said. "Thanks for being so open-minded."

"It's not a matter of open-mindedness but honesty," the pastor said. "I would counsel you, however, to use discretion in revealing your avocation to other church members. Human nature being what it is, this kind of information would spread very rapidly through the congregation. While most would shrug and say no big deal, some parishioners would consider this juicy gossip and be secretly titillated by it. A few would probably condemn it as scandalous."

"There's another family in the congregation who knows about us," he said, "but that's because they go to the same camp."

"Don't tell me their names," Terp said.

"I have no intention of doing that," Wake said, "but I will tell them I've talked with you about nudism, and you've assured me that we're welcome in the church in spite of being nudists."

"You are welcome in the church, ***period***. Neither in spite of nor because of who or what you are or your choice of lifestyle," Terp said.

A week later, Kina Wickham came to see Terp. Kina was a Maori woman from New Zealand, married to a white man from England. Living in Arizona was a geographical compromise for them between their far distant countries. They had a boy eight and a girl ten.

"Wake told me he talked with you, and how graciously you responded," Kina said, "We're the other nudist family in your congregation."

"Thank you for telling me," Terp said.

"I want to show you something," said Kina. She pulled a copy of Healthy Nudist magazine from her purse and opened it. "Here are the Wickhams and the Dolmens together."

Terp looked at the photograph of four naked adults and five naked children standing with wide grins in front of a volleyball net.

"Does this shock you, Pastor Terp?" Kina asked.

"No," said Terp quietly. "It gives me encouragement."

Kina handed the magazine to Terp and said, "You can keep this. There's an article in it you should read about the struggle for topless equality for women; about the social hypocrisy of allowing men to go topless in public but not women."

"Thanks, Kina," said Terp. "Yet another social justice issue for me to be cognizant of."

Lately, Terp had been brooding about developments in the American Calvinist Church. Since the 1930s the denomination had been generally liberal theologically, adopting a series of progressive reforms, including the ordination of women. But the tide was changing, as a wave of more conservative young pastors sought to gain greater influence over the administration of church government.

The denomination had gone through a number of these power shifts over three centuries. Liberals would predominate for a few decades, bringing reforms motivated by grace and social justice. Eventually many moderate folks would begin to sense the church had become too lax, and conservatives would gain power to reign in the perceived excesses of the liberal regime. Greater attention would be given to enforcing church law and maintaining orthodoxy. In time, the conservatives would become too narrowly controlling, and liberals would rise from the ashes to loosen things up.

Momentum in the denomination was definitely with the conservatives as the decade of the seventies drew to a close, and Terp was unhappy with what she saw as their regressive and self-righteously pursued agenda. Occasionally she entertained the idea of resigning and going over to the NCC but believed the American Calvinist Church carried out vital mission work and maintained an influential witness to the world much greater than the capacity of the tiny Natural Christian Church. These would be diminished, she reasoned, if liberals like her left the ACC. Yet she did not relish the prospect of spending the next three or four decades of ministry enveloped in bitter theology wars.

In June, Terp and Cloud received an invitation to a barbecue at the Wickhams' home. The Dolmen family would be there also. Dress was likely to be ***very*** casual Kina told Terp, but she and Cloud were under no obligation to disrobe. Zara stayed home with Mary, and the pastor and her spouse devised a surprise presentation for their hosts.

Kina and her husband John, both in the buff, greeted them at the front door. They escorted Cloud and Terp through the house to the backyard patio, where equally nude Wake and Aimee stretched out in lawn-chairs. Their naked children were cavorting around the lawn.

"We thought we would ***expose*** you to the nudist lifestyle," said John with a twinkle in his voice. "Pun very much intended."

Cloud kicked off his loafers and Terp did the same with her sandals. Without a word, Cloud removed his polo shirt and undid the top button on his khaki shorts. Terp reached down for the hem of her sundress, and in carefully choreographed movements, she pulled the dress over her head while Cloud simultaneously unzipped and dropped his pants. Neither had on underclothes.

The children watched their pastor and her husband strip and made hearty thumbs up signs of approval.

"Whoa!" said Kina. "No tan lines! I am shocked! I was sure both of you would be cottontails. Pastor Terp, I figured you for wearing a bikini rather than a one-piece, but..."

"No ma'am. I wear a no-piece. A cottontail, huh?" quipped Terp.

"Nudist slang," explained Aimee. "Cottontails are new naturists who have tan legs and backs but pale white fannies."

"Oh, I know the term," said Terp. "That was a long time ago in a different life."

The adults gathered chairs in a circle and sipped cold bottles of Lucky Lager beer while Cloud and Terp told them about the Natural Christian Church.

"Terp is an American Calvinist, but my membership is in the NCC," explained Cloud. "It's expected that a pastor's spouse will become a member of the congregation the pastor is serving, but I haven't joined First Calvinist, preferring to maintain the Natural Church relationship. The funny thing is, no one at First Calvinist has questioned my non-membership status, and I haven't said a word about belonging to another denomination. Either they haven't noticed or maybe they think I'm an unredeemable heathen."

"Rest assured if you were a pastor's ***wife***, they would notice and comment negatively and often," said Wake. "I saw it happen at a Calvinist church we belonged to years ago. The minister was married to a Quaker who did not transfer her membership, and there was constant carping about her."

"You've probably gotten a break because you are one of that rare, strange breed -a pastor's ***husband***," said Aimee. "And we certainly won't nag you to switch. In fact, we may look into the NCC ourselves. What do you think, Wake?"

Before Wake could respond, Terp jumped in. "You might enjoy attending services at New River every once in a while, but please don't leave First Calvinist. We really need you here."

"Well, if I'd known about the naturist church when we moved to Arizona, we certainly would have gone there instead of First Calvinist," said Kina.

"How come you're a Calvinist and not a Natural Christian pastor?" Aimee asked.

"Long story," said Terp. She told them her faith saga.

"And you were never tempted to switch?" Wake asked.

Terp hesitated to speak, not wanting to reveal her internal spiritual struggle to parishioners, even those she sat around naked with. If pressed for an answer, she decided, she would say she took it as a rhetorical question and make a joke about the temptation of no dry cleaning bills for clergy robes in a nudist church.

Diplomatically changing the subject to avoid putting Terp in an uncomfortable position, John said, "What are you reading these days, Cloud?"

"I just finished a book I plan to assign to my wilderness ecology students: ***The Man Who Walked Through Time.*** An inveterate hiker named Colin Fletcher wrote it about his trek through the Grand Canyon the long way, the entire length west to east."

"I know that book," said Wake. "On part of the trip he hiked naked."

"Across the Tonto Platform," said Cloud. "Initially, he stripped down to hat, socks, and boots to cool down from the warm May sun, but he discovered a sense of freedom without his clothes -an Adam-like simplicity, I think he called it- and it improved his observation of the world around him. I hiked to the bottom of the canyon once, the short way. Fletcher's book made me long to do it again. Not the entire length like he did, but some ancient and remote stretch of it -naked of course."

"We hiked naked in the Olgas -Kata Tjuta- in the center of Australia," noted Terp. "So even though this is the first I've heard of it, I assume Cloud's planning on taking me along on his nude hike in the Grand Canyon."

"Absolutely yes, and Zara too," he said.

CHAPTER TWENTY-SIX

At the Annual Meeting of the American Calvinist Church in July, the extent of conservative resurgence became clear. The commissioners narrowly passed a series of resolutions that tightened denominational control over ministers. Divorced pastors must undergo detailed evaluations to determine if they were innocent victims of the break-ups. Only if their spouses could be found at fault could the pastors remain in ministry. And the acceptable grounds for divorce were limited to adultery, physical abuse, and desertion.

All kinds of sexual activity outside of marriage, particularly homosexual behavior but including masturbation and unchaste kissing (any touch anywhere on the body involving the tongue), were strictly forbidden and constituted grounds for dismissal for ministers and elders. Candidates for Ministry committees would now be required to ask about the sexual habits of unmarried people seeking to come under care, much to their mutual embarrassment.

One evening not long after the Annual Meeting, Terp and Cloud went to dinner at the Nabi's home in the woods. Terp was upset by developments in her denomination, and Darla encouraged her clergy colleague to vent.

"What narrow-minded, legalistic, moralistic hypocrisy!" Terp ranted.

"Are you feeling vulnerable because of your association with the naturists?" asked Yonah.

"Maybe a little," said Terp, "but it's more about other people than me. A lot of fine ministers may have their careers destroyed by these new rules."

"I enjoyed reading the booklet about the NCC," Yonah continued. "It didn't change my mind about Judaism, but the social context of the church is intriguing."

"I wasn't trying to convert you," said Terp. "Just acquaint you with a different model of religious behavior."

"This isn't about doctrine," Cloud said. "Naturism can be practiced within the framework of nearly every major world religion and a lot of minor ones too."

"I think this naturism talk is a plot. Cloud, you've been wanting to see me naked since tenth grade," Darla joked. "You're just trying to get me to take my clothes off."

"You're completely wrong, Darla," Cloud responded. "It was ninth grade."

They all laughed.

"At any rate," Yonah said, "I find the concept of social nudism acceptable, even beneficial for some, but I wouldn't be personally comfortable with it."

"It's not for everybody," said Terp.

That summer, a member of the Board of Elders at First Calvinist moved to another state, leaving an unexpired term to be filled. The Church Nominating Committee asked Jenny Mast to fill the vacancy on the board. Jenny, a high school physics teacher, had been a member of the congregation for twenty years and was known to be faithful in attendance and generous in her financial gifts to the church. A special congregational meeting was convened and Jenny was duly elected to the board. Terp heard a muffled no from the back corner of the sanctuary when she called for the vote, but the ayes were overwhelming.

Elders in the American Calvinist Church are ordained to that office. Thus, on the Sunday following Jenny's election, Terp ordained her in a special rite during morning worship, in which Jenny knelt for the laying on of hands and prayer.

The only glitch in this otherwise unremarkable scenario was that Jenny Mast was a lesbian. Jenny and her partner Gwen had lived in the same house for decades, and they always sat together in church. Their relationship was no secret in the community. Terp had anticipated that some opposition to Jenny might surface during the congregational meeting, but no one had risen to question the action.

The United States Government accepted 30,000 Vietnamese refugees in September. Through the national office of the ACC, Terp and Cloud volunteered to sponsor an orphan, but as a result of the random machinations of church and national bureaucracies, they were assigned, instead, a nineteen year-old young man who had been living in a camp in Malaysia. They drove to Los Angeles to meet Tran Huu Den.

Since Cloud spoke Vietnamese, they had an easy time communicating about basic needs. Den had already picked up a little English, and Cloud began teaching him more of the language on the drive back to Strange Haven.

Mary, Terp, and Cloud kept their clothes on around the house after Den arrived.

"He's suffering from enough culture shock without having to deal with a bunch of clothes-free Christians," Cloud said.

Mary, however, hated to stay dressed while working in her studio. It would be easy enough to keep Den out of the place while she was painting, but redressing every time she went out to check on Zara seemed an inconvenience. After a week, Mary sat down with Den and explained in the simplest terms she knew that inside the house, family members did not have to wear clothes.

"You can keep your pants on," she said. "No problem. But I'm going to get comfortable." Mary slipped out of her jeans and tee shirt.

Den blushed and said, "I grateful be guest here. I not tell."

When Cloud arrived home, Mary greeted him nude and said, "You need to have a talk with Den in Vietnamese. I'm not sure he understood my explanation in English."

"***Chung toi nguoi theo chu nghia khoa than,***" Cloud told Den.

Den expressed comprehension and added some comments.

Cloud said to Mary, "I told him we are naturists. He understood you the first time, and he wants the family to be comfortable and not to feel constrained by his presence. He thinks of himself as a temporary guest, and he doesn't want us to be angry with him. Besides, he saw a lot of nudity in the overcrowded refugee camp."

Cloud disrobed, and when Terp arrived home, she did too. Den, however, maintained his modesty. Three days later, Den inadvertently forgot to dress after his shower and appeared naked for breakfast. From that day forward, Den was part of the family, and no one gave a thought about him moving to his own place.

The challenge to Jenny Mast's ordination came in the middle of September. The Clerk of the Presbytery called Terp to say that Mrs. Bowdler had filed a formal allegation of malfeasance of office against her. The specific charge was violating the constitution of the denomination by ordaining a known homosexual person.

"I am required to inform you, Terp," the clerk said apologetically, "that we are constitutionally obligated to conduct an investigation into the allegation, and if sufficient evidence is found, this would lead to an ecclesiastical trial."

The trial took place at a church in Phoenix in late October.

Mrs. Bowdler testified that she had voted no at the congregational meeting, which gave her the right to bring charges against the pastor for her deliberately improper action. "It is widely known in the congregation that Miss Mast is living in sin with Miss Jones," she said under oath. "Certainly the reverend knew that at the time of the ordination."

"Please tell the court how you personally came to know that Jenny Mast is -as you phrase it- living in sin," Terp's attorney said to the witness.

"I've seen her holding hands in church with Miss Jones, and the church directory lists them both cohabiting at the same address," Hortense answered.

"These are inferences," the lawyer said. "Many people hold hands in church. What information do you have to substantiate your allegation about Miss Mast?"

"Well, once at a potluck supper I overheard Miss Mast talking with Rev. Morgan. I didn't hear what it was the reverend said, but Miss Mast burst out laughing and said, 'What? An old dyke like me?'"

"Has Miss Mast ever told you directly that she is sexually active with Miss Jones?" the defense attorney continued.

"No," Mrs. Bowdler said. "She and I are not close."

"Have you ever observed her engaging in any kind of sexual behavior?"

"No." she admitted, "...except for hand-holding. I think that's sexual."

"Do you have evidence of any kind indicating Miss Mast has participated in acts involving her own or someone else's genital organs?"

Hortense Bowdler huffed in offense. "Of course not. I would not stain myself with anything so filthy. People don't talk about such things in polite company."

Terp then took the stand. The prosecuting attorney asked, "Rev. Morgan, were you aware of Miss Mast's homosexuality when you officiated at her ordination?"

"I was aware that she affirmed herself as a lesbian. However, I was and remain fully unaware that she has ever engaged in any homosexual acts," Terp responded.

"Can you not reasonably infer from her statements and the fact that she lives with another woman that she has indeed engaged in such conduct?" the lawyer asked.

"Objection," Terp's lawyer proclaimed.

"This is a church court, not a civil trial," said the judge. "In ecclesiastical proceedings witnesses may be asked for opinions and conclusions."

"I'm not in the habit of making such inferences," Terp answered. "I've done too much pastoral counseling with married couples who go for years without engaging in sexual relations to assume that people are sexually active simply because they live in the same house."

Following two hours of deliberation, the court acquitted Terp of ministerial malfeasance. In announcing its verdict, the judiciary panel reported, "In the absence of anyone, including the accuser, speaking to the contrary at the congregational meeting, the congregation acted properly to elect Jenny Mast to the office of elder. It thus became Rev.

Morgan's responsibility to ordain the woman, pursuant to the action of the congregational vote. In addition, no evidence was brought to the court that Miss Mast had engaged in any specific disqualifying behavior at a particular time and place."

Hortense Bowdler was furious and vowed among her small group of supporters to find a way to get rid of the pastor. Terp took no pleasure in the verdict, because she knew it had been made on technical grounds, and other trials were bound to follow throughout the denomination. Many pastors were in jeopardy of losing their careers.

Veterans Day, or as Cloud insisted on calling it, Armistice Day, fell on a Sunday in 1979. On the afternoon of November eleventh, the sixty-first anniversary of the armistice that ended World War I, Terp and Cloud drove to New River to seek guidance from Adam and Evelyn.

Terp poured out her frustration with the ACC. "I've been wondering if the NCC would receive me as a minister," Terp said at the end of her litany of woe.

"Adam and I would count it a great blessing for you to be a minister in our denomination," said Evelyn. "There's no question about your qualifications. The decision would have to be made by the National Assembly, of course, but I envision only one snag."

"What's that?" Terp asked.

"You need a call to a congregation or some other approved ministry in order to be received," Adam explained.

"Oh, I know that," said Terp. "It's the same in the ACC. I wouldn't expect to be recognized as a minister until I had a call."

"What are the prospects for a church for Terp?" Cloud asked. "We are willing to move."

"You'd have to give up teaching at Anasazi," said Adam. "It might be hard to find another position like that."

"I like teaching there," Cloud said, "but I'd give it up in a heartbeat if Terp had a call to a church somewhere."

"Let me tell you a secret," said Adam. "The NCC has been scouting possible locations to establish new congregations, and right at the top of the list is Sedona, Arizona. We've been dreaming of a new church there for years. But we haven't had the right pastors to do it."

"That would be convenient," said Terp. "I'm very interested in being considered for a new church development in Sedona."

"Actually," said Evelyn, "we have something else in mind."

"Oh," said Terp with a note of disappointment.

"What we would like to propose to the denominational office," said Adam, "is that the two of you be called as co-pastors of a new church in Sedona. Cloud, you could be ordained on the basis of your education. You are well respected in the denomination, and you could continue to teach at Anasazi while helping get the church going. And the NCC would do back-flips in heavy traffic if that's what it would take to get Terp into our denomination."

"Oh how exciting!" said Terp.

"I have to admit it's an appealing concept," said Cloud. "But I suspect there may be a few roadblocks along the way."

"The biggest roadblock could be the lack of a suitable and affordable facility. That could end the whole project right at the beginning," Adam said.

"We'll need to meditate and pray about this," Terp said.

"In the meantime," said Cloud, "go ahead with whatever preliminary inquiries you need to make with the New Church Board about calling Terp and me."

The next day, Cloud and Terp drove to Flagstaff to confer with Firstlaugh and Cedar Cradle. Both thought the proposal was worth pursuing, and Cedar Cradle was particularly enthusiastic.

"As soon as you mentioned it, I had a good feeling about the idea," she said. "I have a warm sensation in my body just thinking about the two of you being co-pastors. It seems inevitable to me."

A week later, Evelyn called to say the way was clear with the NCC. "If you two say yes, I'll make arrangements for your examinations by the National Assembly when we meet at Malibu in January."

They said yes.

"I have an idea for a location," said Cloud. "Would it be premature for us to begin exploring the possibilities right away?"

"Go for it!" said Adam. "I'll give you the financial parameters."

Cloud invited Prasada and Darshan to dinner early in December. After the meal, they retired to the studio to exchange foot rubs.

Darshan winced when Cloud pressed firmly below the ball of his left foot. "You're storing a lot of tension in your body," Cloud said.

"My stomach," groaned Darshan. "Business problems take an awful toll on me."

Cloud knew from lunchtime conversations with Prasada that the resort was struggling financially. "I imagine the current national economic malaise would negatively affect occupancy in luxury resorts."

"That's for sure," said Darshan. "People settle for less expensive luxuries in such times. Instead of a weekend in Sedona, they will eat specialty ice cream at home."

Cloud worked his thumbs on Darshan's foot, gently at first then with increasing pressure, and the hotelier felt his body relax.

"Would you be interested in leasing your entire resort to an outside organization for its exclusive use?" Cloud asked.

"I would be interested in learning the details," Darshan said noncommittally.

"A closely knit church group is looking for a long term lease on a location about the size of your place," Cloud said. "I'm confident they could work out a financial deal that would guarantee keeping the property in your hands."

"Ouch!" yelled Darshan.

IV

THE CHURCH IN THE VORTEX

Tis the gift to be simple, 'tis the gift to be free.
'Tis the gift to come down where you ought to be.
And when we find ourselves in the place just right,
It will be in the valley of love and delight.
Joseph Brackett, Jr.

Naked people have little or no influence on society.
Mark Twain

Natural religion is the voice of God.
William Blake

CHAPTER TWENTY-SEVEN

"**Sorry**," said Cloud. "Did I press too hard on your big toe? You must be having trouble with headaches too."

Darshan said, "Yes to both. My toe is sore, my head hurts, and what you just said about keeping the property in our hands hit a nerve. Our financial situation is tight right now, and I've had bouts of insomnia worrying about losing the resort."

"Massaging your toes can relieve the headache," said Cloud. "And a lease could go a long way toward relieving the tension regarding your property. But aren't you giving away your bargaining position by telling us about your precarious finances?"

"Not at all," said Darshan. "You know some of this already. You are a man who does his homework. What I have really done is whet your appetite for making an offer."

"Tell us more about this closely knit church group you spoke of," said Prasada. "Is it connected with the church you serve, Terp?" She was relaxed as Terp massaged her left foot, experiencing none of the soreness that her husband felt. The potential bankruptcy of the luxury lodge did not carry the same emotional weight for her as it did for Darshan. Ownership of property was less important to Prasada. Nevertheless, she wanted her husband to succeed in his chosen career.

"No connection at all. It's called the Natural Christian Church," Terp answered. "They're looking for a facility in the Sedona area to develop a new congregation."

"I presume they would need space for Sunday only," said Darshan.

"No," said Cloud. "This congregation would need exclusive use of the entire place seven days a week. You couldn't take in guests not associated with the church, but the comprehensive lease they want would represent significant payments to you."

Terp said, "We'd better explain what the NCC is." She told them about the denomination's practices.

"Some Christians are very odd," said Darshan. "Hindus don't worship naked."

"Oh yes they do," said Prasada. "In Chandragutti thousands of women come every year to worship nude. They bathe in the river and process naked to the Temple."

"OK, I forgot about that," Darshan confessed.

"And historically, many Hindu temples have combined worship with the erotic arts," she added. "Shiva is certainly known for prancing naked around the universe."

"The gods can do what they like," Darshan said defensively. "OK, so some Hindus are very odd also. But tell me this. How would this affect Prasada and me? We live at the resort. Would we have to move out if we leased to this naked church?"

"I don't think so," said Cloud. "The church is clothing optional. Not everyone is bare all the time, and many visitors keep their clothes on, at least for a while. You would have to tolerate naked people running about the place, but you would not have to take your own clothes off. I suspect church officials would prefer that you stay on the premises to keep an eye on the place. And church members would take over a lot of the maintenance, kitchen, and maid service responsibilities, so you wouldn't have a large payroll. Whenever outside help would be needed -plumbers, electricians, and the like-they would put their clothes on."

"How are you two connected with this church?" Prasada asked suspiciously.

Terp grinned and said, "We're going to be co-pastors of the new congregation."

"You mean you're going to prance about naked while praying?" Darshan asked.

"Yes," said Cloud.

"I'd have to see that with my own eyes to believe it," Darshan said.

"OK," said Cloud and Terp in unison.

They set aside the feet they were massaging, stood, and removed their sweat pants and shirts. Terp bowed her head and prayed, "May God grant blessed lives to our dear friends, Prasada and Darshan. Amen."

Cloud and Terp sat and nonchalantly resumed massaging the feet of their speechless companions.

"Now, about the possibility of a lease," Cloud said, "I'd like to have a proposal to present to the national board, since they would be funding the project for the first three years. What terms would you require?"

It took a moment for a stunned Darshan to regain his voice. "I'll need time to work up the figures. Prasada and I will discuss the matter. Come to my office day after tomorrow at noon, and we'll have an answer. Either a flat no or a preliminary proposal."

Precisely at twelve on the appointed day, Cloud and Terp knocked on the door to Darshan's office.

"Who's there?" Darshan asked.

"Terp and Cloud."

Darshan opened the door wide enough to let them slip in sideways then quickly closed it. He and Prasada were naked.

"I guess you have a proposal for us," Terp said.

Terp called a special meeting of the Board of Elders preceding worship on the Sunday after Christmas to announce her intention to resign. If she were leaving for another pastoral position in the denomination, she would need the approval of the congregation and the presbytery, but since she was resigning from the denomination, no action was necessary. The American Calvinist Church would not transfer her to the Natural Christian Church, so her only recourse was to abandon her ordination by renouncing the authority of the church.

"I intend to resign as your pastor effective Monday January

seventh," she said without preamble. "I will announce this to the congregation at the conclusion of worship today and preach my last sermon next Sunday. I will deliver my letter of renunciation to the Presbytery Clerk in person on the seventh."

The elders sat silent and bewildered in their chairs. After an uncomfortable interval Jenny ventured a question. "Is it because of your trial?"

"Not directly," said Terp. "I'll have more to say about why I'm leaving next Sunday. It does not have anything to do with any of you. I'll miss you all very much."

"What will you do?" Jenny asked.

"We'll move to Sedona, and Cloud will continue to teach at Anasazi College. As of now, I do not have another position, but I anticipate accepting a pastorate with another denomination. That's all I can say for the moment," Terp responded.

Before pronouncing the benediction at the end of the service, Terp made her announcement. An anguished chorus of voices followed with expressions of grief and regret. In the last pew on the left, however, Hortense Bowdler smiled in satisfaction.

The matriarch did not smile that evening, however, because her phone rang continuously with calls from angry church members who blamed her for the pastor's resignation.

The sanctuary was filled to overflowing the following Sunday.

"I don't want to use worship time for personal remarks," Terp said before the invocation, "but if anyone can stay after the benediction, I will explain why I have decided to leave my beloved American Calvinist Church."

Not a single person left at the end of the service.

Terp moved from the chancel to the floor of the nave and began to speak. "I've had visits and phone calls all week from people who want to lay all the blame for my departure on Mrs. Bowdler."

The matriarch sat up in her seat, mindful that she was very unpopular at the moment but reveling in the thought that she had indeed caused the pastor's capitulation.

"I need to make it crystal clear that Mrs. Bowdler is not responsible for my decision to resign. Whatever she has done, including filing charges against me, she did out of deeply held beliefs. We all hold certain things dear to our hearts, and among the members of this congregation, many of those beliefs are contradictory. The fact that Hortense Bowdler and I are on different sides of the theological spectrum is not unusual and not grounds for either of us to leave this congregation."

Terp looked at a face in the last pew. "Mrs. Bowdler, I want everyone here to know that you did not run me out of First Calvinist Church of Prescott, Arizona. So, please, everyone, let her worship in peace."

Terp could have spoken no more devastating words than these to Hortense Bowdler. The woman's countenance changed from a triumphal gloat to a bitter scowl. ***How dare she dismiss me that way***, the matriarch thought.

"I am deeply sorrowful about developments in this denomination," Terp continued, "and my resignation comes in part as a result of distant decisions that affect each of our congregations across the country. Our church has come under the control of leaders whose visions of ministry are narrow and exclusivist. It is very difficult to preach the good news of the gospel when the church has shackled it with reservations, qualifications, and stipulations about who may participate. Some among us seem obsessed with moral purity, or at least moral purity as it pertains to human sexuality. A warped view of moral purity at that, in my estimation. However, they pay little heed these days to morality relating to greed, violence, or lust for power.

"My natural inclination in the face of these developments is to stay and stand up for justice and grace. This congregation has been very supportive of my ministry, as has the presbytery. Clearly the Presbytery of Arizona was embarrassed at having to try me on charges of malfeasance, but rules are rules, and they were obliged to follow them. The thing that causes me the greatest grief, however, is that the charges brought against me are a local symptom of a national disease.

"I see more trials ahead in this denomination. Many ministers, elders, and church members across the land are vulnerable to purges by the purity brigade. I expect many pastors to lose their careers because they have stood up for the marginalized in our society or are themselves secretly members of unacceptable categories of human beings. Watching all this unfold will be very painful, and I do not wish to do so.

"But the desire to avoid pain is not sufficient reason for me to leave. I believe God is calling me in another direction. With your partnership, I have accomplished what God called me to do here, and now it's time to do something else. This church is strong, with an effective Board of Elders. Your witness will continue here without me. I'm not the church. You are. And God is drawing me toward a different kind of ministry.

"I confess the current climate in this denomination makes it easier for me to leave, but the love and support I've received from this congregation make it very difficult. Yet the time has come for me peaceably to withdraw. Farewell and God bless you all."

At the NCC Annual Meeting in Malibu, Terp was received quickly on the basis of her education and pastoral experience. There were no questions from commissioners when she stood before the plenary session.

Then it was Cloud's turn. Terp had already been ordained by another denomination, but Cloud was a lay member of the NCC. Since he was seeking approval for ordination, the questioning would be more rigorous. As it turned out, his reputation throughout the denomination influenced his examination.

Petrus Dort stood to ask the first question. "Let me compliment you on your hymn writing, Cloud, as well as your distinguished tenure on the faculty of Pacific Crossroads Seminary. I see also that you have taken courses in pastoral care and spiritual practices, but academia is a far land from parish ministry. What makes you think you have what it takes to be a pastor?"

"First, I was an adjunct at PCTS and not a tenured member of the faculty," Cloud clarified. "With regard to being a pastor, I believe that I have functioned somewhat as a pastor in non-church settings all my life. But it's not my personal belief that brings me here today. A dozen other people, some of whom are in this room now, have told me they see the gifts for ministry in me, and it is because of their affirmations and encouragement that I stand before you."

Dort continued, "There are certain aspects of NCC practice that are hidden from the public, so to speak, which makes evangelism more difficult. Please tell us your views on this reality."

"I am suspicious of any religion that has secret doctrines or private rituals for an inner circle. What have they got to hide? Inside a church, nothing about beliefs or practices should be hidden or reserved for a selected few," Cloud said. "And I don't believe that the NCC should be a restricted society. With very few exceptions, anybody who wants to attend should be free to do so.

"The exceptions are the same for any church, synagogue, temple, mosque, or faith community. Those who present physical dangers to themselves or others should not be seated among vulnerable people. Pedophiles are an obvious example. Seriously mentally ill individuals are another. We need to find ways to reach out to such people without presenting risks to other worshipers. Perhaps services in structured environments could be devised for such unhappy souls.

"At any rate, the NCC appeals to a relatively small group of seekers. Most people are more conventional with regard to religion, and we need to respect their sensibilities. Our goal should not be to convert the world to NCC beliefs but to be a model of religious honesty and provide a safe place for people who want or need to practice their faith and experience spirituality in this free way. We have, as it were, a ***natural*** constituency."

This last remark was greeted with groans throughout the hall.

"Tell us your understanding of the Bible," said another commissioner.

"I have no quarrel with those who believe the Bible literally, as long as they don't insist that everyone else must also. For the most part, I understand the Bible as metaphor, but this does not diminish its authority in any way. The miracles of Jesus, for example, are more powerful and life enhancing for me when taken metaphorically than if they had to be accepted literally or not at all. The transforming energy of the Bible comes from reflecting on its stories and images and not from the historicity of its words."

"Well then, if Jesus' miracles are not literally true," asked another minister, "what good is Christianity?"

"Communities organized around the healing vision of Jesus do enormous good in the world. Regardless of disputes over doctrines and the exact nature of Christ, there is a salutary dimension to the Christian life. People's lives have been enriched. Society has been changed in healthful ways. But we must always be ready to acknowledge that the Christian church as an institution throughout the centuries has caused a great deal of suffering and death as well.

And it has been when the Church has clung too hard to strict dogma and claims of absolute truth that it has done the most harm."

Dort took the floor again. "So, in matters of doctrine it should be anything goes?"

"No," said Cloud. "But I believe enforcing a narrow orthodoxy is abusive. Fear-based religions that use force or state laws to keep adherents in line are bankrupt, of course. Those that use mind control devices such as guilt and peer pressure to motivate members are also guilty of harm. A confident and strong religion is not afraid of the free flow of ideas and is open to exploring areas of doubt and changing its institutional mind.

"Doctrines can be quite useful for building beneficial models for worship and living, but institutions need to be wary of them. Religious doctrines bear watching and need to be re-examined regularly. Doctrine, after all, is a human invention."

"That view dishonors the saints who received the faith from God," Dort sputtered.

"Saints are not always saintly, I'd say," Cloud responded. "The human dynamics that create religious traditions are not always salutary. I could make up a set of absurd doctrines and with a little persuasion could gather a band of believers. A few of my followers, mostly males, would end up using all their psychological energy to defend the truth of these absurd doctrines, and my imaginary tenets would become orthodox truth."

"That's secular humanist nonsense," Dort responded. "How can you...?

Evelyn Rarom interrupted and said, "I move the examination be arrested."

Cloud and Terp were excused from the room, only to return three minutes later to thunderous applause. The vote was overwhelmingly in favor of ordaining Cloud. Dort asked to be recorded as abstaining but everyone else voted aye.

Cloud, Terp, Zara, Mary, Den, and their pets moved into the Sedona resort at the end of January. When they left Strange Haven, the property owner lamented that he would never find another tenant without investing a great deal of money in renovations. Lloyd solved that problem by buying the place as a summer home and winter getaway when they wanted to enjoy four seasons. Terp and Cloud were pleased, because they had come to love the old place and would now be able to visit it from time to time. Lloyd and Nissa volunteered to help get the new church started, thus they lived like nomads, moving in various configurations among homes in Paradise Valley, Prescott, and Sedona.

The resort offered plenty of meeting and living space and had two pools, one indoor and one outside with a connecting gate. Also outside were a tennis court, a spa, and a sauna. Darshan converted a sunny corner room into a studio for Mary. He was interested in keeping her productive, as he had opened a shop in town to compensate for loss of revenue from the now closed gift shop in the resort.

Mary's paintings sold well, and in time she became a local celebrity, making a great deal of money from her art.

Cloud was ordained at a service in New River. He saw no mystical white light, but Cedar Cradle, Zara, and Prasada each saw a gold aura around his head immediately before hands were laid on him. Terp reaffirmed her previous baptism. Zara had been naked when baptized by sprinkling, so Terp took Zara with her under water, completing the nude immersion rite for both.

Members from Phoenix and New River salted the inaugural service at Sedona. Skye sat with Mary. For the anthem Skye played guitar as he and Mary sang "Morning Has Broken" in soul-piercing harmony.

Lloyd and Nissa acted as greeters. Edna Echo and Clark Hyfrydol made the drive up, as did Dagmar and Quinn. Cedar Cradle, Firstlaugh and their children attended. As residents of the facility, Prasada and Darshan sat in on the service.

Accepting Cloud's invitation, Emily Congo and Bookman Donne came out of curiosity, dressed in their finest Sunday attire. They were the only worshipers who remained in their clothes that day. Since the temperature outside hovered near freezing, the heat was turned up in the sanctuary so the naked worshipers would be comfortable. This also provided incentive for those who stayed clad to remove at least some of their garments. Emily and Bookman, however, kept everything on.

Having been tutored in the art of homiletics by Terp, Cloud was excited to preach the congregation's first sermon. His text came from John 13, the account of Jesus washing the feet of his disciples at the Last Supper. "Jesus rose from the supper table, removed his garments, and wrapped a towel around his waist," Cloud said solemnly. "He then proceeded to wash his disciples feet, using the towel to dry them. What do you see in your minds when you hear these words? This is a sacred scene to stimulate our memories when we're invited to eat and drink in remembrance of Jesus.

"Meditate on his movements around the table. See him shuffling on his knees from one pair of feet to another. This is about more than humility. A brilliant teacher and healer who was as full of God as a human could be, stripped himself naked and caressed the crusty feet of his students.

"Do you think he removed the towel to wipe their feet? It's a logical progression as we mentally fill in the blanks in the text. This evokes an image of intimacy and vulnerability. But for the sake of those who do not wish to think about Jesus working nude, imagine that he kept the towel around his waist and used one end of it to dry the wet feet of his friends. This, then, creates a situation of even closer touch than the naked Jesus wiping their feet from a slight distance.

"Either way you imagine it, this is a holy tableau, as holy and sensual as the parallel scene in John 12, where Lazarus' sister Mary washes Jesus' feet with nard and then wipes them with her hair. Jesus said, 'If I then, your Lord and Teacher, have washed your feet, you also ought to wash one another's feet.' At face value, this has as much sacramental significance as baptism and communion. The church should engage in foot-washing far more often. I have to wonder why it's never been made a sacrament.

"In any case, this account is a call for followers of Jesus to present themselves to one another with authentic vulnerability and intimacy, both of which require considerable trust. My prayer is that we can build that kind of mutuality in this congregation. Already we have begun to do that, most of us, by laying aside our garments. Yet there is much more to creating true intimacy than removing clothes. In search of God's love, let us wash one another's feet literally with our hands and figuratively with our prayers."

As a result of the enthusiastic response to this sermon, Cloud and Terp immediately instituted a monthly foot-washing exchange as part of the worship liturgy. They would celebrate communion the first Sunday of each month, and the assembled worshipers would pair off to wash each other's feet the third Sunday.

Emily and Bookman returned the second Sunday in February, dressed more casually. They kept their clothes on during worship but appeared nude at the fellowship time afterward.

"I really like the services," Emily said, "but I'm having a hard time with the idea of being naked in church. I guess it's my strict Baptist upbringing."

"Don't fret about it," said Cloud. "You're under no obligation to disrobe -ever. If you need to have clothes on for worship to be meaningful to you, no one will question that. There is one exception, however. If you join the church, you must be naked for baptism or renewal of baptism, both of which are done by full immersion."

"Now ***that*** I don't have a problem with," she said. "I was dunked fully clothed, and I remember thinking I would rather have been naked. What a soggy mess I was."

Darla called Terp that week to see how she was doing. In the course of the conversation, Terp told her about the upcoming foot-washing service, and Darla expressed curiosity about the ritual.

"Why don't you and Yonah come and observe," said Terp. "You can sit in the back with your clothes on and no one will mind."

A dozen basins and towels were set around the sanctuary for the foot-washing portion of the service. At the appointed time, parishioners moved their chairs around to make room for the ritual. Cloud and Terp demonstrated on each other then invited the congregation to participate with pre-selected partners.

Darla and Yonah sat in the back of the room, dressed in casual clothing as Terp had advised. Darshan and Prasada, who were naked, observed the proceedings from a spot near the Nabis. The Hindu couple got up and approached the rabbi and her husband.

"We're not Christians either," said Darshan. "And we do not make this request out of faith in Jesus as the Messiah but as an expression of deep friendship. Would you do us the honor of allowing us to wash your feet? You need feel no obligation to reciprocate."

Yonah looked at his wife and she nodded. They removed their shoes and socks. Darshan lowered Yonah's feet into a basin one at a time drying them carefully with a towel. Prasada did the same with Darla.

Darla then said, "We would be honored to do the same for you." The couples traded places, and the Jews washed the feet of the Hindus.

Nissa paired up with Emily Congo and Lloyd with Bookman Donne. The professors had decided to try worshiping nude to see what it felt like, and this seemed a fitting occasion for the experiment.

Skye was commuting regularly to Sedona to be with Mary. On a trip in late February, he brought with him a packet of photographs his brother Cochise had taken at Cloud's ordination. Foremost among them was one of the central acts of ordination, which showed Cloud kneeling, surrounded by unclad ministers who had their hands on his bowed head. Bill and Cathy Blake and their new associate pastor, Malama Kohana had flown from Honolulu for the occasion, so they were in the picture. Terp, Adam, Evelyn, and Kwan-yin were the other clergy included in the laying on of hands ritual.

A rainbow of auras shimmered around the bodies of the assembled clerics, including Cloud. Shades of purple, blue, gold, red, violet, turquoise, tan, and orange radiated from the photo, and so interwoven were the hues that the human eye could not perceive which color belonged to whom. The brilliant spectrum, it seemed, fell upon all of them collectively.

Another picture showed Terp placing a red stole around Cloud's shoulders. A single gold aura extended over their heads.

Cloud savored these images but was ambivalent about displaying them. Eventually, he framed and hung the one of him and Terp in their bedroom. The rainbow of clergy photograph was enlarged and placed on his office credenza.

Argyle Watts retired from the ministry in 1979. When he learned through a denominational newsletter that Terp had renounced the jurisdiction of the American Calvinist Church, he wrote to her last known address. The letter was forwarded to Terp in Sedona. He expressed concern about his protégé and wanted to know what she was doing.

Terp wrote him a long, honest letter about her ecclesiastical trial, her concerns about right wing ferment in the ACC, and her new call in the NCC. His reply expressed sorrow about her experiences in the Calvinist Church and dismay that she may have become involved in a cult. She responded by inviting him and Ruth to visit Sedona and learn first hand what life was like in a naturist congregation.

"What do you think about this, Ruth?" he asked his wife after she had read Terp's latest letter.

Ruth had known about Terp's involvement with the NCC for nearly three years, as a result of conversations with Nissa. Thus she was not completely surprised by this development. "A visit to Arizona with room and board provided free is too good to pass up. More importantly, I know how deeply you care for Terp, and the only way your heart will ever be at rest is by talking with her in person."

He booked the flight.

By the end of March, less than two months after the inaugural service, the congregation had quadrupled from twelve to forty-eight regular worshipers. Baptism and renewal of baptism rites were scheduled for the fourth Sunday of every month.

The pastors instituted an afternoon reflexology program on foot-washing Sundays, and this quickly became popular, resulting in additional visitors who decided to return for worship. Darla and Yonah visited once a month for the foot-washing ritual and stayed for reflexology in the afternoon. The third Sunday in May they shed their clothing.

Cloud sent announcements about the new church to all the secular nudist resorts in central Arizona. This is how the Wickhams and Dolmens learned what Terp was doing, and the nine of them came to worship the first Sunday in April and brought a dozen friends with them.

Terp was delighted to see her former parishioners but told them it would be unethical of her to ask them to leave the Calvinist congregation.

"People leave churches all the time," Kina said. "You didn't contact us about coming here. We found out on our own, and we want to be a part of this new congregation."

Word of Terp's co-pastorate with Cloud circulated selectively around her former congregation, resulting in Jenny Mast and her partner Gwen Jones showing up for worship one Sunday and becoming regulars thereafter. Two other families from the Prescott congregation also learned of Terp's new call, and though they had no previous experience with naturism, visited in early April. They kept their clothes on the next three Sundays in a row, before deciding to disrobe and become members.

Cloud believed the church needed a program staff to continue the pattern of growth. He and Terp developed a personnel model that included specialists to work in the areas of physical, emotional, and spiritual health.

"If humans are created in the image of God, as Genesis suggests," Cloud said, "then the church needs to help people keep their brains and bodies in good shape. Taking care of body, mind, and spirit is a way of honoring God."

"It's a form of worship," Terp said, "unless it turns to conceit. Then it's idolatry."

The first person they recruited was Cedar Cradle, who became the Parish Massage Therapist.

One of the regular worshipers was a former Army medic who became a Registered Nurse. He now worked at a clinic in Flagstaff. Thus, broad-shouldered, six-feet-two Ian Cumming became the congregation's part-time Parish Nurse.

"What we need now," said Cloud, "is a Spiritual Director."

"And where do you intend to find one?" asked Terp.

"I'll make inquiries in Phoenix," he said.

Late one afternoon in April, Cloud, Terp, Firstlaugh, and Cedar Cradle were on the roof of the resort with their children, enjoying a spectacular view of bright red rocks and clear blue sky.

"Look!" said Firstlaugh, "An eagle! That's a good sign."

Zara spotted the bird soaring high in the sky but misheard Uncle Firstlaugh's identification of the creature. "Come down here, angel! I'll make you a nest!" she called out. This is how the church facility came to be known as Angel Nest.

—o—

Terp and Cloud met Ruth and Argyle at Sky Harbor Airport in Phoenix. In the car on the way to Sedona, the couples talked at great length about life in two denominations, the American Calvinist Church and the Natural Christian Church.

"Now, you will definitely encounter nudity at Angel Nest," Cloud said. "So if you're offended by this, it might be better for you to stay at Strange Haven in Prescott. Dad and Nissa live there now."

"Well then," Ruth said, "we'd encounter nudity there too, wouldn't we?"

"Why?" Argyle asked. "We stayed with them before and saw no naked people."

Ruth had never told her husband about her conversations with Nissa and became flustered. "Well..."

Immediately, Terp came to her rescue, saying, "I believe I said they're helping out with the new church. It's a logical and correct assumption that they are naturists. But they're staying at Angel Nest at the moment, so you can have Strange Haven to yourselves if you want."

"At any rate," said Cloud, "if you stay at Angel Nest, there will be no pressure for you to disrobe. No external pressure that is. A lot of people who visit seem to discover an inner compulsion to cast off their clothes. The services are clothing optional, and a few people choose to keep their pants on."

"That's certainly comforting to know," said Argyle wryly. "Under the circumstances, we may as well stay with you in Sedona. We wouldn't learn much about your social and religious practices living in isolation sixty miles away."

The Calvinist pastor and his wife arrived at Angel Nest on Tuesday. By Thursday afternoon, Ruth was running around the place stark naked and taking great delight in doing so. She would have disrobed sooner but wanted to give her husband a little time to adjust to the place before she abandoned his standards of propriety.

More quickly than he had imagined possible, Argyle became accustomed to seeing nude people of all ages, shapes, and sizes moving about the house, quietly tending to the tasks of their ordinary lives. Feeling a bit like a field anthropologist, he accepted the nakedness as normative for the peculiar society he was studying.

He did not, however, see any need to shed his own clothing and insisted on wearing a three-piece suit to Sunday worship. In part this was because of a traditional sense of what was appropriate attire for worship. Going to church without a necktie felt recklessly casual to him. Going naked was for South Pacific natives. But the sanctuary was temperature controlled for the comfort of unclad people, and Argyle's profuse perspiration during the service resulted in his suit needing to be dry-cleaned. Given the cost of dry-cleaning, this eventuality clashed with his sense of financial stewardship.

Accordingly, on Sunday afternoon, Argyle changed into a polo shirt and Bermuda shorts. He also dressed this way on Monday, when he made his way to the pool for a pre-lunch swim. Wearing no bathing trunks under his shorts, he eased into the practice of naturism by slipping out of his clothes and diving into the refreshing water.

After his time in the pool, he appeared nude in the kitchen to make himself a sandwich. "Nothing like a brisk swim to make a man hungry," he said offhandedly to the collection of Angel Nest residents engaged in various stages of lunch. No one commented on his lack of raiment.

CHAPTER TWENTY-EIGHT

Since she was serving on the staff of the church and her family had moved to Angel Nest, Cedar Cradle felt the need for a more formal relationship with the NCC. She said to Cloud, "I want to be baptized. Firstlaugh would like to be baptized with me, but he has reservations about the Trinity."

"I'll talk to him when he gets home from work," said Cloud. "That was my hold-up, too."

Cloud explained to his friend that a metaphorical understanding of the relationship among God, Jesus Christ, and the Holy Spirit was acceptable in the NCC.

"I see God in relationship with all creation," Firstlaugh said. "I perceive the Spirit in the world as a demonstration of the presence of God. And I believe that Christ is an authentic expression of God's love."

"If you desire it, I would be honored to officiate at your baptism," said Cloud.

Firstlaugh embraced Cloud. "I desire it."

The last Sunday in April, all four Begays entered the indoor pool for baptism. Wakhan leaped from the edge into Terp's arms, while

Tzek, Cedar Cradle, and Firstlaugh jumped in feet first. After the questions had been asked and answered by the parents for themselves and on behalf of their children, Cloud immersed Firstlaugh and pronounced a Trinitarian formula over him. Terp did the same for Cedar Cradle, while Tzek held his little sister.

Since all four adults were dripping water, their profuse tears of joy were not evident to the congregation. Terp then baptized Tzek and Cloud immersed Wakhan. As the pastors held the children in their arms, Firstlaugh and Cedar Cradle embraced Cloud and Terp. Zara jumped off Mary's lap and dove into the pool and joined the group hug.

After the service, Mary said, "From the time Firstlaugh went under till Wakhan emerged from the water, a shaft of bright sunlight shone through the window right over the spot where you all were gathered. It disappeared when the hugging started."

"Does that surprise you?" Terp asked her sister.

"I've been around you guys too long to be surprised by anything," Mary said.

Cloud wrote a want ad for a Spiritual Director that concluded with: MUST BE COMFORTABLE COUNSELING NAKED PARISHIONERS. He sent it to Kwan-yin and Evelyn. Through an unlikely string of circumstances that involved Kwan-yin passing it to a parishioner who gave it to his psychotherapist, who handed it on to the tennis pro she was having an affair with, who in turn put the ad in the hands of the Episcopal priest he was giving lessons to, Cloud received an inquiry about the position on the church staff. Cloud asked Kwan-yin to make an initial evaluation, and if the applicant looked promising, he and Terp would drive to Phoenix to conduct an interview. As a result, Cloud and Terp met Tallis Bede at the NCC estate in Phoenix.

The naked clergy couple waited in the conference room for Kwan-yin to escort Tallis in. By prior arrangement with Kwan-yin, the applicant, too, was unclothed. The twenty-nine year-old woman was pale white from face to toes.

"I considered working on a tan in preparation for the interview," Tallis said, "but decided it'd be more honest for you to see me as I am now and not as I may become."

"I can see you both ways," said Cloud. A mystical glow radiated from his eyes. Tallis saw it, causing an excited fluster, as always happened with her psychic discoveries.

"I believe you can," Tallis said, now calm and peering directly at him. "At any rate, as I noted in my resume, I'm a former nun."

"What religion?" Cloud asked.

"Roman Catholic, of course," said Tallis in a surprised voice.

"It's not a matter of course," Cloud said. "Catholicism is not the only religion or even Christian church with nuns, and there's more than one Catholic denomination."

"You're right," said Tallis. "I need to let go of the conceit that the particular church I happen to be rebelling against is the only authentic religion in town."

"Forget about denominational labels. Tell us about the faith search that has brought you to this place and time," said Terp.

"I went to Parochial elementary and high schools, then into the convent and college simultaneously. Eventually I received a Master of Spiritual Direction degree. The more I worked with people on their spiritual struggles -especially priests- the more my own beliefs changed away from the doctrines of my church. I'm a rather progressive thinker and have become somewhat Protestant in my outlook, although not doctrinaire about it. Apart from that, I had a major problem with time."

"Say more about time," said Terp.

"In the convent, time is structured according to a strict discipline. The system is arranged so that everyone knows exactly where she is supposed to be every second of the day. Certain things, like daily prayer, happen at the same time every day. It's not difficult for those sisters who have a strong need to be told by higher authority where they should be every minute. Some of the sisters would get very anxious if they had free time to do with as they wished. It seemed somehow sinful to them, but the system drove me crazy.

"I wanted time to unfold naturally. I like to get up with the sunrise, but in the convent we rose according to the unvarying clock regardless of the natural rhythm of the solar system. I wanted time to just ***be*** without having to ***do*** anything in particular. I guess I flunked obedience once too often, and I was encouraged to rethink my vocation.

"Two years ago I left the convent, intent on making my own way in the world and taking time as it unfolded rather than filling it artificially. I got an efficiency apartment, joined an Episcopal congregation, and set up practice. Most of my clients are clergy."

"What do you see as the biggest spiritual issue facing clergy?" Terp asked.

"A sense of entitlement," Tallis said without hesitation. "Catholic, Protestant, or Orthodox -too many men of God think the world owes them deference."

"What about women of God?" Cloud asked.

"I haven't met enough women clergy to form an opinion," Tallis said, "but I've not encountered that expectation in my very limited contact with them. Catholic sisters have a whole set of control issues but generally without the narcissism that so many priests display."

"Why are you interested in providing spiritual counseling to a bunch of very liberal Christians who go to church naked?" asked Terp.

"I miss living in an intimate community," Tallis answered. "Kwan-yin gave me a lot of material to read about the NCC, and it seems to me there would be less sexual tension in an environment where men and women went about their business unclothed. In a context where bodies were hidden and forbidden, I saw priests and sisters regularly exhibit repressed fascination with bodies of whichever sex they were oriented to. Besides that, if I'm going to rebel, I ought to do it in grand style. My parents already think I've jumped off the edge of the world. I may as well see what life is like on another planet."

Cloud and Terp looked at one another and without words came to a decision.

"We want to offer you the position," Cloud said. "There is no salary, but we will provide full room and board and medical insurance, and you keep all the honoraria you receive from spiritual directing."

Tallis stood and extended a hand to each pastor. "I accept," she said.

Though she was not destitute, Narcissa's financial situation was far from comfortable. The market for patriotic beauty supplies was weak at the moment. She was able to get a group together for gossip and sales once a month or so, but this was not enough to sustain her. Her savings account had dwindled to nothing from the expense of working through the circles at NAT-SASS and making generous contributions to Arms for Jesus Ministries, Incorporated.

She spent the month of May lounging around her house without bothering to put on clothes, drinking up a once substantial stock of wine and liquor. One entire week elapsed when she forgot to take a shower or brush her teeth. For days at a time she fasted from solid food in haphazard manner. The solitude provided ample opportunity to reflect on the direction of her life. As a result of this soul searching she came to the realization that Lloyd was responsible for everything that had gone wrong.

"I can't understand why he left me," she said out loud. Sometime in the second week she began conversing vigorously with the walls and expounding trenchant insights to the furniture. "He walked out on me with no cause and took up with that silly nudist. They must have been rutting like dogs for years behind my back. I'm much better looking than she ever was."

After several days of verbally castigating her former husband, she grew weary of him, and turned her attention to her parents. "All I ever wanted to do was be a model. But would they give me money for modeling school? Nooooooo. The selfish pigs. Go to college, they said. Go be a teacher or nurse or some stupid thing like that. But I got them good. 'Hey Ma! Hey Dad! You failed your only child by raising her in a backwoods trash heap. Whadya think of that? Are you good and ashamed of yourselves?'

"No wonder my life's a mess. They forced me to grow up in a stinking mining town. And they think they're so good. Smug bastards! 'Oh, Narcissa, go to college and we'll pay for everything.' Bullshit! Let me go to modeling school! 'Oh no, dear that's not a legitimate school. It's a racket.' If I told them once I told them a thousand times I was too good for their grubby world, but would they listen to me? Hah!"

The first Monday in June, Narcissa sobered up enough to call her regional sales manager. "Clive, dear, I'm not getting enough sales opportunities. Demand for red white and blue lipstick seems to be waning. I need a new line of products. What have you got for me?"

"I got nothing for your current clientele," the manager said. "Their tastes are limited. You gotta develop a bunch of new ones if you wanna make more money. The repeat business falls off after a while."

"Surely there are other options, new gimmicks, something to boost sales," Narcissa said.

"Well, if you're really interested in expanding your horizons..."

"I'm interested in expanding my commissions," said Narcissa testily.

"The Ladies' Patriotic Beauty Society has a wholly owned subsidiary called Please Your Man Products. They market lingerie and related supplies. Very profitable. But a completely different customer base. You interested?"

"How different?" Narcissa asked.

"These clients would not read the society page of the newspaper," said Clive. "Hell, they wouldn't read ***any*** kind of paper except for maybe grocery store tabloids."

"You know I'm a damn fine sales representative," she said. "I can sell to any demographic. I'll take a whirl at it. And I'll keep at the patriotic line too. The residual business is still worthwhile."

And so it happened that Narcissa soon became the company's leading Arizona sales producer for PYMP. The product line was not to her personal liking. Crotch-less panties, push-up bras, g-strings, whips, spiked collars, and handcuffs seemed rather pointless to her, but they sold well and the commissions were substantial.

Her acting ability helped her put over the sales scripts. "Girls, you will drive your man wild with passion with our latest candy-striped paper panties. They come complete with safety pins so he can change his baby's sexy diaper. I must warn you, though. Don't let him drool too much, because they dissolve in water."

She sold her entire inventory of this new and improved item and had to reorder.

Late at night after a particularly successful sales party, Narcissa began to wonder if men really liked the products she was selling. Opening her sample case, she took out a few items. Soon she was dressed in leopard skin pantyhose with a heart-shaped piece of nylon missing at a strategic place and a pink bra that pressed her breasts practically to her neck. She slipped into high heels and snapped on a spiked leather necklace. Twirling a pair of handcuffs in one hand and cracking a black leather whip in the other, she pranced around the house.

"OK, Lloyd," she crooned to an empty room, "The goddess of passion knows what you like. Come and get me! Maybe I'll let you lick my toenails. But you'll have to beg first!"

Skye's appearances in Sedona area clubs made him a local celebrity. After the owner of the Red Vortex Café signed the folk singer to six months of Friday and Saturday night performances, he decided his life was stable enough to allow him to propose to Mary. She said yes, and the wedding was set for a Tuesday afternoon in June.

Kwan-yin officiated, and Cochise was officially Best Man, but as he was also photographing the event, Cloud stood in for him during the ceremony. Terp and Penny were Matrons of Honor, Cedar Cradle was an attendant, Wakhan was flower girl, and Zara was ring bearer. In addition to Cloud on the groom's side, Randall, Lloyd, Firstlaugh, and Tzek served as ushers.

At the reception, Penny said to her daughters, "Now mother and both daughters have had naturist weddings. Someday we ***must*** sit down and look at each other's wedding albums."

Cloud moved to Penny's left side, extended his arm around her right shoulder and gave her a quick sideways hug. "This is my mother-in-law," he said. "Can you believe that? She could be my twin sister."

A very pleased Penny said, "Liberal use of sun-screen does wonders for your skin. Naturists never leave home without it." An active sex life takes years off one's age, she thought but did not say aloud.

At the Red Vortex the next Friday, Mary joined her new husband in a duet of his original composition, "The Apache Wedding," that brought thunderous applause. Though the song was a lyrical fantasy having nothing to do with their own nuptials, the audience identified the attractive couple with the fanciful imagery of the piece. Skye's soaring falsetto combined with Mary's harmonic alto in the chorus caused a massive epidemic of goose bumps among patrons in the nightclub.

"Can you do that every night?" the owner asked.

"This was just a freebie to celebrate our getting hitched," said Skye.

"I'll add a hundred bucks to your pay if you two do that number every night," the owner offered.

"This is Skye's gig not mine," Mary said, "but I'll sing an occasional duet with him for free if you extend his contract for another six months."

"Deal!" said the owner.

In 1969, songwriter Colin Glee had a top ten hit with "Dancing with Lady Luna," a song celebrating the first lunar landing. Since then he had produced a few minor hits among the hundreds of songs he penned. Although he was well respected in the community of pop-folk-country music composers, he was not widely known by the public. To remedy this, in 1979 Colin began performing his own material in clubs throughout the western states, and in due course, he was booked for a Monday to Thursday night gig at the Red Vortex in Sedona.

Skye and Mary liked to check out the weeknight acts at the club, and as a result, they met and quickly came to like the singer-songwriter.

"I used to do 'Lady Luna' in my road act," Skye told the composer. "But after the near disaster with Apollo XIII, I slowed the tempo way down and made it wistful. The audiences loved it."

"Cool!" said Colin.

The trio met for lunch Thursday. While munching on a cactus French fry, Colin said, "I've been held over for another week, which is good. It's a whole lot better than being told to slink out of town and never come back. But I gotta find a new place to stay. My motel's booked solid next week."

"I'm sure we can find a room at Angel Nest where we live," said Mary. "But there's a catch."

"What's that?" asked Colin.

"It's a church facility," she said.

"Hey, I believe in God," Colin said. "If you live there, it must be OK."

"It's a clothing-optional church," said Skye. "If you're bashful about your body or if nudity offends you, it would not be a suitable place to stay."

"Oh wow!" said Colin. "I was naked in a pew once. In college I dated a preacher's daughter for a while. One Friday night we snuck into the church and got a little carried away."

"In this church, people attend worship in the nude," Mary said, "and there's nothing titillating about it. They're expressing spirituality in a natural way."

"I'm sorry. Bad example," said Colin. "The truth is I'm not offended by nudity. There's plenty of it backstage in show business. And I really appreciate your offer of hospitality and would like to stay at Angel Nest."

Colin demonstrated no inhibitions about shedding his clothing. He attended Sunday worship and was deeply moved by the graceful and grace-filled liturgy, which included Skye and Mary singing "Peace in the Valley" while Terp danced to it. They changed the song's pronouns to plural, and sang about peace for all rather than for me.

At lunch that afternoon, Colin said, "Cloud's sermon really made me think. I've been asking myself a lot of questions lately about God and the meaning of life, but I'm chasing my tail about what I really believe."

"You need to confer with Tallis," Mary said. "She's our Spiritual Director."

Providentially, Tallis Bede, now sporting a golden tan, walked by the table at that moment, and Mary grabbed her arm and pulled her into the next chair. Thus Colin found himself revealing his deepest spiritual longings to the former nun.

A week later, he was on the road again, but he returned to Angel Nest as often as he could.

A fellow teacher at the high school where Arquimedes Shapiro taught Spanish, German, and Vietnamese gave him a flyer for a veteran's rap session group that met at a store front office in downtown San Diego.

"It's a bunch of Viet Nam vets who get together to let off steam about the war," the colleague, also a Viet Nam veteran, explained. "You ought to check it out. A minister who was in the Korean War coordinates it, but all the rest are from Nam."

The Korean War veteran, Arquimedes discovered the first time he attended a rap session, was Petrus Dort, pastor of the Natural Christian Church. Dort didn't say anything about his congregation, however. He focused his entire attention on the concerns and traumas of the former soldiers. They needed to talk, and his job was to listen not proselytize.

At the third session, Arquimedes spoke about his injured left arm. "They told me I'd never be able to use it again," he said. "But I've gone through a lot of spiritual healing services at my church, and I can make it move in little circles now. I have faith that someday I'll be able to lift it above my head."

After the session, Petrus asked Arquimedes to stay and tell him more about the Church of Motherly Healing. "I'm interested in the relationship between religious faith and physical health," the minister said. "There are a couple of women pastors in our denomination who do anointing with oil at healing services. But they focus on mental and emotional healing. They say any physical cures are incidental to improved mental health and lifestyle changes."

"My church wouldn't make a distinction between mental and physical healing," said Arquimedes. "We're already perfect and whole in the mind of God. It's error that causes us to see ourselves as sick or wounded."

The two veterans of different Asian wars talked for three hours. Arquimedes told Petrus more about his church and Petrus described the NCC to Arquimedes. Not long after that, Petrus attended a Wednesday evening prayer service at the Church of Motherly Healing, where he silently prayed for a cure for what he believed was his damaged psyche. Nothing changed internally, but he felt better after the service.

Arquimedes felt obliged to reciprocate by visiting the naturist congregation. Exposing his body was intimidating, however. Baring his genitals was not the problem. Rather, his scarred and paralyzed arm embarrassed him. He knew he could attend halfway, remaining clad in the back row, but the need to match Petrus' gesture was strong. Arquimedes disrobed, and no one stared at his wounds.

In the worship bulletin that Sunday, Arquimedes found an insert with information about "Our Newest Congregation." The glossy half-sheet contained an appeal for contributions to support denominational mission. What caught Arquimedes' eye, however, was not the colorful picture of the church facility in Sedona, but a photo of his former boss in the 1007th MI Detachment, Captain Cloud Morgan, next to an attractive woman wearing granny glasses. They were co-pastors of the mission church.

CHAPTER TWENTY-NINE

After gaining the needed contact information from Petrus, Arquimedes telephoned Cloud and arranged to visit Angel Nest the next weekend. The injured veteran took delight in showing Cloud how he could now move his left arm. By the time he returned to San Diego late Sunday night, Arquimedes was at last comfortable addressing Cloud on a first name basis. He had experienced foot-washing, reflexology, and a special prayer service in which Terp anointed him with oil. His arm did not improve, but he was filled with joyful exuberance and deep satisfaction with his life. This experience, he believed, did not detract from his faith in his own church but added something to it. Arquimedes Shapiro was enchanted by the ethos of Angel Nest and would return frequently.

Zara's third birthday was a warm Indian summer day in October. Cloud proposed a picnic hike to celebrate. "For a long time I've wanted to find the place where I encountered that mountain lion west of Slide Rock," he said to his wife and daughter. "I'd like to show it to you."

Cloud pulled the station wagon onto a patch of dirt and gravel at the side of Highway 89A a half mile south of Slide Rock in Oak Creek

Canyon. He pointed west and said, "That's where we're going."

"We're at the bottom of Oak Creek. Are we going to climb over the canyon wall?" Terp asked with a note of incredulity in her voice.

"No," said Cloud. "We'll use the Sterling Pass trail. We'll gain about eleven hundred feet in our climb. That's less than the elevation rise climbing Camelback Mountain over a shorter distance. Given our physical shape, this is no big deal."

"As long as you're the one holding Zara," said Terp.

He carried his daughter in a sling during the arduous, single-file trek up to the pass and then down bushy, clover-covered slopes into a red-walled canyon. He set her down to creep through the fissure that led to an enclosed valley. As soon as she saw the shallow pool carved out of gold-hued rock, Zara skipped across the stone plain toward the ledge above the pond.

"This is the place!" Cloud said. He caught up with Zara and took her hand. Terp held her other hand as the three approached the basin of water.

As Cloud had done more than two decades earlier, he and Terp removed their hiking boots and socks and plunged their feet into the cold water.

"Brrrrr that feels good!" said Cloud.

"The water's icy, but the sun is warm on this rock," Terp said. "Let's get naked."

No sooner had they stripped and settled their rumps onto the smooth stone than a mountain lion wandered onto the ledge and ambled toward them. All three humans immediately sensed that all was well. There was no fear among them. The lion approached Cloud and sniffed at his right armpit, then sniffed at Terp's face before nuzzling Zara's forehead and plopping down in front of her to be petted. As Zara ran a tiny hand across the tawny feline's back, the large cat purred.

Terp turned to Cloud and said, "I think you have a talent for discerning openings that no one else can see -fruitful, promising pathways. Not only passes into hidden valleys, but spiritual doors as well."

"Really?" Cloud responded. "I just thought I was a weird utopian dreamer. And I wouldn't agree that no one else can see the peculiar things I see. Only a few, maybe. But ***you*** can see them too!"

"That's only because I'm also a weird utopian dreamer. As Emily wrote, 'Then there's a pair of us! Don't tell! They'd advertise -you know.'"

"Ah yes, what would we do without Miss Dickinson's insight?" said Cloud.

Terp held up a hand and said, "Shhh. I have a sense we're not alone here,"

"Besides the four of us you mean?" Cloud asked, patting the flank of the mountain lion.

"Yes," said Terp. "Something benign." Feeling mildly euphoric, she stood and walked around the lip of the pool toward a cave in the vertical face of the mountain.

Before she could reach the entrance, a voice emanated from the cave. "Nobody seems to be afraid of anything anymore. What ever happened to awe?"

The Old One crawled out of the grotto, rose to a standing position, then took Terp's arm and walked with her to the place where Cloud, Zara, and the mountain lion were resting. Cloud judged the being with a large triangular shaped head to be six and a half feet tall. The Old One was as naked as every other sentient being around the pool.

"Hello Terp. Hello Cloud. Hello Zara. Hello [the Old One addressed the cat in a strange language]. I thought this would be an opportune time for more conversation. I know you have questions stored up for me."

"Hello Old One," Cloud said. He spoke in an unsurprised manner, as if he had last chatted with the mysterious being the previous week rather than seven years before. "Let's start with the immediate situation. Are you influencing the lion's behavior?"

"No. Zara is."

"Did you make that other lion smile all those years ago?" Cloud asked.

"No. You did, Cloud. She was really very amused with you. I was watching but you didn't need my assistance," the Old One answered.

"Are there others like you in the world?" Terp asked.

"Oh yes," the Old One responded. "I don't know the exact population, but I would judge about two million all together in communities throughout the planet."

Terp looked at the Old One's genitalia while trying to formulate her next question. "How do you reproduce?" she asked without the elegance she hoped for.

"Slowly by human standards, but yes, we bear children," the Old One said. "I have produced as father to one child born a century ago and living now in Tibet. I hope to produce as mother someday."

"Last time we met, you evaded my question about being an angel," Terp said

"The word angel carries misleading connotations," the Old One replied. "We are beings with a mission to observe people who are of particular interest to..." The Old One paused to find the best term. "...the Transcendent One. Those I watch are connected in some way or are likely to meet in the courses of their lives. We deal in probabilities, however, not predestined fates. And we are acutely aware always that intervention leads to unexpected consequences. If one unhappy thing is prevented from happening, other worse things may occur as a result. So we have to be wise about using our influence."

"That's what makes the concept of sin so slippery," Cloud said.

"Quite so," said the Old One. "And in that context, I confess we are supposed to care for everyone equally, but in reality we all have our favorites. You three are especially dear to me and are among the very few who have actually seen and spoken with me. Only a small number of those we watch over ever perceive us mentally and fewer actually meet one of us. Most remain completely unaware of our presence their entire lives."

"Who among those in your charge do we know personally?" Cloud asked.

"Both of your extended families," the Old One replied. "Firstlaugh, Cedar Cradle and their children are also especially dear to me. Den is too. You might be interested to know that when he was a small child, I influenced Den to turn aside from a booby trap he was intent on inspecting. Cloud, you later interrogated the guerrilla fighter who set the trap, and he confessed to a life changing experience. That was my intervention."

"I remember him!" Cloud said. "Pham van Hai. He said he was tired of war."

"When Den escaped from Vung Tau in that boat," the Old One continued, "he and his companions were in grave peril, but I suggested to a ship's captain that he change course to find the boat people. I also influenced a government bureaucrat to assign him to your family, contrary to your instructions. I apologize for disappointing you."

"To the contrary," Cloud said, "we are so grateful to have Den in our lives."

"I know," said the Old One with confidence. "There are other interferences I'm responsible for. Prasada's position at the college is my doing. That's enough for now. You will likely learn more of my mischief in the future."

"Wait a second. Given all these connections you've made with our minds, are you responsible for our prescient dreams?" asked Cloud.

"Not really," said the Old One. "I will confess to planting certain images and suggestions relating to the prospects for various people eventually to meet one another. But dreams about political assassinations and historic events come from another source far beyond my meager ability. This is a gift I do not have the power to bestow."

"Nevertheless, you regularly mess with people's minds," Cloud said with a chuckle. "And no doubt without their knowledge or permission."

"It is possible to close off one's mind so that telepathic information cannot be received," the Old One said. "Anyone can do this, although few do. Most humans remain open to receiving telepathy either because they don't believe in it or they intuitively desire communication with lovers or some transcendent source."

"Many people do shut off ***portions*** of their minds," Cloud said. "They compartmentalize, preventing one part of the mind from engaging with other parts so they can maintain massive contradictions without having to think about them."

"Beliefs in the realm of religion are especially prone to this," the Old One concurred. "However, one can do this with the entire mind. If you no longer desire my occasional communications, you have the ability to -what is the phrase?- tune me out."

"You know I don't want to tune you out," Cloud responded.

"Why don't people see you?" Terp asked.

"Mostly they don't look. The few who do keep it to themselves or reveal it only to selected folks who won't think they're crazy."

"What's your name?" Zara asked.

"Let me save that for another time," the Old One said.

"What is your...uh...species?" Cloud asked.

"That's difficult to answer," said the Old One. "The name in my language would mean nothing to you. Sometimes we play games making the name for our species into puns in various human languages. I'll talk with colleagues and create a suitable English pun for you. Ninety-nine percent of my DNA is the same as yours, however."

"Earlier we talked about reproduction," said Terp. "Will you elaborate on your sexual nature?"

The Old One answered, "Delightedly! My species is blessedly fully male and fully female. We have special mating rituals in which partners impregnate each other. It is physically impossible for me to inseminate myself -by natural means. I am monogamous, although not all of us are. Some among us engage in periodic bouts of promiscuity. Rather than two partners mating with one another, they've been known to create circles of several dozen, so that each receives semen from the one behind and gives it to the one in front. My soul-mate and I prefer an exclusive relationship."

Zara reached over and touched the Old One's breasts. "You look like both mommy ***and*** daddy," she said.

Noting the concern in Terp's mind, the Old One said, "It's alright."

"I worry about her inordinate curiosity," said Terp. "I don't want her to get in trouble violating other people's boundaries."

"Zara will always be exceedingly curious about the world. There will come a time when you will not be able to protect her," the Old One said. "But if it's any consolation, you need not worry about her harming other people. And for the record, she asked permission to touch my breasts and I gave it."

"So, you two are carrying on telepathic conversations in front of mom and dad," said Cloud.

"It is so," said the Old One. "And I know that all three of you are curious about my body. Come and touch anywhere you like." The Old One reclined supine on the sandstone shelf.

Zara put her hands on the Old One's face. "Oooh, you have a big head," she said.

Terp, Cloud, and the Old One laughed. "That's what your mother called me when she was a little girl," the Old One explained to Zara.

With soft strokes, the humans explored the contours of the Old One's body. "Your skin feels like ours," Cloud said, "but with a sensation of electricity about it."

"My skin is the same as yours. What you sense is energy within me," the Old One said. "Through my skin it is easily transferred to living and inanimate things."

"Can you...? Do you ever...? I mean, does it ever happen that...beings like you have sex with humans?" asked Terp.

"It is biologically possible and has happened from time to time, although not with me," the Old One said. The ancient being reached out and playfully petted the mountain lion. "Of course the results are almost always tragic."

"Almost means there have been exceptions," Cloud said.

"Yes," the Old One acknowledged, " but I'll leave it for you to speculate on what that may mean."

"Would you like to touch us?" Terp asked.

"That is kind of you to offer," the Old One responded. "It would provide me with heightened memories of you."

Cloud and Terp lay on their backs and the Old One explored their bodies with extremely light but energy-laden touches. Each one, husband and wife, experienced highly pleasurable sensations from the ancient one's fingers in contact with their skin, particularly approaching their genital areas. Rather than sexual arousal, however, they felt acute sensual satisfaction.

While this was going on, Zara climbed on the lion's back and played with the feline's ears. When the Old One was finished caressing her parents, Zara climbed down and said, "Do that to me too."

She lay on top of Terp, and the Old One used a finger to trace the lines of Zara's face and body, skipping over the little girl's genitalia.

"She sent me a message to touch between her legs," the Old One said to Cloud and Terp, "and I told her grown-ups should not touch children that way."

"I understand," Zara said. "I won't let a bad person touch me there. But you're not a bad person. I can tell."

"Bless you, Zara," the Old One said, "but I will not touch that part of you. In my society as in human society it is a serious transgression for adults to fondle children's sexual organs." This last remark was directed at Terp and Cloud.

"OK," said Zara. "When I'm grown up?"

"If you wish then," said the Old One.

"I ***will*** wish," Zara declared.

The mountain lion rolled over and began kneading the air with his paws. "He wants to be touched too," said Zara. "He wants a belly rub."

The Old One complied with the creature's request.

"I have an ontological question," said Cloud.

"You doctors of philosophy love ontological questions," said the Old One. "Yet they seldom have clear and simple answers."

"That's true," said Cloud. "What I want to know is are we on the right path?"

"We would not be having this conversation right now if you were evolving in an unproductive direction," the Old One replied. "All three of you are explorers at heart, however, and would feel cheated if I determined the course for you. Do not be afraid of getting lost or making mistakes. You are intuitive enough to find your way home."

"We would like you to meet the people we love," said Terp. "But I suppose you already know them."

"I do know them," the Old One said, "and I hope to meet with them in person someday, just as I have with you. I shall meditate on the probabilities."

"And we'd like to meet your soul-mate," Terp added.

"A pleasant prospect residing at the farthest edge of possibility," the ambisexual one said enigmatically then kissed Zara, Terp, Cloud, and the lion on their foreheads and disappeared in a flash of light.

CHAPTER THIRTY

Colin Glee told his business partner, Asher Shepherd, about Skye, and as a result Asher and his wife Hylli, traveled from Los Angeles to Sedona to sit in on Skye's act at the Red Vortex. That night, Mary joined her husband singing "The Apache Wedding."

Two things developed from this audition. First, Asher told Skye, "Your material and delivery are very good. I want to sign you to a recording deal, on condition that Mary joins you in the wedding number on the first CD."

They quickly reached agreement on terms. Asher recommended Skye have another attorney look over the contract before signing it. "I want you to hear from someone else that it's fair. Don't take my word for it," Asher said.

Second, Mary and Skye invited the Shepherds to stay at Angel Nest. So eager were the entertainment lawyer and his Icelandic wife to enjoy the naturist facility that they began disrobing in Skye's car while stopped at the traffic light at the busy intersection of Highways 89A and 179, much to the delight of the pick-up truck driver in the lane beside them. Asher and Hylli ran naked and giggling from the parking lot to the front entrance of the church resort.

"When I was growing up in Reykjavik," Hylli said after a few sips of Lambrusco, "in winter my brothers and I used to run naked from the sauna into the yard and make steaming snow angels."

"What fun!" said Terp. "My mom always made me put on four layers of clothing before I could go out and romp in the snow."

The introduction of the Shepherds into the household that night provided the excuse for an impromptu party. The children were fast asleep, so the twelve adults could play. The married couples were Cloud and Terp; Firstlaugh and Cedar Cradle; Skye and Mary; Darshan and Prasada; and Asher and Hylli. The two singles were Colin and Tallis.

"Let's do foot rubs!" Mary gleefully suggested.

Six pairs quickly formed and the oily exchange of massages commenced.

Tallis paired off with Colin, with unanticipated results. As he sat with his feet in her lap, Colin gazed at Tallis' face, absorbing the wisdom of her eyes and the character of her mouth and brow. By the time she had finished kneading his second foot, he was in love with his spiritual director.

She knew intuitively that something had changed inside the composer-singer, so she scanned his face with intensity while he performed a reflexology workout on her feet, looking for signs of what was going on in his mind. What she perceived proved irresistible, and she fell for him as well.

"I'm kind of dehydrated," Colin said. "I think I'll get some water."

"I'll go with you," Tallis said.

No one saw either of them again until breakfast.

Cloud massaged Hylli's feet. This was a first time experience for her, and he asked her to note what he did so she could do the same to his feet later. Halfway through attending to her second foot, he felt it pushing insistently against his hands and saw her other foot jerk back and forth. Looking at her face, he saw that she was having an orgasm. The others were intent on giving or receiving relaxation therapy, so no one else noticed the event.

Neither Cloud nor Hylli spoke, but she knew he was aware of what had occurred. Later, when Cloud went to the kitchen to get pitchers of water for the group, Hylli went along to help.

"I've never known that to happen before," Cloud said.

"You're the expert," said Hylli. "I would have guessed it happens a lot."

"I've done this many hundreds of times, and your response was unprecedented," he said.

"It must have been something I thought," she said with a chuckle.

"Be sure to think those thoughts the next time Asher rubs your feet when you two are alone. He'll be glad you came," Cloud responded.

The party broke up around midnight. Terp, Cloud, Cedar Cradle, and Firstlaugh settled into the king-size bed to debrief the events of the day.

"Hylli climaxed while I was rubbing her left foot," Cloud said. "What do you make of that?"

"She's a rather spontaneous person," said Terp. "She probably felt carried away by the pleasure of the massage."

"I think she wanted it to happen," said Cedar Cradle. "Probably she was fantasizing the whole time you were doing her feet."

"Nothing wrong with that," Firstlaugh said, "as long as she doesn't act out her fantasies. Of course, she might think of Angel Nest as a place to do that."

"It was probably the initial excitement of lying around with a bunch of naked people doing something sensuous," offered Terp. "If we act normal, she'll pick up the ethos of the house and do just fine."

"I think you three are very wise," said Cloud. "I'm honored to be among you. But I've got an eight o'clock lecture, so I'm going to curl up and nod off." He kissed Terp and rolled over. Within thirty seconds he was asleep.

Terp's approach to Hylli worked well. The Shepherds stayed through worship on Sunday. Hylli maintained her outgoing and spontaneous personality but there were no more instances of sexualized behavior.

Asher put a large check in the offering box in the narthex. "We'd very much like to visit from time to time," he said. "This is the perfect get-away for us. We feel like we're among trusted friends."

"You've all been so nice," Hylli enthused as she hugged everyone.

"I'll give you a call when I get studio time scheduled, Skye," Asher said. "You and Mary will be our guests when you come over. I want you to be rested and in perfect voice for recording."

"Give me a call when you want to come back," Darshan said, "and I'll make sure there's a room available for you." He drove the Shepherds to the Sedona airport for their chartered flight to Phoenix, where they boarded a jet to Los Angeles.

The night Tallis and Colin fell in love, they lay together in her bed, mostly talking but caressing one another as well. Tallis made it clear she was not ready for sexual intercourse, and Colin honored her statement. Nevertheless, he became sexually aroused and so did she. So great was their mutual interest in exploring one another's minds, however, that they allowed the erotic sensations to sift throughout their bodies without release, prolonging the pleasure for hours.

Sometime after two in the morning, Colin said, "Being here with you like this, I'm feeling the afterglow of making love, even though we haven't."

"That's an incredibly romantic thing for a man to say," Tallis said. "But I think we have made love. We haven't engaged in coitus but we've certainly expressed loving feelings in a physical way."

"I yield to the wise woman," he said and lightly kissed her lips, which parted in response and ardently welcomed his mouth and tongue. She reached down and wrapped her thin fingers around his engorged penis, and he burst in response, spewing semen all over her, the bed and himself.

"Sorry," he said.

"Don't be," she said. "I'm not. Will this stuff make us stick together?"

"You bet," he said.

She pressed her breasts and pelvis against his body. "Let's try to get a little sleep," she said.

They slept for several hours, and when they awoke, they were indeed stuck together. Gingerly they separated. Tallis lay on her back, with her hands behind her head, grinning. Colin began to caress her breasts and when she made no effort to stop him, he moved his hand through her muff and began massaging her clitoris. Within seconds she reached orgasm.

"Now we're even," he said.

They curled up again and slept until dawn.

Colin awoke to the sensation of Tallis gently rubbing his day-old beard with her fingers.

"I need a shave," he said.

"I like the prickly feel of your face," she said. "Can I watch you shave?"

"Sure," he said. "You'll have to come down to my room, though."

"OK. Let me gather a few things first." She jumped out of bed and tossed a hairdryer, shampoo, a brush, and assorted grooming items into a flight bag.

"Moving in?" Colin queried.

"No. I just thought it would be fun to shower together."

Colin washed Tallis' hair in the shower. They stood side by side before the bathroom mirror while he lathered his face and shaved and she dried her strawberry blonde tresses.

With the dryer off, she continued to brush her hair. "There are all sorts of ethical issues with this," she said. "Spiritual directors are not supposed to become romantically involved with their directees."

"Is that what I am?" asked Colin. "A directee? It sounds like a dominance/submission kind of game."

"What do you think our relationship was before we crawled into bed together?" Tallis asked.

"I saw myself as a seeker, someone searching for God, who came to sit at the feet of an enlightened woman."

"I'll accept that," she said, putting the brush down and pressing her hips playfully into his side. "But the truth is, you're wise in ways I'm not and vice versa. We have many things to teach each other. It's clear, however, that I can no longer provide you spiritual guidance. Before you get on the road again chasing gigs around the country, I think we'd better sit down with Cloud and Terp and seek their guidance about our relationship."

"Why is that?" Colin asked.

"Because a member of the church staff has compromised her professional position by falling...getting emotionally involved with...a..."

"Directee," said Colin.

She laughed. "An image just flashed through my mind of an old couple in matching rocking chairs chortling over the word directee."

"Speaking of chortles, let's go get breakfast and face the household," Colin said. "I imagine our disappearance last night has fueled some speculations."

Residents of Angel Nest fended for themselves at breakfast, and Cloud was the only one in the kitchen when Tallis and Colin arrived.

"Have you been out in the sun, Tallis?" Cloud asked. "Your face is glowing."

Simultaneously pleased and flustered by the remark, Tallis blurted out, "OK. If you want to know, I spent the night with Colin, but I'm still a virgin."

"The status of your hymen concerns me not at all," said Cloud. "You're an adult."

"What about professional boundaries?" Tallis asked.

"You're entitled to fall in love, Tallis. If it happens to be someone you're directing, my advice is once is wonderful. Don't make a habit of it," Cloud said.

Wearing a mischievous smile, Tallis replied, "I gave up habits a long tim ago when I left the convent. But who said anything about falling in love?"

"You both have. Not with words, but your faces are shouting it to the rafters," Cloud answered. "Bonus points for the pun, though."

The three sat at the table drinking decaf and cranberry juice and eating oatmeal. As they rinsed their dishes in the sink, Colin said, "I have to go to L. A. for a couple of weeks to sell some songs and do a few gigs. When I get back, I want to be baptized and join the church. Then I'd like to make this my home base. It's a great place to write songs."

"What if I moved back to Phoenix?" Tallis said. "Would you still want to join this church and move in here?"

"If you were moving to get away from me, it would break my heart," said Colin. "But I'd still want to be baptized. That's very clear in my mind. And I can't think of a better place to be than Angel Nest to tend to a broken heart."

"You see why he's such a good songwriter," Tallis said to Cloud. "He's so romantic." She turned to Colin and said, "I'll be the first one to greet you when you step out of the baptismal pool."

"Why don't you stand beside him when I dunk him?" Cloud said.

And that's exactly how it happened shortly after Colin returned from Los Angeles towing a rented trailer with all his worldly possessions.

"We're making renovations in your old room," Cloud said to Colin. "Would you mind switching to the room next to Tallis?"

Colin did not mind. The room had an inside door that converted the two rooms into a suite. After two weeks of endearments via telephone, Tallis was ready for another kind of intercourse when Colin slipped into her bed the first night he was back.

Cloud was feeling stressed. Balancing two full-time jobs was proving more difficult than he had imagined. He thoroughly enjoyed teaching at the college, but the administrative responsibilities required more time than he liked. Meanwhile, increasing membership at the church led to greater time demands for worship and sermon preparation, pastoral counseling, teaching, program planning, weddings, staff supervision, and administration of the church.

Members of the congregation were healthier than the general population, so, thankfully, there was little demand for hospital visitation other than the maternity ward. To date, neither he nor Terp had been called on for a funeral service. Terp was working all the time as well, and they found less and less time for one another amidst their busy schedules.

At the December meeting of the Sedona NCC Board, Cloud presented a proposal for a new membership category. "Darla and Yonah Nabi are Jewish, and Prasada and Darshan Pratyaksha are Hindu. All of them have expressed the desire to be part of our philosophical and faith-nurturing community but not of the church ***per se***. I propose we create a special membership roll for them."

"What would we call them?" Kina Wickham asked.

"We've been playing with the idea of having two rolls, one for church members and the other for affiliated partners," said Terp. "People who participate regularly with us but who can't for doctrinal reasons join the church could be recognized in a ceremony during worship and be placed on the community roll."

"I like that," said Wake Dolmen. "It respects where people are in their faith journeys."

"This would be great for church growth," enthused Nissa. "People with doubts or even no religion could join our church without any pressure to accept specific beliefs. But I bet some of them would eventually want to be baptized."

The board approved the proposal, and the next Sunday, Darla, Yonah, Prasada, and Darshan stepped into the pool not for baptism but to enjoy goblets of olive oil ritually poured over their heads as a sign of welcome to community membership. A blessing prayer for each followed the anointing. The community roll soon grew as Arquimedes Shapiro, a member of the Church of Motherly Healing, joined, along with Hylli Shepherd, a member of the Church of Iceland, and her husband Asher, who was not a member of any church and who was struggling with what to believe about God.

A week before Christmas, as the last faculty meeting before the holiday break concluded, Mito Picaron took Cloud aside. "Could you meet with me in my office for a few minutes, Cloud?" the short, barrel-chested professor of religion asked.

They walked together down the hall and entered a cluttered study, with books, magazines, and loose papers piled everywhere. Mito removed a stack of journals from a side chair and invited Cloud to sit.

"A rumor has come to my ears," Mito announced with dramatic intonation, "that you are involved in a nudist cult? Is this true?"

"From whom did you hear this rumor?" Cloud asked evenly.

"What is the phrase reporters use? A reliable source," Mito said.

"I ignore anonymous letters," Cloud said, "so why should I respond to anonymous rumors?"

"Because they can hurt you," Mito said with a note of sadness in his voice.

"Is your source secret? If so, what is he or she hiding from?" Cloud asked.

"The information came from my wife, Alada," Mito offered. "I do not know where she heard it."

"Well," said Cloud, "the rumor is partly true. I am an ordained minister in the Natural Christian Church, which practices naturism. It is not a cult but a progressive Christian denomination. In your academic field you are well acquainted with the hallmarks of a cult. We do not use mind control techniques or isolate members. Visitors are welcome, subject to a few prudent gate-keeping rules. People come and go at will. All offerings are voluntary and we do not use guilt or social pressure to get people to give more. We have no secret rituals or inner circles."

"Yet people run around naked in your church?" Mito inquired.

"Yes," said Cloud. "There's nothing immoral about that. This does not constitute grounds for my dismissal from the faculty, if that's what you're thinking about. President Bergen is aware of my religious practice. He would rather not have a lot of publicity about it, but he's not going to tell me how I can or cannot worship God."

"To be truthful," Mito confessed, "Alada did not identify your church as a cult. That was my word. She called it a church where people go naked to worship. And I heard you use the word naturism. How is that different from nudism?"

"It's not, really, although the term naturism seems to convey a greater sense of spirituality than does nudism," Cloud answered.

"I question the spiritual value of nudity," Mito said.

"Then keep your clothes on," Cloud said.

"But if I wanted to come to your church, I would be forced to take them off," Mito countered.

"Not at all," said Cloud. "Worship is clothing optional -except for baptisms. You would, however, have to accept that most of the people in the sanctuary are naked."

"How do I know this is not a cult?" Mito asked with skepticism in his voice.

"Even if it were, it would be none of your business. I don't tell you how to worship, so what gives you the right to pass judgment on my faith?" Cloud said.

"Because it might be harmful to people," Mito responded.

"The religion you used to serve as a priest has a long history of torturing and killing people in the name of the faith. I suggest that is exceedingly harmful to people," Cloud retorted.

"Ah yes, and you Protestants have done your share of bad deeds as well," Mito said. "My concern is not for past mistakes but for present ones. And since you brought it up, I harbor significant reservations about the practices of my former faith, beginning with the obvious issue of priestly celibacy. At any rate, out of care for your well-being, I would like permission to visit your church to judge for myself whether it provides a legitimate expression of Christianity."

"You don't need to wrap your curiosity in a rationalization about my welfare," Cloud said. "You're welcome to come to our Sunday morning service, and you can keep your duds on the whole time. There is one requirement, however. Since you are married, your wife must accompany you. We don't allow married people to visit without their spouses. We don't want to create secrets between husbands and wives. Our congregation is a family, and we don't want to do anything that might divide existing families."

"This sounds like Protestant Pharisee rules to me," said Mito. "You Protestants allow birth control and approve of sex for reasons other than procreation. Why can't you allow me the scholar's privilege of investigating a religious phenomenon?"

"So, one minute we are a cult and the next Protestants," Cloud responded. "Which is it, Mito? But I guess you can't answer that until you've seen for yourself. You are most welcome at the Sedona NCC, and you don't need to hide behind scholarly research. But you do need to bring Alada with you. And neither one of you needs to disrobe."

Mito sighed heavily. "Perhaps you and your wife could come to dinner at my home to discuss the matter with Alada and me."

They set a date for the following evening.

Alada greeted Terp and Cloud at the door. She was a slightly built woman, somewhat beyond the age of forty, and tiny, like a ballerina.

Though diminutive in size, Alada was not small in personality. She poured ice cold Coronas into pilsner glasses for her guests. "This will prepare your stomachs for the meal," she said.

Cloud and Terp sipped the beer.

"Mito's talk is full of ***machismo***," Alada said, patting her husband on the knee, "but let me tell you he is a lamb around the house. He does his own ironing, washes the dishes, and cleans the bathrooms."

"Those are habits from my days as a priest," he explained.

"Don't you believe it," Alada said. "I know all about the

housekeepers that tended to you priests," Alada said. "My dear husband is full of bluster, but that's a cover for his gentle saintliness."

"I detect a great deal of love in your words, Alada," Terp said.

Alada swallowed a mouthful of beer. "Yes, I love this man with all my heart." She tussled his straight black hair with her free hand. "But let us speak of other things. In addition to you, Cloud, I've heard that three other Anasazi faculty members attend your naked church. Prasada Pratyaksha, whose husband owns the property, Emily Congo, and her husband Bookman Donne. Emily and I are dear friends, so I trust my information is accurate. Emily, in fact, has been trying to get me to bring Mito along to observe a service."

"I've invited Magnus Bergen to attend," said Cloud, "but so far he's declined. He has his presidential image to uphold, and his wife would throw a fit at the prospect."

"I told Alada about your Protestant rule that husbands and wives must attend together," Mito interjected.

"Catholics have rules too, dear," Alada said, "and this one seems very sensible to me. Besides, Emily told me this long before you did."

Cloud said, "It's interesting that you perceive us as Protestants, Mito. Terp does too. I think of the NCC as Christian but not necessarily Protestant, although its historical roots are in Protestantism. Nevertheless, I don't think the long-established Protestant churches want to claim us among their partners. We tend to be lumped into an oddball group of denominations that don't fit into a recognizable mold, such as Quakers, Christian Scientists, Unitarians, Jehovah's Witnesses, Mormons, and the like."

Terp turned to Alada. "Mito has already said he wants to check us out," she said. "The question is, Alada, are you willing to go along with him?"

"Most certainly," Alada replied. "And not out of scholarly interest or to find out if it's a cult. I want to see for myself how you worship God without clothes on."

They adjourned to the dining room, where Alada served baked trout, brown rice, and steamed vegetables.

"Apart from celibacy, Mito, what are your disagreements with your former church?" Cloud asked.

"Regardless of canonic decree, I still consider myself Catholic,"

Mito huffed. "I'm a Küngian Catholic, admiring the work of German theologian Hans Küng. I refuse to close my mind to ideas simply because they challenge Church doctrine. I cannot bind my conscience to certain dogmas, particularly concerning power and authority."

"What doctrines do you question?" Terp asked.

"No man is infallible," Mito pontificated, "even while sitting on a sacred throne, and the Church is not God's only vessel of salvation. I also agree with Protestants that the gift of sex is for more than simply procreation, and thus artificial birth control is acceptable. I don't understand homosexuality, but considering all the good, faithful priests I know who are burdened with that sad orientation, it must not be quite the abomination the Church claims. Naturally, I favor married priests, although my liberal conscience hesitates at the prospect of women priests."

Alada and Mito visited the Sedona NCC the first Sunday after Christmas. Though he was no longer a priest, Mito sought to strengthen his role as a professor of religion doing academic research by wearing a clerical shirt and collar. Alada came dressed in slacks and a sweater. Emily and Bookman invited the Picarons to sit with them. The visitors remained clad throughout the service. In their private conversation later, Mito deemed the service liturgically deficient, while Alada found it elegant in its simplicity.

When everyone had moved into the fellowship room for post-worship refreshments, Alada slipped back into the sanctuary, stripped off her clothes, and knelt before the empty cross above the chancel. She entered into a time of deeply meditative prayer. Amid the silence, she communed with God. The former nun prayed for wisdom, but knowledge did not come to her. Instead, an electric sense of liberating grace and love suffused her body. This was a holy moment in her life, and she wept for joy.

Some time later, she rejoined the others, who were chatting while sipping coffee and nibbling on cookies, and in doing so neglected to don her garments.

"What are you doing, Alada?" Mito asked sternly. "Put your clothes on!"

She kissed his cheek. "Control yourself, dear," she said.

A few minutes later, Mito reported his impressions to Cloud. "So far, I don't see any signs of cultic activity, but, of course, observing a single mass does not provide sufficient information to form a firm evaluation. I'd like to gather more data."

"Gather ye data while ye may," Cloud quipped. "I suggest you meet with our spiritual director, Tallis Bede. She used to be a Catholic sister."

Alada grasped Mito's arm. "I'd love to meet her. I'm sure we must have a lot in common."

Cloud signaled for Tallis to join them and made the introductions. Soon thereafter, the erstwhile priest found himself ensconced in an alcove with two naked former nuns, one his wife.

"Wouldn't you like to take at least ***some*** of your clothes off?" Tallis asked him.

"I can't do scholarly research unclad," he responded.

"Bullshit!" Tallis said. "You're not doing scholarly research; you're exercising your God-given curiosity. Why don't you go ahead and experience the whole thing?"

Secretly, Mito felt an urge to disrobe, but his stubborn streak got the better of him, and he said, "No, I don't think so."

"Well, it's your loss," Tallis said.

The next week, Mito and Alada attended worship again, with Alada doing so naked. Mito did not wear clerics but kept his clothes on the entire time they were at Angel Nest. The third week, owing to the excessive warmth of the place, he explained to Alada, Mito stripped to a modest bathing suit.

The fourth time they attended was a foot-washing service. Mito appeared wrapped in a large towel. "I have girded myself after the same manner as our Lord when he humbly washed the feet of his disciples," he announced to Alada.

When the congregation stood to sing a hymn, Alada reached over and undid Mito's wrap and pulled it away. "I don't think Jesus wore a terrycloth beach towel," she whispered in his ear. Mito chose not to make a scene.

CHAPTER THIRTY-ONE

Because of rapid growth in the congregation, the room used for a sanctuary had to be enlarged by tearing out a wall and merging it with an adjoining room. The Board also decided to call an additional pastor to assist with programs and integration of new members into the life of the community. As a result of this decision, a search committee presented the Rev. Malama Kohana to be elected by the congregation as Associate Pastor of the Sedona Natural Christian Church.

Terp was delighted to have her seminary classmate and dancing partner join the church staff. Since graduation from Pacific Crossroads, Malama had been serving as Associate Pastor of the Honolulu NCC, where Penny and Randall Owen had become actively involved. Terp's mother and stepfather used the occasion of Malama's installation service in Sedona as an excuse to visit their Arizona family.

Malama's first sermon was based on the story of blind Bartimaeus, who when summoned to Jesus, threw off his clothes before approaching the rabbi. "Jesus' response to the naked blind man," Malama said, "was not to chastise him but simply to ask, 'What do you want me to do?' The blind beggar said, 'Master, let me gain my sight.' And Jesus restored the man's vision, and the naked man then followed Jesus on his way toward Jerusalem.

"Jesus' act of healing is central to this narrative, of course, but the little detail of the beggar throwing off the only garment he possessed is revealing. There is something in the human spirit -a deep-seated urge- to be naked in the presence of the holy. Bartimaeus knew that Jesus was a holy man, and when he was called before him acted instinctively by removing his robe.

"We have largely repressed this urge in modern industrial society, much to our spiritual detriment. For when we approach God insulated by layers of protective clothing, or worse, by fancy suits and dresses, we are tempted to cover our deepest longings and most profound confessions as well. And it's not that God doesn't know what we're hiding; it's that we obscure them from ourselves."

After the service, Ian Cumming, the parish nurse, thanked Malama for the sermon, telling her that he hadn't been able to offer the most troubling of his combat memories to God until he began worshiping naked. Sensing the beginning of an important conversation that could benefit their professional relationship, Malama invited Ian to sit with her in an alcove and talk about his experiences in Viet Nam.

They spent the rest of the afternoon telling stories about their lives. Malama learned that Ian had been stationed at Schofield Barracks in the center of Oahu and that while there he had taken a Polynesian culture class in which he learned the male version of the hula. Excited by this serendipitous discovery, Malama suggested they dance together in a church service.

They practiced evenings for two weeks, then performed the hula, unencumbered by grass skirts, as a sacred movement anthem in worship. The congregation was enthralled by their dance. Even Mito Picaron pronounced it a stunning evocation of the human spirit.

The congregation also came to see Malama and Ian as a couple, which was an accurate perception, because the pastor and nurse developed great affection for one another. Neither fell wildly and passionately in love. Rather, their feelings developed slowly and steadily over the months until Malama and Ian each realized they were soul-mates.

"I don't think there was a specific time before which I was not in love with you and after which I was," Ian said to Malama. "The feeling just grew in me until I could no longer deny it."

"That's what happened to me too," she confessed to Ian.

—o—

Over the years, Cloud and Terp had approached their wedding anniversary in a haphazard manner. By their reckoning, they had three anniversaries, the spiritual date, the naturist one, and the Calvinist one. They never decided which was the real one, and it became a matter of whimsy as to which one they celebrated in any given year. In 1981, they decided on the spur of the moment to do something special for the eighth anniversary of their naturist nuptials.

"Let's exchange memories of something we did together," suggested Terp, "the way you shared memories of Xuan with me and I gave you images of my dad."

"Can I suggest the experience?" said Cloud.

Terp wrote a few words on a piece of notepaper and folded it up in her hand. "Go ahead," she said.

"How about the first time you danced for me to ***Lara's Theme***?"

She handed him the paper on which she had written, "dance for the sad poet."

Cloud's eyes and mouth crinkled in joy. "Thank you dearest Terp," he said. "In the midst of all this stress we've been carrying, it's good to be reminded that we still think -and dream- alike."

They retired to their bedroom, already aroused at the prospect of linking in this special way. Terp climbed into Cloud's lap and guided his erection inside her. Each meditated silently, focusing their minds on the event in which Terp had removed her clothes while dancing in front of Cloud, fulfilling prescient dreams each had experienced years before.

When their foreheads touched, Terp's mind was immediately filled with an image of herself in the act of removing her bra, revealing firm rounded breasts. She perceived Cloud's gasp of pleasure at the sight. Then she removed her panties in front of him for the first time and danced around him in a circle. Cloud's remembrance of that moment filtered into her consciousness. ***Oh my God! What an entrancing body! What incredible beauty I am privileged to witness!***

Cloud's mind was flooded with the sight of himself removing his clothing. ***May I have this dance***, he heard himself say as he took Terp in his arms. ***Next dance -horizontal and a capella- ravish*** *me!* he heard her say. He saw the top of his head descending the length of her body as he kissed her breasts and navel and delta. Then he saw his face from Terp's perspective as he entered her for the first time. Terp's memory of her thoughts at the sight of his face in that moment blossomed in his head. ***Oh God! The love in his face! The joy bursting from grief! This is a holy moment! I love him more than I can stand!***

When, at last, they separated foreheads and opened their eyes, each saw tears streaming down the face of the other.

"I still feel that way," Cloud whispered.

"Me too," answered Terp.

Their mouths crashed together in a deep kiss that progressed quickly to even more impassioned choreography. Terp arched backward on the bed, pulling Cloud on top of her. His thrusts grew in force and she received the escalating movements eagerly, until they burst with pleasure at the same instant.

For a long time afterward, they lay together in silence, savoring the experience. When Cloud got up to go to the bathroom, he came back with a tube of Terp's lipstick. "Close your eyes and lie still," he said to her. He then used the cosmetic to print words backwards from right to left on her body. "Look in the mirror," he said.

Terp stood and saw in red letters: "Dearest T, I love thee. C."

She grinned in response. "Give me that tube, now that you've ruined my favorite shade," she said, "and lie down like a good boy!" She drew stick figures labeled C and T in a series of erotic conjunctions. "This is what I think of you, buster!" she said as he admired her artwork in the mirror.

They fell into each other's arms and began to laugh, long and deep. In due time the red images on their bodies were smeared beyond recognition.

"To the showers, woman!" Cloud bellowed.

This anniversary celebration brought Cloud and Terp four kinds of cleansing. Tears opened their senses to the treasures of their pasts. Passionate lovemaking washed away accumulated stress that had numbed their feelings for too long. Playful laughter scrubbed away the weariness stored in their bodies. And then they gently washed and rinsed each other's bodies in a nurturing shower that used far more hot water than they would have thought prudent in different circumstances.

Toward noon on a Saturday in June, Cloud and Terp visited Darshan's art gallery downtown to deliver two paintings Mary had recently completed and to take a look at a new series of photographs that Cochise had taken of mountains and canyons around the state. They were drawn to a partial view of Camelback Mountain that Cochise had captured from a northwesterly, afternoon perspective showing the outcrop of rock known as the praying monk half in radiant sunlight and half in ominous shadow.

"That's eerie," said Cloud.

"It certainly is," said a man who was browsing in the gallery. He walked over to Cloud and continued, "I was looking at that a moment ago. I'm thinking of buying it."

"The photographer is a close friend of mine," said Cloud. "He is a true artist with the lens. His works are on display all over the world."

"Would you mind telling that to my partner? He loves the photo but is a little hesitant to spend that much money for it," the man said.

"Is he around?" Cloud asked.

"In the next room. I'll get him," the man said. Fifteen seconds later Keefe Keelan returned with Theo Gynt.

"Wow, Theo," Cloud said. "It's been, let's see, sixteen years since we've seen each other and you look maybe four years older. But I hear you're reluctant to invest in a work created by my friend Cochise Burns."

"Cloud Morgan!" Theo shouted. He ran to Cloud and embraced him in a firm hug. Cloud returned the gesture and soon introductions were made all around.

"Cloud has spoken of you fondly," Terp said to Theo.

"Let me introduce you to the owners of the gallery," said Cloud. "I'll bet you can get that photograph for considerably less than what's on the tag."

Prasada was in the back room, helping her husband with inventory. Soon she and Darshan had been introduced to Cloud's college friend and his partner.

"For a friend of Cloud, the Burns piece is yours for half price," said Darshan. Keefe made the deal, and Darshan gained a nice commission. "Now go and get some lunch, and I'll have it wrapped for you when you return," the merchant added.

"Good idea. Can you join us for lunch?" Theo asked Cloud and Terp.

Over garden salads with a large side of cactus fries shared among the four of them, Cloud and Theo brought each other up to date on their lives since college.

"My mother suspected you were gay," Cloud said to Theo. "But I had no clue."

"I never met her," Theo said and then laughed heartily. "My hunch is she suspected ***you*** might be homosexual. According to the common wisdom in America, you very well could have been. At that time, society claimed that men became homosexual because they grew up in families with domineering mothers and passive fathers."

"You're right," Cloud admitted. "It was me she worried about."

"Ironically, by that standard, I should have turned out straight and you queer," Theo said. "I grew up with a strong willed father and a meek mother. I'll confess I loved you, Cloud, but it was crystal clear to me that you were hopelessly straight, and besides, I knew intuitively that you were not my soul-mate. I know now that Keefe is."

Keefe beamed and then said, "I think homosexuality is simply one of many naturally occurring variations in the human endocrine system. There's such a broad spectrum of innate sexual expression among people. It's got to be biology."

"An elegant solution," said Cloud. "By far the simplest explanation, and simple explanations are usually correct. And I've come to the conclusion that there is inherent social value in having a portion of the population being homosexual. Begetting children is not the only evolutionary survival advantage. Procreation includes ideas, inventions, art, and technology. Homosexuals provide the needed creative edge for civilization."

Terp changed the subject. "I'm curious about your work after seminary, Theo."

"I did post graduate study in alcohol and drug addiction and was called to a ministry doing recovery work with street addicts. Six years ago Keefe and I moved to Phoenix, and I'm doing a similar kind of ministry in the Valley," Theo explained.

"When were you ordained?" Terp asked.

"My denomination, the Scandinavian Protestant Church, only ordains closeted homosexuals," Theo said. "I'm openly gay and thus disqualified by my honesty."

"That's one reason I left the American Calvinist Church," Terp said. "You ought to explore ordination in the NCC. We don't discriminate because of sexual orientation."

"I've been a loyal SP all my life," Theo said. "I flirted with the Quakers in college but missed the liturgy. I still have a dream that my church will ordain me before I die."

"In the meantime," said Cloud, "why don't you two come to Angel Nest for dinner? It would be great if you could stay the night and attend worship in the morning."

"That's assuming we're comfortable with group nudity," said Keefe.

"All you have to do is say your schedule does not permit you to visit," said Terp.

"Oh, but it does!" said Keefe. "And having conferred with my partner without need of words, we wouldn't miss it for the world!"

During the fellowship time after worship the next day, Cloud said to Theo, "I remember your insightful critiques of worship when we were in college. What are your thoughts on our ordinary naturist service?"

"A little light on liturgy for my taste," Theo said, "but very strong on spiritual profundity. What would an extraordinary service be like?"

"Each first Sunday we celebrate communion by intinction -as a commemoration of Christ, not real or spiritual presence. On third Sundays we do foot-washing. We have total immersion baptisms any time, and liturgical dance at least monthly," Cloud said.

"Well then it looks like we'll need to come back," Theo responded.

"And I want to introduce you to some people in Phoenix," Cloud added.

During the following week, Cloud set up a conference call with Kwan-yin, Adam, and Evelyn at one end and Terp, Malama, and himself at the other. "NCC churches have been focusing energy and resources inwardly during our early years of development," Cloud said to his colleagues. "But we're growing up now, and it's time we emulated the major denominations by investing in mission work outside our own congregations."

"Knowing you as I do, I assume you have something specific in mind," said Kwan-yin.

Cloud told them about the addiction recovery ministry that Theo was involved with. "Half a dozen denominations contribute to the mission," Cloud said. "So it's not a fly-by-night independent operation. Our financial contribution would be welcome, of course, but there's another way we might be able to enrich the ministry."

"Actually, this part is my idea," said Terp. "I'll take the heat for being out of line. The director of the addicts' ministry is an SP with a Master of Divinity degree, but he can't be ordained because he's homosexual. If he were ordained, he could provide a sacramental dimension to his work that could be life changing for some people."

"And you want ***us*** to ordain him," said Adam.

"The thing is," said Terp, "he has high hopes to be ordained in the SP Church sometime in his lifetime. He may not want our ordination. But I think we should meet with him to explore what we can do for his ministry."

"We do have a provision in our constitution for non-parish ministers, although we've never had one in the denomination," said Evelyn. "It would be useful to explore the possibility, even if we never follow through with it."

They arranged a meeting with Theo in New River on Saturday afternoon. Keefe came along and was invited to participate in the discussion, which lasted several hours.

After describing his work in detail and providing financial reports and other documents, Theo said, "I would welcome monetary contributions from the NCC to the ministry. As to the possibility of ordination, which Terp has raised, I have mixed feelings. I am open, even eager, to learn more about the NCC and explore the possibilities for ordination, but I don't want to mislead any of you about my loyalty to the Scandinavian Protestant Church. I haven't given up on them yet."

"I have an idea," Evelyn said. "Cloud, are you teaching any courses at Anasazi this summer?"

"No," he answered.

"Would you tutor Theo in the history and polity of the NCC?" she asked.

"Certainly," he responded. "That's a great idea. Theo taught me so much about analyzing religions when we were in college. It would be great fun to turn the tables and have him sit at ***my*** feet for mentoring."

"I'd love it," said Theo.

"There is a potential problem down the road," Adam said. "There's nothing about it in writing, but the expectation in our denomination is that ministers will be married, or if not, that they will lead circumspect lives. Theo and Keefe are not married but are living together openly, which, arguably, does not meet the definition of circumspection."

"Well, so are a lot of our members," huffed Kwan-yin.

"Yes but they're not ministers," said Adam. "Petrus Dort, who is single and very circumspect, will make that distinction very clear on the floor of the Assembly."

"What if they were married in an NCC ceremony?" asked Malama.

"The state of Arizona would not recognize it, of course, but I'm willing to bet our National Assembly would for purposes of ordination," said Cloud.

"Well, you're the expert on polity," said Adam.

"So, Theo and Keefe," said Terp, "ordination aside, how would you two like to be married in an NCC ceremony?"

"My heart turns somersaults just thinking about it," said Keefe.

"It would be a blessing beyond measure," said Theo.

The third Saturday in July, Terp and Cloud co-officiated at the wedding of Theo Gynt and Keefe Keelan at Angel Nest. All the NCC ministers and church staff members in Arizona attended the service, and Cochise photographed it for posterity. Lloyd and Nissa came, bringing Mandy and Tenny along to observe the historic occasion. For the same reason, Terp invited Jenny Mast and Gwen Jones. At the conclusion of the service, Terp said, "You may kiss one another." They did, very tenderly.

Four days later, Gwen Jones suffered a stroke so severe that she was quickly transferred to a hospital in Phoenix. The nurse in charge of the intensive care unit decreed that only immediate family and clergy were permitted to visit Gwen, and this very specifically did not include Jenny.

Terp lent Jenny one of her clergy shirts with clerical collar, and by wearing this, Jenny was able to gain entry to the room and hold hands with her life-partner and caress Gwen's forehead.

Gwen rallied on the third day and was moved to intermediate care. Cloud, Terp, and Jenny gathered around Gwen's bed and held hands, including Gwen in the circle, and prayed. Terp anointed the stroke patient with oil. Gwen was not able to speak, but she blinked her eyes in comprehension of the love and care given to her by these three.

In the middle of the night, when she knew no one else was in the room, Gwen chose to let go of her will to live and quickly suffered another stroke and died.

Most Natural Christians opted for cremation and having their ashes scattered over some beloved spot. A few preferred to be buried nude, and the NCC cemetery at New River accommodated these people. Gwen had made it clear she wanted to burn like a Viking and have Jenny strew her remains in the Prescott National Forest. This she did.

Later that week, Cloud and Terp conducted their first memorial service at Angel Nest. "This is not a funeral," Terp said to the assembled mourners. "It is our testament of belief in the immortality of the human soul. The eternal part of Gwen Jones has left her earthly body for good. Now she knows in ways that we do not what communion with God means. We will all miss her, none more profoundly than her beloved Jenny. Yet our task at this moment is as much to celebrate her life as it is to grieve her passing."

"She was a crusty lady," said Cloud, "and she didn't mince words." Scattered chuckles of recognition rippled through the congregation. "I loved her directness and her curmudgeonly ways. You could always rely on Gwen to be provocative and interesting. Anyone who craved boredom or daintiness steered clear of Gwen Jones. And she scared the pants off of hypocrites." Cloud's eulogy coaxed more laughter from the people.

Then Mary and Skye sang a duet of "Abide with Me," which caused tears to flow in equal proportion to the foregoing laughter.

Among those attending the naturist memorial service were many couples from the lesbian community in north-central Arizona. Some among them shed clothing for the occasion while others remained in their mourning attire. At the conclusion of the service, Cloud invited everyone to surround Jenny with their hugs and prayers, and singly as well as in twos, threes, and fours, male and female, clothed and naked, the assembled guests did so. More than an hour elapsed before the hugging came to an end.

Jenny said later that this exchange of physical and emotional energy buoyed her spirit for an entire week following the service. The growing congregation benefited also, because seven lesbian couples started coming to Sunday morning worship as a result of attending Gwen's memorial.

CHAPTER THIRTY-TWO

Aldous Askeladd, Cloud's high school classmate, had become a successful writer, with three best-selling science fiction novels and two biographies to his credit. Film rights to one of his novels, ***Alien Crater***, had been sold to a famous director for future production as a movie. During the past decade he had been living in Los Angeles with his wife and two children, but in the summer of 1981 he decided to give up the hectic life of megalopolis and return to his roots.

Encantadora Santa Alma Askeladd was also a graduate of West High in Phoenix, having been a freshman when her future husband was a senior, although they had not known each other then. They met in 1968 at a party hosted by mutual friends from the Arizona ***avant-garde*** artists community shortly after Encantadora graduated from the University of Arizona in Tucson.

Encantadora called herself a bohemian Latina and delighted in shocking people with her acerbic tongue, but inside beat a tender, humanitarian heart. Tall, angular Aldous was grace in motion when he played his banjo and sang protest songs at the ***soiree***, thereby enchanting Encantadora. But when he sang Buddy Holly's "Everyday," smiling and looking directly into her eyes, he won her heart completely. It was not lost on her that Buddy Holly married a Latina.

Before that tumultuous summer came to an end, they said wedding vows in front of a justice of the peace in Phoenix. Their daughter Huxley was born the following year and son Savage in 1972.

As Aldous built his writing career, Encantadora made her way through the world of commercial art, developing a specialty as an illustrator for science fiction and fantasy book covers. Her bold, colorful artistry was much in demand.

It was she who broached the idea of moving back to Phoenix. "Neither of us needs to be in L.A. to do our work. Phoniness and backstabbing are sapping our creative energies. Let's go somewhere life is simpler, more natural, and less stressful."

They took a short-term lease on a townhouse in the Arcadia district on the east side of Phoenix and began looking for a home to buy. One afternoon, Aldous turned on the television for a respite from unsuccessful efforts at outlining a new novel. Arizona Afternoon was on, and the host, Dagmar Solbrent, was interviewing her husband, Viet Nam War veteran Quinn Queensbury, about the rap groups being formed around the state to help combat veterans deal with post-traumatic stress.

"Hey, I went to high school with that guy!" Aldous shouted. "Dora, Hux, Sav, come and look!"

"Tell us some of the locations where veterans who need to talk about their combat experiences can join a group," Dagmar said to Quinn.

"He was a showoff in high school, would do anything on a bet," said Aldous. "Now he's in a wheelchair. I wonder what happened."

Quinn listed a string of locations before saying, "And there's a meeting on the campus at NAU in Flagstaff. That one's facilitated by my high school classmate, a vet with two Purple Hearts, Reverend Cloud Morgan."

"Once again," said Dagmar, "for more information call 800..."

"***Reverend*** Cloud Morgan?" said Aldous. "Did he say reverend?"

"He did, Dad," said Huxley.

"Cloud was my best friend in high school. I've often wondered what the hell happened to him," Aldous said.

"Apparently not hell," Savage quipped, "if he's a minister."

"I have to find out about this," Aldous said. He looked up

Quinn's number in the phone book and called him that evening. As a result of this conversation, he telephoned Cloud in Sedona.

"Wow!" said Cloud. "I wondered where on earth you ended up. I've got to be in Phoenix tomorrow for a tutoring session. Are you free for lunch?"

They arranged to meet at Macayo's on Central Avenue.

"I read ***Alien Crater***," said Cloud, "about the narcissistic beings from another planet who land in Meteor Crater and use it as a base for colonizing the earth."

"Actually, they created the crater as a nesting place for their floating space colony and later disguised it to look like a meteor had crashed there. My aim was to produce a set-up so preposterous that no one would believe it. That way the reader could concentrate on the ironic by-play between the mutually dysfunctional aliens and humans," said the author.

"I noticed the multiple layers in the text," said Cloud.

This was the highest praise a writer could hear, and Aldous was pleased.

"Tell me how you got to be a minister," Aldous said. "I remember you being rather irreligious in high school."

Cloud laid out the story for the author: Viet Nam, Xuan's death, years of solitary grief, Adam and Evelyn, the Natural Christian Church, meeting Terp, and more.

As Cloud talked, Aldous began to form the outline of a book in his mind. "I remember you had a dream about Buddy Holly and the others dying in a plane crash before it happened," Aldous said. "Did you ever have dreams like that again?"

Cloud told him about other prescient dreams. He did not, however, mention out-of-body experiences.

"I've been searching for a subject for my next book," Aldous said. "I think I just found it. Would you allow me to work up a proposal for the story of war hero turned minister Cloud Morgan and the nudist church he serves?"

"I'm flattered," Cloud said, "but I have trouble with the hook you've devised on several counts. First, I'm not a war hero, and my work in the war zone was routinely boring. Not much of a story there. Second, the NCC is a lot more than one minister or a single congregation. I'm one of three pastors at my church. Apart from those concerns, however, I'm open to talking with you about ideas for a book."

"There are so many directions your story could unfold," Aldous said. "I'm really intrigued by the narrative possibilities."

"One more thing," Cloud said. "I can't give you permission to write about the Angel Nest community without conferring with the people who live there. Issues of personal confidentiality need to be considered. Not matters of doctrine, belief, or practice, but the privacy rights of individuals."

"Could I at least come up and take a look around?" Aldous asked. "You know, do some preliminary research?"

"How long would it take to do ***all*** the research you needed to write a book?" Cloud asked.

"With interviews, cross-referencing, gathering historical records, location notes, and so on, it could take six months, probably more," answered Aldous.

"Assuming the residents are OK with it, you could stay indefinitely at Angel Nest and do interviews and whatever else you needed to do on the scene, but there's a catch."

"What's that?"

"You'd need to bring your family with you," Cloud said.

"You mean move to Sedona?" asked Aldous.

"If you want to write authentically about the Angel Nest community, you'll have to move in and live with us, not just visit. And we don't allow husbands to stay without their wives. The public schools in the area are not so bad, by the way," said Cloud.

"You're telling me that my whole family will have to become nudists if I want to write a book about your church," Aldous said.

"Yes," said Cloud. "And it well may be the simpler, more natural life you seek."

Aldous paused a moment to think before asking, "When is your appointment?"

"In two hours," said Cloud.

"Come over to my place right now. I want to talk to Dora and the kids about this, and I may need you to answer questions. They may think I've gone loco."

When Aldous laid out the project and the naturist living environment to his family, the first thing Encantadora wanted to know about was a suitable place for her work. She was delighted to learn about Mary's studio. Huxley and Savage conferred for less than a minute and came back with a verdict. "Let's go for it, Dad!"

"You're all rather quick to leap into this radical adventure," Aldous said.

"It's not so radical," said Huxley. "At one time or another, you and Savage and I have all posed nude or nearly nude for Mom's paintings."

"But none of the naughty bits showed in the final product," Aldous said. "And I seem to remember, Dora, when ***I*** posed for you, you painted my body but put the head of a lion on it."

"I should think you'd be pleased to have your body associated with such a courageous creature," Encantadora responded.

"Well, both my face and body are on the cover of ***Nymphets of Narian***," Huxley boasted. "That's totally cool."

"But artfully posed," said Aldous.

"Of course," said Encantadora. "But what I want to know is whatever happened to leisurely perusing the Sunday paper with all four of us naked and piled into one bed?"

Aldous replied, "As I recall, that tradition began before Huxley and Savage came along and drifted to an end about the time Huxley started second grade."

"I really miss those times," said Savage.

"Me too," said Encantadora. "Our no pajamas Sundays were a blessing for the family -and it looks like they will be again, only seven days a week."

The Askeladd family moved in to Angel Nest in time for Huxley and Savage to enroll in school. Mary was delighted to share the studio with Encantadora, and Darshan was thrilled with the prospect of another artist to supply his shop. Savage quickly developed a friendship with Tzek, who was in his class in school and lived down the hall at Angel Nest.

Mary soon discovered that her artist colleague was a passionate and opinionated woman, who did not suffer fools gladly. Fortunately, Encantadora's views on the state of the universe were similar to

Mary's, so they enjoyed interludes of raucous laughter at the expense of national and local leaders.

"I've used every member of my family as models," Encantadora told Mary, "and they're tired of sitting for me."

"You'll love it here," said Mary. "You'll find lots of people willing to pose."

As the autumn unfolded, the fantasy artist produced a series of wild and weird canvases that Darshan sold as fast as he could display them. She also completed a number of covers for novels.

Aldous and Encantadora were not religious in the traditional sense of the word, although they were drawn to spiritual ideas and mystical experiences. The adjustment of the Askeladds to naturism was complete within twenty-four hours, but becoming comfortable with the ethos of prayer and worship took longer.

Just as Encantadora found many willing models for her artwork, Aldous discovered that many members of the church, though not seeking publicity for themselves, were eager to be interviewed about their lives and beliefs. They also had plenty of affectionate stories to tell about Cloud and Terp.

Cloud proved to be the most difficult interviewee. He held back information about experiences in Viet Nam. Anything that could be construed as laudatory toward himself Cloud dismissed as insignificant or refused to talk about, except for his relationship with Xuan, which he discussed at length. Lloyd slipped Aldous a copy of the Arizona Republic article about the medals Cloud had received. This was the piece that Narcissa displayed in her foyer, and Cloud hated it. One Sunday Arquimedes appeared for the weekend, and Aldous discovered a goldmine of information when he asked the Californian about Cloud's activities in Viet Nam.

Slowly the puzzle that was Cloud Morgan came together in Aldous' notes. Hidden from the author, however, were the most dramatic elements of the story: the out-of-body experiences and the existence of the Old One.

In order to reduce the stress in his life, Cloud accepted a reduction in pay in exchange for a part-time teaching load and elimination of most extra assignments and administrative responsibilities at the college. Magnus Bergen told Cloud he hoped this was a temporary situation, because he wanted to grant Cloud tenure and promote him to full professor, but he couldn't do that as long as Cloud was working less than full-time.

Dagmar and Quinn spent a weekend at Angel Nest in the fall in order to pose for a portrait they had commissioned from Mary. Aldous took advantage of their presence to interview them about both Cloud and Terp. While researching Cloud's life, the writer had learned so much about Terp that he had decided his book must be about the two of them.

Dagmar wanted Mary's painting to explore the nuances of their faces and ignore their bodies, and Mary complied with this wish. The final product depicted a twin saguaro cactus with a single root but two trunks branching out into four arms. Near the top of the right trunk she painted Quinn's face without a hint of his long brown hair that he usually kept tied back in a ponytail. At the same place on the left trunk she painted Dagmar's face, also without her trademark blond tresses.

The effect of paring away the elements that framed their faces and concentrating on their eyes and mouths was stunning. Quinn and Dagmar appeared as a man and a woman filled with the knowledge of good and evil yearning for the good to prevail. Each was shown as strong and resolute but with a hint of impishness around the edges of their mouths.

"Perfect!" enthused Dagmar. "Absolutely perfect!"

Quinn was exceedingly pleased as well.

Dagmar provided Mary a bonus by displaying the painting on her program and then interviewing the artist on Arizona Afternoon. This caused the phone in Darshan's shop to ring off the hook with inquiries about Mary's paintings. Dagmar said nothing about the Angel Nest naturist community in the interview, referring only to Mary's studio in a secluded area near Sedona.

The album that Skye had recorded for Asher Shepherd was doing well in its market niche, and Asher had approached Skye about putting together material for a second album. "Apache Wedding" started to get airplay on radio stations west of the Rockies, so Asher released it as a single.

All things considered, this was a good season for Mary and Skye. Their professional lives were successful and satisfying, and their love life was even better. All they wanted now was a child, but Mary was having trouble conceiving.

Cofflynn McCarthy was curious about his neighbors behind the twelve-feet-high privacy wall at the back of the Arms for Jesus church property. On a Sunday afternoon in September, after everyone from his congregation had gone home, he climbed onto the roof of his church, and using binoculars, spied out the backyard of the Natural Christian Church facility. A row of palm trees and strategically placed lemon and orange trees obscured most of his view, but here and there he caught fleeting glimpses of naked people wandering about. This disturbed him so much that he stayed on the slanted roof for thirty minutes, attempting to make a count of the naked flashes he observed. His feet ached from the unnatural stance he was forced to assume in order to gather intelligence of debauchery, but Cofflynn dutifully stayed at his post. His legs wobbled on the ladder on his way down to earth, and he nearly fell off. But God was with him in this mission, he thought, and he kept his balance.

The next day, he asked a member of his church to make a check of public records, thereby learning the nature of the organization on the other side of his wall. Armed with this information, Cofflynn paid a call on the Phoenix Police Department.

"Captain, I have evidence that a nudist cult is blaspheming the Holy Bible in the heart of a respectable neighborhood in Phoenix," the minister said. He handed the officer a typed report of his findings. "How soon can you execute a raid on the offending premises?"

The captain spoke slowly, drawing out his words with care. "Well, Reverend, the Natural Church folks are well-known to the police. There's nothing illegal about what they're doing, and they've behaved like model citizens in the area. The department has received no complaints about them from neighbors concerning noise, parking or anything else. On the other hand, we ***have*** received complaints about your church. Some of your neighbors called to complain about members of your congregation discharging firearms in the air on the Fourth of July. The city ought to have an ordinance about that. It's a dangerous practice. People could be struck by falling bullets. There have also been angry calls alleging that members of your church have littered the lawns of near-by residents with Arms for Jesus flyers."

"You can't intimidate me, captain," said Cofflynn. "We have a constitutional right to bear arms and a right to free speech."

"No citizen has a right to endanger other people," the officer said. "If a stray bullet fired from your property struck a child in the neighborhood, the Constitution would not protect you from liability. As to your flyers, if I were you, I'd ask your folks to be more careful about how they distribute them."

"May I assume from your response that you do not intend to do your duty and shut down this depraved organization?" Cofflynn asked in a huff.

"We have no cause for action," the captain said.

Cofflynn stormed out of the police station ready to implement plan B. He telephoned all the local television stations announcing a press conference the next morning. One television news organization noted for frequent reporting on sex and gore, sent a correspondent to cover the event.

Cofflynn directed members of his church to march in front of the NCC estate, carrying picket signs and shouting slogans. He stood before the television camera denouncing the den of iniquity in the midst of this quiet, God-fearing neighborhood.

Within minutes, a dozen residents called the Police Department to complain about Arms for Jesus people disturbing the peace.

The episode made the Six O'clock News. The story began with pan shots of the Arms for Jesus sanctuary and the front of the NCC property, with the reporter's voice-over setting up the conflict. Then Cofflynn emoted for the camera about the evils of public nudity, followed by scenes of picketers with signs bearing such messages as "Naked Communists," "Pinko Nudists," and "God says shame on you!" A sound bite of the reporter's interview with Kwan-yin came next, after which the reporter summed up the situation with inane and melodramatic verbiage about a clash of cultures.

From the news manager's perspective, it was a good two-day story that kept the viewers tuned in. Cofflynn was frustrated, however, because several of his members were cited for disorderly conduct and no allies rushed to his defense. Kwan-yin received more than a hundred inquiries about attending NCC services, and she had to enlist the assistance of Adam and Evelyn for mid-week screenings of prospective church visitors. The end result of the flap was fifty new members for the Phoenix NCC congregation.

Late in the afternoon on the day Cofflynn held his press conference, Narcissa sat in bed brooding about growing old. She was fifty-nine and dreaded the prospect of turning sixty some months hence. For weeks she had eaten very little. Clinical depression had robbed her of an appetite. On the positive side, she had stopped drinking alcohol, but this had more to do with feeling numb already than it did with improving her health.

A month earlier Narcissa had resigned from the Ladies' Patriotic organization, abandoning both her red white and blue lipstick clients as well as her crotch-less panty customers. These are empty enterprises, she told herself. Selling silly things to gullible people brings no personal satisfaction. My life has been a waste!

Apart from occasional trips to the bathroom to pee and drink tap water from her toothbrush cup, Narcissa had been in bed for three days. "This is stupid!" she said out loud. "I may as well kill myself." Her words were met by the silence of an empty house. Summoning a burst of energy fueled by anger, she made her way to the bathroom and rummaged through her medicine cabinet, looking for pain pills or anything else suitable for a lethal overdose. Nothing! In a fit of rage, she scooped everything from the shelves, scattering tubes, bottles, bandages, clippers, and sundry items in all directions.

Narcissa staggered to the kitchen in search of a bottle of vodka. All gone! "Shit! Shit! Shit!" she wailed. "I'll have to get cleaned up and dressed to go out for pills and vodka." She shuffled toward the shower, but halfway there, a thought entered her mind from somewhere outside herself. Silent words flashed in her brain: "A shower is too much work right now. Get back in bed and watch TV for a while." The advice was strangely compelling and she obeyed. Narcissa switched on the television and flopped her naked body into bed.

"Coming up next," the news anchor said, "local nudists under attack from anti-communist minister -right after these messages."

Narcissa was hooked by the teaser. Of course, the story did not come up next as promised but was aired at the end of the broadcast, following another round of commercials. Nevertheless, Narcissa stayed tuned, cursing impatiently through the sports and weather reports, which she hated, in order to hear the only story that had captured her interest.

"Naked people are the devil's playground," Cofflynn ranted to the news reporter. "Imagine orgies on the altar of Christ! We must put a stop to this sacrilege!"

The scene shifted to Kwan-yin's office, where the minister, wearing a gray business suit, looked directly into the camera and said, "We are peaceable folk who simply want to worship the way God created us."

"Cofflynn, you stupid son of a bitch," Narcissa shouted at the screen, "you're a tight-assed blithering idiot!"

Deep anger welled up from her gut, turning into tears that washed down her face. One by one she named the people in her life she felt had deceived or betrayed her. T. C. Smith, Dante Kherbet, Barry Goldwater, Malachi Hinny, Cofflynn McCarthy. Other names poured out, women as well as men, Clive and Marybelle among them. At last, the image of Lloyd appeared in her mind. In a flash of desperate honesty, she admitted to herself that her ex-husband had not been unfaithful to her. "He's a good man," she said aloud.

This sudden release of anger produced contradictory effects on Narcissa. For a time she felt better than she had in months. Honest confession seemed to have lightened her soul. But as she pondered what she had done with her life, and how she had pushed away a gentle and decent husband and alienated her only child, she could see nothing left to live for.

"Forget booze and pills," she announced to the four walls of her bedroom. "I'll just slit my wrists and be done with it."

She went to the bathroom and fumbled with her safety razor, trying to get the blade out. Her hands were unsteady, and she sliced her right index finger. "Shit!" she yelled, throwing the razor to the floor. "My stupid finger won't bleed enough to do any damn good!" She searched for a bandage strip and discovered that she had thrown them in the toilet during her earlier angry foray in the bathroom. She scooped the wet bandage box from the toilet bowl and hurled it against the mirror. "Oh God, I can't do anything right," she moaned. Narcissa slumped to the floor and wept bitterly.

Two more silent words appeared in her brain: "Call Evelyn."

"Evelyn who?" she shouted to whoever was playing games with

her mind. But she knew which Evelyn. She tried to ignore it, but the message repeated with greater insistence.

Narcissa gave up trying to block the command and stumbled back to her bedroom and yanked the top drawer from her nightstand. It fell to the floor with a loud thud. On her knees rummaging through it, cursing all the while, she pulled out an old address book. Under "R" she found Adam and Evelyn Rarom. With trembling hands she dialed the number.

CHAPTER THIRTY-THREE

Evelyn picked up the receiver on the second ring. "Hello?"

"I don't know why I called. I'm sorry to disturb you. Good-bye," said Narcissa.

"Please don't hang up," said Evelyn with a calm, cheerful lilt. "I'm sure you had a good reason to call. How can I help you?" The pastor did not recognize the voice at the other end of the receiver, but from years of pastoral experience she recognized the sound of human desperation.

"Are you Pastor Evelyn?" Narcissa asked.

"Yes. I'm sorry. I should have identified myself."

"This is Narcissa Morgan. You probably don't remember me. It's been so long."

"Of course I remember you, Narcissa. It's good to hear from you," the pastor said.

"I don't want to bother you, but this...thing...in my head said call..." Narcissa did not continue her thought.

"Where are you, Narcissa?" Evelyn asked.

"At home in my bed. I haven't been well. I'm going to kill myself and I just wanted someone to know, that's all."

"I'd like to know about it," said Evelyn. "What made you decide to kill yourself?"

This question opened a floodgate of words from Narcissa. As Evelyn listened, she put her hand over the speaker and whispered to Adam, "Go to the office phone and call Kwan-yin. Tell her to get over to Narcissa Morgan's house pronto. Suicide threat."

He turned to go but turned back and mouthed, "Do we have her address?"

"Yes, dear, I know what you mean," Evelyn said to Narcissa. Covering the speaker again, she said softly, "In the old newsletter mailing list, I'm pretty sure."

Adam rushed out and three minutes later returned flashing a V sign.

Narcissa prattled on, and when she paused to catch her breath, Evelyn said, "I'd like to listen to you in person. Would it be OK if I dropped by later this evening?"

"I'll probably be dead by then," Narcissa said. "Besides that, the house is a mess and I haven't showered today, so I'm not presentable for company."

"Don't worry about that," said Evelyn. "You should see the mess my house is in at the moment." She kept Narcissa engaged in conversation for another fifteen minutes until she heard the faint sound of a doorbell echoing through the receiver.

"Someone's at my door," Narcissa explained. "I'll have to go."

"Don't hang up," Evelyn instructed.

Narcissa dropped the receiver onto her pillow, and without considering the fact that she was naked, obeyed the insistent repeating command of the bell and went to see who was ringing it. "Who's there?" she called out from behind the door as she peered through the peephole.

"Kwan-yin Burns. I'm a friend of Evelyn Rarom," she said.

"You're the lady I saw on TV a little while ago!" Narcissa shouted. Anyone who appeared on television qualified as a celebrity in Narcissa's mind, and she would not be rude to a celebrity. Momentarily unaware of her appearance, Narcissa opened the door and invited Kwan-yin into the house. "I've been sick, so please forgive the mess in the house. Please, sit down," Narcissa said, and then she fainted.

Kwan-yin cushioned her fall and saw to it that she was comfortably positioned on the carpet. Evelyn's voice called out from the phone in the bedroom. "Hello? Narcissa? Who's at the door?"

The pastor dashed into the bedroom. "It's me. Narcissa let me in then passed out. She looks like she hasn't eaten in a week. She's a real mess -hair all matted, face pasty, hasn't bathed in a while. Whew! Pretty gamy -and stark naked. She answered the door that way."

"I'm on my way," said Evelyn. "I'll be there in less than an hour."

Kwan-yin moved Narcissa into bed then went into the kitchen to make soup. After spoon-feeding the chicken noodle broth to Narcissa, Kwan-yin placed a call to a private number.

Dr. Ed Lumen, family physician and member of the Phoenix NCC answered the phone.

"Ed, it's Kwan-yin. I need a house call. It's important but not a stat emergency. Are either you or Kay available? Palmcroft district."

"Kay's at a meeting. Give me the address. Twenty minutes OK?"

She gave him the address. "It's Cloud's mother. Thanks, Ed."

Evelyn and Ed pulled up in front of the house a few seconds apart.

"She says she hasn't eaten in three days," Kwan-yin explained to the physician, "but I think it's been longer than that."

After examining the patient, Ed said, "Rest and nourishment, Narcissa. Mostly nourishment. And plenty of fluids. You're dehydrated."

"That hardly matters, since I'm planning to kill myself as soon as you all leave," Narcissa said.

"You came close, Narcissa," Ed said, "but you know full well that you're not allowed to do yourself in once you've been rescued. Rules of the game."

"Yes, doctor," Narcissa said meekly. She was beginning to enjoy the attention.

In the foyer on his way out, Ed said to Kwan-yin and Evelyn, "I gave her an injection to boost her strength. Here's a sedative. Make her take it before you leave."

"Would it be alright if we took her to New River for a few days?" Evelyn asked.

"That would be great, but do yourself a favor and give her a bath before you put her in your car."

"OK, Narcissa," Evelyn announced, striding into the bedroom, "it's just us girls now, and we're going to clean you up."

Kwan-yin and Evelyn slipped off their clothes and stood Narcissa up. Taking positions on either side of her, they walked her into the bathroom careful to avoid the mess on the floor, turned on the shower and climbed in with her. The ministers soaped, scrubbed, shampooed, and rinsed the depressed woman. After toweling her off, they dried and brushed her hair. Narcissa decided she liked the attention very much indeed.

Although the outside thermometer registered ninety degrees that night, Evelyn and Kwan-yin bundled Narcissa in winter clothing due to her frail condition. Kwan-yin went home, and Evelyn drove Narcissa to the camp at New River.

On the way, Evelyn said, "You've been experiencing a deep spiritual crisis, Narcissa. The fact that you called me is a sign of great hope, but you're not out of the woods yet. I'd like you to meet with a friend of mine, Edna Echo, on a professional basis, and I can offer you prayer and a special healing and anointing service -just for you."

"I'd be careful offering something just for me," Narcissa said. "I got off on the wrong track a long time ago thinking the world owes me something special."

"You hit bottom tonight, Narcissa. What you just told me is your first step out of the pit," Evelyn said.

The next morning, with Narcissa's permission, Evelyn called Cloud to tell him what had happened with his mother. He and Terp drove down that afternoon to visit her. Narcissa greeted her daughter-in-law with unfeigned affection.

"How's my granddaughter doing these days?" she asked. "I think it's time she got to know her...uh...grandmother...er...at least this one of her grandmothers."

Before returning to Angel Nest, Terp held her mother-in-law's hand while she prayed for her, and using oil, marked the sign of the cross on her forehead. Narcissa wept and hugged Terp, not wanting to let her go.

Cloud said to Evelyn, "Tell Edna to send the bills for mom's therapy to me."

Narcissa returned home after a week of restful sunbathing in New River. She had gained five much needed pounds. The next month was a blur of activity for her. Counseling sessions with Edna Echo, long talks about religion and spirituality with Evelyn and Adam, Sunday worship at the NCC in Phoenix, savoring Kwan-yin's insightful sermons.

She called Cloud one evening and said she wanted to visit her parents, who were now living in a nursing home in Prescott. "I haven't seen them since you were in elementary school, Cloud. I need to make amends with them, but I don't want to go alone. Will you go with me?"

"I think that's a wonderful idea, Mom. Why don't you drive up here and spend a little time with Zara, then you and I can zip over Mingus Mountain to Prescott," said Cloud.

And so it happened.

When Narcissa and Cloud arrived at the nursing home, they learned that Bill Cloud was near death. His wife, Minnie, was beside his bed in a wheelchair.

"Dad, it's Narcissa," the wayward daughter said. "I know I treated you and Mom badly when I left home. I was a selfish brat, and I'm very sorry. Please accept my apology. Will you forgive me?"

Tears welled up in the old man's eyes.

"You too, Mom. Please forgive me." Narcissa took her mother's hand and kissed it. Standing, she bent down and kissed her father's forehead.

"Yes," the dying man whispered. "We never stopped loving you, Narcie."

"He's right," Minnie said. "I'm so grateful you came to see us. Now he can pass in peace. And you too, Cloud. My how you've grown into a handsome young man!"

The four of them, representing three estranged generations, joined hands while Cloud prayed for God's blessing upon this reunion. In the early hours of the following morning, Bill Cloud died. Less than twenty-four hours later, Minnie, unable to consider life without her husband, lapsed into a coma and soon joined him in the world beyond.

Narcissa continued to make progress with her therapy and in November visited Lloyd and Nissa. "I need to apologize to both of you," she said. "Lloyd, I blamed you for the break up of our marriage, but I know now that it was my own doing. I am sorry."

"What's done is done, Narcissa," Lloyd said. "We've all grown a lot since those days."

"You have no need to apologize to me," Nissa said.

"If you knew what has gone through my mind about you, Nissa, you'd understand why I need to apologize to you," Narcissa said.

"Don't tell me," said Nissa. "I'll take your word for it."

"Lloyd, I'm glad you've found happiness with Nissa. I wish you well. And I've never acknowledged your generosity. Thank you for paying off my mortgage with money I tried to prevent you from earning. I was wrong about the land."

Early in the new year of 1982, Narcissa gained employment as a receptionist in Ed and Kay Lumen's medical office and became actively involved in the Phoenix NCC congregation. At an earlier stage of life, she would not have joined a congregation with a pastor of another race, but now Kwan-yin's Chinese ancestry seemed a blessing to her.

In a moment of insight with Edna Echo, Narcissa said, "I'm not particularly interested in sexual relations with anyone, but I know now that I want affection. I want to be touched and appreciated...and loved."

"We all want to be loved," Edna said. "How do your granddaughter's hugs fit in with your needs?"

"Perfectly," said Narcissa. "She calls me Grandma Narcie, and as much as I hated it when my father called me that, I cherish it from Zara. The last time I visited Cloud and Terp, they did a reflexology workout on me, and between having my feet massaged and Zara hugging me, I am a very satisfied woman."

In the spring, Narcissa attended a foot-washing service at Angel Nest and made a point of washing Nissa's feet. At lunch that day, surrounded by her family, Narcissa said, "The people I thought had all the answers told me I was special and deserved praise, but they were only using me to gain my allegiance or get my money. But I kept chasing after them, willing to pay anything to hear them say I was special. In the end, they all abandoned me. And the great irony is that paid compliments are all lies. And people who claim to possess the absolute truth are all liars. Some of them are only lying to themselves, but they manage to hurt other people anyway."

—o—

Two years after its founding, the Sedona Natural Christian Church had become the largest congregation in the denomination. Average worship attendance hovered around three hundred, with many more coming for Christmas and Easter services. People came to hear Terp and Cloud preach, and for the healing services, and for the music program, and to experience the dance choir. The foot-washing services attracted a committed following, including many non-Christians. The community roll included nearly a hundred Jews, Hindus, Buddhists, Taoists, Native American religionists, Christians of other denominations, spiritual seekers, and agnostics.

"When we get our first Muslim and Mormon participants," said Cloud, "then we can begin to talk about being truly religiously inclusive. I feel sure this will happen."

In July, three months before her fifth birthday, Zara overheard her parents talking about their out-of-body experiences. "Teach me to float," the precocious child said with determination.

Terp and Cloud looked at one another, conducting a detailed but wordless conversation.

"OK," Cloud said. "Come with us to the bedroom."

Little Zara lay supine on the giant bed and listened intently to the instructions her parents provided. "Let me try, now," she said. She closed her eyes and entered into a period of slow, deep breathing. For about five minutes nothing happened, but all at once Terp noticed the change in Zara's face.

"She's gone," Terp said. "On her first try! I'm jealous."

Mom and dad lay back, one on each side of their daughter, and within a minute popped out of their bodies.

"Zara, where are you?" Cloud transmitted telepathically.

"Here, Daddy!" She had already left the bedroom and was hovering near the ceiling of the studio. Terp and Cloud surrounded her with their spirits.

"Where would you like to go, dear?" Terp asked. "What would you like to see?"

"Let's go see that eagle I thought was an angel," Zara said.

They sailed off in search of the majestic bird. Though they flew beside several hawks that day, they failed to find any eagles.

Nevertheless, Zara had great fun exploring the skies around Sedona.

When they returned to their bodies, Terp said, "Zara, this is a special gift and you must use it wisely."

"I know, Mommy. You and Daddy will show me," the child said.

"Promise us you won't do this by yourself until we tell you it's OK to solo," said Cloud.

Zara hesitated. She had already begun to contemplate floating again soon -by herself. "I...I...want..."

"I was a little older than you the first time I floated," said Cloud, "but I didn't float outside my room until I was a teenager."

Zara started to argue but restrained herself.

"We understand your desire to explore," said Terp, "but there are dangers in being out of your body too long or flying too far away."

"Is it dangerous because you meet dead people?" asked Zara with a touch of eagerness.

"In three decades of travelling without my body, I've never encountered any," said Cloud. "I suppose it's possible, but they'd have to have died ***very*** recently, within seconds or minutes at the most. I suppose if you floated around hospitals you might see them."

"Let's compromise on soloing," said Terp. "You may leave your body by yourself if you promise to stay within the borders of Angel Nest. If you want to go further, one of us or Aunt Cedar Cradle or Uncle Firstlaugh must go with you until we decide you're ready to go alone."

"That's cool," said Zara. "But I didn't know Aunt CC and Uncle F could float too. What about Tzek and Wakhan?"

"No, but I suspect there will soon be great agitation in that regard," said Cloud.

And there was. Zara shared a bedroom with Tzek and Wakhan, and she wasted no time telling her adoptive cousins about her experience floating. Firstlaugh and Cedar Cradle thereupon taught their children how to leave their bodies, and the seven souls spent the rest of July exploring Oak Creek Canyon and the purported vortex sites around Sedona, without taking their bodies along.

A regular Saturday morning ritual developed around floating. Instead of watching cartoons on television, the three children stretched out on the carpet in their bedroom, nestled in between their parents, and popped out of their bodies to explore the world.

One Saturday, as they mentally convened in the studio before sailing off to examine the ancient Anasazi cliff dwellings known as Montezuma Castle, the adults sensed another presence hovering in the area.

"Who are you?" Cedar Cradle asked.

Silence.

"The presence is benign," said Terp to her soul-family. She then focused attention on the alien soul and said, "Don't be frightened, whoever you are. We're friendly."

"It's moving away from us," Firstlaugh said. "But I don't pick up any fear. It's more a feeling of shyness, or perhaps embarrassment."

"Please come back," signaled Terp. "We've never met anyone else while floating out of our bodies."

"Are you dead?" asked Zara.

No communication came from the other entity but Firstlaugh sensed the being had stopped moving away.

"Say your names, everyone," suggested Tzek. "I'm Tzek! Who are you?"

Each of the others announced their names to the unknown presence.

The silence continued for another minute, and then Huxley Askeladd passed through the wall into the studio. "I thought I was the only one who did this," she said. "In fact, I didn't know I could communicate with anyone while spiriting."

"Hi Huxley! Is that what you call it?" asked Cloud. "I first left my body when I was six, and back then I called it floating and the term stuck. But I like spiriting. It has a nice resonance to it."

"I started when I was nine," Huxley said. "I'm thirteen now."

"We're going to Montezuma Castle. Would you like to go along?" Terp said.

"I've never gone that far from my bedroom before," said the teenager. "But if I'm with you, I guess it would be alright. My parents know I sleep in on Saturday mornings, so they won't disturb me. My body should be safe."

"Did you drink enough water before you left your body?" Cedar Cradle asked.

“Yeah, I think so,” said Huxley. “By the way, my parents don’t know about this. Are you gonna tell on me?”

“No,” said Cloud. “That’s your decision to make. And for what it’s worth, they don’t know about us either. It would be difficult for us to tell on you without revealing how we found out.”

“Thanks,” Huxley said. “Someday I’d like to tell them, but I’m not sure they would believe me. Now let’s go see some cliff dwellings before the adobe crumbles.”

CHAPTER THIRTY-FOUR

Thirteen months after running into Cloud in Darshan's shop, Theo Gynt stood before the summer National Assembly of the Natural Christian Church, meeting in Las Vegas, to be examined for ordination. Having been mentored by Cloud, who had received a stiff interrogation under similar circumstances, Theo was prepared to answer the toughest doctrinal questions.

A tacit understanding prevailed among the representatives that Petrus Dort would ask the first question. He had jumped to his feet so often in past examinations that everyone had learned to sit back and let Petrus get his concerns out of the way first.

"In your biographical statement," said the eager minister, "you say that you are married and also that you are homosexual. Would you clarify for the assembly whether Keefe is a man or a woman?"

"Oh, that's an easy one," Theo quipped. "I was expecting a difficult question about explaining some complex theological construct." Laughter reverberated through the hall. "Keefe is one hundred percent male."

"How then did you come to be married?" Petrus continued.

"Cloud and Terp Morgan officiated at a wedding service for us at the NCC sanctuary in Sedona," Theo explained.

Petrus had anticipated murmuring from the representatives at the disclosure of this information, which he already knew, but nearly everyone else also knew it, and there was no reaction.

"Given that the state does not recognize the validity of your marriage to another man, please provide the assembly with a biblical defense of this unprecedented event," Dort said.

"Render unto Caesar that which is Caesar's," said Theo, "and to God that which is God's. My love for Keefe is a gift from God, the true spouse of my soul. Whether or not the secular law or even other church authorities approve, I wanted to acknowledge that gift and pledge faithfulness to the man I love -before God and in front of other believers who would be a cloud of witnesses."

"What about those texts that describe homosexuality as an abomination?" Petrus pressed.

"The Bible also says eating certain foods, such as shrimp and lobster, is an abomination, and I'll bet most of the people in this room are guilty and unrepentant of ingesting those abominable creatures," said Theo. "But if you'll carefully study the Bible verses about unacceptable sexual behavior, you'll find that most of them have to do with cult prostitution and idolatry. I'm neither a prostitute nor an idolater, and I do not believe that the nurturing physical love that Keefe and I enjoy as marital partners is sinful in God's eyes."

"I respectfully demur from your interpretation," Petrus said, "but I'll stand aside now, because it's time for someone else to ask a question."

After a full minute of silence, Cloud rose and moved that the examination be arrested. When the vote was taken to approve Theo for ordination, Petrus abstained and everyone else voted yes.

At the same meeting, a proposal for a new organizational design for the denomination was discussed and debated. Many in the growing denomination felt the need for more structure. They had been operating like a large family where everyone knew everyone else, with things generally decided by consensus. Now there were so many new faces among clergy and lay leaders that they could no longer do that.

The plan ultimately approved divided the NCC into four regional districts, which would provide representatives to annual meetings based on the number of members in their churches. Arizona, Utah, and Nevada were combined into one of these regions. The Assembly also created a national administrative office to be directed by a Presiding

Bishop. This Presiding Bishop, soon known informally as the Grand PB, had limited power but many opportunities to be persuasive.

Texas and California both sought to have the national office located in their respective states, and in a compromise, the assembly decided upon Phoenix as the headquarters city. A nominating committee was elected to find the first Presiding Bishop.

Cloud brought a proposal that the NCC recognize foot-washing as a traditional Christian rite that should be encouraged in worship. Ultimately, Cloud wanted the practice to be recognized as a sacrament, but he knew this would take a long time. The assembly approved his proposal by a wide margin.

Four weeks after the close of the assembly, Terp received a phone call from Agnes Day, co-pastor with her husband of the NCC congregation in Eugene, Oregon. "As you may know, Terp," Agnes began, "I am serving as chairperson of the search committee for our first Presiding Bishop. We've been engaged in a discernment process to find the right person. We began with the roster of every minister in our denomination and through prayer and discussion winnowed it down to a small list. We have now come to the unanimous view that you are the person we seek."

"Me?" Terp said with a note of disbelief in her voice. "Surely not me."

"Yes, surely you, Terp. We would like to present your name for election at a specially called assembly this fall," said Agnes. "What do you say?"

"Well, I'm flattered," said Terp, "but I feel very called to the work here in Sedona. How long do I have to meditate and pray about this before you need an answer?"

"Is forty-eight hours enough time?" replied Agnes.

Terp convened an ***ad hoc*** council of Cloud, Cedar Cradle, Firstlaugh, Malama, and Tallis to help her think this through. Each one confirmed their perceptions that she had the requisite gifts for such a role and encouraged her to be open to the prospect.

She was nevertheless reluctant to accept the call to denominational leadership.

"Do you have any doubts about your adequacy to do the job?" asked Tallis.

"None at all," said Terp. "I know I could do the work. But parish ministry is my first love. This is what motivates me and makes me leap out of bed in the morning, anticipating the new day. What we're doing now -all of us together- is incredibly fulfilling for me. Thank you all for your affirmations, but the truth is I don't ***want*** to be Presiding Bishop. If you all tell me I must do it for some greater purpose, then I'll give it a try, but that's how I would approach the work, not as a call clearly perceived and freely embraced but as an obligation accepted for the good of the body."

"The position is an experiment," said Cloud, "and the denomination is not in dire straits. If we needed a Churchill for this moment in our history, I would urge you to say yes. But under the circumstances, I would rather see you follow your bliss."

Terp said no, and the search committee turned to an equally qualified minister, Cathy Blake. Cathy said yes, and after being elected to the position, she and Bill moved to Phoenix. The Honolulu congregation called a recent graduate of Pacific Crossroads to be their next pastor, and life continued on in the church.

Needing some work to keep busy with, Bill Blake volunteered as a part-time associate pastor at the Phoenix NCC congregation, providing Kwan-yin with much needed assistance.

Cathy's first ecclesiastical act as Presiding Bishop was to officiate at the ordination of Theo Gynt. Also present to lay hands on the kneeling Theo were the other Arizona pastors, Kwan-yin, Bill, Adam, Evelyn, Cloud, Terp, and Malama. The major surprise of the day came when Petrus Dort drove over from San Diego to take part in the service.

"I still have reservations about this," he said, "but being here is a way for me to acknowledge the nearly unanimous decision of the National Assembly. The collective wisdom of the church calls me humbly to submit, and in the scheme of the universe, I confess, this issue of sexual orientation is a small matter compared with violence and war, and besides that, my relationship with peers in the NCC is more important."

"I am deeply honored by your participation, Petrus," said Theo.

"To be honest," said Petrus, "given your church background, Theo, I suspect that you and I may be natural allies on some doctrinal issues that will come before the church in the future, and I don't want to make an enemy of a potential friend."

In the spirit of the moment, Petrus and Theo embraced.

"Wow!" Theo commented a few minutes later. "The most orthodox pastor in the denomination just hugged a liberal homosexual and lightning didn't strike either of us."

Dr. Bookman Donne, professor of English at Anasazi College, developed an adult Bible study class at Angel Nest. He called it "The Bible as Literature," and it soon attracted a committed following. In fact, Bookman dealt with more than the literary values in scripture, venturing into the history of how the Bible came to be written and canonized, as well as various methods of interpreting biblical texts. His class was especially popular among the non-Christian community members, who found his approach engaging, illuminating, and a non-threatening way to learn about biblical content.

On the warm mid-spring Sunday afternoon when Bookman lectured on the erotic love poetry of the Song of Solomon, there was standing room only in the classroom, so they had to adjourn to the sanctuary in order to accommodate everyone.

"Let me begin in a personal way with chapter one, verse five," Bookman said. He held the Bible before him and read, "I am very dark, but beautiful, O daughters of Jerusalem, like the tents of Kedar, like the curtains of Solomon." He lifted his glasses to his forehead and peered into the mass of assembled naturists. "My genetic roots are in Africa, and I confess that when I read these words, they stir my soul. Thus am I drawn into the earthy and overtly sexual imagery of this breathtaking book of the Bible. Of course, if I were writing the poem, I'd say dark ***and*** beautiful. The ***vav*** in verse 1:5 can be translated as ***and*** or ***but***. Alas, historically the European translators of this text have preferred the ***but***, which reveals, I surmise, a certain bias against the charm of the dark.

"Let me say at the outset there are risks associated with sitting in a room full of naked people and listening to some of these passages. The Song of Solomon has been known to cause sexual arousal in certain circumstances. Thus warned, anyone who feels uncomfortable with the subject matter and would like to leave the class may do so now."

Not a soul or body stirred.

"Among those inclined to read the Bible literally are some who make specific exception for this book. These sensual love poems are so disturbing to certain people that they feel the need to interpret them allegorically. These erotic verses are declared to be Israel's love for God or Christ's love for his bride, the Church. I find it very difficult, however, to read these descriptions of physical love that way. And it tests the limits of human credulity to imagine that the ancient poets who wrote about mountainous breasts, fragrant vulvas, and moist penises were lost in contemplation of Israel's love for the Creator or the Lord's passion for his Church as they composed these lines.

"Nevertheless, Christian theologian Hippolytus, early in the third century, wrote that the reference to breasts in the Song of Solomon represented the Old and New Testaments. One implication of that metaphor, carried to its logical conclusion, is one breast considerably larger in volume than the other. Well, no one's perfectly symmetrical, I guess. In a bizarre interpretation, Saint Jerome said these poems taught sexual abstinence. But perhaps the oddest interpretation of the Song of Solomon came from Martin Luther, who said the book was written to encourage peasants to be obedient to their divinely ordained masters.

"On the other hand, hardnosed, no nonsense John Calvin argued against allegorical interpretation, saying this book described the beauty of God's handiwork, which, according to Genesis, God declared very good.

"The Song of Solomon, or Song of Songs as it is also known, is a series of erotic love poems woven into a dialogue between a man and a woman, interspersed with comments from a chorus. The collection dates to sometime in the third century before the birth of Jesus. Some poems hint that the lovers may be betrothed, but others provide no indication of marital status. The one thing that is quite clear, however, is that the man and woman are intimately acquainted with each other's bodies.

"It has been theorized that this book originated as a marriage manual for newly-weds. It is certainly explicit enough, although the anatomical references as translated into English are not clear to the modern reader. For example, in chapter five, verse two, the man says to the naked woman on the other side of her bedroom door, 'my head is wet with dew.' The average English reader is not likely to catch the

Hebrew euphemism used here. He is saying that the head of his penis is moist with seminal secretion. To put it less delicately, he is so aroused that he's ready to ejaculate.

"By the time the woman gets her door unbolted, her lover has gone. One can only speculate on what might have motivated him to leave the scene. Parenthetically, another Hebrew euphemism appears suggestively in Ruth chapter three, where Naomi tells Ruth to visit Boaz secretly at night and uncover his feet, lie next to him and do whatever he says. Feet in that case refer to genitals.

"The term garden used throughout the Song of Solomon refers to a woman's vulva and vagina. In verse 4:15, the linking of flowing streams of Lebanon with the woman's garden indicates that she is well lubricated and thus prepared for intercourse."

Bookman took the class through the text, substituting plain English words for the flowery translations of Hebrew euphemisms, including references to aphrodisiacs. Then he and Emily read the male and female portions of the Song as a dramatic duet. As a result, modesty towels were much in evidence, and many men lingered after class to chat casually about baseball statistics and automobile maintenance.

An unexpected result of Terp declining the offer to become Presiding Bishop was increased influence in the denomination for her and Cloud. The work of the search committee was supposed to be confidential, but somehow Terp's refusal leaked out and spread like wildfire through the churches.

This was taken as evidence that the Morgans were not seeking power or influence, which ironically, gave them more of both. Cathy Blake called Terp and said she knew she was the committee's second choice, and knowing who had been asked first, she was content with that position. As the months passed, ministers and lay leaders around the denomination checked in with Terp and Cloud about their views on various matters. People wanted to know where the Morgans stood on things before moving forward with new proposals.

In Arizona, the legal name of the Natural Christian Church had "(BA)" standing for "Born Again" appended to its name to distinguish it from an independent church in Tucson, which had incorporated as the Natural Christian Church prior to the denomination seeking that status. The unaffiliated church added "(ER)" -"Eden Rite"- to its name as a demonstration of Christian cooperation.

In June, Presiding Bishop Cathy Blake received a phone call from Michelle Valentine, a woman who identified herself as a member of the Eden Rite congregation in Tucson.

"I don't know if it's the right thing to contact you, but we need help," Michelle said. "I don't know where else to turn."

"What kind of help?" Cathy asked.

"First let me say that I'm Secretary of the Church Council, and the Council has authorized me to talk with you," said Michelle.

"That sounds ominously official," said Cathy. "Is this a legal matter?"

"Well, it could have legal implications down the road, but not against you," Michelle responded. "We fired our pastor, and we think we're on solid ground about that. He's not in any position to sue us. But we need advice on where to go from here."

"And since your congregation is unaffiliated, it seemed sensible to touch base with the nearest naturist denomination," Cathy suggested. "That's what I would have done too. How can we help?"

Michelle preferred to talk about the sensitive situation face-to-face, so a meeting was set for the next day in Phoenix. The NCC denominational headquarters consisted of two rooms at the Phoenix NCC church, down the hall from Kwan-yin's office.

CHAPTER THIRTY-FIVE

Ensconced in Cathy's office, Michelle said, "The founder of our congregation, Pastor John, was a saintly man who died of a malignant melanoma five years ago. Tick Tackerman, was Secretary of the Council at the time Pastor John died, and Tick sort of named himself as the next pastor, and in the midst of the turmoil and grief swirling around the congregation, nobody objected. It felt good to have someone in charge."

"And it was this second pastor who was fired?" asked Cathy.

"Yes. He didn't prove to be as saintly as Pastor John," continued Michelle. "He had a bachelor's degree in psychology but no ministerial training. He simply announced to the congregation that God had ordained him to be the next pastor, and his supporters shouted hallelujah and the council went along with it because he had a popular following, and also for the sake of peace."

"Tell me about his termination," said Cathy.

"A few months ago the council held a secret meeting to deal with complaints. Actually, some of the council members were involved with the problems, some were fed up, some were scared, and others were ashamed," Michelle said. "First let me say that our congregation has always been fairly liberal about sex. We think it's a natural part of life, and nobody gets upset if a couple of adults sneak off to a secluded corner of the compound and get intimate. We think masturbation is normal and not sinful. We're not promiscuous, and we don't condone orgies and adultery, but we're far from puritanical as some nudist organizations are. A few of our members have engaged in group sex and stuff like that. Not many and never on church property, but I know it's gone on."

"I see," said Cathy.

"It took Tick about two years to gain complete authority over the congregation," Michelle explained, "and once he did he introduced selected members to what he called sexual reforms. How he picked the couples to participate in his reforms I don't know, but he led them on with promises of church sanctioned sex parties. Before they were allowed to participate in his 'sacred love-ins' he had to test them first. The test was that Tick would have intercourse with a wife or girlfriend while the husband or boyfriend watched. Tick's wife was off-limits, however."

"How many people did he...test?" Cathy asked.

"We don't know," said Michelle. "We've discovered fourteen couples so far, but most people are keeping mum. He tried to recruit my husband and me, but we turned him down flat. That was right after my mother died, and I was an emotional wreck. I was upset that such a kind woman should suffer so horribly from lung cancer. I told Tick about my anger at God for allowing cancer, and he suggested sex therapy. My best friend let Tick screw her while her husband looked on. That was right after their son was arrested for marijuana possession. They were so upset afterward that they dropped out of church and never did participate in Tick's group sex parties."

"Why do I have a feeling you haven't told me the worst yet?" Cathy said.

"Most members didn't know this was going on," Michelle said. "Tick was careful about who he tried to recruit. It just occurred to me that all of the cases I know about involve people who were having problems of some kind when Tick approached them. I wonder if that's significant? Anyway, things exploded a few months ago when Tick fired the youth director and took over youth work himself.

"He started a coeducational sex education class for high school students. For the first class he had them sit in a circle and watch each other masturbate. Then he asked for a girl volunteer to give him a hand job. I've been told that no one wanted to do it, so he ordered one of the girls to massage his penis -as an educational experience- and she obeyed. He told them the next week they would learn about oral sex.

"Luckily, several of the kids had the good sense to tell their parents about the class, and next week's episode never happened. That's when the council met secretly and decided to fire the pastor. We told him if he tried to fight it, we would go to the police."

"What was his reaction to that?" Cathy asked.

"He brought in an agreement for us to sign saying he would go away quietly in exchange for keeping everything secret. No police notification. Some of the council members wanted to sign it but I refused and no action was taken," said Michelle.

"Good," said Cathy. "Even if you had, it would not be binding, but you need to talk to the girl's parents about filing a complaint with the Tucson Police Department."

"We already have," said Michelle. "They're not willing to file charges. They're afraid the District Attorney would turn this into a crusade against the congregation. And they don't want their daughter dragged into the spotlight. That might be more harmful to her than Tick's actions. The other parents feel the same way. They don't want their kids traumatized by the legal system and the inevitable publicity. The teens are just embarrassed by it all."

"By the way, it ***is*** significant that he only seemed to go after vulnerable people. I can recommend an excellent counselor to work with the youth group," Cathy said. "With a little bit of help they'll be OK, thanks to swift action by your Council, but I suspect many of the adults will have a harder time with the trauma caused by the pastor."

"Thanks," Michelle said. "The thing is, dealing with Tick is not the help we need right now. The reason I called is because our congregation is falling apart, and we need leadership to hold us together. The council wants to explore the possibilities of becoming part of your denomination."

"We'd be very happy to talk with you about that," said Cathy, "but whether or not you realize it, your congregation very much needs help dealing with Tick and the aftermath of his abuse. That's why your congregation is acting the way it is. Who's leading the congregation right now?"

"Members of the council are taking turns leading worship, but attendance is way down, and people are complaining about everything. Some who don't know the whole story are complaining that the council forced out a good man. They won't believe we had sound reasons to fire him."

"I have an idea," said Cathy. She dialed a number on her desk phone. "Bill, do you have time to meet someone in my office?"

A few minutes later, Cathy introduced Michelle to her husband, who was currently underemployed. Before the afternoon was over, Michelle had arranged for Bill Blake to visit the council of the Tucson congregation for a conversation about interim ministry and congregational dynamics in the wake of sexual abuse situations.

A week later, Bill signed a contract to serve for one year as interim pastor of the troubled church, to help them work through their trauma. Edna Echo and Clark Hyfrydol spent time working with the youth group and with abused couples. Bill Blake arranged a series of congregational meetings to clear the air, provide factual information, and put false rumors to rest. He also reestablished traditional elements in worship, providing an atmosphere of reverence that helped worshipers focus on the transcendence of God. Gradually, unhappy members came back. As the congregation grew more confident, members began to invite friends to visit. This was heartening to the members, because for the past four years most of them had been too embarrassed by their pastor to invite guests to worship.

Before the year was out, the National Assembly of the NCC accepted the petition of the Tucson church to be part of the denomination, and the (ER) and (BA) appendages were dropped from the official names of the Arizona congregations.

Sarai and Abram completed their junior years at Arizona State University in the spring of 1982. Abram was majoring in psychology and Sarai in anthropology. Both intended to enroll in seminary when they graduated from college. Evelyn insisted they do more than sit around the pool all summer, preferably by getting jobs. Unfortunately, there were no summer jobs in New River, and neither had a car for commuting to Phoenix for work.

Cloud solved the dilemma by engaging the twins as summer interns at Angel Nest. "I've got a project I've been itching to do but don't have the time for," he explained. "It involves a little bit of psychology and some anthropology as well, so the two of you could be a big help."

"What do you want us to do?" asked Sarai.

"We have the names, addresses, and phone numbers of several hundred people who have visited the church but have not joined. Some are regular visitors, and some have come once or twice and not returned. I'd like to find out what motivated them to visit in the first place, what their impressions of the church are, and why they have not come back or joined. I'd like you to develop some interview questions and go out and talk to these people."

"In person?" asked Abram.

"Preferably," said Cloud. "Telephone interviews are OK if that's the only way to get information, but face-to-face is the best way to learn from and about people."

"What if they don't want to talk?" Abram continued.

"Thank them and go on to the next person on the list," said Cloud. "Not everyone will participate, but I'll bet most of them will be pleased to tell you what they think."

"But we don't have a car," said Sarai.

"You can use my VW," said Cloud. "I'm not teaching any classes this summer, so Terp and I can make do with one car."

Abram and Sarai spent the summer conducting interviews and learning about motivations of the human psyche. Most dropouts praised the church. A few thought it too conservative and an equal number viewed it as too liberal. Some preferred worship that allowed them to be more passive, as if watching television.

The most common reason people gave for ceasing attendance was dissatisfaction with their own bodies. Significantly, Abram noted, they were not troubled about exposing their genitals but embarrassed by other parts of their bodies, such as thighs and bellies.

After dinner one evening midway through summer, Sarai found Terp alone on a balcony.

"I'm enjoying the sunset," Terp said "This is such a beautiful and peaceful place, don't you think?"

"Indeed," agreed Sarai. They stood in silence a few minutes admiring the play of prismatic light on the pigmented rocks. Then Sarai said, "May I ask a personal question?"

"Certainly, but I may choose not to answer it," said Terp.

"I've noticed that your family and the Begays gather in the children's room on Saturday mornings, and don't come out for a couple of hours, but there's never any noise. I'm having a hard time imagining what you could do that would keep kids quiet that long."

"We've been wondering how long it would be before somebody noticed," Terp said.

"Abram's noticed too," Sarai said.

"Is this a topic of speculation around Angel Nest?" Terp asked.

"Not that I know of," said Sarai. "I passed Mary in the hall once - in front of the kids' room- and asked, 'what's going on in there?' She said, 'I can't say.'"

"Bring your brother to my room in an hour, and we'll tell you about Saturday mornings," said Terp.

When Abram knocked on the door of the master bedroom, Cedar Cradle greeted him and Sarai. Firstlaugh, Cloud, and Terp were seated in chairs, and there were chairs across from them to which the twins were directed.

"We need to ask you a few questions before we reveal our family activities," Firstlaugh said. "Your answers will affect the direction of our conversation."

"Don't worry," said Cloud. "There are no wrong answers. We simply want a sense of your own experiences before we tell you about ours."

"Have either of you had any mystical or extra-sensory experiences?" asked Cedar Cradle.

"Sure," said Abram. "Both of us. Every so often I fall into a deep meditative state, without trying to, and feel a sense of complete oneness with the universe. It's like I'm filled with peaceful knowledge of God and creation and so connected to everything that I -whoever I may be- don't end but extend out into the cosmos."

"I've experienced the same as Abram," said Sarai, "but not at the same time. This seems to happen to us individually, not when we're together."

"Anything else?" asked Terp.

"Not unless you count dreams," said Abram.

"What dreams?" asked Cloud.

"Oh, you know, the usual twin dreams," said Sarai. "Every so often I'll have a dream about something happening at school, but it doesn't happen to me; it happens to Abram."

"And vice versa," said Abram. "Little things, like when I spilled my juice in the cafeteria. Sarai didn't tell me she'd dreamed that until it actually happened."

Cloud, Cedar Cradle, Firstlaugh, and Terp looked at one another and held a wordless conference. A moment later, Cloud began to unfold the story of their out-of-body travels. As he spoke, Terp seamlessly picked up the account in mid-sentence, followed in turn by Firstlaugh and Cedar Cradle adding to the tale.

The twins' eyes grew large as they listened. When Cedar Cradle came to the end, Sarai and Abram said simultaneously, "Will you teach us?"

"Hop up on the bed and lie on your backs," Cloud said. "As soon as you mentioned your encounters with the cosmos we knew you would be apt students."

Filled with instructions and surrounded by the energy of four experienced floaters, Sarai managed to leave her body in ten minutes, followed ten seconds later by Abram. Soon the other four joined them hovering near the ceiling.

"That's just like Sarai," Abram communicated to the group. "She was first out of the womb too."

The next morning, Abram and Sarai, without their bodies, reconnoitered in the children's bedroom with the Begays, the Morgans, and Huxley Askeladd, before setting off to explore Munds Mountain.

"I'm having another crisis of faith," Cloud said to Tallis, "and I need some guidance."

"Reverting to your scientific atheism?" Tallis asked.

"No," said Cloud meekly. "It's coming from the other direction. I've been reading John Calvin's ***Institutes*** and Karl Barth's neo-orthodox work, and I'm beginning to wonder if the conservatives may be right after all."

"Calvin was a radical liberal in the context of the Reformation," Tallis said. "To claim that Christ was not bodily but only spiritually present in communion was a huge departure from the orthodoxy of the day. Calvin was no conservative but a speculative theologian who was not afraid to let his mind explore forbidden territory."

"Intellectually I know that," said Cloud. "It was his followers a century later who distorted some of his speculations and cast them into concrete. But I keep asking myself: what if I'm wrong and the fundamentalists are right? What if God is only interested in saving people who manage to find and believe the exact truth about Jesus Christ? What if the Bible is literally true?"

"Even in those places where scripture contradicts itself?" Tallis asked. "How can it be literally true when the Gospels provide distinctly differing chronologies for the same events?"

"You're right, of course," Cloud conceded. "The truth of scripture is found in interpreting the meaning arising from the words not the words themselves. And I don't know why I'm dithering about this right now. It's just that I am continually trying to integrate my belief in God and my trust in science, trying to smooth out the inconsistencies, and it's hard work. Why do I always have to make things so complicated? A simple absolute faith would be so much easier."

"The credo of science," Tallis said, "is to remain completely open to new discoveries and correction of faulty assumptions. It takes integrity and intellectual honesty to do that. Why shouldn't you grant the same to God?" She lifted a Bible from her desk. "Do you believe God is limited by the words printed on these pages? Is the reality of God constrained by the perceptions of humans who lived thousands of years ago? Surely the totality of God is greater than that."

"You're right again, Tallis. We owe God the best of our reasoning ability," said Cloud. "The thing is, I find it easy to believe in the God whose energy transcends material existence. It's the details of religion that I struggle with. And as a practical matter, simply believing in God is not enough. What one believes about the nature of God makes a great deal of difference. Some of the things people declare about God and about Jesus are painful to consider."

"And therefore?" Tallis asked.

"Well, what if my openness to people of other religions is a mistake?" Cloud said with a note of concern in his voice. "What if the Bible, contradictions and all, is the only window to the true nature of God?"

"Do you really believe you're on the wrong track?" Tallis asked.

"No," he said. "Every sinew of my brain tells me the literalists are irrational and their claims are harmful to the mental and physical health of believers. But I don't want to be like them in unbending certainty that my truth is superior to theirs."

"Don't lose any sleep over it," the spiritual director said. "You're too honest to hide behind absolute religious doctrines, and from what I've heard, you're also not opposed to exploring ambiguities within the laws of physics."

"What exactly have you heard?" Cloud asked.

"That you're not afraid to plumb the spaces between matter and energy," Tallis replied. "Oh, nobody has told me anything explicit, but from snippets of conversation and odd comments, I've developed a theory that you are experimenting with mind traveling."

Cloud sighed and smiled sheepishly. "I confess that I have withheld crucial information from you as my spiritual director." He then told her about his out-of-body practices, which did not entirely surprise her.

"Are there particular locations where it is easier to float than others?" she asked.

"I've never thought about that," Cloud said. "Now that you mention it, however, there are places where I seem to be able to pop out of my body without half trying."

"Thin places," said Tallis with an air of authority.

"I've heard that term," Cloud said. "What exactly are thin places?"

"They are spots on the earth where the usually veiled existence of transcendent reality is translucent, places that evoke mystical feelings in certain people," she explained. "That is if they are open to such experiences."

"I've known places like that," Cloud said.

"Everyone has four regions in the world where thin places are apparent to them. Those who are able to visit each of their four at some time in their lives are especially blessed," Tallis said.

"Why only four?" Cloud asked.

"Four is a useful spiritual number, representing strength," she said. "I think in fours. If pressed, I'd concede the likelihood of more, but more might be unstable."

"OK. What are your four thin places?" Cloud continued.

"Ireland, Scotland, Alaska, and Arizona," she said confidently. "Can you guess what yours are?"

"Those are rather large areas for sheer transcendence to be stretched out," he said.

"Within those broad realms are specific locations of translucence for particular people," she said. "I've found at least a dozen such places in Arizona. Sedona is one, Mount Humphreys another. St. David in Cochise County is also on my list."

"Well, I would venture that mine would be Arizona, Hawaii, Australia, and Viet Nam," he said. "As for eliciting mystical feelings, in Arizona it would be the White Tank Mountains, in Hawaii it would be Haleakala on Maui, in Australia it is definitely Uluru, and in Viet Nam, the My Tho River."

"And Sedona?" Tallis asked.

"Yes of course, and probably two dozen other places in the state," he replied.

Later that day, he told Terp about his thin places conversation with Tallis. She guessed that three of hers would be the same as Cloud's, Arizona, Hawaii, and Australia. "My fourth is certain to be England," Terp said. "Stonehenge has got to be a thin place for hordes of people, including me."

"Yes, I remember you telling me about a rather vivid vision you experienced there," Cloud said.

"One of our many mystical introductions to one another," Terp said. "The other one in England was St. Paul's Cathedral."

Filled with a sense of joyful gratitude, he caressed her cheek. "The ravishing poet. What a blessed introduction. I am so fortunate I can hardly stand it." Cloud swept Terp into his arms and held her in a passionate embrace.

CHAPTER THIRTY-SIX

Conversations about a merger between the Natural Christian Church and the Naturist Church of God had been going on informally between the two denominations for several years. In September 1982 the talk grew more serious.

The only state where both the NCC and the NCoG had congregations was Texas. Otherwise, the NCC was a western denomination and the NCoG a southern one, with congregations in every state of the former Confederacy. Between them, the two denominations extended over the entire U. S. Sunbelt. The NCC, in addition, had congregations in Baja California and British Columbia.

The two churches appointed task forces to work together to develop a plan for union. Cathy Blake convened the NCC team, which included Cloud and Terp, Adam Rarom, Petrus Dort, and Agnes Day. The NCoG team was led by Job Needing, and included Ehud Spartan McRod, Rammage Brand, Jimmy-Jack Bleaux, Gaspar Passman, and a former Miss Florida runner-up, Lurleen Bleaux McRod Bryant.

"Let's begin by identifying those things we hold in common," Cathy said.

"For starters," chortled Job, "we all like to run around in our birthday suits."

Agnes stood between two large easels that were draped in newsprint. With a felt-tipped pen she marked one sheet of paper with a plus sign and the other with a minus sign. Turning to the plus sheet, she wrote "NATURISM."

"What else?" Cathy asked the assembled teams.

"Immersion baptism," offered Cloud.

Agnes wrote that on the plus side.

"Better make a note on the other sheet," said Ehud, "because we don't have a Morgan case exception. We require re-baptism in all cases."

"So noted," said Agnes.

"We're both dedicated to protection of the environment," said Gaspar.

"How about a commitment to making the world a more just and peaceful place?" suggested Terp.

"Yes, world peace," said Lurleen, coming to life at the mention of a familiar theme. "This is something we all pray for."

"Of course the best way to achieve peace is through a strong military," said Rammage. "And a well regulated militia," he added as an afterthought.

"I don't necessarily disagree about a strong military," said Cloud, "although what constitutes strength is open to interpretation. I think Petrus and I are the only war veterans in this august group, and I would say an intelligent Defense Department is more important than a massive one. Petrus may have a different view."

"Well now, we're already drifting into qualifying one another's statements," said Adam. "Let's see if we can find areas of broad agreement and work on the details later."

A long silence ensued that Petrus eventually broke. "I agree with Cloud on the military, but let's switch to a new area. How about openness to people of all races?"

"Sure," said Job. "We have a black family in Tampa and another one in Atlanta. All our congregations are officially integrated."

"Is that all?" asked Cloud. "Are any other races represented in your church?"

"Hey, it's a start. These things take time," said Gaspar.

"We both believe in the full participation of women in the church, including ordination," said Cathy, seeking to keep the conversation on a positive plane.

"That's right," said Job.

"How many women pastors do you have?" asked Agnes.

"Right now we don't have any serving as pastors," said Jimmy-Jack, "but we have two female assistant pastors, one in Miami and the other in Houston. They're bright girls, and some day I'm confident they'll find little congregations somewhere that'll be willing to take them on as pastors. We don't have husband and wife pastors like you all."

This caused Terp to recall conversations with the clergy couples who served as NCC pastors in Austin and El Paso. They were not enthusiastic about the proposal for merger with the NCoG. "Maybe we should take a look at our differences," she suggested. "Once those are clear we can begin to consider what compromises will be necessary."

"Let's start with beliefs about the nature of humankind," suggested Adam. "In the NCC, we believe that all people are flawed in some way. The Calvinists call it total depravity. That term is too extreme for us, but we see human brokenness and imperfection as inevitable and at some level unfixable this side of heaven. As a result, we tolerate failure and rely completely on the grace of God as we go about our daily lives."

"We're a holiness church," said Rammage. "We in the NC of G believe that sin can be overcome by willpower and strictly following the word of God. The Bible wouldn't say 'ye must be holy' unless it was possible to become sinless."

"I don't see any easy compromise on that one," said Adam. "What else?"

"We believe you must be Christian to be saved," said Lurleen. "Salvation comes only to those who rightly profess their faith in Jesus Christ."

"We believe God is sublimely sovereign," said Cloud. "It's presumptuous of us to set limits on what God may do. God will embrace whomever God wishes to embrace. Some of us believe it is God's intention to embrace everyone."

"Not all of us believe that," said Petrus. "Some in the NCC think that not everyone will receive God's ultimate grace. Nevertheless, that grace is extended to all humanity, regardless of their religious professions or lack thereof."

"I hesitate to bring this up," said Lurleen, "but I heard a rumor that you folks out in the West allow homosexuals to join your churches. Is that true?"

"Not only join," said Terp, "but they are eligible for ordination as well."

Lurleen gasped.

"See, I told you so," said her cousin Ehud.

"We do not have anything in writing about homosexuals joining our congregations," Job said. "The reality, however, is that such people are not welcome. Our members believe that individuals with that lifestyle present a risk to our children."

"Pedophilia and homosexuality are not at all the same thing," Terp said.

"Well now, little lady, that's subject to debate," said Job. "It looks to me like we've hit a few snags here. If we're going to make this merger work, it looks like we Southerners will have to bend a little on our holiness and you Westerners will have to give up some of your free-wheeling frontier hippy-dippy ways. But I'm confident we can do that. We have a duty to come together in Christian unity. Brotherhood is our ideal. Men of good will must bind together under the strong rule of Christ."

"Lunch is ready in the next room," announced Agnes. "Let's take a break."

After lunch, Job invited Petrus to go for a walk. "Look," Job said, "we're gonna need some help from your side to come up with sensible rules for a new denomination. I've done some checking on you, Petrus, and you have an admirable record of standing up for sound doctrine. We'd like to support you in any way we can. If you help us on some of these sensitive matters, I can guarantee that when the merger comes to pass, ***you*** will be the Presiding Bishop."

"What are the specific sensitive matters you have in mind?" asked Petrus.

"We know a lot more about you all than you think we do," said

Job. "We're not redneck crackers. We can give ground on the doctrine of sin and perfectibility. We can agree that God may save a bunch of unbaptized babies in Africa that die of starvation. But here's the bottom line. That foot-washing stuff that Morgan started will have to go. And the homos will be gone the day after the merger becomes official. Pastors who coddle fairies will be disciplined and if they won't behave, defrocked."

Petrus said nothing.

"Well? Whaddya say?" asked Job.

"I need time to think about this," Petrus said.

The afternoon session established that family ties -bloodlines- were important markers of identity for the NCoG, while ancestral kinship was not important to the NCC.

"We really don't care who your daddy was," said Adam. "Our church families are not based on blood or marriage. Total strangers walk through our doors and become beloved members of our family."

"Our doors too," said Rammage. "We're not all inbred, as you would paint us. However, not every stranger proves to be righteous and worthy. There are such things as untouchables, you know. Perverts of any kind are simply not acceptable among decent church folks."

"If you're referring to pedophiles and spouse abusers, we effectively screen them out for sensible public safety purposes -but not for doctrinal reasons," said Cloud. "However, I suspect you maintain a broader definition of what constitutes righteousness and worthiness. From our standpoint, no one is perfectly upright and respectable, no one is completely clean, which is why God responds to humankind with grace."

"Speak for yourself," said Gaspar. He tried to say this in a jocular way, but a tinge of sarcasm was evident in his voice.

"It's clear that we are far from any kind of agreement about the shape of a merged denomination," said Petrus. "However, I have something to say that should cut through our differences and get us to the point we desperately need to reach."

All eyes turned to Petrus Dort. Job smiled expectantly then suppressed it, lest he be seen to gloat.

"Job and I went for a walk after lunch," Petrus said. "We talked about many things, including possible ways to get beyond our differences and create a new church unlike either of its predecessors."

Job's smile returned. He liked the way Petrus was spinning their conversation.

"In the course of our conversation," Petrus continued, "Job offered me the position of Presiding Bishop in the new denomination in exchange for my support on issues relating to liturgical practices and the presence of homosexuals in our congregations."

Job's smile vanished, replaced by a deep scowl.

"In truth, I have significant reservations about ordaining ***non-celibate*** homosexuals to the ministry. But I have no doubt that many people are born with same-sex orientations, and there is no reason to exclude them from participation in worship and the life of the church. If anything, it is a scandal to the Gospel to exclude them. And from an ethical standpoint, I am uncomfortable with Job's offer. Therefore, I must decline it."

"The confidential conversation you just revealed won't get us closer to merger," Jimmy-Jack said. "You've just blown it to hell."

"I know," said Petrus. "I said it will get us to the point we need to reach. That point is recognition that a merger will not work. Our differences are much too great. We would all end up unhappy. There are plenty of denominations organized around being miserable together. We don't need to add another one."

They had planned to spend a week designing a new church, but after Petrus had spoken, the gathering produced a unanimous agreement that he was correct. At the end of one day of negotiations, the members of the two teams shook hands, wished each other God's blessings, and went their separate ways.

Though he was actively involved in the life of the congregation in Sedona, Den missed his Buddhist roots. In order to reconnect with the tradition he grew up with, he joined a Buddhist meditation group in town. The leader of the group practiced Tibetan Buddhism, which was different from the Thien Buddhism Den had known in Viet Nam. The Tibetans presented a more disciplined path toward enlightenment than the less structured way he had followed as a child. Nevertheless, Den found the meditation exercises deeply satisfying.

Cloud was impressed by what he perceived as the maturing of Den's soul as a result of practicing Tibetan prayer techniques. One day he asked Den if he had experienced any mystical release during meditation.

"Sometimes I feel almost able to leave my body and soar into the heavens," Den replied.

The following Saturday, Den -without his flesh- joined the rest of the family in their floating explorations of the red rock country.

Now there were eleven floaters at Angel Nest. Late one Saturday morning when they arrived home from soaring over Cathedral Rock, before returning to their bodies, they huddled together to discuss where to go next week.

Tzek said, "I want Savage to join us. He's my best friend, and if Huxley can do it, I bet he can too."

"I did this on my own," Huxley said. "I'd like Sav to come along too, but I'd feel an obligation to get permission from Mom and Dad first. But that means I'd have to tell them what I've been doing all these years."

"Huxley's right, Tzek," said Cedar Cradle. "It's OK for us to teach our own children to float, but it would not be right for us to do that with someone else's child without permission."

"Alright," said Tzek with disappointment registering clearly in his voice.

"Listen, Tzek," said Huxley. "I've been planning to tell my parents one of these days. I'll move that up to right away, and see if we can't get my brother out of his body."

"Alright!" said Tzek with entirely different inflection.

"Oops!" Huxley said. "It just occurred to me that I would be giving away the confidentiality of all you guys. What do you think?"

The group discussed the matter and quickly came to unanimous agreement that Huxley could reveal their names and out-of-body activities to Aldous, Encantadora, and Savage.

Huxley called a family conference that afternoon. The Askeladds did this periodically if any one of them had some matter or concern to express.

"I have something to share too," Aldous said.

"You go first, Dad," said Huxley.

"I have now completed the research and have written a detailed outline of my book. There are three stories that run parallel for a time then merge together, about Cloud, Terp, and the NCC," Aldous reported.

Huxley was aware that his outline was incomplete because it did not include anything about out-of-body experiences. Of course, neither she nor her father knew about the Old One.

"You all moved here to support me in my work. Now that I've reached this point, it's no longer necessary to live at Angel Nest if you would like to move somewhere else. I can do the actual writing anywhere," he said.

Encantadora said, "This place is perfect for ***my*** work. I enjoy sharing the studio with Mary, and the pieces I sell in Darshan's shop provide a comfortable income for us."

Savage said, "I have friends here. Tzek is my best friend in the whole world. I love this place and don't want to move."

Huxley added, "What I have to say will change the status of your research, Dad, so none of us will want to move. I certainly don't want to leave this place!" She paused to make sure everyone was listening intently to her words. "When I was nine, I had an out-of-body experience. I was in my room meditating, imagining that I was swimming in the air, and poof! I rose to the ceiling and looked down and saw my body stretched out on the bed. Since then I've learned how to induce spiriting. That's what I call it. I've left my body pretty regularly to explore the neighborhood. But recently I got caught at it."

"Caught?" Aldous blurted out. "Who saw you? What were you doing?" He was so surprised by his daughter's confession that his mind assumed she was fully visible when out of her body.

Encantadora did not make that assumption. "Yes. Who could catch you if you were...invisible?"

"The Morgans and the Begays caught me," Huxley said.

"How?" Aldous asked.

"They were out of their bodies too, and they perceived me flying around the house," Huxley explained.

"Were you spying on people?" her mother asked.

"No, no! I never go into people's bedrooms or bathrooms or

anything like that," Huxley said. "That would feel...unethical...against the spirit of spiriting."

"You say the Morgans and Begays were out of their bodies?" Aldous said.

"Yes, Dad," Huxley said. "Your book outline has a gaping hole in it. You can't leave now, because you have a whole lot of research to do on an invisible piece of the story." She told her family about the places she had been with the ten other floaters.

"Wow!" said Aldous. "I have so many questions I don't know where to begin. Does Cloud know you're telling us this?"

"Yes," she said. "We all agreed on my telling you."

Savage said, "Hey, I wanna do that too! Will you teach me?"

"Well, Sav, you're the reason I'm telling all of you about this," Huxley said. "Tzek wants you to learn to float -that's what they call it- so you and he can go exploring together."

"Cool! When do we start?" Savage said.

"Now wait a minute!" said Encantadora. "This is a real bombshell. Let's all calm down and think this through."

"Well, I'm elated to have an excuse to stay longer and do more research," said Aldous.

"You don't need an excuse," Encantadora said. "We're welcome here as long as we want to stay. And our financial contribution to the general welfare here is much less than a house payment. You can do all your writing here and take as long as you want."

"Mom? Dad? Can I float too?" Savage asked eagerly.

"Your sister didn't ask permission," Encantadora said. "She just went out and did it." She tried to produce a tone of reproach with her voice but it came out as pride.

"This is different," Huxley explained, "because Cloud and Terp would be teaching you how to do it, and they wouldn't do that without the consent of Mom and Dad."

Aldous and Encantadora looked at each other, grinned, and said yes to their son.

When the time came to teach Savage how to leave his body, Cloud and Terp invited his parents to observe. Savage caught on quickly and was soon hovering around the ceiling. Huxley went up with him for company.

"Do you two want to be next?" Terp asked Aldous and Encantadora.

Encantadora feared that her husband would not be successful at it, and she did not want to do it without him, so she said no. Aldous worried that his wife wouldn't be able to leave her body and also declined.

"You know, Aldous, you caught me out of my body once," Cloud said.

"When was that?" Aldous asked, feeling perplexed.

"Senior ditch day in 1961. We went hiking in the White Tanks," Cloud explained. "I was sitting on a big rock on the side of the mountain, and you yelled at me and waved your hand in front of my face."

"Oh yeah, I remember that!" Aldous exclaimed. "You really snapped at me. You said you were meditating, but there was a totally blank expression on your face."

"That's because I had left my body and was exploring the desert. I heard you yelling and raced back and popped back into my skin," Cloud said.

"I never would have suspected what you were actually doing, but I always knew there was something odd about your eyes that day," Aldous added.

Terp said, "Any time either of you change your mind and want to give floating a try, just say the word."

"Does Mary do it?" Encantadora asked.

"No," said Terp. "She's chosen not to, but she knows about it."

"Maybe someday we'll try it," offered Aldous, "but I for one want to ***meditate*** on the matter first."

"What are you reading?" Terp asked Cloud with genuine curiosity.

Engrossed in a novel, Cloud occupied the length of the couch, with his head on one arm and feet dangling over the other. Terp swept his legs aside and sat beside him.

"Oh, it's a book I abandoned when I met you," he said.

"The one I knocked out of your hand in the drugstore?" she asked with surprise in her voice.

"Yes. I saw it in the bookstore the other day and felt the need to tie up a loose end after all these years," he said, holding up the cover for her to see.

"Isaac Asimov. ***The Gods Themselves***," she read aloud.

"I like Asimov's strong females," he said. "And I'm tickled by his description of male and female characters merging their ethereal bodies in ways that remind me of both our floating and our unique way of sharing memories. You'll be interested to know also that according to Isaac, social nudity will be the norm when humans colonize the moon."

In late October, Terp experienced a vivid dream that stayed with her upon awakening. Their Volvo station wagon had breasts in place of headlights, and a penis came out from the tail pipe. Female genitalia replaced the spare tire. She and Cloud were nestled inside each other's bodies behind the wheel together as they drove the automobile down the highway. The vehicle would not stay on the road, however, but flew into the air. A destination came to her mind. They were trying to reach Los Angeles, but they were moving eastward, in the opposite direction of the California city. Yet she sensed they were going in the right direction. It wasn't Los Angeles they were seeking but ***Los Angeles Extranos***.

The car swerved and looped and dipped as they traveled through the air, but they were not afraid. Zara was riding on the hood, where the ornament should be, and this did not cause concern either. Two babies were riding peacefully in the back compartment. All five of them were human and something beyond human at the same time.

V

SOJOURNER

The Soul selects her own Society
Then shuts the Door

Emily Dickinson

Jesus said to his disciples: When you make two into one, and when you make the inner like the outer and the outer like the inner, and the upper like the lower, and when you make male and female into one, so that the male will not be male and the female will not be female...then you will enter the realm of God.

The Gospel of Thomas, Saying 22

Jesus said: When you remove all your clothes without shame and like children put them under your feet and stomp on them, you will see the son of the living one and not be afraid.

The Gospel of Thomas, Saying 37

CHAPTER THIRTY-SEVEN

Syd Darwin hit the lottery for a hundred thousand Australian dollars, and to celebrate, he proposed taking his family on holiday in America. Alice and the children quickly decided Arizona must be their destination. Since the Darwins and Morgans had maintained correspondence over the years, he knew how to reach them in Sedona, and so Syd telephoned Cloud to inquire about visiting during the last week of 1982.

"This is wonderful news and perfect timing!" Cloud responded. "As it happens, we're having a family reunion then and we'd love to have our Aussie relations here. And naturally, we especially want to meet little Terp."

"It'll be good to be out of the wet for a spell," said Syd. "There'll be six of us, counting the wee one. That won't be too much trouble will it?"

"No," said Cloud. "We're expecting more than sixty people all together, so you'll blend in nicely with the rest of the family. Many of them are anxious to meet you. And while I'm thinking about it, you could do us a great favor."

"Anything," said Syd.

"Look up Geneva Andrews in Alice Springs and see if she'd like to tag along with you. She's a missionary with no money, but we'll pay her fare," Cloud said.

"No, I can't do that," Syd said.

The unexpected response threw Cloud off balance. "I'm sorry I asked, Syd. It was presumptuous of me. Just forget about it," he said.

"Oh, I'll look up Geneva and bring her along if she wants to come," Syd explained. "But I won't let you pay for it. This is my treat. It would give me great pleasure to share a bit of my lottery loot with a missionary. How do you think she'll like hanging round a pack of nudists?"

"She's used to it," said Cloud.

And so Syd and Alice, Kuranda and Nuoc with their daughter Terp, Koah, and Geneva arrived at Sky Harbor Airport in Phoenix on the twenty-eighth of December. Cloud, Terp, and Skye met them there.

Amid group hugs, handshakes, and cooing noises about the beautiful little four-year-old Terp, Geneva said, "I hope you don't mind. We snuck in an extra guest."

A trim, quietly confident sixteen-year-old Aboriginal girl stepped out from behind Koah.

"Oh my God!" shouted Terp. "Amoonguna!" Terp threw her arms around the teenager, and then made room for Cloud to hug both of them.

"I guess it was a bit of alright for us to bring her along then," Geneva said with a note of mischief in her voice.

Cloud let go of Amoonguna and Terp and turned toward Geneva. He embraced the missionary, and with his arms locked around her waist, began to spin her around so that her feet and calves were off the ground. "You have to watch out for these Calvinists," he announced to the rest of the entourage. "They're full of surprises. Bless you, Geneva."

When Cloud eventually stopped and put her down, Geneva said, "You're the first man in all my sixty odd years to ever hug me that way. I have to admit I like it."

They stowed their extensive luggage in the bed of Skye's pick-up truck, and he returned to Sedona with Koah riding shotgun. The rest of the Aussie travelers crammed into the station wagon for the trip north.

The next two days required more shuttles back and forth between Sky Harbor and Angel Nest. Argyle and Ruth Watts arrived on a flight from New Jersey. Penny and Randall flew in from Honolulu, bringing with them Isadora Coryphee, Terp's liturgical dance professor at Pacific Crossroads and theology professor Ogden Cobbhart. Asher and Hylli drove over from Los Angeles, as did Arquimedes and Petrus from San Diego.

Lloyd and Nissa, as well as Narcissa, came for the reunion. Adam and Evelyn were there, along with Kwan-yin and Cochise, Cathy and Bill, Theo and Keefe, and the twins, Abram and Sarai. Dagmar and Quinn motored up for the event, as did Darla and Yonah. Edna Echo, Clark Hyfrydol, Ed and Kay Lumen, and their daughter Vala represented the Phoenix NCC congregation. Anasazi College faculty members present included Emily Congo, Bookman Donne, and Mito Picaron along with his wife Alada.

Jenny Mast, still grieving the loss of her partner Gwen, came to the party and quickly developed a friendship with Geneva. The full-time residents of Angel Nest included the Morgan, Begay, and Askeladd families, Darshan and Prasada, Mary and Skye, Malama and Ian, and Tallis and Colin.

The entire troupe gathered in the large family room on New Year's Eve afternoon. The day was bright, clear, and cold outside. Many sat around the fireplace, enjoying its crackling warmth. Others lounged on couches or gently swayed to and fro in rocking chairs. Some reclined on rugs near the potted live Christmas tree, which was beautifully unadorned. People chatted amiably, exchanging reminiscences or foot-rubs.

Syd led the Aussie contingent singing "Waltzing Matilda" and then engaged everyone to join in on "Angels We Have Heard on High." Aldous produced his banjo and sang "A World of Our Own," with a dozen others soon harmonizing with him.

Youngsters swooped around the room, playing hide and seek. Huxley, at thirteen, circulated back and forth between the active chatter of children and the subdued conversations of adults. Eventually she made alliance with Amoonguna, the only other teenager in the place.

Despite wintry weather outside, no one wore a stitch of clothing. The room was warm and cozy as much from mutual affection and feelings of well-being as from the solar-paneled heating system.

Mary engaged in serious conversation with the Lumens. "For the longest time I tried to get pregnant," she explained to the physicians, "but I couldn't conceive. We had extensive testing, and they couldn't find anything wrong with either Skye or me, but no matter how hard we tried, nothing happened. So three months ago I completely gave up the idea of ever having a baby of my own. We talked about adopting, and bingo! I got pregnant."

"It often happens that way," said Kay. "Trying too hard has a way of blocking success."

Mary wasn't the only pregnant woman in the room on the last day of 1982. Tallis and Malama were also expecting. So were Emily, Prasada, Darla, Kwan-yin, Dagmar, Cedar Cradle, and Kuranda. Terp was carrying twins. The family would be growing larger in the coming year.

Out of the blue, Cloud felt a strong desire to tell everyone about the Old One. Suspicious about the origin of the idea, he looked across the room at Terp, who chose that moment to stare expectedly at him.

Without speaking, they carried on a conversation. Are you thinking what I'm thinking? Yes. Do you suppose? Could be. Let's do it.

Terp and Cloud maneuvered their ways across the crowded room and met in front of the fireplace. Cloud clapped his hands to gain the attention of the room.

"On this auspicious day," Cloud said, "Terp and I want to reveal to all of you, whom we love dearly, an intimate and heretofore very private part of our lives. A few of you in this room know part of the story, and two of you have firsthand knowledge of it, but this afternoon seems like an opportune time to tell the whole thing to all of you."

Aldous leaned over to Encantadora and whispered, "He's going to tell everyone about floating."

Cloud did indeed begin the narrative by describing his first out-of-body experience when he was six. But he added a wrinkle Aldous knew nothing about. Cloud talked about a conversation with an imaginary friend he called the Old One. Terp then spoke of her childhood encounter with the Old One in the desert west of Phoenix. All across the room people listened in rapt attention, feeling their skin tingle as the story unfolded. Terp revealed the visit she and Cloud made to the Old One's shack in 1972.

Cloud said, "Mary, do you remember that summer you slept in a sleeping bag in our old apartment in Tempe? Soon after you arrived, you had a dream in which Terp and I got married in a naturist ceremony."

"Sure. It bowled me over when you showed me the actual photos that Cochise had taken. I loved curling up in that corner," Mary responded. "It was next to your old Army footlocker. I always felt such a sense of blessing when I slept there."

"You were sleeping next to the scraps of the Old One's robe that were inside the footlocker," Cloud said. "That's what caused you to feel euphoric and have the dream."

Evelyn said, "I felt the same as Mary when you opened the locker and showed us those scraps. I wanted to dance for joy."

"As I recall, you did in fact dance for joy, and it was profoundly beautiful," said Terp. She paused and then added, "And Adam sang, also beautiful, of course."

"What you have described were childhood encounters. Have either of you seen the Old One since you became adults?" asked Clark with carefully professional curiosity.

"I think I saw the Old One in Hyde Park when I was eighteen," said Terp. "But it was from a distance, so I'm not completely sure."

"We've had two face-to-face meetings since then," said Cloud. "Once on our honeymoon in the Outback. Amoonguna was with us on that occasion. And then again in a wilderness area west of Oak Creek Canyon two years ago. Zara was with us that time."

"Well, now there's another huge hole in my research," said Aldous, throwing his hands in the air. "And it creates a major problem. The out-of-body stuff will stretch the imagination of my readers, but in the end most of them will accept it. No one will believe this story about an Old One. Maybe I should just chuck the whole project."

"Why don't you do what you're gifted at and write it as a fantasy novel. People will suspend their disbelief if they think it's fiction," suggested Cloud.

"Yes!" said Aldous. "That's a great idea! Their skeptical defenses will be down, but the secret will be that it's a true story settling pleasantly into their open minds."

"What does the Old One look like?" asked Evelyn. "You would

never tell us much about the Old One's appearance before."

As if on cue, the Old One materialized in the flesh, standing next to Terp and Cloud. Addressing the couple, the Old One said, "Don't concern yourselves about that. They can all see for themselves now." The Old One was naked and visibly pregnant.

Preacher, the Australian shepherd, and the two cats, Poet and Painter, trotted from their respective corners of the room directly to the Old One. Preacher's tail was wagging happily. Poet and Painter rubbed their cheeks against the Old One's ankles while Preacher's nose probed a bit higher.

"This reunion has proven irresistible to me. I simply could not pass up the opportunity to see you all in one place at the same time," the Old One said.

The assembly lapsed momentarily into astonished silence.

Cloud spoke first. "Has every one of us has been assigned to your care?"

"Yes," the Old One replied. "Each one here plus many more whom you have not met. But never in all my centuries have so many of the people whose lives I've been following come together like this. This occasion is extraordinary, much too full of creative possibilities to resist showing myself."

"Speaking of showing yourself, when are you due?" asked Terp. With familiar affection, she placed a hand on the Old One's belly.

"By your calendar, next July," the Old One responded. "Incidentally, my gestation period is about five weeks longer than yours. And I take note that by the time I give birth, eleven of the women in this room will have given birth also. Congratulations to all of you, and a special commendation to you, Terp, for conceiving twins."

The news that the Old One knew she was carrying twins sent Terp into a momentary reverie concerning the circumstances of her becoming pregnant. Her eyes closed and a wide smile covered her face as she thought about that night. She and Cloud had just returned from a faculty reception at the college and were still in their evening clothes. A month earlier, Cloud had again spoken of his strong desire that Zara not be an only child, and with mutual eagerness they had agreed to discontinue birth control at an opportune time.

Terp's only reservation was about timing a pregnancy so that delivery would coincide with the lightest season of the church calendar. As they considered this factor, however, they realized that there was no such period for their congregation. Typically, churches experienced lower attendance and little or no programming during the summer, but summer attendance actually increased for the Sedona NCC. Many visitors from other NCC congregations took vacations in the Sedona area and thus swelled the numbers in the pews.

"I guess it doesn't really matter ***when*** we do it," Terp ultimately declared.

The night of the reception, now home in their bedroom, Terp turned so that Cloud could unzip her dress, and with no words exchanged between them, he undid the button at the top. A sudden and intense erotic sensation flooded her nervous system. Shivers ran down her back as his hand descended with the zipper down her spine.

"Cloud, I'm ovulating," she whispered. "Let's make a baby!"

Without replying, he took the hem of her dress with both hands and slowly lifted it up along the curves of her body and then over her upraised arms. When the dress was off, he wadded it into a ball and playfully tossed it across the room. He unhooked her bra and hung it on a lamp and then with his hands on her hips slipped her panties down.

Terp turned around and undid Cloud's tie, draping it over her neck as she seductively unbuttoned and removed his shirt, which she casually flung somewhere over her shoulder. Slowly she pulled the tie across her breasts and then rolled it up and pitched it underhand into the dirty clothes hamper. She pressed her breasts into his chest as she maneuvered his undershirt above his raised arms and let the garment fall as they kissed with great ardor, both sets of arms still in the air. She broke away from his face and in a downward movement kissed his neck, chest, and abdomen. Now on her knees, she opened his belt and undid the fly of his trousers. Once his pants were off, she tied the legs into a knot and threw them at the bathroom door. After sliding his boxers to his feet, she caressed his organ with her lips.

Somehow the knowledge that Terp could easily get pregnant from this lovemaking increased their level of arousal. Terp fell in a backward bounce onto the bed and parted her legs. Cloud teased her delta with kisses.

"This is double the pleasure," Cloud enthused as he entered her.

Terp had already experienced an orgasm before he got that far and within seconds of feeling him inside her enjoyed another one. His ejaculation occurred quickly. Lying sated with Cloud resting on top of her, Terp said, "This was twice as good as our usual spectacular connections."

Neither was surprised when Terp's obstetrician confirmed with an ultrasound examination that she was carrying twins.

Now realizing that she had tuned out her guests, Terp opened her eyes to see if anyone had noticed her mental absence.

Apparently not. The people who had been scattered around the room were now gathered in tight semicircles around the fireplace, mouths agape at the appearance of the gravid hermaphrodite who had materialized seemingly out of nowhere.

Zara ran up and exuberantly embraced the Old One. "I remember you!" she said excitedly. "Do you remember me and the mountain lion?"

"Yes, Zara, I remember you most fondly. The lion sends his regards."

Amoonguna approached quietly and held out her hand, which the Old One took and held gently. "G'day, Amoonguna," the Old One said. "You've grown into a fine young lady. I am so pleased."

"Thank you, dear friend," she said and curtseyed.

Terp said, "You know all of us, but not everyone here knows you. It looks like an introduction would be in order. Several times I've asked you your name, beginning when I was five, and you said I couldn't pronounce it. Will you please tell us now?"

The Old One's tiny mouth produced a generous smile. "I suppose I have delayed this revelation long enough. My name is [a rapid series of guttural noises and unusual yet strangely musical sounds came forth]. Cloud, with some of your linguistic gifts, I imagine you can reproduce a little of what I have spoken, but probably not all of it. The closest translation of my name into English misses the nuances and rich associations inherent in my native language, but it nevertheless contains some noble sentiments. You may call me Sojourner."

Displaying scientific curiosity, Ed Lumen asked questions about Sojourner's intersexual body, gestation, and method of delivery, and Sojourner answered cheerfully.

"Other than the length of gestation, nothing you have described falls outside the range of human biology," Ed said. "But apart from natural anatomy, I notice that your foreskin is intact. Is that the norm in your society?"

"Among my species, circumcision has never been practiced," Sojourner said with a tinge of vocal emotion. "In fact, we do not engage in any disfiguring behavior relating to our bodies. No tattoos, no flesh piercing, no bones in the nose, and so on."

"Do you base that on religious, cultural, or scientific reasons?" Kay asked.

"Yes," Sojourner replied.

Kay then laughed. "Sorry, badly phrased question. On what do you base your aversion to circumcision and other body-altering practices?"

Sojourner sighed. "It would be difficult to answer without some of you inferring criticism of human behavior. I intend no disrespect, but comparisons are unavoidable. Unlike humans, our civilization never passed through primitive tribal stages in which belonging was maintained by identifying disfigurements. Our religion honors the whole body as formed and cannot conceive of...God...demanding any kind of mutilation or peculiar adornment."

"Most of us males had no choice in the matter of circumcision," said Cloud. "When I was born it was routine for hygienic reasons."

"I am sorry for your loss," said Sojourner, "and I do not believe that you would ever have suffered hygiene problems had the custom been otherwise."

"People with both male and female organs occur occasionally among humans," Ed said. "Is this normative or exceptional for your species?"

"We think of ourselves as fully-sexed, as opposed to humans who are half-sexed. We are all this way," Sojourner answered. "Those among you who have studied philosophy may remember that your Greek philosopher Plato claimed that in the beginning there were three sexes, male, female, and the combination of male and female," Sojourner continued.

"I seem to remember something about the third sex becoming powerful and rebelling against the gods," said Cloud.

"Yes," responded Sojourner. "And to punish them all, Zeus separated them into male and female, and then discovered, much to his chagrin, that the separated ones spent all their time trying to become one again. Of course, Plato was mistaken in his mythological pronouncement. Zeus did no such thing. My belief is that Plato must have heard tales about my species, but since he never encountered one of us himself, he decided we must be extinct. He was right about the powerful part, though. The historical truth is Plato was not well considered. He possessed a somewhat unpleasant personality, and my ancestors avoided him."

"I remember something from a study of Genesis in seminary about Adam and Eve originally being one person with both male and female attributes," Terp said. "Have you ever heard anything about that?"

"It had to do with the Genesis account of humans being created in the image of God. Since God is a unity, Adam necessarily must have included Eve in one body," said Sojourner. "But the solitary creature was lonely, so like Zeus, God separated the inclusive Adam-Eve into male and female humans. The difference is that Zeus did it for punishment and God did it for compassionate reasons. This idea arose among a number of ancient Jewish and Christian scholars but fell into disfavor. It surfaced again in the seventeenth century among a few German mystics."

"You seem to know everything, like what they call omniscient. Are you a divine being?" asked Nissa.

"Thank you for asking, Nissa," said Sojourner. "That is a very important question. And the answer is definitely no. I am not divine or holy or venerable or anything of the like. And not omniscient either. Please stifle any urge to worship me or any of my kin. We are finite, imperfect beings, subject to errors and poor judgment similar to you humans. Worship only God."

"Then God truly exists?" Aldous asked.

"I believe so," said Sojourner.

"That's not a definitive answer," said Aldous. "In fact, it seems deliberately ambiguous."

"I've been accused of evasive answers many times over the centuries. It's one of my weaknesses. It proves my point about being imperfect. So, I'm afraid that's the most you'll get from me on the subject of God's existence."

"Definitive about God or not," Ogden sighed, "now I'm going to have to rewrite the entire anthropology section in my book. I suppose I will never be done with it."

"That prospect should make you happy," Isadora said. "I don't think you want to finish it. How many thousands of pages is it now?"

"Some artists have a hard time letting go of their creations," Sojourner noted.

"Theologian as artist," Ogden mused. "How splendid! There's another chapter!"

Mary, Encantadora, and Cochise had been conferring in a corner, and they now approached Sojourner. Mary spoke for the three of them. "You know the work that Dora, Cochise and I do," she said. "As artists, we try to tell the truth about life, often indirectly. Your beauty is extraordinary, otherworldly, and for some, no doubt, disturbing. Would you be willing to sit for the three of us so that we can paint and photograph you?"

"I know you well enough to be confident that your motives are honest," Sojourner said. "If I allow you to make images of me, I trust you would not use them to exploit me or anyone else. I will say yes if every human in this room will solemnly promise that any such representations of my likeness will be used exclusively for and within this community. They must not be displayed in public or in connection with the church. I do not want anyone to become confused and redirect spiritual energy toward me."

"Is there something wrong with the church?" asked Cloud.

"No, not at all," said Sojourner. "But the congregation needs to be focused on God. Pictures of me would become a distraction and are likely to be misunderstood. So many of God's communications with the world have been badly misinterpreted through the millennia. I don't want to be the source of further distortions."

A quick survey produced suitable promises to honor Sojourner's conditions.

"But what about our unborn children?" asked Terp. "And what about those who are strangers now but who will become part of this community in the future? Must we keep this secret from them?"

Before Sojourner could respond, Cloud added, "Yes, one of the pillars of our theology is that we have no doctrinal secrets. Our church's wisdom is open and accessible to everyone."

"First ask yourself why you have chosen to keep knowledge of me confidential for so many years," said Sojourner. "You already know that some things are better left unsaid. More to the point, I am not a piece of doctrine. Theology is about God. I am not God or even godlike. If I may use a rough metaphor, I am related to your family not your church. Our mutual affection is family business, not an ecclesiastical matter."

"Thank you, Sojourner. I understand the difference," said Cloud.

"In response to Terp's question, I think when the time comes you will know -all of you- how to handle sharing my identity with others. But if ever in doubt you need only ask and I will give you an answer," Sojourner said.

"Ask like in prayer?" asked Cedar Cradle.

"I would not call it that," said Sojourner. "It's more like the way you communicate when you're floating. Something like telepathy."

"If you're just an ordinary being," said Cloud, "then why do fragments of your robe have residual power? Why does the sand you sat on years ago in the Todd River stay warm even in the freezer? And why do I feel like I'm in the presence of holy grace when you're here?"

"Every sentient being exudes energy," said Sojourner. "In time it fades, though. When was the last time you checked the sand you brought from Australia? All the so-called relics of me that you have so carefully stored away will eventually lose their energy. I say with certainty, they won't be of any use to future generations."

"But they've had a very beneficial effect on this one," said Evelyn.

"Thank you for thinking well of me," said Sojourner. "As to the sense of grace you described, Cloud, others have experienced that also, but some have felt remorse instead, or even terror. Encounters with a being such as I may magnify one's innate state of mind, but it is true that people also enjoy or suffer such emotions in the presence of certain other humans. Let me say again, I am not in any way divine."

The terms of his incarceration mandated that T. C. Smith be segregated from the general convict population at the Arizona State

Prison at Florence. Nevertheless, certain guards found ways to get around that requirement as a tool for keeping the peace. From time to time, Smith's keepers temporarily abandoned him to the oversight of inmates with agendas relating to sexual gratification. He wasn't singled out for this treatment, however. Other child molesters at Florence experienced the same occasional lapse in penal management.

T. C. Smith lay on his bunk with angry determination etched into his face. He felt like crying but would not let himself succumb to that dangerous display. Blood and semen oozed from his rectum. He had lost count of the anal rapes he had endured over the course of seven years in prison, but he was dealing with the pain and humiliation in his usual manner by concentrating fiercely on a well-crafted plan of escape. He knew exactly how he was going to do it. The plan was perfect but would require a great deal of patience on his part. The constellation of circumstances needed to bring about his freedom may not come together for years, but he would be ready when it did.

"When I get out," he spoke quietly to himself, "vengeance shalt be mine." A list of his betrayers scrolled through his mind, concluding as always with the unknown enemies responsible for his arrest. "I don't know how they did it," he whispered to himself, "but those damned nudists behind the back wall of my temple had to be involved. When I get outta here, those jaybird bastards are gonna pay!"

Cloud challenged Sojourner's assertion of non-divinity. "I don't think appearing and disappearing instantaneously is something ordinary beings can do," he said. "Perhaps you're being too modest about your status in the scheme of creation. What's the possibility you may be one of those angels on high we sang about earlier?"

"Leaving one's body and traveling through water, walls, and space, as you have been known to do, is not ordinary either," Sojourner said. "Humility is nevertheless an admirable trait. Do not be quick about attributing holiness to beings or things you do not understand. Most assuredly I am a creature of the earth and not of the heavens."

"Well, floating seems pretty ordinary compared with the way you come and go in a flash," responded Cloud.

"The way I transport my body," Sojourner explained, "is different only in degree from what you do when you leave your body. Your human psychological pioneer Carl Jung partially recognized this reality when he noted that the psyche is able to function outside of what he called the spatio-temporal law of causality. The psyche -or soul- can not only leave its body, as you have discovered, but also it can transport its body through other dimensions, as my species has discovered."

Cloud smiled gratefully upon hearing this intelligence and extended a hand to Sojourner, who grasped it firmly. They peered into one another's eyes and recognized profound esteem each for the other.

"Do you have any advice for us?" asked Cedar Cradle.

"One of your Ten Commandments, not properly observed, can be dangerous," the ancient one said. "Beware of that particular one. Be very careful."

"Which one? How? Do you mean that literally?" asked Terp.

"You will know when the time comes, Terp -if it comes," Sojourner responded.

Cloud's mind immediately pictured not the Decalogue but the face of T. C. Smith. Just as quickly, he dismissed that idea because Smith was safely locked up in prison for the rest of his life.

"Do you have any other words of wisdom?" asked Firstlaugh.

"Well, now that you mention it," Sojourner said, as if reminded of something temporarily forgotten, "I think it's time for Cloud and Terp to bring out Mary's painting of them."

"The triptych with the two of us looking like angels merging into one?" Terp said.

"Exactly," said Sojourner. "Hang it here above the mantle for everyone to see. It is a parable for the future."

Mary beamed at this affirmation of her work. She thought of this piece as the best she had ever produced but believed it could never be exhibited. Now it would be viewed by hundreds of people. Having long since offered up the triptych to the oblivion of posthumous recognition, Sojourner's words lifted her psyche with the breath of artistic resurrection.

"Speaking of the future," said Terp, "what should we be preparing for? Where are we heading?"

Sojourner smiled enigmatically and replied, "Where do you want to go?"

HERETICS IN OCCUPIED EDEN

CONTINUES IN BOOK THREE,

THE DANCING CHURCH

About the Author

Kenneth Alan Moe was born in Phoenix, where from an early age he experienced mystical events. At age ten he began writing poetry. His working life has included service in the U. S. Army as a prisoner of war interrogator, in the corporate world as an insurance investigator, and as a mainline Protestant minister.

Consistently underscoring it all, for more than half a century he has practiced the vocation of writer, evolving through pencil, pen, manual and electric typewriter, and computer to produce reams of fiction, non-fiction, and poetry.

About Strange Angel Press

Strange Angel Press is a consortium of writers who act as editors, advisors, and cheerleaders for one another. We pool our collective experiences and talents to help participating writers with the art, craft, and discipline of fully telling the stories that have inspired us to put words to paper.

Visit our websites:
strangeangelpress.com
facebook.com/StrangeAngelPress
facebook.com/HereticsInOccupiedEden

TAKE A WALK ON THE SPIRITUAL SIDE

with

KENNETH ALAN MOE

And the

HERETICS IN OCCUPIED EDEN

THE FLOATING BOY - Growing up in post-World War II Phoenix, Cloud Morgan enjoyed exploring out-of-body, but nightmares of impending tragic events caused him grief. In a dream so vivid he felt compelled to search for her, he saw an enchanting dancer from the East. Two beautiful women with psychic gifts matched the image in Cloud's dream, but which one was the dancer?

THE STRANGE ANGELS - Cloud pursues a career as a history professor, while Terp serves as a mainline parish pastor, until peculiar circumstances draw them toward a previously unimagined vocational partnership.

THE DANCING CHURCH - Rebuffed when seeking to join an ecumenical pastors organization in Sedona, Cloud and Terp launch their own unorthodox group of spiritual leaders, from New Age to Native American. These efforts soon attract the malicious attention of local fundamentalists.

Praise for the Series

"A special genre of fiction that gives respect to our psychic and paranormal world and our need to demystify the body..." - Lawn Griffiths, Journalist

"I have not felt a connection to fiction like this in some time. Perhaps you could say it is a Harry Potter for adults." - Amazon Reviewer

Available in Paper and Kindle editions on Amazon.com

STRANGE ANGEL PRESS

www.ingramcontent.com/pod-product-compliance
Lightning Source LLC
Chambersburg PA
CBHW051537250626
47157CB00001B/84